# FEBRUARY'S ANGEL

## A NOVEL

## L. B. JOYCE

February's Angel
Print Edition ISBN: 978-0-9600311-2-2

made a visit to the Champs-Élysées Fountain of Love to throw in a coin and make a wish.

This, by the way, was something she actually did. And had her wish come true?

Not yet. But she was pretty sure there was no time frame for one of these wishes.

*So you can still hope...*

Yep, there was something about starting out a conversation with "Since I've been living in Paris..." that was enough to have boosted her reputation to not only a person of interest, but one who was also quite knowledgeable as well.

At least back home in Cleveland, she found this held true.

*And you want to be that person. If only in someone else's eyes. Someone special.*

This was why she was now standing at her window, searching the faces in the evening crowds below, hoping to see a familiar face.

*Julian's face...*

Julian was an artist, a very contemporary, abstract kind of artist. His paintings were easily recognized by his signature use of big splashes and broad brushstrokes of color. She had met him when she first arrived in Paris, and liked to think they were very good friends.

This was why she was hoping, at this very minute, he might be on his way to her apartment. He'd changed his mind and would be more than happy to accompany her to Cleveland for Abby and Kevin's wedding. Even though she knew this wasn't an option, since he'd already committed to a showing of his work at a gallery the same weekend.

But this was okay... she got it. Right now, his career came first. At the mercy of the followers of the who's-who-in-the-art-world, he had put everything else in his life on hold. Determined to break through to the top and get the recognition he deserved, it appeared he was finally close to reaching this goal.

But, and he was always so quick to remind her of this, if he slacked off even the least bit, he could very well become invisible once again.

And, as he dramatically informed her, his life would be over.

# CHAPTER 1

Sophie liked to tell people she could see the Eiffel Tower from the window of her third-floor walk-up. Now, maybe this was stretching the truth a bit. Since there were quite a few different factors involved for this to happen.

First of all, you had to smash almost the whole side of your face against the glass to get the right angle. It also had to be a relatively cloudless day.

And finally?

You had to squint really, *really* hard.

But there it was, the Eiffel Tower. Or, as any proud Parisian would quickly inform you, *La Tour Eiffel*. In all its glory.

Okay… so maybe only the top of the tower was visible.

But most people were impressed by this. In fact, she'd found that living in Paris was enough for most people to be in awe of whatever she had to say. Even if she embellished the truth a bit. She could claim she had almost climbed to the top of the Eiffel Tower. Or she had

# FEBRUARY'S ANGEL

*If I knew I would be falling in love with an angel, I would have searched for you harder and found you sooner.*
*~ Anonymous*

# A NOTE FROM L. B. JOYCE

*I would like to dedicate this book to all my readers,*
*as you are what inspires me to keep writing.*
*May you always have romance in your life,*
*and love in your hearts.*

# ALSO BY L. B. JOYCE

This is Book 3 in the series,
Twelve Months, Twelve Love Stories

*A Million Decembers*

*For the Love of July*

*February's Angel*

*Promise Me November*

*An Unexpected June*

*A January to Remember*

*September's Moonlight Serenade*

*Goodbye Heartbreak, Hello May*

*March, a Song and a Dance*

Holidays in White Oaks Valley

*A Grand Slam Kind of Christmas*

Since his paintings were gaining in popularity, she wasn't worried. Even though she still hadn't figured out what message he was attempting to send with his work. So many times she'd tried to match the title to the painting in front of her. But as of yet, she couldn't find the connection.

Not for a single one of his paintings.

Sort of like she wasn't able to connect with him.

*Nothing clicked.*

She absentmindedly fingered the locket he gave her only last week. He had insisted he wanted to give her something to show how he felt about her. But since she so adamantly told him she didn't want a ring, this necklace was what he chose. He had designed the locket himself, inserting photos of them inside. He also had it engraved on the back, with only one word.

*Forever.*

But as much as she hated to admit this, forever was not a word she associated with Julian.

So, why was she so desperately wishing he would change his mind about this trip? Maybe because she was in need of a friend? Someone to show up with, sending out the message the events of last summer? Well, that was now old news. It didn't matter anymore. She had moved on.

*And it frightens you to know how far from the truth this is.*

She turned away from the window. She needed to stop thinking and start packing. Staring blindly at the clothes hanging in her closet, she finally chose her one reliable black dress and her favorite blue dress. All the while, she made it a point to ignore the royal blue evening gown hanging there. It was the dress she had worn when she went to the Children's Hospital Benefit with Chester Mazzori last July. The first of the two times she'd spent with him.

*And it had been wonderful.*

Unfortunately, the second time they were together had gone in the opposite direction, turning her life upside down. She'd compare it to being yanked out of a beautiful dream, to then be thrown right back into her ordinary life.

Raking her hand through her hair, she gave an irritated sigh. She couldn't start thinking about that. This would only lead to thinking about him.

But after she tossed the dresses in her suitcase, she sank down on the bed and closed her eyes.

*Why can't you let it go?*

You'd think her mind would have said enough already, it was time to move on. If only to let her live in peace. But this hadn't happened.

Abruptly leaving the bed, she returned to her closet. Grabbing a couple of sweaters and shirts, her two favorite pairs of jeans, and her leggings from the top shelf, she tossed them in her suitcase. Since her plan was only to be gone for a week, she didn't need to pack much. And if she stopped to think about it, who did she need to impress?

*No one... absolutely no one.*

Almost angrily zipping up the suitcase, she set it by the door.

She checked her phone to see her flight had been delayed again, this time by almost another hour. After she changed the time for her taxi, she curled up in the chair by the window, a sadness creeping through her.

She hated these sudden moods taking hold of her. They left her feeling unsettled, a nagging uncertainty hanging over her. This wasn't like her. She had never been a gloomy, why-did-this-happen-to-me kind of person. But here she was, exactly that.

She knew this was because she wasn't sure what to expect when she was finally back in Cleveland.

*You know you are going to see him again. But what happens next is what worries you.*

Chester Mazzori...

*He had never left your mind.*

And she was beginning to believe he never would.

# CHAPTER 2

*A*fter Chester brought her home from the benefit on that July night, she had been too excited to even think about going to bed.

Because, honestly?

Look at how much her life had changed over the past few days. How was it, through such a random encounter, she would end up attending a formal event with a man she met on the street?

*A celebrity, of sorts.*

Professional major league baseball players would fall under the category of being famous, wouldn't they? Even more so if they were rated as one of the top players in the league?

And there was no doubt about it, Chester Mazzori was good at what he did. He was also, unarguably, the most attractive man she had ever met. Even now, thinking about him, a shiver traveled through her, all the way from her head to her toes.

She had taken a big chance on that hot and humid July afternoon when she made such an impulsive stop on the busy highway. To then run into oncoming traffic to rescue the puppy. But there was no way she would have let the poor little thing get run over. No, she was too much of an animal lover to let that happen.

And how did she and Chester meet?

This had happened when he'd been forced to slam on his brakes in order to avoid running into the back of her stopped car. When he first got out of his car, she could tell by his expression, he wasn't very happy with her.

*Definitely not the best of starts.*

But then everything began to change. At the risk of sounding crazy, it was as though some unknown power suddenly swooped down and *poof...* there was this instant connection between them.

*So, as you can see, this was no ordinary encounter.*

No, they had fallen into the midst of a life-changing experience, one she knew she couldn't let slip away. And she did this the best way she knew how. She began chattering away, about everything and anything.

When they finally parted, he left her with the promise of baseball tickets. And how had she responded? By suggesting he should seriously think of shaving off his beard and trimming the overgrown mop of hair he had going on.

*What were you thinking? Baseball tickets versus personal hygiene advice? This certainly didn't seem like a fair exchange, did it?*

Call it women's intuition, or whatever, but she got the distinct feeling he was using all of that hair as a shield. And as attractive as she already found him, she couldn't even imagine how handsome he would be without it.

If there was anyone knowledgeable about the life-changing power of a makeover, it would be her. She had sat through umpteen classes and lectures on the importance of putting your best foot forward. Be it hair, makeup, and/or clothing.

She knew her stuff.

To say she was thrilled when he called the next day to ask if she would be his date for the Children's Hospital Benefit would be an understatement. And, when he arrived at her door the night of the event, he about took her breath away. Because gone were the unruly hair and beard. And just as she had predicted, he was even more devastatingly handsome than before.

In fact, she had been almost speechless, a trait for her, one that rarely ever happened.

The evening had gone on to be magical in every sense of the word. Until she had gone and made a mess of everything. She asked him to kiss her.

*Who does something like this? Certainly not the type of women he was used to dating.*

But the gentleman he is, he didn't let her down. Granted, it was a very casual kiss. But it was enough for her to know this was another thing he was good at.

Maybe even better than baseball.

So, she told him this… blurted it right out loud.

*Again, not one of your better moves, judging by his amused chuckle.*

Totally embarrassed, she had practically thrown herself out of his SUV. Unfortunately, she was barefoot. She had kicked off her shoes as soon as they got in the car. Since Chester was so tall, she really had no choice but to wear the highest heels she could manage, and her feet had been begging for mercy.

He had tried to persuade her to put on the shoes on for the short walk to her door, but she'd childishly refused. So, he picked her up and carried her to the door.

Now beyond flustered, she invited him in. But he declined. Taking this as an indication she should write off the whole evening and give him the chance to make his escape, she bid him a quick goodnight and slipped inside.

But proof miracles really do happen, he'd knocked on the door. He told her he wanted to see her again, but he wanted to take it slow. Because what they had was too special to hurry.

Yes, these had been his exact words.

And this was when she knew…

Chester Mazzori was the man she was going to marry.


She should have known this had been too good to be true.

Proof of this was the next morning when her life suddenly took a turn in a whole new direction. Beginning with her phone ringing at the ridiculous hour of seven-thirty in the morning.

It was her Aunt Louise. She needed Sophie at the boutique right away. There was something very exciting they needed to discuss.

And no, it couldn't wait.

When she had arrived at The Chic Boutique, the designer clothing store she managed with her aunt, she found her aunt in a panic. She had received a call from a business associate in Paris. A shop was available on the fashionable Avenue des Champs-Élysées, and if she moved fast, the shop would be hers.

It had always been her aunt's dream to open a boutique in Paris. This is where she had studied design and also where she met her husband, Paul. Swedish born, he had been in Paris studying architecture. After a whirlwind courtship, they had married.

But when Sophie's parents divorced and her mother passed away shortly afterward, her aunt and uncle found themselves as the appointed guardians to Sophie and her younger twin sister and brother, Hannah and Brian.

So, they moved back to Cleveland. Louise opened The Chic Boutique and Paul set up his architectural firm.

It was because of her aunt's influence, Sophie had chosen a career in fashion. So, it was assumed once she graduated from college, she would join her aunt at the boutique.

And now there was this new venture in Paris.

But there was a slight problem. Paul was scheduled to undergo back surgery. With the long recovery period to follow, Louise didn't feel comfortable leaving him. This, she told Sophie, was where she came in. She would be the one to go to Paris.

Not only would she undertake the grand opening of the boutique, but she would also stay on permanently as the manager.

It was the opportunity of a lifetime. And who knew? Maybe while in Paris, she would meet someone and fall in love. Exactly like she had fallen in love with her Paul all those years ago.

After all, wasn't Paris known as the city of love?

Sophie was trying to take this all in.

At the same time, she was in denial.

*You don't need Paris. And falling in love? You're pretty sure the man you want is right here. Less than twenty minutes away.*

In her excitement, her aunt hadn't even noticed Sophie didn't seem to share her enthusiasm. She chattered on about how great this would be for their business. It would fly through the roof when their customers found out about the boutique in Paris. This was an opportunity that would take them to the next level. It would label them as a fashion icon here in Cleveland.

She got the chills just thinking about this.

She has also been told there was a furnished apartment available. It was a third-floor walk-up, conveniently located in the same building housing the boutique.

She had also checked on flights. If they got to work right away, set up a plan and ordered merchandise to be sent directly to Paris, Sophie could leave as early as the end of the week.

Everything was in their favor. Including the interior of the boutique, recently painted and ready to be stocked with new merchandise. This would include a line of vintage clothing and accessories, something she knew was Sophie's passion.

Of course, there would also be a new name on the store front.

*Sophie's.*

This was the name she had chosen for the boutique. It was the perfect name. Sophisticated, yet whimsical. Even Paul had agreed.

And this is what drove it all home. When Sophie knew she couldn't let her aunt down. She owed her too much.

But, seriously? Why did this have to happen now?

*A week, or even a few days ago, you would've been thrilled.*

But now there was Chester.

*Yes, Chester. The man you have already decided you're going to marry.*

If, by chance, he did call, how was she going to be able to explain? But there was also a good possibility she would never hear from him again. Either way, the outcome wouldn't be good.

Suddenly feeling both anxious and irritated, she'd glanced over to see her aunt had finished her call. A frantic expression on her face, she was mumbling to herself as she checked off items from a buyer's catalog.

She shoved Chester into the far corner of her mind and went over to help her aunt.

Yeah, as you can imagine, this was easier said than done…

Between working on the plans for the new store, and dealing with the handful of customers who wandered into the boutique, it was late afternoon before Sophie finally had a few minutes to herself. Her aunt was out running errands, so she had the place to herself.

Though she wasn't really alone. For the last two hours, a woman had gone back and forth between the dressing room and the large mirror set up in the corner of the shop at least a dozen times. She had now narrowed her selection down to two dresses. But she wasn't sure if her choice would pass her daughter's approval.

Sophie watched her disappear into the dressing room again, an even more anxious expression on her face. This was exactly why she had convinced her aunt it would be a bad idea to carry wedding dresses in the boutique.

During her internship in a bridal shop, Sophie had witnessed how the high expectations of shopping for a wedding dress could so quickly turn into an episode of drama and tears. To the extent the final profit from the sale hadn't even come close to covering the time and stress involved.

This was also when she'd decided if she ever got married, she didn't want a big wedding. Nope, her plan involved get married on a beach somewhere. With the setting sun as the background. And her family and close friends as the only guests.

The groom would have no choice but to go along with this.

*But it's beginning to look like this is never going to happen, doesn't it?*

With a sigh, she had picked up her phone to check her messages.

And there it was … a voice message from Chester.

Her heart beating a mile a minute, she had leaned back against the counter to listen to his message. The deep, velvety tone of his voice flowed through her, the tension and frustration she'd been carrying around all day slowly fading away.

*Hey angel, it's Chester. I'd like to take you out to dinner on Thursday. I wish it could be sooner, but we have a game both today and tomorrow. Let me know if this will work for you. I can pick you up at seven.*

A few moments of silence passed before he spoke again.

*I've been thinking about you... a lot. So, call me. Until Thursday, then.*

She stared down at the phone, when what she wanted to do was put her head down on the counter and cry.

Even go as far to start sobbing.

But she really wasn't one to cry. She wasn't sure why. Maybe it was because her sister Hannah cried enough for the both of them? Something had to go extremely and horribly wrong for her to break down in tears.

*You should be happy. He called. And this is what you had hoped would happen, right?*

Yes... and then, no.

She'd listened to the message again.

*Thursday...*

Since there was a chance they might forfeit the Paris space if they waited too long, her aunt had already suggested Sophie schedule her flight for Friday. She wanted her in Paris as soon as possible.

So, Sophie had a decision to make.

A small part of her, the logical part, knew she should tell him she was leaving, maybe even permanently. And she would understand if he wanted to cancel. She'd be fine with this.

*What a big lie this was.*

But the rest of her wanted to see him again. If only as a test. After all, this time could be different, the connection no longer between them. Then she would be able to fly off to Paris, knowing she was leaving nothing behind.

*And this was even a bigger lie.*

For a few minutes, she did nothing. Then, picking up her phone, she hit his number. When she was switched over to his voice mail, she left her message.

*Chester, this is Sophie. Hi, Thursday would be fine. I have some unexpected news to share with you. I confess I've been thinking of you, too. Umm... I'll see you then.*

Dropping the phone in her lap, she had leaned back in her chair and closed her eyes.

*Auuugghhhhhh...*

*I confess I've been thinking of you, too? How in the world did you come up with that choice of words? So prim and proper.*

At the sound of someone tentatively clearing their throat, she had opened her eyes. The woman who had been agonizing over her dress choice was standing in front of her.

Her voice firm, she had laid a dress on the counter. "This is the dress. With a few minor alterations, it will be perfect. My daughter will just have to accept my decision."

She sent a glance over at Sophie's left hand. "I see you're not married. When you do decide to get married, promise me you'll be nice to your mother. We aren't all that bad, you know."

Shaking her head, Sophie had taken the dress from her. "I doubt I'll ever get married since I don't seem to do well at relationships. Something always happens to put an end to them before they even begin. I'm beginning to think I'm one of those women destined to be the bridesmaid, never the bride."

For some odd reason, she had then gone on to tell the woman all about the boutique in Paris. And her date with Chester.

The woman, who Sophie learned was Helen Peters, was excited.

"I live right next door to Chester's aunt. Evelyn is her name. She is so proud of him and talks about him all the time. He comes for one of her home-cooked dinners at least once or twice a month. I understand, since her lasagna is to die for."

She frowned. "Evelyn once told me Chester was married when he was younger. But the marriage only lasted for about a year. His wife ran off with another man. Supposedly, he had been madly in love with her and took the breakup really hard."

Her forehead creased in thought. "I think his parents passed away when he was a teenager and since then, Evelyn has been like a surrogate mother to him and his three sisters. His youngest sister is the only one still living in the area, Carrie. She's a beautiful girl. An interior designer, I believe."

This information is not what Sophie had wanted to hear. From what Helen Peters had told her, it sounded like Chester had more than his share of being left behind.

And now she would be doing the same.

*Even though this was the last thing you want to do.*

The dress paid for and an appointment set for the fitting, Helen Peters left the boutique.

Glancing around at the silent shop, Sophie dropped her head on her arms and gave a long, frustrated sigh

*It just wasn't fair.*

# CHAPTER 3

*Once in a lifetime,*
*you meet someone who changes everything.*
*~ Unknown*

At the sound of someone banging on her Paris apartment door, an unwelcome interruption of her daydreams, Sophie nearly d out of the chair.

She opened the door, thinking it was the taxi driver.

It was Julian.

He immediately wrapped her in a big hug. *"Ma chérie!* I am so glad to see you have not left yet! I wanted to see you one last time, just to let you know how much I'm going to miss you."

Claiming her mouth with his, he gave her a long, passionate kiss. Then his eyes slowly roaming over her face, his voice was husky with desire. "Come on, *SO-pheee.* Let me show you how much I love you. This way I will always be on your mind while you are gone."

They were doing a dance with their hands, his trying to bring her closer, hers trying to push him away. His kisses becoming more urgent, he moved them over to the bed, stretching out beside her.

Now as much as she loved how he said her name, *SO-pheee,* and that he called her *ma chérie*, she didn't want to have to fight him on this again.

It just wasn't right.

*He wasn't right.*

*Is it possible you feel this way because he interrupted your dreams about Chester?*

Maybe?

She closed her eyes, giving a frustrated sigh. Okay, so maybe it was because of Chester. But no matter how hard she tried to feel differently, Julian wasn't—nor ever would be—Chester.

*There's no anticipation, no eager flutter in your stomach at the thought of his kiss. Nor does your heart start beating in a frenzy when you see him, almost as if it wanted to leap right out of your chest.*

Nope.

There was no spark.

No desire.

*God, no... if Chester was on the bed with you right now, there is no way you would be able to resist him. Not in a million years.*

Her sigh had Julian pause his onslaught of kisses. He gazed down at her, an inquiring expression on his face.

She scooted out from under him and, sitting on the edge of the bed, she reached out to touch his cheek. "Julian, *please...* I told you before, I'm not ready for this. And I don't know if I ever will be."

He gave a huge groan and, rolling over onto his back, he dramatically threw his arm across his forehead. Then he slowly lifted his head, peering sharply at her.

"From what you're saying, I'm beginning to wonder if there is another man in your life. A man you haven't told me about, *ma chérie.* Could this be true?"

His expression went from thoughtful to determined. "Because if there is, I am sure I can prove I'm the more charming of the two of us. And I can definitely be the better lover. You only need to let me prove this."

He reached for her, rolling them back onto the bed. Swooping in to give her a kiss, he frowned when she turned away, her lips tightly pressed together.

With a sharp intake of breath, he abruptly left the bed. Dragging his hands through his hair, his look was one of disbelief. "There is someone else, isn't there? How could this be? And more importantly, why did you start something with me if you are already in another relationship?"

She left the bed, taking his hands in hers. "Julian, there is really no one else. There might have been, but nothing came of it before I left for Paris. And now, I can't stop wondering what might have happened if I had stayed. If the outcome would have been different."

She shrugged. "Once I'm back home, maybe I'll be able to see things more clearly. I don't know, I really don't. I only know I'm so confused." She slowly shook her head. "Please try to understand."

He took her into his arms and, after a long, drawn-out sigh, he rested his cheek to the top of her head. He wasn't worried, at least not yet. He would let her go home where he truly believed she would come to her senses.

She had to realize he was the one for her. How could she not? Together, they were a perfect fit.

He gazed down at her. "Okay, I will try to be patient. But you do realize I can't wait forever." He frowned. "Don't make me regret I didn't go with you. Instead, I want you to come back, all of this hesitation gone from your mind so you can belong to me. Then we will take Paris by a storm."

Abruptly letting her go, he headed for the door. He was still talking. "And now, I must go. I didn't tell anyone I was leaving, and the gallery is in such a disarray. I don't even want to think about how much work there is to be done before the show."

She followed him to the door, where he turned to frame her face with his hands, his voice a husky whisper. "Tu es l'amour de ma vie."

Since her French was still somewhat limited, she wasn't quite sure what he said. But judging by the tone of his voice, it had to be something romantic. So, she tried to lose herself in the kiss he gave her, hoping she'd feel something.

But again, there was nothing.

*Nope... nothing.*

*Not at all like when Chester kissed you.*

If anything, Julian's kiss left her feeling frustrated. As though something was missing, leaving her with a yearning for so much more. There was no breathless hitch of her heart. Or the feeling she was falling into a moment in time she never wanted to leave.

She went to stand at the window, waiting for him to come out of the building. Once he appeared, moving in his usual quick Julian fashion, he paused to gaze up in her direction. When he saw her, he smiled and after blowing her a kiss, he went sprinting down the sidewalk. Only after he was out of sight, did she finally turn away.

Her hands going to her throat, she fingered the locket.

*Why can't you like him as much as he seems to care for him?*

Evidently, there was something majorly wrong with her, because most women would kill for a man like Julian. He was successful, extremely handsome, and so incredibly sexy. His voice alone, with the bonus of his French accent, was enough to make a woman want to follow him anywhere.

*But for you? Again, nothing clicks.*

Her taxi now due to arrive at any minute, she decided to go downstairs to wait. She slipped into her coat and, picking up her suitcase, she closed the door behind her. Suddenly tempted to turn around and slip right back inside, she quickly began making her way down the stairs, dragging her suitcase behind her.

She never thought going home would make her feel this way, filled with such conflicting emotions.

On the one hand, she was excited about Abby and Kevin's wedding and seeing her friends and family. After all, she hadn't been back since she left for Paris back in July.

On the other hand, she was terrified of what might happen when she saw Chester again. Her only hope was she didn't make a complete fool of herself.

If she did, all the stories in the world wouldn't make her any more interesting.

# CHAPTER 4

*A*bsentmindedly fingering the baseball he held in his hand, Chester watched another gust of snow whip past his window.

What had started out as a few random flakes only a short time ago had now developed into a full-blown blizzard. He hoped the latest prediction this new wave of snow would be long gone before Kevin and Abby's rehearsal dinner on Friday was on the mark.

Today was Wednesday. So, a lot could happen between now and then.

He smiled, shaking his head. Everyone who lived in Cleveland knew how unpredictable the weather could be. And they all blamed it on the lake effect. He wasn't quite sure he went along with this, but knew he was tired of snow. It had started up right after Christmas, and he'd swear it hadn't let up since.

If anything, he was feeling pretty pleased with his decision pick up his tuxedo earlier. He'd actually picked up all the tuxes, seven total. This covered the wedding party, along with Abby and Kevin's fathers. As the best man, it seemed like the logical thing to do, since he and Kevin were the only two in town right now.

No doubt Kevin had plenty of things to keep him busy. Abby would make sure of this.

*Yeah, you're a real Mr. Nice Guy. But then, what else do you have going on right now?*

Sadly, not a damn thing…

Sobered by this thought, he set the baseball down and pushed away from his desk. His hands shoved in his pockets, he strolled over to the window just in time to watch the snowplow rumble past.

This had him wondering … was it snowing in Paris now? Glancing at his watch, he saw it was a little after four. This meant it was a little past ten in the evening there.

*Sophie…*

A familiar feeling of loss coming over him, he closed his eyes.

He could see her so clearly in his mind. Unfortunately, the expression of bewilderment and pain on her face was what he remembered the most. But he had only himself to blame for this.

*You're such a damn idiot.*

Jamming his hands further in his pockets, he stared unseeingly out at the slowly moving traffic.

He wondered… Was she alone in her apartment? Like he was right now? Possibly thinking about him?

*Yeah, right.*

He gave a short laugh. More likely, she was out on a date with this French guy. Julius or Jude, whatever the hell his name was. Abby had let this information slip the other day when he'd helped her and Kevin move into their new condo. From what she said, this guy was crazy about Sophie.

He frowned.

Stupid name for a guy, no matter who he was. Abby said he was an artist. This made it even worse. How did he think he was going to make a living, painting pictures? Let alone support someone?

Sophie deserved the best. And if he could somehow convince her he was the one for her, he would give her everything.

*Anything. Everything. He would give her it all.*

But this was all hopeful thinking on his part. Sophie wasn't his.

And it was beginning to look like a sure bet she never would be. Hadn't she made it clear her career was more important than he was?

So maybe she and this French guy were a better fit after all.

If only he could persuade his heart to go along with this. Then maybe he'd be able to move on. But after the last kiss they shared, he knew this was probably never going to happen.

Nope, the kiss had changed everything.

Sinking down into his chair, he leaned back and closed his eyes.

And once again, he was right back with Sophie on that fateful night in July.

# CHAPTER 5

*Sometimes, love works.*
*But sometimes, it hurts more.*
*~ Anonymously Yours*

After Chester had listened to Sophie's voice message accepting his dinner invitation, he hadn't been able to stop thinking about this 'news' she'd said she wanted to share.

What did she mean? Was it good news? Or bad news? Did it involve him? Them?

By the time he'd arrived at her townhouse the night of their dinner date, he'd prepared himself for the worst.

But his worry had all but disappeared when she opened the door.

Wearing a blue sundress that brought out the blue of her eyes, once again he fell right under her spell.

When she gazed up at him, their eyes meeting, he had been hit by such a strong wave of desire, it took everything he had not to pull her into his arms.

So he could kiss her. Maybe even until she begged him to stop.

Instead, he'd somehow managed to place a casual kiss on her cheek before he mumbled some inane remark about the color blue. It was her color, he told her. Making her eyes even a more beautiful shade of blue. The color of bluebells, he would have to say.

When she only continued to gaze up at him, her expression puzzled, he then had to go on and explain how bluebells were flowers his Aunt Evelyn always insisted on in her garden because of their beautiful coloring.

If he were to be honest, he wasn't sure if he'd ever seen one. And if he had, he probably hadn't paid much attention. But with the way his aunt carried on about them, they had to be pretty spectacular.

Almost as spectacular as the beautiful blue eyes he was now gazing into, unable to look away for the life of him.

Thank goodness, his explanation seemed to have gone over well. In fact, everything continued to go well during the drive to the restaurant, all the way up until they finished their entrées.

They had talked about everything. Their families, the always safe topic of the weather and, of course, baseball. He told her things about himself he had never shared with anyone else. He'd swear she had a way of bringing the words right out of him.

But not once did she bring up the news she told him she'd wanted to share. In fact, she seemed to avoid any talk at all about what she did. Except for her vague comment, she helped manage a women's clothing store with her aunt. Or as she'd referred to it, a boutique. Not much into fashion, he assumed this had to mean fancy. Or more likely, expensive.

Now, Chester is not the brooding type. Or should we say, he's not a pessimistic kind of guy. No, he liked to think of himself as a very positive person. A go-getter. A take-charge kind of person. To succeed at what he did for a living, he needed to be almost overconfident. This was what usually brought out the best results on the field.

His theory on this? No one had ever hit a home run if they hadn't been convinced they were capable of doing so.

But for some reason, he'd begun to feel very apprehensive about how the rest of the evening would go. There was a cautiousness about Sophie he couldn't quite figure out. As if she was keeping something from him.

So, he could only wait.

The waitress had cleared their table and poured Sophie's coffee.

Lounging back in his chair, Chester stirred his Scotch and amaretto. Content to watch Sophie as she studied the dessert menu, he smiled at the seriousness of her expression as she mulled over her choices.

She had finally glanced over at him, her smile shy. "If I order something, will you share it with me?"

Honest, and he would swear by this, he had no idea he would say what he did.

It just came out. "Angel, I'll share anything with you. For as long as you want me to."

And this, unfortunately, was when everything started to go downhill. He could only watch as her eyes seemed to grow bigger and brighter as they searched his face. Then, after staring down at the menu, slowly she'd closed it. Clasping her hands together in front of her, he could see they had started to shake.

*This wasn't what one would call an encouraging sign.*

Her words had come out in a whisper. "Chester, I'm leaving."

At first, he didn't understand. Or maybe it was more like he didn't want to understand.

*She was leaving? When? Now? Where was she going? And why?*

His first instinct to stop her hands from shaking, he'd reached over to grasp them firmly in his. "I don't understand. You're leaving? Where are you going?"

She'd refused to look at him. Her gaze focused on their hands, her voice was so low he had to lean in closer to hear her. "Paris... I'm going to Paris, France. My aunt is opening a boutique in one of the more fashionable areas of the city. This is something that has always been a dream of hers. Since my uncle is scheduled to have surgery, she wants me to go in her place. I couldn't say no. I owe her so much. She has done so much for me, Hannah and Brian. I have to go. I..." Her voice trailing off, she had still refused to meet his gaze.

For a few moments, he was silent, not sure if he understood what she was trying to tell him.

*See? You were right in thinking something like this would happen. Why did you think, for just this once, things would finally work out in your favor?*

Then, giving her hands a gentle squeeze, he responded. "We can still see each other until you have to leave. And we'll keep in touch until you come back. Do you know how long you will be gone?"

Shaking her head, she'd pulled away. "No, no, no... I can't do this to you. It's not fair. Because I think... I..."

She'd paused, taking a deep breath. This should have been a warning, what she had to say next wasn't going to be what he wanted to hear. But again, he was clueless.

Averting her gaze, her words were barely audible. "This may turn out to be permanent, and my flight leaves tomorrow morning. I know I should have told you this, but we didn't make the flight reservation until late this afternoon. And I wanted... I... I should have called you right then to tell you and I know it was wrong of me not to, but I... I didn't want..."

Her words trailing into silence, the silence that followed had been unbearable, as almost in shock, he'd waited for her to say something else... anything. Or at least give him a reasonable explanation for why she hadn't let him know about this from the beginning.

But she did no such thing. Instead, she had remained silent, still refusing to meet his eyes.

He was finally the one to make the first move. Reaching up to run his hand through his hair, he slowly leaned back in his chair.

*What the hell? Why did she wait to tell you this?*

A slow anger began to fill him.

This showed in the frustration filling his voice. "I can't believe this. And I don't understand why you waited until now to tell me this. *God,* Sophie... I would've tried to find time... no, I would have *made* time to see you over the past few days if I knew you were leaving. The hell with the games."

When she didn't say anything, he'd persisted, something now he wished he wouldn't have done. But he was having such a hard time, all of these emotions slamming into him and he couldn't even think straight.

"And here I thought we were on the same track. That there was something between us. Something special." He slowly shook his head. "I thought you felt this, too. But evidently, I was wrong."

Again, he'd waited for her to say something. Again, there was only silence. And damn if he didn't go and make things even worse. "Is this what you have to do? Or is it something you're doing because you feel the need to prove yourself?"

Her head had shot up, her eyes finally meeting his. And this was when he realized he'd gone too far.

But it was too late. Now she was the angry one. Glaring at him angry, her expression one he hoped to never again experience. At least not when it was because of something he did.

*If there was even the chance of an ever again.*

Her voice had been firm, almost clipped. "Yes, it's something I both want and have to do. And I assure you, I am not trying to prove anything. Not to you or anyone else. I've worked really hard to get to this point, and this is a great step in my career. You can't tell me you don't understand, because I'm sure you've also made sacrifices to further your career."

She'd shrugged. "Plus, I can't just quit on a whim. I have bills to pay."

He could only stare at her.

On a whim?

This is what she considered him? A passing fancy?

He'd opened his mouth to say something, but then just as quickly closed it. He'd wanted to tell her, whim or not, he'd gladly pay all of her bills if she decided not to go to Paris. She wouldn't even have to work. God knows he made more than enough money for the both of them. He'd buy her a store or what was it she called it again?

A boutique? Yeah, he'd buy her a dozen of those.

*Thank God, you hadn't blurted this out.*

He could only imagine what she would've said if he had.

Afraid of what else could come out of his mouth, he'd remained completely silent. She'd followed his lead, not uttering another word.

After he'd paid the bill and they left the restaurant, the time spent in his SUV for the drive to her townhouse was complete torture. He'd wanted to say something, anything… but he didn't know what he could say to make things better. A few times, he'd almost reached over to hold her hand. If only to let her know, even if he wasn't sure what to say, he was there for her.

But he did none of this. No, instead he let his own conflicting emotions take over.

She, in turn, kept her face turned toward the passenger window, while nervously clasping and unclasping her hands in her lap.

Of course, now that he'd had the time to think about everything, he knew exactly what he should've said.

Starting out by telling her he understood.

*Even though, at the time, you hadn't.*

He would've convinced her they could make it work. Planes flew back and forth between Paris and Ohio every day.

Okay, maybe not every day. But enough that they would be able to see each other often. After all, they weren't living in the horse and buggy era.

There were a lot of options available out there.

He also would've assured her that he knew the situation wasn't ideal. And it wouldn't be easy. But they could do it. Because he believed, even with the short time they had known each other, they had a future together.

*Finally, you would have told her, if there was the one thing you knew for sure, it was you weren't ready to let her go.*


Before Chester had even turned off the ignition, Sophie was out of the SUV and running up the sidewalk. After breaking into a sprint to catch up with her, he watched as she struggled with the lock. Concerned that her hands had started to shake, he took the keys from her and unlocked the door.

To his dismay, without uttering a single word, she pushed open the door to go inside.

Filled with a quiet desperation, he knew he couldn't leave her this way. Turning her to face him, and pressing a soft kiss to her forehead, her name had come from him in a frustrated sigh.

*"Sophie...*

She'd responded by leaning into him, and closing her eyes, she gave the softest of sighs.

And he was gone. A groan coming from low and deep in his throat, he'd pulled her up against him, covering her mouth with his. When she reached up to wrap her arms around his neck, he'd deepened the kiss. Exploring her mouth with a passion unbeknownst to him ever before, he'd put everything he had into that kiss.

Yes, it had been some kiss, unforgettable in so many ways. Taken to a place he'd never been before, it was a place he never wanted to leave.

He only knew he didn't want it to end, certain she'd felt the same.

*No, you know she'd felt the same. You could feel this in the way she responded.*

But then, what did he do? He'd opened his mouth again.

*A bad move. A really, really bad move.*

Placing his hands on her shoulders, he'd waited until she opened her eyes. His gaze searching, his voice had been rough. "If you still feel the need to leave? Then go. Because I don't know how else to prove to you how I feel."

He turned and walked away.

Unfortunately, the stunned expression on her face was one he would never forget, ingrained in his memory forever

# CHAPTER 6

*C*hester's phone rang. This had him falling right back into the present. Almost in a daze, he picked it up to see it was Kelly. He groaned.

*You can only blame yourself for this. It was a big mistake asking her to be your date for the Winter Snowball Charity Dance.*

Why had he let everyone talk him into doing such a stupid thing? Because ever since then, she hadn't stopped calling. Sometimes two or three times a day.

And this had been going on now for how long? Over two weeks?

Yeah, she was beautiful. If you like the fake, beauty queen kind of look. But her personality had much to be desired. This had become obvious within minutes after he'd arrived at her townhouse to pick her up for the dance.

And talk about high maintenance. They had spent almost the entire night arguing, if only because he was so put off by her constant demands for his attention, along with just about everyone else in the room.

But even after an evening that could only be classified as a total disaster, she still kept calling him.

He sighed, running his hand over his face. He knew she was probably still hoping he would ask her to be his date for Kevin and Abby's wedding. Even after he'd told her he wasn't planning on taking a date.

He had made this very clear. Twice, maybe even three times. He had also told her, quite adamantly, he wasn't interested in starting up a relationship right now. No, he was pretty sure he was done with relationships of all kinds.

*Damn sure.*

When you completely fail at something as many times as he had, it was a sign you needed to throw in the towel and give it up.

*For good.*

He looked down at the phone to see she had left a message. As he was debating whether he should even bother to read it, the phone rang again.

He looked up at the ceiling, a huge groan coming from him.

*Is she ever going to stop?*

He picked up the phone and, without even checking the number, he barked out his hello.

There was a short silence on the other end before Kevin's voice came at him. "*Sheeesh…* is this your new way of answering the phone? If so, it's a surefire way to go about discouraging any future calls."

Running his hand over his chin, Chester gave an embarrassed laugh. "Sorry, I thought it was someone else. And no, it's not necessary for you to know who."

Leaning back in his chair, he swung his feet up to rest on the desk. "So, what's up? Another job for me?" He smiled. "Remember, once you're married, I'll be reverting back to my usual self and there will be no more favors. So, take advantage of this while you can. Speaking of favors, I picked up the tuxes. I'll bring them with me when we meet at the hotel on Friday."

He could hear Kevin talking to someone in the background before he came back on the phone. "Sorry, I'm picking up a pizza. Thanks for getting the tuxes. It's good you got that out of the way with this weather. What's with all of this snow?"

Chester picked up the baseball and, turning it in his hand, he laughed. "You need to even ask? This is Cleveland, remember? You're a Chicago native, so you should be used to this kind of weather. But try to relax, because from what they're predicting, tomorrow the snow is supposed to let up."

Kevin mumbled under his breath. "I hope you heard right, because Abby's going crazy. I'm learning very quickly how even the smallest thing can suddenly escalate into a major problem where a wedding is concerned. She just called me, all worked up about at least a half-dozen new developments. And even though I didn't see what the big deal was, I kept my mouth shut and did what she asked."

He laughed. "I've learned it's best this way. It's also the reason I'm calling. It looks like we could use your help again. And even though I said we, I want you to know I had nothing to do with this request. Nope, this is all Abby."

Tossing the ball up in the air and catching it, Chester smiled. "Sure, as long as you realize I'm keeping tabs on every request you throw at me."

Kevin laughed. "Yeah, I'm sure you are. But I don't know how you're going to feel about this one. It seems Sophie's flight got delayed before she even left Paris. Then a second delay had them re-routed to Pittsburgh. Why they could fly into Pittsburgh, but not Cleveland, I'm not sure. Anyway, as it stands now, she's scheduled to land in Cleveland around seven-thirty tonight. But Abby and I have a final meeting with the caterers at the same time, so we won't be able to pick her up."

There was a slight pause. "So, do you think you can do this? For some reason, Abby is insistent she shouldn't have to take a taxi."

Chester very slowly set the ball down on the desk and just as slowly lowered his feet back on to the floor. Dragging his hand over his jaw, he closed his eyes.

His mind was in an uproar.

*No, you can't. You won't do this. This isn't what you'd planned.*

*Your plan was to keep as much distance between the two of you as you could. And, by your reaction to Kevin's request, even though you thought you'd be okay with seeing Sophie again, it's obvious you've been fooling yourself.*

*Yep, it appears it doesn't matter if she is with you, or somewhere else...*

*Nor does it matter how many times you tell yourself you have to move on...*

*Or you try to convince yourself you don't need her in your life...*

*Your feelings for her are never going to change.*

*Not today. Not tomorrow. Or any day after.*

With all this swirling around in his mind, sort of like the snow he could see outside his window, he couldn't bring himself to speak.

Kevin broke the silence. "Hey, if this is a problem, I can find someone else. You were Abby's first choice, but—"

Galvanized into action, Chester shot up in his chair, his feet hitting the floor. He all but shouted. "No... *no*, I'll pick her up." This was followed by a long, measured breath. "Neither you nor Abby should have to worry about anything but getting married right now. Text me the flight information and I'll take care of it."

Kevin's sigh of relief came through over the phone. "Thanks. And hey, I really appreciate everything you've done so far." He chuckled. "To think I used to have you pegged as pretty much of a jerk."

Chester's laugh was short. "Well, as you have probably now realized, you're one of the few to find my bark is worse than my bite."

He could hear Kevin joking with someone as he paid for the pizza. When he came back on the phone, it was obvious he was impatient to end the call. "Yeah, and from what I've heard, I'm not the only one who has had a change of opinion about you. But I gotta go. Abby's probably wondering where I am. I'll text the flight info. Again, thanks!"

The screen on Chester's phone went blank.

Placing his phone on the desk and picking up the baseball again, he leaned back in his chair. He fingered the ball as he stared out the window.

What did Kevin mean when he said someone else now thought very differently of him? Who? It wasn't Sophie, was it?

No, he seriously doubted this. She'd pretty much made her feelings about him very clear.

His hand reaching for his phone, for one crazy moment he considered calling Kevin to ask what he meant by his comment.

Realizing how pathetic this would be, he pulled his hand back. Kevin could might have been talking about anyone. It could be one of the guys on the team, for all he knew.

*Just forget about it. You're grabbing at straws here.*

In an effort to banish Sophie from his mind, he glanced around the room, taking in the collection of the framed photos lining the walls.

They all had something to do with baseball.

There were photos of him accepting the trophy for his Home Run Derby win, his Rookie of the Year award and a dozen or more other awards. Some were even from college and high school. To look at all of them, you would think all he had ever done in life was played, talked, ate and slept baseball.

He sighed. In a way, this wasn't too far from the truth.

He was still a bit embarrassed by what he felt was such an extravagant display of sorts. After Thanksgiving, his sister Carrie had found all the photos and stuff packed away in his closet and about had a fit, insisting he needed to bring them out for people to see. He should be proud of what he had accomplished, she said, not hide them away in a dark corner of a closet.

Somehow, his Aunt Evelyn had suddenly been in on the project, thinking her opinion was needed. This resulted in everything escalating into a huge production. She and Carrie began having long discussions about paint colors. Asking his opinion on window treatments. Or showing him samples for what kind of area rug he'd prefer on the floor.

He was confused. Wasn't a rug just a rug? Did it matter?

It was suddenly imperative he have a new desk chair. Along with new lamps. And a pair of upholstered chairs for visitors. Who these visitors would be, he had no idea, but rather than argue, he told them to go ahead with their plans and do whatever they felt was necessary.

He had put his foot down on getting a new desk, though. The desk he had was fine. Originally belonging to his father, he was going to hang on to it no matter what they thought. And no baseball themed wallpaper. Or baseball print fabric for the chairs or window treatments.

This would be too over the top. Too cutesy.

*Please... that's the last thing you'd want.*

Everything else they were planning? Hell, he didn't care. It didn't matter to him. He'd only made it a point to stay out of their way. And now with the room finished, he had to admit it looked nice, his favorite addition the new desk chair he was sitting in.

But who wouldn't be happy with a top-of-the-line, extra padded-and-swivel-powered desk chair, all upholstered in a butter-soft leather?

But as he gazed around the room, he realized all the photos and awards he'd accumulated over the years and now on display? These weren't important. They weren't what was going to make him happy.

No, because of a one chance meeting, you want more

After he clasped his hands over his head in a long stretch, he reached for his phone to see if Kevin had sent the flight information. He had, the arrival time now moved to an even later time of eight-fifteen.

He glanced out the window. The snow was still coming down, making him wonder if it might be a good idea for him to leave now. Because if it kept snowing at the rate it was, the roads could become impassable. And if this didn't happen, so what? He'd rather get to the airport early. After the long travel time Sophie had to endure, when she finally got off the plane, there should be someone there to meet her.

If he left now, he would also be able to stop off at the gym and get in a good workout. This might help rid some of this restlessness he had going on.

Picking up his jacket, he hesitated. He wondered... did Sophie know he would be the one to pick her up? And if she did, was she okay with this?

He shook his head. He wasn't going to start thinking about this now. It would only send him right back to where he had been a few minutes ago, reliving everything he'd been working so hard to forget.

He threw on his jacket and grabbing his gym bag and his keys and headed for the door.

# CHAPTER 7

*A*s soon as the wheels of the plane touched down, Sophie let out a huge sigh of relief.

Seriously, if it was possible, she'd run right off the plane and kiss the ground it sat on.

She felt as though she'd been traveling for a month. As it was, she was arriving almost seven hours later than the originally scheduled time. But, peering out the window at the blizzard-like conditions, she was more than thankful to finally be in Cleveland.

She shivered, quickly slipping into her coat as a big gust of wind rocked the plane. She was exhausted and ready to drop, only having slept fitfully during the flight. She also couldn't remember when she'd last had something to eat. Those peanut butter crackers she gobbled down—had this been in London or Cleveland time?

She was wondering who'd be picking her up. She'd assured Abby she'd be more than happy to take a taxi, but Abby had quickly shot this down. She'd already arranged for someone to meet her, so Sophie wasn't to worry. But since this had all been set up according to her original flight time, she didn't know what to expect.

She watched the luggage slowly pass by on the baggage carousel, finally catching sight of her bright pink bag. When it came within reaching distance, she grabbed hold of the handle.

A hand closed over hers. At the same time, a familiar voice vibrated close to her ear, sending a shiver through her. "Here, let me get that for you."

She stopped dead in her tracks, her breath catching in her throat. And just like she'd feared, she was sent spiraling back into a world she had absolutely no control over.

*Chester...*

Chester had been strolling back and forth in the baggage claims area for about forty-five minutes. He had signed about a dozen autographs and posed for about the same number of photos. Now, his collar pulled up in the hopes of remaining as inconspicuous as possible, he stepped back to watch the latest group of arriving passengers flood the area.

He spotted Sophie the moment she turned the corner.

She looked totally exhausted. But at the same time, he only saw how beautiful she was, the royal blue coat she was wearing the exact same shade as her eyes.

*Bluebell blue...*

He wanted to go right up to her and enfold her in a big hug. If only for a few seconds to experience again how it felt to hold her in his arms. Instead, inching closer, he watched as she waited for her luggage. When she reached out to grab the handle of a bright pink bag, he quickly moved to take it from her, his hand covering hers.

This simple contact brought on such a strong emotional response from within him, he briefly had to close his eyes.

*It's still there. She still has a hold on you.*

Whether they wanted it or not, the chemistry was still there.

And from what he could tell?

It was even stronger than before.

Their hands still gripping the handle of her bag, Sophie turned to face him.

He searched her face, looking for some kind of sign. Relieved to see she appeared more surprised than angry or upset when she saw it was him, he slowly let out a long breath.

Sophie didn't know what she was thinking.

Well, she did, but she didn't want to acknowledge this. Instead she quickly averted her gaze, looking anywhere except in his direction. Because if she saw that look in his eyes, the one he always seemed to have for only her, she didn't know what she was going to do.

But then she couldn't help it, she did exactly what she didn't want to do.She gazed up and into his eyes.

*And it was still there.*

Slowly pulling her hand from his, she swallowed. *"Hi..."*

When he remained silent, his gaze still on her, the words came flying out of her mouth.

"I'm so sorry."

He seemed to come to life. Gently pulling her bag from her hand, he took her arm and moved them to a less crowded area.

Only then did he turn to her. "You're sorry? Whatever for?"

As she gazed back at him, she realized there were so many ways she could answer this.

She'd start out by telling him she was sorry they'd parted so abruptly and with so much left unsaid.

Then she'd swallow her pride, and this was a biggie, to let him know, no matter how many times over the past few months she'd tried, she hadn't been able to get the kiss they shared out of her mind.

And how so, so many times she'd wished there was some way they could do the kiss over again. If only to find out if it still made her feel the same way it did the first time.

Finally, she was just really sorry... so sorry about everything.

But she said none of these things. She was too afraid. What if he shrugged it off? Or told her he'd already moved on and it didn't matter anymore? They didn't matter anymore...

*This would about kill you.*

Her heart caught up in her throat, she swallowed again, her smile uncertain. "I'm so sorry you had to come out in this awful weather to pick me up. I told Abby I could take a taxi, but she seemed so upset I'd even suggested..."

She paused mid-sentence, her forehead creasing in thought. Had Abby done this on purpose? Was this her attempt to bring them together?

*Well, look how you tried to help her out when she and Kevin came so close to ending their relationship. So, you shouldn't be surprised, should you?*

She glanced up at Chester to see he had a funny expression on his face. Which made her believe he, too, suspected Abby may have set them up. A faint smile on his face, and with a slight shake of his head, he took her arm and began leading her towards the doors to the parking garage.

He finally spoke. "You never need to say you're sorry. And there's no way we would've asked you to take a taxi. Not after the long journey you've had."

He smiled down at her. It was such a genuine smile. A smile that spread a warmth through her she hadn't felt all day.

"Nope, this wouldn't be right, not at all."

# CHAPTER 8

"*W*oohoo… Chester! Chester Mazzori!" This shrill voice seemed to rise above everything, grabbing everyone's attention.

When Sophie felt Chester tense beside her, she turned to see a woman waving her hand wildly in the air as she pushed her way through the crowded terminal.

"*Damn…*" With this low curse, Chester put his arm around Sophie, keeping his voice low. "I can't seem to shake this woman. She's a local reporter with her own social events column and I don't know how she does it, but she always manages to turn up wherever I am."

He frowned. "You have to be on guard when you're around her. She has a way of getting things out of people they never intended to say. So, let me handle her, okay?"

When Sophie only nodded, a nervous expression on her face, he smiled. "Don't worry, it will be fine."

The woman had come to stand next to them, curiously eyeing Sophie. A huge smile on her face, she held out her hand. "Hello, I'm Susan Carter. And you are?"

Then, shooting a quick glance over at Chester, she laughed. "Wait, I bet this is your baby sister, right?"

Chester tried not to smile at the look of indignation filling Sophie's face at this question. Tightening his hold on her, he swiftly jumped in with an answer. "Susan, it's nice to see you. And no, this isn't my sister. She's a good friend who just flew in from Paris. But now, after a long day of delayed and re-routed flights, we only want to get home. So, I hope you'll excuse us as we continue on our way."

He gave her a big smile as he began steering Sophie through the crowd gathering because of Susan's loud greeting. This didn't stop Susan from throwing out the questions to what she was so determined to find the answers.

"Chester, wait… everyone wants to know. What's going on with Kelly? Are you still a couple? And is it true you've asked her to be your date for Kevin Kardell's wedding?"

Coming to an abrupt halt, he let out a deep hissing breath before he turned to her, fire in his eyes. "Absolutely not, a big no to both of those. Now, please excuse us." He turned back to Sophie. "Come on angel, let's go."

As soon as the words came out of his mouth, he knew he'd made a big mistake. If Susan had caught him referring to Sophie as an angel, there was no doubt in his mind this information would make it into her next column.

*And what did you just get done telling Sophie? Be careful how you answer her? Damn… you couldn't even follow your own advice?*

He tightened his grasp on Sophie's arm and began striding briskly towards the exit doors. She almost had to run in order to keep up with him.

When Chester pushed open the door to the parking garage, a gust of wind came around the corner, sending a shower of snow right in Sophie's face. When she stopped, trying to wrap her coat more tightly around her, Chester set her bag down and stepped in front of her, sheltering her from the blowing snow. After he buttoned her coat and pulled up her collar, tucking her hair inside, he smiled down at her.

"There you go. We can't have the maid-of-honor getting sick."

And, just like that, Sophie was right back to where she had been the night of the Children's Hospital Benefit.

She was totally smitten.

Something, she was quick to remind herself, could very well turn out to be a huge problem. Especially after those questions Susan Carter fired at Chester.

Yes, she was also very interested in finding out the answer to both of these questions. Who was this Kelly? And exactly what was going on with her and Chester?

She wasn't the same Kelly who couldn't keep her hands off of Chester the night of the benefit, was she?

*Because how could you forget how she had managed to work her way to his side every chance she could get?*

Hanging on to his every word, and to him as well, she was sophisticated, beautiful and with a body most women could only dream about.

Yes, Kelly was a threat not to be taken lightly.

*You know you can't measure up to a woman like her...*

She sighed, suddenly feeling very, very weary.


It was a relief to sink into the comfort of the passenger seat of Chester's SUV. Leaning her head back against the seat, this was when Sophie decided she needed to stop thinking about Kelly. She already had enough to handle with Chester in the driver's seat and only inches away.

Close enough to be aware of everything about him.

*Every irresistible inch of him.*

This was when she realized, even though he'd started up the engine, they hadn't moved. She glanced over at him. His arms leaning on the steering wheel, he was gazing over at her, an expectant expression on his face.

She gave him a tentative smile.

He smiled right back at her. "You need to buckle your seatbelt."

Becoming flustered and not knowing why, since this was such an ordinary request, she began fumbling with the seatbelt. When she couldn't seem to get it buckled, he took pity on her, reaching over to help her out.

Overwhelmed by his nearness, she closed her eyes.

He smelled amazing, a combination of soap, shampoo and the sharp spiciness of his cologne coming at her all at once. She wanted so badly to run her fingers through his hair, if only as an excuse to smooth away the melting droplets of snow lingering there. In an effort to keep from doing this, she glanced down, her gaze falling on the console between them.

Her eyes lit up. "You have Lifesavers!"

She smiled over at him. "I love Lifesavers. Can I have one? I don't think I've had one for years. And since I've had nothing to eat, for what now seems like ages, they look like ambrosia to me."

She grinned. "You don't seem like the type of man who carries Lifesavers around with him. Not that you would actually carry them on you, of course. Or you'd go around, handing them out. What I meant is, having them here in your SUV."

Just as she was beginning to think she was acting like a total fool, rambling on about a silly little piece of candy, he leaned back in his seat and smiled over at her.

"As far back as I can remember, my aunt has been a fan of these little rolls of Lifesavers. She told me if I shared with my friends, we'd all be blessed with good luck. She claimed this was the honest truth because they were the colors of the rainbow. And as we all know, rainbows are a sign of good luck."

He chuckled. "In fact, she still gives me a roll when I go to visit her. So, please have one, have two. I can always use some luck in my life."

Picturing him as a little boy, offering the candy to his friends, hoping the luck his aunt promised would be theirs, she smiled. "Well, she must be right. Look at what you've done so far with your life."

She shot him a stricken look. "I'm not insinuating it was all due to luck. Of course, this isn't what I meant. What I'm trying to say is the Lifesavers certainly couldn't have hurt."

*You're starting to babble. Get it together.*

She picked up the roll of candy, and after checking it out, she frowned. "Darn, the cherry one is next. I like the pineapple."

He chuckled, holding out his hand. "Here, I'll take the cherry one. Then you can have the one you want." After a slight hesitation, he leaned forward instead, opening his mouth.

She placed the candy in his mouth. Her fingers brushing across his lips. her whole body trembled at just this slight contact.

She closed her eyes.

*How could something so incredibly simple make you feel the way you do right now?*

Chester felt it, too. Impulsively, he brushed his lips over her fingers. And damn if he didn't start choking on the piece of candy.

He began coughing. In a panic, she patted him wildly on his back, relieved when he waved his hand at her, able to get his breath. "Thanks, you can stop. I think I'll be okay now."

Could he be any more embarrassed?

*No more romantic moves for you. You need to leave this to people who know what they're doing. A segment of the population you're clearly not meant to be a part of.*

Clearing his throat one final time, he gave her a watery smile. "Well, at least we now know they're not meant to be swallowed whole. They certainly won't be saving any lives with the kind of move I just made."

The worry slowly leaving her eyes, she took the next candy from the roll. It was green. She put it in the palm of her hand and held it out to him.

"It's okay. Trust me, it's something that could've easily happened to me. Here, let's try this green one. Maybe red isn't your color." One of those little frowns flitted across her face. "Or maybe it's me. I'm not good luck, at least not for you."

And darn if he wasn't giving her that look again before he gave it one more shot, scooping up the candy with his mouth. He followed this with a soft kiss to her palm. With, thank goodness, not a hint of a mishap.

His confidence restored, he smiled at her. "As far as I'm concerned, you're the best of luck. And from now on, green will be my new favorite. Thanks, angel."

*Angel...*

There it was again... and with the use of this simple little endearment, they both became silent.

Sophie, with her palm still tingling from his kiss and wishing she could get up the nerve to ask him why he chose to call her this.

While Chester was wondering if he had made a mistake by letting it slip.


The snow had now tapered off to a few flurries, but the roads were still snow covered and slick.

Most of Chester's concentration centered on guiding his SUV through the slow-moving traffic, the silence between them began to grow uncomfortable. He sent a glance over at Sophie to see she was studying him. When she swiftly turned to face the window, he searched his mind for something to say.

*Ah... how about the reason you're both here? The wedding?*

After he slowly eased the SUV onto the exit ramp, he spoke. "I think it's going to be a great wedding. Even though, from what Kevin's told me, what started out to be a small affair has now turned out to be a bit more than what they wanted. But I guess this is the norm where weddings are concerned." When she merely nodded at this, he forged on. "I also heard the band is supposed to be good, the bandleader a friend of yours and Abby."

Still totally embarrassed at having been caught staring at him, Sophie gave a sigh of relief. The wedding. This was a safe topic, one she should certainly be able to handle.

She began chattering away. "Yes, Jason. The name of his band is Banded Together. We've all known each other since high school. Since we had no one to play for our school dances, he and his friends formed the band. And I guess you'd say it was history in the making, with the band still at it today, bigger and better than ever."

She smiled. "All the girls went crazy over Jason because they thought he was so hot. They still do. Think he's hot, I mean. I guess he is. Sort of the sexy and brooding type of hot. But not my type at all."

Realizing she may have said too much, she was quick to add. "Not that I have a special type."

Unfortunately, she went on to dig herself in even deeper with what came next out of her mouth. "How about you? Is there something you look for? In a woman, I mean."

She sent him a look of panic. "Not that it's any of my business, of course."

*What are you doing? Everything coming out of your mouth, you wind up apologizing for in the very next sentence.*

Now beyond embarrassed, she closed her eyes, her lips tightly pressed together. If it were possible, she'd sink right down in her seat and disappear. Because what was next? Was she going to ask him how many kids he planned on having? Or what kind of house he wanted to live in?

Or how about, *did he remember the kiss they shared?*

She chanced a glance over at him to see he was smiling.

He cleared his throat. "*Hmm…* well, I guess I'd have to start out by saying, if you'd asked me this about six months ago, my answer would be I honestly had no idea what I was looking for in a woman. But then one day, there she was, standing right in front of me. And I realized I'd found everything I ever wanted."

He slowly shook his head. "But now I'm stumped, not sure of what to do next. Since I'm pretty new at this kind of thing, I worry I'll make a mistake. As it is, I think I've already made a few."

After he passed a slowly moving truck, he glanced over at her. She was staring at him, her lips parted and an uncertain look on her face.

He smiled. "So, what do you think? Maybe you can help me out? Because I really want to get it right this time."

She blinked, closing her mouth.

She wasn't quite sure how to answer him. She so wanted to believe this woman, the one he found standing right in front of him, well, could he be referring to her? But at the same time, she knew she was crazy to even think this. The last thing she wanted was to get her hopes up. It was quite possible everything he'd said could very well be in reference to Kelly.

*You can't think about this now. You need to wait until you can find out more information from Abby.*

She shrugged. "I guess. What I mean is, yes, I'll help you. But I don't know if I'm the one you should be coming to for advice. I certainly haven't had much experience with this kind of thing."

His answer? "*Hmm...* okay. It's a deal then. We'll help each other out. But right now, we're going to get you something to eat. You certainly need more than a Lifesaver after the day you've had."

He'd pulled into a parking lot. Peering out the window, she saw they were at what looked like a small neighborhood bar with the name, *The Home Plate*, flashing from the bright neon sign. On this blustery winter night, it was like a welcoming beacon.

When he came around to open her door and she was about to step down onto the snow covered ground, he scooped her up in his arms.

She could only hang on, a surprised cry coming from her. "Chester! What are you doing? Put me down. You don't have to carry me. I'm more than capable of walking."

He shook his head. This wasn't going to happen.

There was no way he was going to put her down. Especially not now, after experiencing again how it felt to hold her in his arms. Instead, after pressing his key holder to lock the SUV, he tightened his hold.

He sighed. "Sophie... it's obvious this parking lot hasn't seen a snowplow in hours. And you're not wearing boots. The fact you've lived in Cleveland for as long as you have, you should know better."

He grinned. "So, hang on and enjoy the ride."

With her doing exactly that, he trotted through the snow and up the steps to the entrance of the bar. After he put her down, reluctantly relinquishing his hold on her, he gently brushed the snow from her hair.

His smile was teasing. "After watching you almost get run over and more than once finding your choice of footwear, or lack of it, unbefitting to the occasion, I'm beginning to think you need someone to take care of you. Since I'm the only one available right now, I think it's time I stepped in to be your someone."

Before she could respond, he opened the door and his hand going to the small of her back, he gently steered her inside ahead of him. "I hope you like hamburgers, because in my opinion, they have the best around."

# CHAPTER 9

Chester watched as Sophie put the last French fry in her mouth, a look of pure pleasure on her face.

Briefly closing his eyes, he swallowed.

How could the simple act of eating a French fry suddenly seem so damn sexy? Running his hand over his jaw, he tried to ignore the overwhelming onset of desire she'd managed to stir to life inside of him.

Anything at all related to her mouth, even the thought of it alone, made him want to kiss her.

*Thoroughly.*

It would be a consuming, breath stealing, heart racing kind of kiss. A kiss that would finally take them out of this stage of uncertainty they were stuck in. Once this happened, he was pretty sure everything else between them would fall right into place.

*It's a French fry, for God's sake. You need to get it together. Or you're going to wind up doing exactly what you don't want to do. Make a total mess of things.*

The word French brought to mind this man she left behind in Paris, the supposedly "crazy about her" boyfriend. He needed to get her side of the story on this Juke or Jud, or whatever the hell his name was.

He wondered, the necklace she was wearing... did this guy give it to her? And if he did, what did it mean? It looked sort of expensive.

He watched as she placed her napkin on her plate and pushed it away before she glanced over at him. She gave him a shy smile. "Thank you. You're right. The hamburger was delicious."

Lost in her smile, he was again gripped by the feeling he hadn't been able to shake since his hand closed over hers, reaching for her bag at the airport.

The feeling where he wanted to blurt out those words. The words he'd sworn he'd never again say in his lifetime.

*You need to slow down, remember? You've only been with her about an hour and you've already fallen right back under her spell.*

He leaned closer to take the locket in his hand. After studying it, he turned it over.

The inscription jumped right out at him.

*Forever*

*Damn...* if this wasn't enough to throw a damper on his expectations, he didn't know what would be. He could only pray this simple, single word message didn't mean what it implied.

Noting the nervous expression on her face, he slowly removed his hand. He sat back in his chair, the tone of his voice casual. "Nice, is it from a boyfriend? And out of curiosity, what does the inscription on the back mean? Because it sort of implies something pretty serious."

For a few moments, she was silent, her hand creeping up to cover the locket with her fingers. Almost as if she was trying to hide it from him. She finally looked directly at him. "A good friend gave it to me. A friend I met in Paris."

Unsure why she felt the need to give him any further information, the words came tumbling out of her mouth. "Unfortunately, he seems to want more from me than I want from him. I… I'm not sure what I'm going to do. With the two of us, well, it seems like there's something missing. At least for me, there is."

He nodded slowly. "*Ah, I see.*"

And damn if he didn't know what else to say. Probably because, truthfully, he didn't see. Leaning back in his chair, he nodded a few more times as he studied her. He wasn't quite sure what she meant with the 'something was missing' comment.

Then he decided, what the hell. He might as well come out and ask her. What did he have to lose?

*Yeah, what was it they said? Go big or go home?*

Yeah, sort of like playing ball. You give it your all and you either hit the ball out of the park or you strike out. And this was definitely one of those times he could use a home run.

He tilted his head towards her, giving another slow nod before he spoke. "So… what exactly is it you're looking for?"

This brought on such a look of panic, he was quick to reassure her. "Hey, I'm only trying to help you out. Part of the agreement we made earlier. You know, you help me, I'll help you in return. Then hopefully, between the two of us, we'll be able to figure out how to make this whole relationship thing work for us."

Her look skeptical, he continued. "Again, I'm referring to my relationship… and your relationship." He nodded towards the locket. "Or whatever you've got going on with that."

She hesitated, looking down at her hands. Then she looked right up and at him, the words flying right out of her mouth. Words she didn't even know she wanted to say.

Words she suddenly believed with all of her heart.

"I want to be so in love with someone, I'd be willing to do anything for them, with them feeling the same about me. We wouldn't have to think about it. There would be no hesitation because we'd both know it was the real thing. And all of this would happen on the spur of the moment, with no looking back, no thought about the future."

And this is when it hit her. The answer to what she was looking for was sitting right in front of her.

*Oh my God, you want this to be with him. Nothing has changed. He really is the one, the man you want to spend the rest of your life with.*

She blinked, almost holding her breath as she waited for him to say something. But he didn't. He only continued to study her, his eyes holding hers. Finally, clasping her hands tightly together, she leaned in closer.

She had to ask. "And what… what about you?"

He smiled. It was a slow smile. A smile that settled deep inside of her, sending her heart flip-flopping in response.

He reached across the table and took her hands in his. Gently caressing her fingers, his voice was so soft. "I'm beginning to think we both want the same thing. So, maybe we should just wait and see what happens next."

He abruptly pulled his hands from hers and reached for his wallet. After he pulled out some bills and placed them on the table, he stood, holding out his hand.

"Come. We've got to get you home. It's already after midnight. And after the long day you've had, you must be exhausted."


It was only after Chester had dropped her off, coming inside to check out every room, just to be on the safe side, he'd assured her.

And he'd pressed a light kiss to her cheek before he went running through the lightly falling snow to his SUV. Where he turned to wave, as though he knew she'd still be there, waiting …

And she'd watched from the window, as he drove out of the parking lot, his SUV finally disappearing from sight …

Yes, it was only after that she had finally crawled into bed.

But after only a few minutes, she sat up on the bed and reached up to unclasp her necklace. Holding in her hands, she closed her eyes, slowly shaking her head. It was only right she give it back to Julian when she returned to Paris. Because whatever happened next, good or bad, Chester would be the only forever in her life.

After she set the necklace on the nightstand, she settled back under the quilt and closed her eyes.

There was a smile on her face when she fell asleep.



Chester backed out of the parking space in front of Sophie's townhouse. He put the SUV in drive and headed for the main road.

He was trying to figure it all out. Were those words she so passionately delivered in the restaurant meant for him? Or was he was seeing too much into this, setting himself up for another disappointment?

Because, come on … when a man gives a woman a piece of jewelry with the word 'Forever' inscribed on it, well … this was definitely a commitment of some kind.

*But she did say something was missing. And it does take two.*

From what she'd told him, her return flight to Paris was scheduled for the day after Valentine's Day. She was planning to spend the time between the wedding and her departure with her aunt. They hoped to work on the yearly retail plan for the Paris boutique.

There was also some kind of fashion show in the works for the day before Valentine's Day. An annual event her aunt had started over ten years ago, it was now very popular. All the proceeds went towards a scholarship fund for aspiring fashion designers.

So, after Valentine's Day, she would be gone. Back to Paris. And if he didn't play his cards right, she'd again be out of his reach.

And possibly out of his life.

After being with her tonight, it was very clear he only had one option. And this was he had to give it his best shot.

*You want it all … you want that home run.*

The fairy dust she'd unknowingly sprinkled over him the very first time they met? Well, it must be pretty powerful stuff.

Because he hadn't been able to shake it.



Bells were ringing everywhere.

Slowly opening her eyes, Sophie saw her phone was flashing.

When she reached over to grab it off the nightstand, she realized someone was also ringing her doorbell.

She squinted at the phone. It was also only eight o'clock in the morning.

Groggily sitting on the edge of the bed and in the befuddled state she was in, she was having a hard time trying to decide what to do. Should she answer her phone or see who was at the door?

She didn't want to do either. She wanted to go back to sleep so she could fall right back into the dream she was having about Chester.

In the dream, he had carried her through a forest, the ground and all the trees covered in a blanket of freshly fallen snow. Arriving at this charming little cabin, he'd gently set her down on the bed. After sinking down with her into the down filled blankets, he reached over to frame her face in his hands. His mouth swooping in to hover over hers, he was just about to kiss her.

And … *Poof!* Her phone rang. Sending both the kiss and Chester disappearing into thin air.

She frowned. Hopefully, this wasn't a sign of what was to come.

She finally glanced down at her phone to see the call was from Abby. She answered, Abby speaking before she even had a chance to say hello. "Hey, sleepyhead, it's me ringing your doorbell. I have come bearing coffee and donuts. I also have two excited little friends of yours who are very eager to see you again."

Tinkerbell! Popcorn! Her two pups!

Throwing her phone down on the bed, she went racing down the hall. She opened the door to Abby. Laughing, she was trying not to drop the b0x 0f donuts she was holding, two containers of coffee teetering on top. This was while the two dogs, having tangled her in their leashes, were running excited circles around her.

After Sophie separated them and Abby was able to maneuver her way inside, Sophie sat on the floor, happily greeting the two ecstatic dogs.

She finally made her way to the kitchen, the dogs following right on her heels. There she found Abby arranging the donuts on a plate while the coffee was heating up in the microwave.

She gave her a big hug. *"Oh, Abby* ... thank you for bringing the pups. I missed them so much." She laughed, giving her another hug. "I bet you're getting so excited! You always said you wanted a winter wedding, snow and all. It looks like you got your wish."

A big grin on her face, Abby shook her head. "Like they say, be careful what you wish for. But from what I've heard, it's supposed be better by Friday. So, hopefully we'll be all right. My biggest concern is about anyone who is flying in."

She made a face. "Thank goodness Kevin's family is only coming from Chicago and when I last checked, their flights still show the original arrival time. Keep your fingers crossed, because I can't imagine how his mother would react if she was faced with the kind of delays you had to put up with."

She gave a big sigh. "Tonight, they're all staying at our condo. I think Kevin wanted them to see it since we just moved in. But this means we've had to work like crazy getting everything set up. Thank goodness, tomorrow and Saturday night, they've reserved rooms at the hotel like everyone else."

She shrugged. "It should be interesting, I guess."

After failing at her attempt to bribe Abby with money to break it off with Kevin, so he could marry the daughter of a past friend, things were still awkward with Kevin's mother. Abby had hoped this would show his mother how much in love she and Kevin were. Possibly even growing to like her.

But his mother had gone on to shock everyone, insisting Melissa be invited to the wedding. Thank goodness Kevin had adamantly vetoed this. But this had Abby wondering if his mother was ever going to accept her as part of the family.

Sophie gazed at her with concern. "So, Kevin's mom still hasn't come around, huh?"

Abby's smile was resigned. "No, not quite. But I trust Kevin, and he told me I have nothing to worry about. I'm just relieved they don't live close by."

But she didn't want to talk about this.

Swiftly changing the subject, she sent a sly glance over at Sophie.

"It was nice of Chester to pick you up at the airport. Just curious, how did that work out for you?"

Crossing her arms over her chest, Sophie sent her an accusing look. "I knew it! You had this all planned out, didn't you?"

When Abby only shrugged, feigning ignorance, Sophie sank down in one of the chairs at the kitchen table. She reached for a donut and took a big bite.

Her words came out in between bites. "*Oh, Abby* … I feel like we're going around in circles. He doesn't trust me, and I'm afraid to ask him what's wrong. What I'd like to do is tell him to get over it, and kiss me again. But what if this scares him off? Or worse yet, I make a complete fool of myself?."

As she watched Sophie devour the donut, Abby was both amused and skeptical. "I seriously doubt this would happen. Kevin doesn't tell me much, but from what little he has, it sounds like Chester is pretty taken with you."

She shrugged. "Now remember, what I'm about to tell you is coming from Kevin. He said Chester has been moping around, not doing much of anything since you left. He also disappeared for a few weeks after the world series. He wouldn't tell anyone where he was going, only that he needed some time alone to figure out what he wanted in life. Pretty deep, I'd say."

She grinned. "For a man, that is."

Sophie had finished the donut and had now taken a bite out of a second one. When she realized what she was doing, she plunked the donut down on the plate and shoved the plate away from her, a horrified expression on her face. "Oh my gosh, look at me! Why didn't you stop me? Were you going to let me eat all of them and not even say anything?"

At the startled look on Abby's face, she groaned, dragging her hands through her hair. "I'm sorry. It's only that I'm beginning to think he's a lost cause, we both are. Maybe he'd be better off with Kelly. Because seriously? What man wouldn't love to be with a woman like her?"

Sitting back in her chair, she pointed to the plate of donuts. "I'd be willing to bet you every donut on this plate, Kelly would never stuff herself with donuts because of a man." She sighed, gazing over at Abby. "But what am I saying? She probably hasn't been within five feet of a donut in years."

Abby was confused. "Kelly? Mia's sister, Kelly? Chester doesn't like her. Why would you even think this? I know he took her to the Winter Snowball Charity Dance, but only because a few of the guys on the team talked him into it." She shook her head. "Some of those guys can be so relentless at times."

She suddenly burst out laughing. "And let's be serious here, Chester and Kelly together? This will never happen. Not after the disaster that night turned out to be. They argued the entire time. I think it was because he was embarrassed by the act she put on. Like she was the First Lady of Baseball or something. And the dress she wore... seriously? It was so elaborate and form fitting, I have no idea how she could even move. I'm pretty sure it had to be one of her past pageant dresses. I was waiting for her to whip out a tiara."

She shook her head. "Nope, I can't see it. They'd wind up killing each other within a week, if even that."

Sophie plunked her chin down on her hand, giving a big sigh. "According to this reporter who came up to us at the airport, there's a rumor she's Chester's date for your wedding."

Abby frowned. "*Hmm ...* that's news to me. I'm pretty sure Kevin told me Chester wasn't bringing a date. And if Kelly's name was on the guest list, I definitely would've remembered seeing it there. But since all the guys on the team are invited, it's almost impossible to know who's coming with who. We really couldn't tell them who they could bring."

She hadn't even told Sophie she was paired with Chester for the rehearsal dinner, the reception, and the brunch the following morning. Or that Chester was also her partner for the ceremony. The way she saw it, some things were better left unsaid, even up until the last minute. Hopefully, this would lead to a welcome surprise.

She reached over to pick up a roll of Lifesavers on the counter before she smiled at Sophie. "Do you want to know what I think?"

At Sophie's nod, she continued. "I think you should go for it. Make the move. If it doesn't work out, well, then you move on. Otherwise, you're going to drive yourself crazy. Or eventually do something really stupid."

She sent Sophie a wry smile. "I should know. I did some really stupid things with Kevin. Yet, for some reason, he loved me enough to hang around. Even with how crazy everything got."

She waved the roll of candy at Sophie. "You don't mind if I open these, do you? I can't remember the last time I've had one. They used to be my favorite candy when I was little."

She grinned. "I always used to save the red one for last. They're my favorite."

Sophie was surprised. "Where did you get those?"

Abby shrugged. "Right here on the counter. Why?"

Smiling, Sophie shook her head. "It's only … never mind. Sure, go ahead, have one. Maybe it will bring me good luck."

After a puzzled look, Abby began opening the roll of candy. Then she tilted her head. "Is your phone ringing somewhere?"

Nearly knocking her chair over in her haste to get out of it, Sophie went flying into her bedroom. Grabbing her phone off the bed, her hello came out quite breathless.

There was a short silence before Chester's voice flowed through the phone.

"Sophie?"

Her heart lurched in response.

Every time she was hit with the sound of his voice, her whole body got into the act, everything reacting at once. Right now, her heart was racing, and her mind had gone sailing off into space, leaving her without a single thought in her head.

She finally got it together enough to answer him. "Yes, it's me … Sophie."

She took a deep breath. "Hi."

"Hi." He sounded worried. "I'm sorry, you were probably still sleeping and—"

She quickly interrupted him. "Oh no, I wasn't. Abby's here. She brought my pups and we've been eating donuts and drinking coffee. She brought those with her, too."

Here she was quick to add. "It's a long-standing tradition with us since we were kids. Usually, we would have Abby's cookies. But with the wedding, it's donuts from our favorite donut shop. Abby has enough to do right now without having to make more cookies."

She paused to take a breath. "I don't want you to think we sit around and eat cookies or donuts all the time. Because we don't. We only do this for special occasions. Like now."

*Oh no ... here you go again. He doesn't want to hear all of this.*

But could she stop talking?

Of course not. "If I sound like I'm out of breath, it's because I ran to answer my phone. I thought it might be you, and I didn't want to miss the call, so ..."

*Seriously? Now you've given him this image of you sitting here, stuffing your face with donuts. While waiting for him to call.*

She took a deep breath. "What I meant to say, I've been hoping you'd call. Because I couldn't remember if I thanked you for picking me up from the airport. And for the hamburger. I..."

Her hand going to her mouth, she slowly sank down on the bed.

*Stop. Just stop right now. Let him be the one to say something.*

After a short silence, he gave a soft chuckle. "You did thank me. At least twice, I believe. And I assure you, I was more than happy to have been there for you. I'm also interested in trying out this donut shop of yours. For as long as I can remember, donuts have always been a favorite indulgence of mine."

"You want me to take you there now?"

She actually blurted this out.

And now, beyond embarrassed, she groaned.

After another short silence, he chuckled again. "Oh, sweetheart ... that's not necessary. Sometime soon, though. But this isn't why I'm calling. I'd really like to spend some time with you. I don't know what your plans are today, but I thought I could whisk you away this afternoon and then out to dinner afterwards."

Flying back to the kitchen, she found out from Abby what time they were meeting at the boutique to pick up their dresses. After that, Abby had plans with Kevin and his family. So, she would be free.

She did a little happy dance around the kitchen before she spoke into the phone. "Chester, will three o'clock work? I'll meet you at my aunt's boutique. That's where we're meeting to pick up our dresses."

She'd swear she heard a smile in his voice. "Perfect. You'll need to wear warm, casual clothing. Gloves, hat, and boots, okay? I'll see you at three then."

She suddenly remembered… "Chester? Wait … I want to thank you for the Lifesavers."

He chuckled again. "Anytime. *Hmm* … and look what happened. I do believe that move may have brought me the luck I was looking for. Until three, then."

After she hung up the phone, she glanced over at Abby. Leaning against the counter, she had a big grin on her face. "My, my, my … he certainly isn't wasting any time, is he? Why do I have a feeling this is going to get really interesting?"

She walked over to Sophie and placed the roll of Lifesavers in her hand. "Even though I'm not sure what's going on with these, it looks like they did bring you luck. So, you should probably hang on to them."

Slipping into her coat, she turned to give Sophie a big hug. "I've got to get going if Kevin and I want to get to the airport on time to pick up his family. I'll see you at the boutique as planned. I'll be bringing Kevin's sister, Katy. Lisa and Chloe are meeting us there."

Clutching the roll of candy in her hand, Sophie wasn't really listening. Instead, she was trying to remember where she put the baby blue hat, scarf and mittens her sister had crocheted for her. She was pretty sure she hadn't taken them with her to Paris.

Chester was partial to her in blue.

# CHAPTER 10

$\mathcal{C}$hloe was in heaven.

Twirling around in circles, her smile couldn't be any bigger as she watched her reflection in the boutique's full-length mirror. She was in the dress she would be wearing for her role as flower girl in the wedding.

It was any little girl's dream dress. Tea length, the red velvet bodice had short puffy sleeves. A wide red satin ribbon at the waist tied in a big bow in the back. But it was the skirt of the dress Chloe was in love with. Made up of layers and layers of white sparkling tulle, with every move she made, it floated around her like a soft, fluffy cloud.

Laughing out loud, she held the child's sized snow-white fur muff up to her cheek as she made one more turn.

Watching her, Sophie began to laugh, too. "You should ask Abby if you can dance down the aisle. You're so good at it. I can see those dancing classed paid off."

Lisa, who was busy packing her bridesmaid dress into a garment bag, shook her head as she grinned over at Sophie. "Sophie, please … don't give her any more ideas. Ever since she first put the dress on, she has talked about nothing else but how she can't wait to dance the night away."

Chloe, who'd finally agreed to stay still while Sophie helped her out of the dress, was all smiles. "Daddy promised he would dance with me as much as I wanted."

She quickly glanced over at Lisa. "But don't worry, momma. He told me he'd have to save a few dances for you, too."

Kevin's sister, Katy, who was listening to all of this, started to laugh. "So this is what I have to look forward to when Olivia gets a little older. As it is, she already has Stephen wrapped around her tiny little finger and she can't even walk or talk yet!"

Lisa rolled her eyes. "I believe it starts the first time they make eye contact. If I get one dance, I'll consider myself a lucky woman."

"And here she is…"

With this announcement ringing through the room, they turned to see Abby enter with Sophie's Aunt Louise following behind and holding up the train of her wedding dress. Katy, known for her ability to cry at the drop of a hat, put her hands to her face, her words coming out in almost a sob.

"*Oh, Abby…* you look absolutely stunning. Kevin is going to fall in love all over again when he sees you coming down the aisle."

As they all gathered around her, oohing and aahing, Abby smiled over at Sophie. "All the credit goes to Sophie. She found the dress, insisted I try it on and it was love at first sight. But then, how could someone not feel beautiful in this dress?"

The dress was all appliqué and lace, except for the wide band of dupioni Silk draped across her shoulders. Accented with crystal beading and pearls, the body of the dress was form fitting to her hips. From there, it gradually flared to the floor, the back hem slightly longer to form a train. The veil, falling to her waist, was of the finest tulle, attached to a narrow headband covered with more crystal beading and pearls. The elbow-length gloves she was wearing completed the whole look of what one would expect of a winter bride.

Grabbing a tissue from the box Lisa passed around, Sophie's aunt wiped the tears from her eyes. "You look absolutely beautiful, sweetheart. I hope this Kevin realizes what a lucky man he is."

Her hands going to her hips, she sent a stern look over at Sophie. "I wish you'd consider adding wedding dresses to the Paris line. Look at how good you are at this."

Sophie shook her head. "Nope, I only like doing this for friends. I remember too much of the drama that goes on with bridal wear from my internship. No wedding dresses for me."

She walked around Abby, her eyes intently scanning the dress, inspecting every detail. After she reached over to adjust the buttons lining the back of the dress, she nodded. "I think we might need to add one more hook at the top so it fits more snugly. Everything else looks perfect."

After the dresses, shoes and accessories were all packed up and ready to go, Abby filled all of them in on the details they needed to know for the rehearsal dinner the following evening.

Just as she finished, and they were about to put on their coats, Chester opened the door and walked into the boutique.

For a brief moment, a look of panic crossed his face when everyone turned, their attention zeroing in on him.

Then he saw Sophie.

Their eyes meeting, she smiled at him.

Suddenly, for Sophie, all she was aware of was Chester. It was at this moment she realized there would never be anyone else she would rather see walk through the door and on their way to see her, than him.

She wasn't sure… was this what it felt like to be in love? Because, truthfully, she had never felt like this before. No man had ever caused her heart to start fluttering with such excitement at only his mere presence. Or make her feel so incredibly happy at just the sight of him.

She only knew when she looked into his eyes, the message she saw there did something extraordinary to her. She felt safe. She felt wanted. And she felt like her heart had fallen into the right hands.

She continued to smile at him. When what she really wanted was to walk right into his arms.

*And please... then he would kiss you. A kiss like he gave you on the night before you left for Paris.*

When she realized everyone in the room was watching them, she shot a desperate glance over at Abby.

Abby went right into action.

"Chester, you're right in time to help us carry all of these bags and dresses out to our cars. You don't mind, do you?"

Chester didn't hear a word she said.

He was still watching Sophie. Something had happened, and he wasn't quite sure what it was, only between them everything was different. It had to do with the way she was looking at him. As though she suddenly saw something about him she hadn't noticed before.

He felt like maybe, just maybe, they had reached a turning point in this somewhat shaky relationship they were stumbling through together.

And suddenly, he was filled with an incredible feeling of hope.

The sound of Abby loudly clearing her throat brought him back to earth. With a slight tilt of his head and an absentminded smile, he turned to her.

"I'm sorry. What did you ask me? I didn't quite get it."

Abby grinned. "*Hmm...* I can see this. I asked if you could help us take these dresses and bags out to our cars."

After shooting another quick glance over at Sophie, to see she was suddenly very busy doing who knows what, he walked over to Abby. "Sure, anything for the bride, I've been told." He winked. "Tell me what goes where."

A thoughtful expression on her face, Sophie's aunt was watching Sophie and Chester. She sent a questioning look over at Lisa, to be met with a big grin and a nod.

She patted her hair in order and, with a look of determination on her face, she made her way over to him. She held out her hand. "Hello, I don't believe we've met. I'm Louise, Sophie's aunt."

He gave her a big smile as he shook her hand. "It's so nice to meet you, Louise. I'm Chester. I play baseball with Lisa's husband and Abby's fiancée. I also like to think I'm a very good friend of Sophie's."

"*Ah...* I see. A very good friend. *Hmm...*" Nodding, she then proceeded to give him a thorough once over, a smile slowly spreading across her face.

Becoming a bit uncomfortable with this, Chester hesitantly smiled back at her before he glanced over at Sophie, his eyes sending her a plea for help.

Immediately sensing trouble, knowing how assertive her aunt could be, Sophie walked over to join them.

"Aunt Louise …"

Louise waved her hand dismissively at Sophie as she continued to smile up at Chester. "Not now, dear. I have a favor to ask this handsome man of yours."

And to Sophie's complete dismay, she began fluttering her eyelashes up at Chester, the tone of her voice becoming very flirtatious.

"Have you ever done any modeling? Because we could use you as one in our fashion show. We're short on male models and from what I can see, you'd be perfect. The show is the day before Valentine's Day." She tilted her head, her look as persuasive as one could get. "Please say you'll help us out. The proceeds go to a very good cause, and one very near and dear to my heart. And also to Sophie's."

He looked over at Sophie.

She shook her head. "You don't have to do this. Really, you don't."

Seriously? Right now, she wanted to throttle her aunt. What the heck was she doing? There was no doubt in her mind the last thing Chester wanted to do was be a model in a fashion show. Which meant it was up to her to let him know he was in no way obligated to go along with such a crazy idea.

A mischievous gleam lit up his eyes.

*Uh oh...*

Casually crossing his arms over his chest, he was smiling as he addressed Louise. "A model, huh? *Hmm* … I must say, I've never been asked to be a model before."

He turned to Sophie, one eyebrow raised. "So, tell me, will you also be one of the models in this show?"

Before she even had the chance to open her mouth, her aunt jumped in with an answer. "Of course she will. In fact, I'll make you a promise. If you agree to join us, I'll make sure you and Sophie are partners. The crowd will love it. Together, you make such a striking couple."

She winked at him. "It's really too bad we're not modeling wedding dresses. Because, honestly? I hope I don't embarrass you by saying this, but you're every woman's vision of what the perfect real-life-cake-topper-groom should be."

She gave a vague nod towards Sophie, whose mouth was now open in shock, an expression of horror on her face. "Don't worry about her. She's a natural at modeling and always enjoys being in the show. And if you agree with my request, I know she'll be thrilled."

Her pitch delivered, she continued to smile up at him, waiting.

Chester glanced over at Sophie to see her eyes were now closed, a blush tinting her cheeks.

And suddenly, there was nothing he wanted more than to be a model in a fashion show.

*With the promise of such a desirable partner, how could you even think of passing on this?*

Holding out his hand to her aunt, he nodded. "Louise, you've got a deal."


Sophie moved into high gear, her goal to get Chester out of the boutique before, heaven forbid, something else happened. She picked up the garment bag holding Chloe's dress, her plan to hand it to him.

But Chloe managed to get to him first, and was trying to get his attention, pulling at his jacket. Surprised, he looked down at her grinning face.

He grinned right back at her. "Hey, little one… what's up?"

She mimicked his stance, crossing her arms over her chest. Aiming a very serious look up at him, her voice carried clearly through the now silent room.

"So, everyone wants to know … are you and Sophie going to be the next two to get married?" She turned to Lisa. "Right momma? Didn't daddy say he and Kevin are betting on this happening soon?"

Closing her eyes, Lisa gave a half laugh, half groan. "Oh, Chloe…"

*"Oh no…"* The only other sound in the room, this came from Sophie.

She wanted to die… *just die.* Because honestly? This would be the only thing that could possibly save her right now.

*Could things get any worse? First Aunt Louise asking him to model and now this from Chloe? The poor guy probably wants to turn around and high tail it right out the door.*

She watched Chester try to hide a smile as he squatted down next to Chloe. He cleared his throat, the sound almost echoing in the hushed silence.

"Ah, Chloe… sometimes it's not all that easy. I think I should probably get to know her a little better before I bring up the idea of marriage, don't you?"

After taking a few seconds to think about this, Chloe nodded.

He, in turn, nodded back, his expression thoughtful. "You see, for some people it takes little longer to realize what they've been looking for is right there in front of their nose."

Though it was barely discernible, he gave a quick nod in Sophie's direction. "So, it's best to wait until they figure it out for themselves. Then you can make your move."

He shot another look over at Sophie to see she hadn't moved, her eyes now closed.

He smiled and, turning back to Chloe, he reached over to tweak her nose. "You can't hurry love, princess. I want you to remember this. Because I have a feeling, as pretty as you are, you're going to break a lot of hearts when you get older."

This brought on a big grin before she frowned. This was followed by a very dramatic sigh. "I don't know if this will ever happen. Daddy's already told me I don't need to have any boyfriends."

This made everyone laugh, a welcome break in the silence. Smiling at Chloe, Chester ruffled her hair with his hand. "I can very well imagine him saying this."

As though nothing was amiss, he reached for the garment bag Sophie was holding. "So, now where am I taking this?"

Sophie had been very quiet since they left the boutique.

After Chester turned his SUV onto a road leading to a local park, he glanced over at her. She had a worried expression on her face.

Easing his foot off the gas pedal, he reached over to take her hand. "Hey, why so serious? What are you thinking about?"

Slowly shaking her head, she let out a long sigh. "I'm really sorry about what happened back there in the boutique. My aunt always speaks her mind. And Chloe... you've got to remember, she's only seven. At her age, it's all about fairy tales and living happily ever. With Chloe, it's probably even more so, with the vivid imagination she has."

He was quiet for a few moments. "So, I take it you don't believe in any of that?"

She closed her eyes.

*Do you believe in fairy tales or happily ever after? Oh Lord... you're not sure. Maybe a little? But not necessarily happening to you.*

She glanced over at him, but with the way he was studying her, as though he was trying to figure her out, she almost couldn't remember what she wanted to say.

She shrugged. "I think most woman believes in the magic of fairy tales from the minute they're born. There's always that hope we'll find someone and eventually fall in love. After that, if we're lucky, the happily ever part will fall right into place."

Shooting him a quick glance, she shrugged. "You just never know."

He was quiet for a few moments. Then he cleared his throat. "Well... I'd have to say that's an unusual way to look at it. I think men are more cut and dried when it comes to such things. We see what we like and go for it. It's all about keeping it real, I guess."

She was smiling. Which had him smiling. "But about this fashion show, maybe you'd rather I didn't do this modeling thing for your aunt?"

Shaking her head, she turned to face him. "Oh, nom... of course not. I'm sure you'll be a big hit. Sometimes I wonder if the women come for the fashions or only to see the male models. A few years ago, when we had the whole company of a local fire department participate, I thought a riot was going to break out. After all, there's something about a fit and attractive man in a tux that drives most women wild."

He chuckled. "Wild? And do you include yourself in this group of most women?"

She swallowed, suddenly feeling very hot and bothered. How the heck was she going to get herself out of this one? Her next words came out in a sputtering mess. "Gosh, I … I'm not sure. I guess it depends on the man. What I mean, with some men, it doesn't make much difference. But, with others…"

Now she was completely flustered, with no idea of where to go with this. And the sudden vision flooding her mind, of Chester looking so amazingly hot in his tux on the night of the benefit, certainly wasn't helping matters. 'Fit and attractive' didn't even begin to describe his appearance that night. He had taken her breath away.

*This was also the night you gave him your heart, no questions asked. Admit it.*

She sighed. She might as well come right out and say what she was thinking. At this point, what did she have to lose? "Where you… well, take you for instance. You look good."

His voice was low … and *so* deep. Along with a hint of a smile coming through. "*Hmm…* good? Just good?"

She shook her head, before revealing more than she probably should've. "No, you … well, you look amazing. But then you always look amazing to me."

In the silence following, it occurred to her they had come to a stop. In front of them was a huge hill, packed with people of all ages. On toboggans, sleds, inner tubes and even cardboard boxes, they were flying down the hill at what appeared to be an extremely dangerous rate of speed.

Is this what he had in mind? Sledding?

*Really?*

*Oh dear, obviously, he has no clue as to how uncoordinated you are. Outdoor sports, or even indoor sports for that matter, have never been your best of friends.*

But at this point, she'd gladly jump on one of those sleds. If only to make a quick getaway from this new predicament she'd managed to get herself into.

Chester had leaned over the console and gently cupping her chin in his hand, his face was suddenly so dangerously close to hers. She closed her eyes as his voice drifted around and over her, caressing her with his words. "You look amazing to me, too."

The kiss he gave her was more of a brush of their lips than what you'd call a kiss. And, before she even had time to react, it was over.

She almost groaned aloud.

*Not fair... it's so not fair. You didn't even get the chance to kiss him back.*

Hiding her disappointment, she watched him pull on a knit hat and grab his gloves from the console. Then he was out of the SUV and opening her door. As she stepped down, he looked down at her feet, shaking his head.

Puzzled, she looked down at her boots, then back up at him. "What's wrong? You said boots. And these are boots, are they not?"

He sighed. "Yes, they are, if your intention is to make some kind of fashion statement. I guess they'll have to do for now. But we should probably see about getting you some good, reliable outdoor boots."

He tilted his head, a thoughtful look coming over his face. "Or maybe even snowshoes. Those are always fun. And we certainly have the snow here to make good use of them."

She sent him such a horrified look, he burst out laughing. "Just kidding, just kidding. Don't worry, I get it. You're not the loving-the-outdoors type of woman. So, I won't even think of bringing up white water rafting or camping in the wilds. This will come in time."

The urge to touch her, coming on so strongly, he reached over to run his knuckles lightly against her cheek. "But, be warned … I can be very persuasive when I want something, even more so when you're involved."

Before she could respond, he had gone to the back of his SUV to open the trunk. He pulled out a sled and, dragging it behind him, he took her hand. "For now, we'll start out slow."

He smiled down at her. "I haven't been sledding in years and something tells me, for you, it's been even longer, if ever. Come on, it will be fun."

Sophie wasn't necessarily afraid of heights.

But standing at the top of the hill as Chester lined up the sled, she decided this could very well be the one time she was. It looked like a long, long way down to the bottom. Such a long and very dangerous way to go.

She closed her eyes, wondering if this might be the time to say a little prayer.

When Chester turned and saw the worried look on her face, he wondered if he'd made a mistake bringing her here. He'd racked his brain, trying to think of something different and fun for them to do. Where they could relax and not have to worry about each and every word coming out of their mouth. Maybe even share a laugh or two.

There was no denying the tension between them was becoming close to unbearable. For him, it was wondering how much longer he'd be able to hold off from making his move. And this would be to kiss her like she was meant to be kissed. A kiss filled with all the passion that had been building inside of him since his first glimpse of her at the airport. Or, if he were to be completely honest, going all the way back to when they first met. When she'd been so intent on rescuing the puppy.

Yep, and he'd make sure it would definitely be some kiss. Rivaling the kiss he'd given her right before he walked away from her that July night.

It had almost killed him to reign in on the kiss he gave her only minutes ago. But honestly? If he hadn't, any control he was barely hanging on to would've gone up in smoke. And he was way past the stage of his life where making out with a girl in a vehicle would be considered cool.

*Well, you're committed to this sledding thing, so get on with it.*

He smiled at her. "Okay, are you ready? It's going be fun. Just remember to hold on to me and you'll be fine."

When they first started down the hill, it was.

Fun, that is.

With Chester's arms wrapped around her, holding her securely against him, she found she was more than happy with the whole experience.

In fact, she was actually beginning to enjoy the ride.

This all came to an abrupt end when a sled carrying two little girls came to a dead stop right in front of them. Both girls tumbled into the snow and in his attempt to avoid hitting them, Chester tried to make a sharp turn around them. Something he quickly realized was not one of his better moves.

Their sled flipped, sending both him and Sophie flying through the air. With Sophie somersaulting through the snow and eventually landing flat on her back. Where she remained completely silent, not moving.

In a panic, he half crawled, half stumbled over to her, to find her eyes were closed. "*Oh my God*, angel … are you all right? Please, sweetheart … say something."

Slowly opening her eyes, she stared up at him. Right before she began to giggle. "Oh, Chester… I'm fine."

He closed his eyes and bowing his head, he gave a huge sigh of relief. "You scared the hell out of me. I…"

And the next thing she knew, he was kissing her.

For Sophie, the kiss was everything she'd been waiting for. While for Chester, it was everything he'd been holding back. All of this taking place, right smack dab in the middle of the hill, with no regards to all the sleds and toboggans flying around them.

She wanted to touch him. Frantically struggling to remove her mittens, she finally freed her hands. Tangling her fingers in his hair, she pulled him even closer, her mouth searching his with a passion she didn't even know she possessed.

There was one thing she did know.

She didn't want the kiss to end.

His face resting in the curve of her neck, Chester's breathing was finally almost back to normal.

He knew he should get them up off the ground before someone ran into them, but the feel of her hands in his hair was so sweet, he couldn't seem to make the move.

*The kiss was right... so right. And what was even sweeter? You know she feels the same.*

When Sophie felt his mouth curve into a smile against her neck, she realized she was also smiling. Slowly moving her hands from his hair to his shoulders, her voice registered faintly in his ear. "Chester? Maybe we should move?"

With a reluctant sigh, he lifted his head and, after pressing a quick kiss to her mouth, he got to his feet, pulling her up with him. He retrieved her mittens, handing them to her before he went over to get the sled.

When he returned, he gave her a sheepish grin. "I guess this wasn't the best idea." At her sudden look of concern, he was quick to add. "I'm referring only to the sledding, of course. I thought, well, I hoped it would be something different. And it seemed like a good idea with all of this snow we have."

He shrugged, not knowing what else to say.

She reached up to press her fingers to his mouth. "I think it turned out pretty well."

His eyes searched hers. Evidently liking what he saw, he reached for her hand, a slow smile coming over his face. "You know what? You're absolutely right. But for now, how about we give up the idea of sledding and go somewhere where there's a fire in a fireplace, some soft, comfortable chairs and wine. I think we deserve this."

She grinned up at him. "I would love that."

With him still holding her hand, they made their way back to his SUV. After she buckled her seatbelt, she glanced over to see he was watching her.

When she smiled, he leaned over to catch the corner of her mouth in a kiss.

He winked at her. "I know how you feel about being impulsive."

Sophie was studying the dessert menu.

Reminded of the last time he'd watched her do this, Chester took big gulp of his whiskey and amaretto. His hope was the slow burn of alcohol down his throat would help erase the memory of what had taken place right after.

He turned his head, his gaze resting somberly on the fire in the fireplace.

*This isn't all that different, is it? Again, she'll be leaving. But this time, you'll have her with you for a little longer. So, you have more time to prepare yourself.*

His gaze returning to Sophie, he slowly shook his head.

*You're a fool if you believe this.*

Yep, he was a bigger fool than he gave himself credit for.

Sophie looked up from the menu to find Chester was watching her, a preoccupied expression on his face.

When his eyes finally met hers, she smiled at him. "As usual, I can't make up my mind. So, will you share something with me?"

A faint smile appearing on his face, he reached over to take her hands in his. After he gazed down at them for a few moments, he decided, what the hell… why not throw caution to the wind and tell her what he so longed to say.

Lifting his head, he looked right into her eyes. "Angel, like I told you once before, I'll share anything with you. Forever, if you'll let me."

She looked down at their hands before she gazed back up at him, her eyes wide, intently searching his. She started to say something, but then she had to stop, the words catching in her throat.

He could feel her grip tighten on his hands before her answer finally came out in a whisper. "What are we going to do? About us?"

He had no answer to give her. This was only because, as usual, he was at a complete loss of what to say.

There was also the fear of whatever he did manage to come up with, well, it would be wrong. He'd made this mistake the last time and was now well aware, once the words were said, how everything could spiral completely out of control.

Sophie's heart had begun to beat in a panic. With his silence, she had no idea what he was thinking. But one of them had to say something.

Briefly closing her eyes, she shook her head. "I'm sorry. I thought… well, I guess I'd hoped you might be feeling the same, that there's something between us. Something out of our control. A connection of some kind. Maybe even magical."

She shook her head again, while at the same time, she tried to pull her hands away from his. "Ignore what I said. It's okay. I understand. I don't want you to feel you're obligated in any—"

Somehow, he was next to her, his hands framing her face. His lips hovering over hers, his groan was deep, his words urgent. "I'm so sorry. It's only that I'm so damn afraid I'll say the wrong thing. If you remember, I didn't fare very well at this kind of thing when you left back in July."

She remained silent, her eyes so big and so bright, he'd swear he could drown in them. Something he realized he'd be more than fine with, as there was no other place he'd rather be.

His thumbs caressing her cheeks, his lips continued to taunt her, tease her, dropping soft kisses over her face. "But there's one thing I'm sure of, and this is I don't want to even think about you leaving right now. Instead, let's enjoy every minute, every single second we have together." He ran his thumb slowly over her bottom lip. "Please, angel… let's do this. Somehow, we'll figure it out. Or something will change."

Held spellbound, not only by his words, but by the message he was sending with his eyes, she slowly nodded.

After the sweet, lingering kiss he gave her, he realized this wasn't enough. He wanted more, if only to be able to hold her in his arms. He needed to feel her against him so he could pretend she belonged to him. If only for a little while.

He gave a swift glance around the room. The band had finished setting up and were about to play their first song of the evening. A slow song, a few couples were already moving out onto the dance floor.

He swiftly rose to his feet and, reaching for her hands, he gently pulled her up out of her chair. "Come dance with me. This way, I can hold you in my arms. I can't even begin to tell you how many times I've dreamt of being able to do this again."

They began to dance, his hands holding her firmly against him, the beat of his heart so steady and sure next to hers. Mesmerized by the of feel of him, she slowly began to relax, giving a long, contented sigh.

When he pressed a soft kiss in her hair, she reached up to clasp her hands behind his neck. Gazing up at him, she smiled. It was a smile that reached all the way to her eyes.

"I do believe we've both been dreaming about the same thing."

<h1 style="text-align:center">CHAPTER 11</h1>

*Family and love go hand in hand.*
*~ Unknown*

"Y ou need to listen to me."

Chester was furious. And worried.

If he took time to calm down, he'd realize he was actually a lot more worried than furious.

His hands gripping the arms of his desk chair, he leaned back, closing his eyes.

*What can you possibly say to make her realize you're only acting like this because you're concerned?*

Finally, he opened his eyes and, resting his arms on his desk, he looked directly into his sister's sullen face.

"Carrie, come on... I'm only telling you this for your own good. But the way you're reacting, you'd think I told you your life was over."

She stared right back at him, her arms crossed over her chest. "Well, essentially, it might as well be."

She gave a frustrated sigh. "You know, just because you're my brother and older than I am, doesn't give you the right to tell me who I can date. Now I know why I waited until now to tell you this."

He sighed. "Carrie, he's not a nice person. Take it from me, I know. If you heard the way he talks about women, bragging about how he can have any woman he wants, you'd be horrified. He's a player with a capital P. Hell, I've heard stories..."

A disgusted look coming over his face, he shook his head. "Stories I'm certainly not going to share with you. Most of the guys on the team bite their tongue when he gets started. But one of these days, all hell is going to break loose and there's going to be a confrontation. I certainly don't want it to be between him and me, because of my little sister."

She immediately bristled at this. "Quit referring to me as your little sister. In case you haven't noticed, I am twenty-six years old. This means I'm a woman and not a little girl anymore. And I'm certainly not as naïve as you seem to think I am."

He leaned back in his chair, studying her. Let's face it, she would always be a little girl to him, *his little sister*. And the way she was carrying on right now, she was acting the part to a tee.

But he certainly wasn't going to tell her this. He hadn't grown up in a house full of women to not know when to keep his mouth shut.

*This, as you know from experience, adds up to the majority of the time.*

There were times he actually found himself wondering how Carrie could be a member of their family, as she in no way resembled any of them. Or acted like them. A free spirit, she marched to the beat of her own drum and always had.

A wry smile appeared on his face as he remembered the time he got into trouble for telling her a bunch of gypsies must have dropped her off on their way through town, since she was so different from either of their other two sisters. Only eight at the time, she had gone running to their mom, sobbing hysterically. He, in turn, had been grounded for a week. At the time, this had been the worst possible form of punishment since it happened to be baseball season.

But getting back to Carrie, if anyone were to see her for the first time, they would most likely guess she was a dancer. It was the way she carried herself, with such elegance and grace, while at the same time, making it appear as if this required no effort at all on her part.

And though a career in dancing was something she would've excelled at, this wasn't what she wanted to do.

She wanted to design things, she'd said. So, she'd went on to pursue a career in interior design and with her services now already in high demand, it was apparent she'd made the right choice.

She had a classic oval-shaped face. Her eyes, an unusual shade of deep violet, were framed with outrageously full and sweeping lashes. Add to this her long, dark and naturally wavy auburn hair, reaching halfway down her back, and you had a striking combination that always brought a second glance from everyone who saw her.

Now you'd think with all of this going for her, she'd be full of confidence. But she wasn't. Always second guessing herself, she was too quick to settle for less than she deserved. Which resulted in a series of bad relationships with just about every guy turning out to be a total loser. And, using her own words here, breaking off another piece of her already tortured and worn out heart.

Should he also mention she was extremely dramatic?

*But then again, do you know a woman who isn't?*

And now there was this thing with Doug, one of the guys on the team and whom, she'd informed him, asked her to be his date for Kevin and Abby's wedding.

This was not good.

*No, this was bad. Really bad.*

There were red flags everywhere when it came to this guy.

He sighed. "He's only asking you because of me. It irritates the hell out of him when I refuse to give him the time of day. But he's the last person I'd ever want as a friend. Because, believe me, he's not the kind of guy I want to be associated with."

This brought her up out of her chair, her hands going to her head as she began to pace back and forth. "I can't believe you. Why can't you see, maybe, just maybe… he might possibly like me for myself. With nothing to do with you?"

Crossing her arms over her chest, she glared at him. "You make me so mad. What gives you the right to be judging someone? From what I've heard, you haven't been very successful lately when it comes to women. So, maybe you should start worrying about your own love life than trying to control mine."

As soon as these words left her mouth, she regretted it, noting the pained look flashing across his face. "Oh, Chez … I'm sorry. I shouldn't have said that. Any woman would be lucky to have you. I mean this. Honest, I do."

He waved his hand at her. "Don't worry about it. You're definitely right on that account. But I'm not giving up, still hoping for the best. And I want the same for you. This is why I'm so concerned about you having anything to do with this guy, kitten."

She sighed. Every time he called her kitten, he had her. He'd given her this nickname when they were growing up and it still stuck.

He saw her face begin to soften, this followed by a smile. It was a reluctant smile, to be sure, but it was still a smile.

Reaching for the roll of Lifesavers on the desk in front of him, he tossed it to her. "Here, take these. You'll need them if you're determined to go to the wedding with this knucklehead. Only promise me if he drinks too much or starts acting up, you'll turn around and walk away. Don't even *think* of trying to reason with him. Or, *God forbid*, get in a car with him. Come to me or any one of the other guys. Okay?"

Stuffing the roll of candy in her jeans pocket, she nodded.

Then, as she turned to leave, his phone rang. A mischievous smile on her face, she quickly reached over to grab it off the desk. She hit answer, delivering her greeting in a very breathy and sexy tone of voice. "Hello. You've reached Chester Mazzori and you're speaking with his *purrrr-sonal* assistant, Candy. May I ask who's calling please?"

He groaned, closing his eyes.

She glanced over at him, her eyebrows raised. Holding her hand over the speaker of the phone, she gave him a curious look. "And who, may I ask, is Sophie?"

"Give me the phone." This came out in a growl as he almost dove across the desk in an attempt to grab the phone out of her hand. A big grin on her face, at first she held it out of his reach. Then she quickly relented, handing it to him. She knew the look on his face too well. She wasn't going to win this one.

*Let's face it, you never have... and probably never will.*

Curious, she watched as he spoke into the phone.

"Angel, can you hold a minute?" Holding his hand over the phone, he pointed at Carrie and then at the door.

"You. Out. Now."

She headed for the door, only to stop and give him a big grin. When he gave her another warning look, she dug the roll of Lifesavers out of her pocket and tossed it to him.

"I think you should hang on to these. At least during your conversation with Sophie." Her hand shot up to her mouth. "*Ooops... my bad.* It should be angel, not Sophie, right?" The grin still on her face, she blew him a kiss as she slipped out of the room.

He shook his head before speaking into the phone. "Hey, sorry about that."

He'd called Sophie earlier to let her know when he'd pick her up for the rehearsal. When his call went through to her voice mail, he momentarily considered leaving a message, but he suddenly found he wanted to hear her voice.

So, he'd left a message for her to call him.

She'd been on his mind ever since he'd dropped her off at her townhouse last night. He'd gone to bed with a smile on his face and when he woke up this morning, he was still smiling. He'd be willing to bet it was the same smile.

And now here he was, smiling again.


At first, Sophie thought she had hit the wrong number. Who was this woman, with this very sexy voice, answering his phone? Then after a rustling noise in the background Chester had spoken into the phone.

So, she was relieved. Well, sort of... Because there was still the fact he had an assistant who went by the name of Candy. This immediately bringing up a vision she didn't want to think about.

But she was being silly. It was only a name. A name with a sexy voice, nothing more. And, come on... she had no claim on him. If anything, she should be thankful it hadn't been Kelly who'd answered the phone.

She'd have a lot more to worry about if that had happened.

So, now her response to Chester was a little tentative. "Hi, I hope I haven't interrupted anything?"

His answer was swift. "No, you haven't and you never will. And to clarify, that was my sister Carrie who answered the phone. She's my youngest sister. I have absolutely no idea how she came up with the name Candy. She likes to fool around and, as you just witnessed, she has the tendency to get carried away."

Was it only his imagination, or did he hear her give a sigh of relief at this?

*Or maybe you're getting a little carried away, thinking, maybe even hoping, she might be jealous.*

This possibility bringing a bigger smile to his face, he settled more comfortably in his chair. "I called to let you know I will pick you up tonight around six. I guess I could've left a message when I called, but I wanted to talk to you. If only to hear your voice."

Glancing out of his window, he saw it was starting to snow again. He chuckled. "And now, I'm really going to go out on a limb here and ask you to please wear your boots tonight, since I see the snow is starting up again."

After a slight pause, she spoke. "And if I don't?"

He leaned back in his chair, closing his eyes. The soft breathiness of her voice and the hidden significance of her comment brought on his response in a husky whisper. "You know how I feel about holding you in my arms, angel."

Then, clearing his throat, he was quick to add. "And of course, I would never want to be responsible for any danger befalling the maid-of-honor before the wedding. After all, I do have a reputation to withhold, the nice guy I'm rumored to be."


After he ended the call with Sophie, Chester sat at his desk, idly watching the snowflakes drift past his office window.

He abruptly came to his feet and, grabbing his keys from the desk, left the room.

He had a plan.

But to do it right, he needed help. And he knew the perfect person for the job.

Ten minutes later, he was in his truck and pulling out of his condo parking garage.

The snow-covered roads didn't bother him like they usually did. In fact, he realized he was whistling as he drove.

He had every reason to be optimistic.

Yep, all was right in his world.

# CHAPTER 12

$\mathcal{C}$hester pulled his SUV up the driveway of the small ranch-style house and turned off the ignition. He was relieved to see the snowplow service he'd hired had already made their rounds, clearing both the driveway and the walk to the front door. This was one of the many little jobs he took over for his Aunt Evelyn. It was a small price to pay for all she'd done for him and his sisters over the years.

He glanced over at the garage, relieved to see her car was parked inside, safe and sound. He wouldn't put it past her to go out in this kind of weather as nothing, certainly not a few inches of new snow, ever seemed to hold her back. At the age of almost eighty-five, she still showed no signs of slowing down.

He opened the side door of the house and, before stepping inside, he vigorously stomped his feet on the mat to shake off as much snow as possible. His aunt would have a lot to say, and nothing of it would be good, if he left a trail of snow over what looked like her recently mopped floor. He could hear the sound of the TV coming from the living room, so passing through the kitchen, he headed in that direction.

He found his aunt, watching the news on TV while eating her

lunch. By the enticing aroma filling the house, he was pretty sure she'd made her famous chili. This had him realizing how hungry he was when he knocked on the doorjamb to get her attention. "Hey, auntie… do you have enough for me?"

She didn't skip a beat, as though it was completely normal for him to suddenly appear in her living room in the middle of the day. In fact, she didn't even take her eyes off the TV screen as she waved him towards the kitchen.

After he filled a bowl with chili, he sat beside her. He leaned over to kiss her on the cheek before he began to eat.

A commercial came on, evidently a sign conversation was now allowed. She turned, giving him a curious glance. "So, what brings you here? It's not like you to drop in without giving me at least some kind of notice. And how's the chili? Enough chili powder?"

After finishing another spoonful of chili, he gave her a thumbs-up. Then, setting the spoon back in the bowl, a sheepish grin came over his face. "I need your help. Can you give me a quick course on how to make a nice dinner? Preferably, one with a romantic theme?"

She looked puzzled. "What? Now you suddenly want to learn how to cook? What brought this on?"

Then her eyes lit up. "Wait a minute… a romantic flair? Chester, have you met someone? And now you're telling me you want to make her dinner? A romantic dinner?"

Her hands going to her head, a huge grin lit up her face. *"Oh, my Lord...* this is serious stuff. Could it be my prayers are finally being answered?" She clasped her hands to her heart. "So, tell me more. What's her name? How long have you known her? And could she be the one?"

He held up his hand in protest. "Hey, hold on. Don't get too excited." Then, he couldn't help it… he was grinning, too. "Her name is Sophie and yes, I really like her. But we're both pretty new in this relationship thing and nothing has really happened yet. I thought instead of taking her out to some restaurant and fighting the crowds on Valentine's Day, I would invite her to my place and make her dinner."

Noting her skeptical look, he shrugged. "Hey, you're the one who keeps telling me I need to entertain more now that Carrie has finally finished with all the decorating."

When she continued to study him, he started to wonder if maybe it wasn't such a good idea after all. He picked up his spoon. "Well, it sounded like a good plan in my head."

He went back to eating his chili, obviously enjoying every spoonful.

As she watched him eat, a feeling of happiness came over her. She was never happier than when she was feeding someone. A great believer sharing a meal brought people closer together, this was her way of showing her love.

She slowly nodded. And wasn't this something the world needed these days? More love? Lots of it. You only had to watch the news to know this.

And now this request from Chester. A romantic dinner? Who would've thought?

She leaned back on the sofa, the TV now completely forgotten. "My, my, my…" When this drew a questioning glance from him, she shook her head.

"You can't learn how to cook a fancy restaurant style meal in such a short time. Especially since you don't know diddly squat about cooking. Not, may I remind you, from my lack of trying to teach you over the years."

He had the grace to look somewhat ashamed. But before he could say anything, she put her hand on his arm, the look on her face one he knew well. Whatever she was going to say, this was the way things were going to go.

"Let me make the dinner for you. It can still be just as romantic. This way, you won't take the chance of goofing it up. Because something tells me, by the look on your face and the fact you're actually willing to learn how to cook for this woman, she must be pretty special."

Picking up his spoon and then putting it down again, he nodded, a faint smile on his face.

"I can't believe I'm telling you this, but she is. I don't know how she did it, but she has me. Like, what is it they say? Hook, line and sinker? I've never felt like this before and I don't want to goof it up."

He suddenly frowned. "I already let her slip away from me once, and I have no intentions of letting that happen again."

She reached over to give him a hug. "And it won't. But only if you turn the dinner over to me. Somehow, we'll get you involved so you can claim you had a part in it, too" A frown creased her forehead. "How, I don't know. But we'll figure it out."

Relieved, he returned her hug. "Okay, you've got a deal."

He stood. "I'm going to get more chili. Do you want anything? Then maybe we can talk about what you're planning to make for this dinner. The one thing I do know, she loves desserts. The more chocolaty, the better. And preferably, one we can share."

A slow smile worked its way across his face. "This is her request, not mine. But one I gladly go along with."

As she watched him leave the room, she gazed upward, sending a silent prayer of thanks to the big guy above. Then her mind kicked in, sorting through all the possible menu plans and recipes, always on file and ready to go.

She smiled. She couldn't wait to meet this woman who'd finally broken through the armor Chester had been hiding behind for so long.

She was pretty sure she was going to like her.

How could she not? Chester said she loved desserts, the more chocolaty, the better.

With this going for her, Sophie was already a winner in her eyes.

# CHAPTER 13

*I realized I was thinking of you and*
*I began to wonder how long you'd been on my mind.*
*Then it occurred to me, since I met you,*
*you've never left.*
*~ Anonymous*

Sophie gave one last look in the mirror.

She twisted around to check out the back of the dress, sending the skirt floating up in a cloud of chiffon before drifting back around her.

She had to give her aunt credit.

It was perfect.

A deep, royal purple, the fitted satin bodice and three-quarter length sleeves had an almost iridescent sheen. Paired with the chiffon knee-length skirt of the same color, the total effect was one of a classic cocktail design. Classic vintage, it was a dress she could very well imagine Audrey Hepburn would've worn.

Her aunt had surprised her by bringing the dress over earlier in the day, insisting it would be perfect for the rehearsal dinner. But Sophie suspected her visit was more of an excuse to get information about Chester, since she'd spent the entire time talking non-stop about what a wonderful young man he was.

He was so polite and, *oh my... so* incredibly handsome. She couldn't wait for the fashion show. She already had the perfect ending lined up for the show. It would feature the two of them together, their walk down the runway leaving the audience dreaming of the love of a lifetime.

They were going to be the hit of the show.

Which reminded her, when Sophie saw him tonight, she needed to find out if he had a tuxedo. He probably did, but if not, they would be more than happy to provide him with one. A man like him needed to have the best possible fit in order to show off his magnificent physique.

Sophie shook her head.

*His magnificent physique? Let this be a warning to never leave your aunt alone with Chester. Heaven knows what she might say.*

Throughout her aunt's visit, she'd either nodded or shrugged at almost everything she had to say about Chester. She was hesitant to share. With their relationship so new, she wanted to keep it all to herself, if only for a little while longer.

There was also the fact everything was so up in the air right now, any plans between them on hold. She felt like they were tip-toeing around each other, trying to avoid facing what they really needed to talk about.

But now was not the time to think about this. Not tonight. No, tonight, she only wanted to enjoy this time they had together. Hopefully, Chester was right when he said things could change.

She ran her brush through her hair and put one final dab of perfume behind her ears before she glanced around the room to make sure she wasn't forgetting anything. Since she was spending the night with Abby at the hotel, her suitcase was packed and waiting by the front door. And her pups had already been dropped off at her aunt's house for the weekend.

She removed her coat from the hall closet and reached for her boots. Then she hesitated, a slow smile spreading over her face. Leaving the boots where they were, she closed the closet door.

She was still smiling when the doorbell rang.

Sophie opened the door.

It was Déjà vu all over again, sending her right back to the night of the Children's Hospital Benefit last July. The only difference was the light dusting of snow in Chester's hair, giving him an almost ethereal glow.

As if he'd been sprinkled with glitter.

*Might you even suspect there's some kind of magic in the air?*

She took it all in, her gaze slowly traveling over him. He was wearing a dark grey suit under his perfectly fitted and hand tailored, dark grey cashmere overcoat.

*Oh my, he looks so good. Or, if he were to ask... he looked amazing.*

He gave her a slow smile. When she didn't move, he reached over to run his fingertips lightly down her cheek. "Hey beautiful, are you going to let me in?"

After a flustered laugh, she quickly stepped aside so he could enter.

Now it was his turn to inspect her. His gaze slowly traveled over her, everywhere, before he smiled. "You look absolutely gorgeous, angel."

She moved closer, wanting nothing more than to feel his touch. Tilting her head, she smiled up at him. "And as always, you look amazing. I just..." She became silent, her gaze dropping to his chest.

Noting her hesitation, he rested his hands on her hips to pull her even closer. Like her, he wanted to feel her touch. "What is it? You can ask me anything."

Intrigued, he watched as a blush began to build in her cheeks. She gave another breathless laugh and, though it was totally unnecessary, she nervously began adjusting his tie before going on to smooth the lapels of his jacket. When she realized what she was doing, she pressed her hands against his chest and gazed up at him.

"It's silly, I know. And I guess it's not a big thing. But I'm curious and I guess… well, I don't understand. Why do you call me angel?" She shook her head. "Not that I don't like it. I do. But I don't see it. Me as an angel, I mean."

His hands framing her face, he gazed into her eyes. "*Ah,* but you are… so much so. You came into my life, your blonde hair framing your face like a halo and your eyes shining like stars. You not only saved the puppy that day, you saved me, too. And, of the two of us, I believe I was the one who most needed saving."

Here he stopped to give her a soft, lingering kiss. "And now I'm a true believer. You will always be my special angel."

He stepped back, reluctantly dropping his hands from her. "But now, as much as I would love to stay right here, just the two of us, to continue this conversation, we should get going. The roads have turned a little slick since it started snowing again. We don't want to be late."

This was when he looked down to see she was wearing red suede open-toed heels. A sudden gleam in his eyes, he cocked his head towards her, his eyebrows raised. "*Hmm…* and what's this? No boots?"

She'd picked up her coat from where it was draped over the sofa. It was only after he helped her slip into it and he'd reached for her suitcase, she gave him a casual glance, a tiny smile hovering on her lips.

"Oh yes, about that… I guess I thought I'd take my chances."

Chester tightened his grip on Sophie, while at the same time, he managed to push open the door of the church with his shoulder. After he gently dropped her to her feet in the vestibule, he reached over to brush the snow from her hair. He smiled at the rosy glow of her cheeks, brought on by their brief time in the frigid night air.

Breathless and laughing, they had been arguing good-naturedly about her insistence there was really no need for him to carry her. But after losing her footing a few times in the icy parking lot and almost taking him down with her at least half of those times, he'd finally scooped her up in his arms. With her protests coming at him only halfheartedly, he carried her the rest of the way to the church.

Her eyes still sparkling with laughter, she turned to him and, holding her finger to her lips, she whispered. "*Shh...* we need to be quiet. After all, we are in a church."

His only response was to drop a quick kiss to her mouth before he took her arm to lead her to the front of the church. The first to arrive, they removed their coats and sat in one of the front pews facing the altar.

He put his arm on the back of the pew behind her, his fingertips resting lightly on her shoulder. In the hushed silence, they took in the beauty of the centuries-old church.

She finally smiled up at him. "I've always loved this church. If you close your eyes and stay really quiet, you can almost feel all the history that took place here. All the weddings, baptisms, holidays and even funerals, each such an important part in the lives of so many people."

Her expression turned wistful. "This is one of the things I love most about Paris. There's so much history and beauty surrounding you, no matter where you are. It's amazing that what we think of as being old here in this country, isn't even close to what's considered old there—hundred's of years old."

Noting her serious expression, he pulled her into a quick hug. "Someday, maybe you can show me some of these places. One I would like to visit is Italy. My aunt has spoken many times about the relatives who still live there, somewhere in the countryside outside of Florence."

She smiled. And then darn if she didn't open her mouth again to say what she really shouldn't be sharing with him. But somehow, he brought out this trait in her.

Every single time.

"When I get married, I'd like to go there for my honeymoon. I mean, our honeymoon." She shot him a stricken look. "I don't mean ours as in yours and mine. I'm referring to whoever I marry. You know, the groom."

And then, no surprise here, she kept on digging herself in even deeper. "Of course, we'd both have to agree on this. I don't expect you… I mean the groom, to go along with everything I want. He really should have an equal say in everything, too."

*What is your problem? Why do you keep blurting things out like this? Next thing you know, you'll be asking him to marry you.*

Running his fingers lightly through her hair, he smiled down at her. "I have a feeling you'll have no problem swaying this groom of yours over to your way of thinking."

They were both silent for a few moments before he cleared his throat.

The tone of his voice was hesitantly curious. "So, what else do you have in mind for this future wedding of yours? You know, the one with this groom you mentioned? The same groom who will be unknowingly corralled into agreeing with all your plans?"

She laughed, making a face at him. "Now you're making me sound pathetic. But if you really must know, I don't want a big, fancy wedding. I want to get married on a quiet beach somewhere. With only my closest family and friends there to share the day. We'd say our vows just as the sun was setting. And afterwards, everyone would party and dance the night away."

She gazed up at him, her expression suddenly so serious. "Because it should all be simple, don't you think? All about the bride and groom, the love they share and the life they are about to start together as husband and wife. It shouldn't be all about expensive dresses, elaborate venues and fancy food. Or all the pressure to invite people you don't even know or haven't seen for years."

Her words suddenly trailing off into silence, she gazed down at her hands

*And bingo… once again, you've said entirely too much.*

When he didn't respond, she glanced up at him. The look he was gave her was so intense, she was caught up in his gaze. She wouldn't have been able to look away even if she tried.

And Chester?

For him, everything was suddenly all so perfectly clear… and *so right.*

Maybe it was being surrounded by the beauty and the serenity inside the church. Or watching Sophie's earnest expression as she so passionately described the kind of wedding she wanted.

Or maybe because they'd soon to be celebrating the wedding of their close friends.

He only knew he'd never loved anyone as much as he loved this woman now sitting beside him.

*He wanted everything with her.*

Starting with the beach wedding she described. And the honeymoon in Italy. After that, he wanted to be able to share the rest of their life together so he could love her as she was meant to be loved.

Cupping her chin in his hand, he placed the gentlest of kisses to her mouth. *"Ah, angel..."*

A blast of cold air came at them, while at the same time, the sound of voices floated through the church. Pulling apart, they turned to see the rest of the wedding party appeared to be arriving, and all at the same time.

When Kevin and Abby began making their way down the aisle, with everyone else following behind, Chester rose from the pew. He pulled Sophie up with him and keeping her hand in his warm grasp, he leaned in to press a kiss behind her ear.

Followed by his whisper. "Later."

A shiver running through her with the promise of this one word, she glanced up at him.

And darn if he wasn't giving her that look again.

Later couldn't come soon enough.


The waiters had cleared the tables and the speeches were now finished.

The sound of laughter and the buzz of conversation filled the reserved section of the restaurant. Since most of the wedding guests were staying at the hotel where the restaurant was located, no one was even the least bit concerned about the snow still coming down outside.

His conversation ending with Chris Gardner, Kevin's longtime friend from Chicago and also a member of the wedding party, Chester turned to see Sophie was chatting with Lisa and Katy.

As he watched them, he was beginning to wish he hadn't committed to the impromptu bachelor party Alex had planned for later. Drinking with the guys wasn't how he'd like to spend the rest of the evening.

He reached for Sophie's hand. As she turned to him, her eyes wide and questioning, he tucked a stray curl behind her ear.

"Hey…"

*I miss you…*

She smiled, and without even thinking, she leaned over to press a kiss to his cheek.

Realizing what she did, and embarrassed by her impulsive show of affection, color flooded her face. She gave a swift glance around them before her eyes came back to meet his.

"Hey…"

*I'm right here…*

The breathy tone of her voice about did him in. Between this and how she always became so shy or flustered with any affectionate move or words from him, well … let's just say this sent his mind right into a frenzy, scrambling to think up a way he could get her to himself. If only for a little while. Bringing her hand to his mouth, he grazed her knuckles with his lips.

Observing all of this, Lisa smiled over at Chester. "Have the two of you had a chance to visit the observation deck they added when they remodeled this hotel? You should go check it out. It offers quite a spectacular view of the city. It can also be very romantic."

She was quick to add. "Be careful, though. I don't know if you're aware of this, but you made Susan Carter's social column in today's paper. 'Heavenly' was a word she used to describe how life is treating you these days, Chester. This, along with a few other interesting revelations. If you get a chance, you should check it out."

A brief flash of irritation crossed Chester's face before he shook it off, sending Lisa a smile. "Thanks. I guess I'm not surprised. She's one determined lady."

He held his hand out to Sophie. "Come on, let's go check out this view."

Leaning against the railing of the observation deck, Sophie gazed out at the panoramic scene in front of her.

A light snow still falling, it was as though the city had been captured inside a giant snow globe at the magical hour of midnight. A soft blanket of snow covered the buildings, a the perfect setting for what seemed like millions of lights, sparkling in every color of the rainbow.

Leaning against the railing next to her, Chester wasn't admiring the view.

No, he only had eyes for Sophie.

The delicate curve of her cheek, her beautiful eyes—now a deeper shade of blue against the purple of her dress—held him spellbound. He was also very aware of her mouth, her lips parted as though waiting for his kiss.

All this, combined with the intoxicating scent of her perfume, and one he now only associated with her, was pulling him in, a longing for so much more taking over his senses. He wanted nothing more than to pick her up and carry her off to a place where he could make love to her.

Mad, passionate love.

*The rest of the world be damned.*

Closing his eyes, he took a long, steadying breath. When he opened them, it was to find she was watching him, a curious expression on her face. So, when she smiled, the kiss he gave her was inevitable. A kiss that almost, but not quite, made up for the time he'd spent during the evening imagining a moment such as this.

With a deep sigh, he rested his forehead against hers. "Angel, I've been waiting to do this all night. How did I ever fool myself into thinking I only needed one kiss from you and I'd be satisfied? I now know this will never happen."

*"Mmm..."* Her eyes closed as she leaned against him, she decided

she was perfectly happy with what he just said, content to stay right where she was and in his arms.

He put his finger under her chin, lifting her face up to his. The look in his eyes sent her heart into high gear, beating even faster. She moved closer, her lips parting, anticipating his kiss.

*Umm... maybe this is when you should probably tell him one kiss wasn't going to do it for you, either?*

His smile was slow and satisfied. With her cheeks flushed and her eyes wide and gazing into his, he was almost positive she was waiting for another kiss. But first, there was something he needed to do, something he wanted to ask her.

His hands spanned her back to bring her even closer. "I have a favor to ask of you. After the fashion show, I want you to keep the rest of the day open. For me only. I want to have you all to myself. We'll celebrate Valentine's Day together. And yes, I know it's the day before. We'll consider it Valentine's Eve or something."

He smiled down at her. "Will you do this for me?"

Honestly? If he kept looking at her like he was? Why, she'd do just about anything he asked. Her hands going up to clasp behind his neck, her answer came out in a sigh. "I'll do whatever you want."

This immediately had her all flustered.

*Oh, no... remember? You need to think before you speak.*

No sooner had these words come out of her mouth and watching the blush rise in her cheeks, his lips curved into a smile.

He chuckled, pulling her even closer. "Whatever I want, huh?" He cleared his throat. "Well, this is something I'm definitely going to keep in mind."

Deciding this was as good as any to take her up on her invitation, his mouth hovered over hers. "Maybe we can start on this right now. An early Valentine's Eve request, shall we say?"

The kiss he gave her was enough to warm up even the coldest of Februarys.

# CHAPTER 14

Chloe was having the best time ever. It was official, being the flower girl in a wedding was the most exciting thing to have happened in her whole life. This life consisting of the grand total of seven and a half years.

She'd already inspected every inch of the suite Abby had reserved for them and was now sitting on the bed, eagerly going through the items in the gift basket delivered to their room only minutes before.

Even though her mom wasn't going to stay with them, she was so excited to be sharing the room with Abby and Sophie. Her mom was staying with her dad, though she did promise she'd stay with them to party for a little while.

She watched as her mom and Abby took their dresses out of the garment bags so they wouldn't be wrinkled for the wedding. As she went skipping over to look at her dress, the door to the room opened and Sophie walked into the room.

The dress forgotten, Chloe went running over to give her a big hug.

Abby grinned over at Sophie. "So, you finally decided to join us, huh? We were beginning to wonder if you were even going to show up."

Sophie laughed. "I wouldn't miss this for anything."

After Chloe pulled her over to see the gift basket, chattering about what it contained, Sophie plopped down on the bed. Kicking off her shoes, she gave a big sigh of relief. "Chester and I went to the observation deck and then walked around a little bit."

Color filled her face. "You know, just talking and everything."

Lisa came over to sit on the bed. She tried to hide her smile. "Uh huh, of course. I knew you'd enjoy the view."

She handed Sophie a folded newspaper. "Here, I wanted to give this to you before I forget. I thought you'd like to know what Susan Carter wrote about Chester. And about you, too. Read it out loud."

Hesitantly, Sophie took the newspaper from her and began to read.

*Hey all, I was at the airport yesterday and who should I run into, but Chester Mazzori. He was there to pick up a woman who had just flown in from Paris. A woman he addressed as angel. After further investigation, I found out this heavenly companion of Chester is Sophie Michaels, a fashion designer and co-owner of The Chic Boutique here in Cleveland. She has been in Paris for the past six months overseeing the opening of a new boutique. She is also a very close friend of Abby Evans, the fiancée of Kevin Kardell, whose wedding will take place this Saturday. Both Chester and Sophie are in the wedding party. So, this means all of those rumors flying around about him and Kelly aren't true. Because when a man calls a woman 'angel' there must be something really magical going on between them. Until next time, Susan*

Abby was frowning. "Wow, this is so not fair. It's a heck of a lot better than what she wrote about me." She shook her head. "Somehow, she always managed to get me and Kevin at a bad time."

Lisa nodded over at Sophie. "Yeah, I'd say you're pretty lucky. Susan must have seen something about you she liked, because as Abby just indicated, she can be quite snarky at times. Especially since Chester rebuked one of her passes a short time ago."

She laughed at the annoyed expression on Sophie's face. "Oh, Sophie... I think she scared him half to death with the brazen way she went after him. I have to give him credit with the gentlemanly way he handled the whole situation." She smiled. "For someone who comes across as being so rough and tough, Chester is very sensitive to other people's feelings. And once he finds what he wants, there is no stopping him."

She paused, her voice thoughtful. "*Hmm…* so what are you going to do? Because it's no secret, for Chester, you're the woman he wants. And it's obvious you're just as crazy about him. Have you talked about what will happen when you leave?"

Sophie sighed. "I really don't know. He told me maybe things would change and until then, we should enjoy the time we have. But so far, nothing has changed. So, taking that route may have been a mistake. But I'm just as guilty, going along with him. I guess now I can only hope for a miracle of some kind."

"You two need to spend some quality time together. Find out if it's the real thing. Then you set up a plan. The last thing the rest of us want is a frustrated Chester moping around, always in a lousy mood."

Sophie and Lisa both whirled around, their mouths open in shock.

Because this observant statement hadn't come from Abby. No, it had come from Chloe.

Abby, who had come over to join them, burst out laughing as she threw herself back on the bed.

Lisa groaned, and putting her face in her hands, she shook her head. Then she reached over and pulled Chloe into a hug. "*Oh, Chloe…* you're going to be the death of me."

Chloe shrugged. "I'm only repeating what daddy said."

She gazed up at Lisa, her expression puzzled. "What does he mean by quality time? And why is Chester frustrated?" This last question was directed to Sophie.

Still laughing, Abby looked over at Sophie. "Yeah, Sophie, why don't you tell us… exactly what did Alex meant by those comments? Why is Chester so frustrated?"

Lisa, trying to keep a straight face, shook her head. "Abby, stop it."

Totally embarrassed at this point, Sophie smiled over at Chloe. "Oh Chloe, I… *umm,* what I think…"

She stopped to take a deep breath. "Let me start over. Sometimes, when two people really like each other, they're afraid they'll make a mess of things. So, they don't talk about what they're really thinking. And this is what Chester and I seem to be doing. So, Chester is… *ah*… let's say he's confused. Which is another word for frustrated, I guess?"

She glanced over to see both Lisa and Abby had big grins on their faces.

More like huge grins.

For a few moments, Chloe was silent, thinking about what Sophie said.

Then she nodded. "You need to go see him right now and let him know how much you really like him. Then he won't be frustrated anymore."

Satisfied she'd solved the problem, she resumed her inspection of the items in the gift basket. Then she looked up at Sophie, a big smile on her face. "You could take him a gift. Let me see if I can find something in here. Unless you already have something else you think he'd like?"

Sophie was at a loss for words. Her gaze darted over to Lisa and Abby, only to see they were trying not to laugh and wouldn't be of any help.

Finally, Abby took pity on her. Sliding off the bed, she went over and picked up a white bakery box from the wet bar. She held it out to Chloe. "Don't worry, Chloe. Sophie and Chester will figure it out. But, look what I have. These are the same cookies I made for the wedding favors. They're extras, so I brought them for you to sample. I need your honest opinion of how they taste."

After Chloe went diving off the bed to take the box from her, Abby smiled over at Sophie. "Listen to Chloe. As young as she is, she always seems to hit it right on. Trust me, I should know."

Searching through the gift basket with Chloe, Lisa pulled out a bottle of wine. She handed it to Sophie. "Here, it will be your job to open this wine. I believe we could all use a glass right now. We have so much to celebrate, with friendship and love topping the list."

She beckoned to Chloe. "Hey, bring those cookies over here. I want to try one, too."

The morning of the wedding greeted them with blue skies, the snow sparkling like glitter in the bright sunshine.

After a quick breakfast, the rest of the morning passed in a flurry of activity with a trip to the hotel beauty salon for makeup and hair appointments. This was followed by a leisurely lunch in the suite Abby had reserved.

Then everything began to move at a much faster pace.

The photographer arrived.

Sophie's Aunt Louise showed up shortly after, taking on the job to make sure everyone was dressed properly and ready to go when the limousine arrived to take them to the church.

Abby was radiant, counting down the minutes until she would see Kevin. They had been texting back and forth all morning.

This had been something Abby was a little hesitant about at first. She thought this might fall under the category of bad luck for the bride and groom.

Because wasn't it sort of like seeing each other before the wedding? After Kevin assured her he was pretty sure it was fine, and he wasn't worried, she began texting him even more.

Chloe was excited, but now beginning to feel a little nervous. What if she didn't throw the rose petals the right way? She walked too fast? Or too slow? Or her biggest concern, she tripped and fell?

Everyone assured her this wouldn't happen. And even if it did, it wouldn't matter. The ceremony would still be beautiful.

Her only job was to have a good time.

As usual, Lisa was busy keeping everyone and everything in order. She was the one who realized Abby had left her bag, containing her makeup, brush, and all the other essentials she would need, in the hotel room. So, she sent a hotel employee to retrieve it. She was also trying to keep a close on Chloe, who she thought was starting to look a little pale.

Katie was trying not to think about Olivia, hoping she was behaving for Stephen and his parents. She had been so fussy during the morning. And even though Stephen assured her everything would be fine, she was worried. Yes, she knew she was being silly, but after all, Olivia was only a baby. And this was the first time they'd spent this much time away from each other.

And Sophie? Right before the ceremony, this is the text she received from Chester.

> Miss you. Even though this is Abby's day, you'll be the one I'll be watching walk down the aisle. Save a dance for me, angel.

Smiling, this was her reply.

> Miss you, too. When you see me, my smile will be for you. And every dance I save will be yours, too.

They both meant every word they said.


As Katy had predicted, as soon as Kevin caught sight of Abby coming down the aisle with her father, he fell in love with her all over again. There wasn't a dry eye in the church after the emotional greeting they shared when they met at the altar.

And as for everyone else?

Chloe nailed her job as flower girl without a single mishap. This meant Lisa was finally able to relax.

Katy found out she'd been worrying for nothing, since Olivia hadn't make a single peep during the ceremony.

And Chester?

As soon as Sophie had started her walk down the aisle, lost in the dazzling smile she sent him, he'd only had eyes for her. He had to keep reminding himself to stay where he was, fighting the urge to leave his place at the altar to go meet her.

It was when Abby and Kevin began to exchange their vows, he

finally tore his gaze from hers. He closed his eyes, moved by the promises Abby and Kevin's made to each other on this memorable day.

*You are the one I've chosen, because you are the one I love. And on this day, I promise to stand by your side, to share your joy and your sorrows, in good times and bad. And always I will respect and cherish you. Through all the days and nights of our lives.*

When he finally glanced over at Sophie, he saw her eyes were also closed, a faint smile on her lips.

He liked to think she was thinking of him.

Listening to Kevin and Abby's vows, Sophie was filled with a yearning for the same.

She slowly opened her eyes and gazed over at Chester. The message in his eyes was more meaningful than anything he could say.

Applause broke out, spreading through the room. A joyful response to the announcement Kevin and Abby were now officially married, the celebration was ready to begin.

Chester reached for her hand. A smile tugging at the corner of his mouth, he leaned in to whisper in her ear. "There's a lot to be said about all of this wedding hoopla, don't you agree? Maybe you and that future groom of yours should discuss your options." At her quick glance, he grinned. "Just sayin'…"

She reached up to kiss his cheek. "I'll be sure to take that into consideration."

# CHAPTER 15

*The first time I saw you, my heart whispered,*
*"That's the one."*
*~ Unknown*

The Grand Ballroom of the Regency Party Center had never looked better. Keeping with the time of year, the room had been turned into a winter fantasy, with a few subtle touches of red in a salute to Valentine's Day.

Miniature twinkle lights were everywhere. They were in the sheer gauze draped across the ceiling and in the trees positioned about the room, glitter coated snowflakes hanging from the branches for even more sparkle. If you took the time to look closely, you would notice a bright red cardinal, with its less colorful mate, perched in each of the trees.

The tables were draped with sheer gauze, sprinkled with snowflake and heart shaped confetti. The place settings were fine white china, rimmed in silver and the glassware, an assorted mix of fine cut crystal.

The centerpieces, an assortment of white branches, were anchored by clear marbles in a clear glass vase. Tiny lights strung on silver coated copper wire were draped among the branches, a pair of cardinals and glittered snowflakes adding the finishing touch.

At each place setting was an official team logo baseball cap, a cellophane bag containing two of Abby's homemade cookies, nestled inside. The cookies, each in the shape of a heart, were monogramed in decorator's icing, one with the letter K, the other with the letter A.

There was also a permanent black marker tucked inside the cap. Since quite a few of the guys from the team were in attendance, it was the perfect opportunity for guests to get an autograph or two.

Yes, everything was set for the evening ahead.


Chris Gardner casually sauntered into the ballroom, making his way over to check out the wedding cake on display. He chuckled when he saw the cake topper. The groom, a baseball player, was chasing after the bride who was carrying a basket of cookies. After he checked out the groom's cake, a very realistic and detailed rendition of Cleveland's baseball stadium, he moved over to where he had a better view of the wedding guests entering the room.

After a few minutes of this, he gave a resigned sigh. From what he could see, he wouldn't be exaggerating if he made the claim he was about the only one attending without a date. This made him almost regret his decision not to bring Lauren.

*Yeah, maybe not such a good move? Because here you are, dressed to the nines, but at the same time, alone and looking pretty much like a loser.*

He knew Lauren had been waiting for him to ask her to come to Cleveland with him, but he just couldn't do it. They'd only been dating for about two months and by asking her to be his date for this wedding, he would be making some kind of commitment.

Nope, this was something he definitely didn't want to do.

*You might as well come right out and admit it... the two of you? It's not working.*

He liked Lauren. He did. Their interests were similar and they usually had a lot of fun together.

She was also the kind of woman any man in his right mind would be a fool to give up. A dancer in one of the shows currently playing on Broadway, she was blonde, blue eyed and gorgeous. When he first met her, he couldn't believe she even took the time to speak to him, let alone agree to go out on an actual date.

But as hard as he tried to get serious about his feelings for her, he couldn't. There was no spark, no chemistry. There was no 'this is the woman I want to spend the rest of my life with' revelation coming at him.

As corny as he knew this sounded and even more so coming from him, she wasn't the woman for him.

Maybe he was expecting too much? He wasn't sure. But the one thing he did know… a long-term relationship with Lauren was not in his future.

So, here he was, on his own, somewhat of a new experience for him. Not because he was what you'd call a lady's man. Or what women referred to as a player, jumping from one woman to the next, with no intentions of settling down.

*Lord, no… you're neither of these.*

The reason he never lacked companionship was due in part to his sister Emily. She was always setting him up with someone. Having married the guy she met when she was a sophomore in high school, and now the mother of a four-year-old son, she was hell-bent on getting him married off.

*She wants you settled, she said. The fact you're not getting any younger is the reason for her sudden concern. Or, so she says.*

He was beginning to wonder if she might be on to something. It seemed like almost everyone he knew was married by now. Over the past year alone, he had attended more weddings than he would've liked and with half of these, he had been a member of the wedding party.

He was honored to have been asked, but enough was enough. This wedding was the exception. Friends since elementary school, he was more than happy to be here for Kevin.

*Nope, you wouldn't miss this for anything.*

He shook his head. This would explain why he hadn't been the least bit insulted when his partner for the wedding turned out to be the flower girl. He rather enjoyed Chloe's company. Her candidness was refreshing.

He chuckled. Chloe's biggest concerns were how many dances she could fit in with her father before the end of the evening, and when they were going to cut the cake.

That she'd promised him a dance was an honor he didn't take lightly.

He sighed. He should probably get a drink before everyone else got the same idea and bar got too crowded. Heading in that direction, he sidestepped a couple who were arguing. The woman's blond hair reminded him of Lauren.

*Was this an omen?*

Yep, he needed to talk to her when he got back to New York. Start fresh.

Because he still had hope. Somewhere out there, a woman was waiting for him. Just like he was waiting for her. He only needed to be patient.

Who knew?

It could even happen tonight.


Carrie was furious.

She was so mad, she wasn't even aware she was mumbling out loud as she marched her way towards the Grand Ballroom. It was only when she arrived at the entrance, and one of the wedding guests gave her a worried look, she realized what she was doing. She glanced around, relieved to see no one else appeared to have noticed.

So, Doug thought she was crazy, did he?

*Well, hopefully he won't find out just how crazy you can get.*

She couldn't believe he had dropped her off at the front entrance because he wanted to park his car. When she asked him why he didn't have the valet service do this, he became almost belligerent. She must be crazy if she thought he was going to trust his car to some kid, he told her.

Did she have any idea how much he had paid for the car?

Then—this almost sending her right over the edge—after she got out of the car and began walking up the steps to the entrance, he beeped his horn to get her attention. Shouting out loud enough for everyone to hear, he told her to find out where they were sitting, and get him a beer before the bar got too crowded. Because, as he so eloquently put it, he was ready to party, babe.

He topped this off with a grand show of gunning the accelerator as he took off towards the parking lot.

Could she be any more embarrassed?

*And babe? Yes, this I exactly what he said... Babe. Evidently, you are one crazy babe.*

She hated that he called her this.

She gave a frustrated sigh. It looked like once again, Chester was right. She should have listened to him.

But there was no way she was going to tell him this. Or ask for his help. No, she got herself into this mess, so it was up to her to find a way out.

After checking the list to find their table number, she made her way over to the crowded bar, inching in as close as she could. That she was about the only woman in line, certainly wasn't making her feel any better. To make matters even worse, she was practically pressed up against the guy in front of her.

She gave a frustrated sigh.

*If only if you could go home...*

She closed her eyes. A prayer might be in order. If only to ask for a little help to get through the rest of the evening.

Or a miracle.

*Yes, a miracle is definitely what you need.*


Drink finally in hand, Chris turned to leave the bar.

And, damn, if he didn't run right into the woman behind him. Though he tried to prevent this from happening, his glass tipped, almost his entire drink spilling down the front of her dress.

She let out a horrified cry before she looked up at him.

And she fell right into his eyes.

But this was okay. Because he fell right back into hers.

And at this exact moment, he knew…

*She's the one.*



Frozen in place, for Chris and Carrie, it was a moment they'd both been waiting for.

Call it fate, destiny… it really didn't matter. What mattered was that they both felt it at the same time.

With a slight shake of his head, Chris took her arm and moved them away from the crowded bar. Even then, he still kept hold of her arm, afraid if he let go, she would somehow slip away from him.

Or worse yet, she'd disappear into thin air.

*Because, truthfully? For all you know, she might be a figment of your imagination.*

Nope, he wasn't going to let her get away, real or not. At least not until he found out as much as he could about her.

*Everything… he wanted to know everything.*

He glanced down at her. Shaking her head, she opened her mouth as though she wanted to say something. Instead, she gazed down at his hand

When he realized he might be scaring her, he quickly removed his hand from her arm.

*Hell, you're even scaring yourself. You need to calm down, take control of the situation.*

He took a deep breath. "*Damn,* I'm so sorry. Let me get something from the bartender so we can wipe some of the drink off your dress."

Unable to catch her eye, he was quick to add. "You stay right here. Promise me you won't leave."

She nodded.

After giving her one more glance, he turned, shoving his way through the crowd to get to the bar.

He only knew he had to hurry.

*If you don't, you might lose her.*
*And there was no way he could let this happen.*


Carrie watched him disappear into the crowd.

He asked her to not leave? Well, he had no reason to worry. She wouldn't be able to move, even if she tried.

She had no idea what was wrong with her, having never felt this way before. She should be furious he spilled his drink on her. But there were so many other things going on in her mind right now to be worried about the state of her dress.

She felt as though she'd stepped into a dream, as though this was happening to someone else. She almost couldn't breathe, her heart now beating in a frenzy. She wanted to laugh out loud. Or maybe even cry… but this would be with pure joy.

This stranger, this man she knew nothing about, had awakened something in her like no one ever had before.

And everything she had believed up until now?

This had all changed.


A million thoughts were running through Chris's mind as he made his way back to Carrie, towel in hand.

Who was she? What was her name? Was she here with someone? A date? Hopefully, she wasn't engaged? Or worse yet, married?

These, along with so many other questions, were coming at him so fast, he couldn't even think straight.

He felt like he was about to begin a whole new chapter in his life. A chapter holding the promise of something wonderful.

As long as it was with her.


Chris reached Carrie's side, relief flooding him to find she hadn't disappeared. He handed her the towel. "Here, this is the best I could do. Again, I'm so sorry"

He smiled, a crooked smile. And sexy... unfortunately, for her, it was just so darn sexy, sending her heart beat into high gear.

She glanced down at the towel as though she had no idea what to do with it before she sent him a shaky smile.

He gently took the towel from her and began patting the spill on her dress. "Here, let me do it for you. You seem to be a little shaken. Again, I'm so sorry. I can be such a klutz at times. And now, it looks like I've gone and ruined not only your dress, but maybe your evening, too."

The distraught tone of his voice was what broke through the bemused state she couldn't seem to shake. She swallowed, her voice coming out huskier than usual. "I think it will be fine." She ran her hand over the stain. "See? You can hardly tell."

For a few moments, they both stared down at the dress. It was obvious this was far from the truth. The stain was definitely visible and it was sure to become even more pronounced as it dried.

But this wasn't important. She didn't care about the dress. What mattered was this incredibly handsome man who was standing next to her. Because of him, what had started out as a disastrous evening, had now turned into a chance meeting of a lifetime.

*Maybe this is why you're here? Proof there really is such a thing as fate? You've heard people talk about this, but never did you think it could happen to you.*

Chris was studying her, thinking how her voice was the perfect match to her incredible beauty. An almost smoky tone to it, it was low and seductive, stirring something deep within him.

*You want to hear more.*

This had to be the reason for his next move. Gently, taking her hand in his, he proceeded to do the most impulsive thing he'd ever done when meeting a woman for the first time.

His gaze holding hers, he brought her hand to his mouth and placed a slow kiss to the inside of her wrist. His voice came out low and husky."I hope I don't frighten you by what I'm about to say. After all, I don't know who you are, or even know your name. But you are the most beautiful woman I've ever had the pleasure of spilling a drink on. And now, I want to know everything about you. Starting with … I hope you're not already taken?"

He glanced down at her left hand as he said this, his crooked smile coming at her again. "I see there's no ring? So… maybe, if I'm lucky, this means there is no fiancé? Husband? Or boyfriend?"

Blushing like crazy, her response was a breathless spill of words. "No, not married. Not engaged. And no boyfriend."

The look of relief on his face, filling her with confidence. She began to study him.

What was it about a man in a tuxedo? Especially this man. But then again, he'd look good no matter what he wore. Her imagination taking over, she went as far to wonder how he would look wearing nothing at all.

But what was she thinking?

*Dear Lord, get a hold of yourself. This isn't a romance novel you're living. Though you're beginning to understand there might be some truth in what these writers come up with. Love at first sight? It's all starting to make sense.*

This man could certainly fill the part of a hero in any romance story. He was tall, at least six inches taller than she was. His dark blonde hair, cut in a shaggy, carefree style, curled slightly over the back of his collar. His eyes were a deep, sapphire blue, his face chiseled in all the right places. And his mouth?

It was perfect… the possibility of his lips meeting hers in a kiss was enough to make her feel faint.

But, just as he knew nothing about her, she knew nothing more about him… his name, or why he was here.

She gave him a tentative smile. "My name is Carrie. I'm a friend of both the bride and the groom." She tilted her head to look up at him. "And you? Are you a friend of Kevin's? A member of the wedding party?"

A frown flashed across her face "Unfortunately, I missed the ceremony, but I'm sure it was beautiful."

But she didn't even want to get started on this. Twenty minutes before Doug was to pick her up, he called to say there was a change in plans. Since he was still trying to recoup from partying last night, they were going to skip the ceremony. It was no big deal, since the reception was the most important part of the whole wedding thing anyway.

She almost cancelled out on him right there on the phone.

*And now you're so glad you didn't,*

She smiled.

It was a brilliant smile.

And she aimed it right at Chris.


When Carrie smiled at Chris, his mind went completely blank, what she'd asked him, sailing right over his head. Hoping to pull himself together, he glanced down at his tux. This was enough to remind him of why he was here.

He smiled. "Yes... to both. The ceremony was beautiful. And I have been friends with Kevin since grade school. We played baseball together."

He chuckled, shaking his head. "Unfortunately, 'played' is a bit of an exaggeration when it comes to my skill at the sport. I spent most of my time on the bench. After high school, even though we have gone our separate ways, we still keep in touch. I am very happy for Kevin and Abby. And honored to be a part of their celebration."

He aimed another smile at her. "Carrie... such a beautiful name. It fits you. My name is more ordinary, Chris, short for Christopher. It turns out my mom was a great fan of Winnie the Pooh. I am thankful she chose James as my middle name instead of Robin."

After a slight hesitation, he completely surprised himself with what he came up with next. "I don't know how it is with you, but it seems like everyone I know is getting married. It makes me wonder if I should start thinking more seriously about doing the same."

*What? Why the hell did you say that? You just met her. What next? Are you going to propose?*

*Briefly* closing his eyes, he almost groaned aloud. Because, crazy as it may sound, he could actually imagine doing such a thing.

This meant he had now gone completely off the deep end. Confusion filling him, he looked down at their hands, his still holding hers.

*Come on, you need to get it together. You're going to scare the poor woman away.*

That she wasn't backing away, trying to think up an excuse to leave, was a miracle in itself.

Carrie was actually wondering the same. But she decided this was only because he was still holding her hand. She certainly didn't want to insult him by pulling it away. Nor did she want to leave. Because something was going on between them. Something magical and out of their control.

She smiled. She knew exactly how to respond. "You and I should make a pact. If both of us still aren't married three years from now, we'll marry each other. It will be a big wedding with all the hoopla that goes along with it. Maybe having this plan to fall back on will take the pressure off in the meantime."

Once these words left her mouth, she regretted them.

*He probably thinks you are one of those girls who want to get married only for the wedding.*

But he surprised her. Once again, he brought her hand to his lips. But this time, the kiss he planted to the inside of her wrist was much slower. And so, *so* seductive, it had her almost swooning in the process.

*Yes, you heard right, swoon... there was no other way to describe how this simple kiss made you feel.*

Could this possibly mean he was going to agree to what she had proposed?

Chris would be the first to tell you, yes, he was.

Absolutely he would agree to this. If this meant he would be able to see her again, spend more time with her?

He was in.

*For real.*

He gently squeezed her hand. "You've got a deal. And we'll start by making our first promise to each other tonight. I want you to save a dance for me. Can you do this?"

She nodded.

*Anything... you would dance with him now if he asked... Music or no music.*


An arm abruptly snaking around Carrie's waist, she was engulfed in a crushing hug.

She sent Chris a startled look, while at the same time, she pulled her hand from his. Then she turned to find she was face to face with Doug.

A very irritated and scowling Doug.

His voice was loud, too loud. More than enough to make several of the guests turn around to stare. "What the hell, babe... I've been looking for you. I thought the plan was for you to be at our table, holding a beer for me. Instead I've been forced to get it myself. Then I find you roaming around, trying to make new friends."

As if to make his point, he raised a can of beer to his mouth. After taking a big swig, he sent a curt nod in Chris's direction. "So, who the hell are you? And why are you hitting on my date?"

Embarrassed beyond words, Carrie glanced over at Chris. He was eyeing Doug warily, a puzzled expression on his face.

Chris didn't understand. This was her date? Why? It didn't make sense. This wasn't the kind of guy he'd expect her to be with. More importantly, this wasn't the kind of guy she *should* be with. No, she deserved much better. So, so much better.

*Like you...*

Carrie wanted to cry. With Doug's arrival, every amazing minute she and Chris spent, had now been ripped right out from under them. She couldn't even imagine what he was thinking.

If she could, she'd grab his hand and run. Anywhere. As far away as they could get from this awful situation.

She slipped out of Doug's hold and after giving him and Chris a bright smile, she made the introductions. "Doug, this is Chris. He is Kevin's friend from Chicago. And Chris, this is Doug. He is on the baseball team with Kevin. He asked me to be his date for tonight."

She turned to Doug, her hands going to the front of her dress. She gave an embarrassed laugh "I bumped into Chris, knocking his drink out of his hand. Unfortunately, it spilled down the front of my dress."

When Chris shot her a puzzled glance, she gave a slight shake of her head.

He was immediately concerned. Was she afraid of this guy?

Feeling the need to protect her, he quickly jumped in to give his version of what happened. As far as he was concerned, this would be the correct version. "I believe I was the one at fault. It's because of my clumsiness, Carrie's dress is now covered with scotch and soda."

After making a big production out of crushing his empty beer can in his hand, Doug drew himself up to his full height. His expression was almost ridiculous with how threatening he tried to be. "I hope you have plans to compensate her for this. Dresses don't come cheap, you know."

Carrie was horrified. She didn't care about the dress. It was only a dress. Chris could spill a drink down every dress she had if he so desired.

*You don't care...*

After giving Doug a long look, Chris nodded... very slowly he did this. "*Ah...* no need to worry. I always own up to my mistakes. I'll definitely take care of the cost of cleaning Carrie's dress. Or replace it, if need be."

Carrie frantically shook her head. "No, you don't have to do that. There's no—"

Doug cut her off, his remark directed to Chris. "You're damn right you will."

This was when Carrie realized, from this moment on, her date with Doug was only going to get worse. She didn't even want to think about what was going to happen once he had more to drink.

But for now, she needed to get the two men away from each other before Doug did something really stupid.

She held out her hand, sending Chris a brilliant smile. "We should let you go. I'm sure the rest of the wedding party is wondering where you are. It was so nice meeting you."

When he took her hand, his firm grasp almost did her in. She didn't want to let go. But her eyes pleading with him to understand, she finally withdrew her hand.

Chris was torn. His instinct was to tell this Doug to get lost. Then he'd whisk Carrie away with him. But the unspoken message she was sending made him respond just as casually.

"It was nice meeting you, too. And don't forget our pact, starting with tonight." He cleared his throat, his eyes holding hers. Almost in a dare. "Because I assure you, I won't."

At Doug's sharp look, he gave him a quick nod and a smile. "You're a very lucky man. Take good care of her."

He turned and was gone, swallowed up in the crowd.

For Carrie, it was as if all the life had gone out of the room. She closed her eyes, Doug's rambling comment barely even registering. "Seems like a decent guy. But you make sure he reimburses you for the cost of getting your dress cleaned. Even if it was an accident. He looks like the type who can afford it."

Then he let out a loud laugh. "Hell, what am I saying? You'll never see him again." He grabbed her arm. "Come on, let's go join the rest of the guys. You did find out what table we're at, didn't you? I hope it's a good one and we're not stuck with a bunch of losers."

At a complete loss for words, she could only stare at him

*Losers? How ironic. Right now, you're pretty sure the two of you fall in that category—hands down.*

She didn't want to join the rest of the guys. She wanted to go home.

But this wasn't true. She now had a reason to stay, a very important reason.

*"Don't forget our pact, starting with tonight. Because I assure you, I won't."*

She wanted that dance...

# CHAPTER 16

$\mathcal{E}$veryone was looking for Chloe. Somehow, she appeared to have completely disappeared.

It was Sophie who finally found her, only a short distance away, curled up and sound asleep on one of the sofas in the hallway. Carefully settling next to her, she sent a text to Lisa to let her know she had no reason to worry. Chloe was safe and sound and she'd stay with her.

She also sent a text to Chester to let him know where she was.

It was a relief to escape the crowded ballroom. As much as she loved to dance, especially to Jason's band, she had finally had enough. And if you weren't dancing, conversation was impossible. You had to shout to be heard over the music.

Her feet were also killing her. She gazed down at her red suede heels, a perfect match to her red velvet bridesmaid dress. She loved the shoes, but they certainly weren't suited for the day long marathon this wedding had turned out to be.

*Make that eight hours, soon to be nine.*

She kicked off the shoes and, resting her head back against the sofa, she closed her eyes.

She was suddenly being kissed by a very familiar pair of lips. She opened her eyes to see Chester leaning over her. Reaching up to clasp her hands behind his neck, she smiled.

He gave her a slow smile. "Well… what do you know, it worked, just like Sleeping Beauty. One kiss and you're awake." He kissed her again. "Maybe there really is some truth in all of this fairy tale stuff, huh?"

As she gazed up at him, the only thing she was capable of thinking was how much she loved him. He was the kindest, sweetest, and let's not forget, sexiest man she'd ever known. If she could, she'd spend the rest of her life with him.

*In a heartbeat.*

A sadness flowed through her.

*How will you be able to leave him again?*

Chester sat down next to her and put his arm around her. "Hey, why so sad? What are you thinking about?"

She gazed up at him, her eyes searching his. Her answer was simple.

"Us."

This response giving him immediate cause for concern, he pulled her closer, his voice soft and soothing. "When I think of us, I find it hard to believe I would have such a sad expression on my face. No, I think I'd look happy, thinking how thankful I am to have met you back in July. And how when I'm with you, I know all is right in the world."

He dropped a kiss in her hair. "Most of all, I thank God, from the deepest part of my heart, for sending me an angel to warm me in this cold month of February."

Again, he had no idea where all of this was coming from. But he was beginning to think all the credit should go to her.

*She brings the words right out of you.*

And her response? She closed her eyes, lifting her mouth to his. "Kiss me…"

So, he did. Framing her face in his hand, he gave her the sweetest kiss. This had her dropping her head on his shoulder, a dreamy smile on her face.

He noticed her shoes on the floor. He chuckled. "I can see, once again, the shoes are off. I don't understand. What exactly is it with you and shoes? And your inability to keep them on your feet?" He reached down to pick up one of the shoes and, after studying it, he slowly shook his head. "Though I must say, with the height of these heels, these could be a challenge to even the most determined and fashion-conscious woman."

She smiled up at him. "I need to wear heels when I am with you, the higher the better. I don't know if you've noticed, but I'm quite a bit shorter than you are."

Then she sighed. "I can't help it... I love shoes. There is nothing like a new pair of shoes to lift one's spirits. And these shoes are very special to me."

He set the shoe back on the floor and, settling next to her, began running his fingers slowly through her hair. "How so?"

She leaned more comfortably against him. "When I first arrived in Paris, I was so homesick. I worked almost twenty-four-seven, hoping if I didn't have any time to think, I wouldn't be so unhappy."

She didn't tell him, besides being homesick, she hadn't been able to stop thinking about him. Wondering if she might have made the biggest mistake in her life by leaving with so much left unsaid. Those first few weeks, she would've given anything to see him again. If only to talk to him about what happened between them.

And now here she was, knowing she only had to ask and he would kiss her.

She reached up to press a kiss to his cheek.

He raised an eyebrow, the corner of his mouth twitching in a faint smile. "And what was that for?"

Smiling, she shrugged. "Oh, I don't know. I guess I felt like being impulsive."

When he gave her that look, you know the one, she quickly continued her story. "After I was in Paris for about a week, I finally got up enough nerve to venture out on my own to pick up lunch. This was when I saw these shoes. They were in one of the little shops right down the street from my aunt's boutique."

She smiled at the memory. "They were the only items in the window, displayed like the rarest of jewels on a white satin pillow. And I fell in love with them. I know it's silly, but I felt like they had been put there just for me. I went into the shop, tried them on, and they were a perfect fit. So, I bought them. I didn't even blink an eye at the price and believe me, they are by far the most expensive shoes I have ever bought. But I convinced myself they were my reward for all the hard work I did, setting up the boutique and getting it ready to open."

She shrugged. "I feel good when I wear them. Well, maybe not after wearing them as long as I have today. I think they may be more for show than comfort. But aching feet and all, I still love them."

Before she had any idea of what he was going to do, he lifted her legs up onto his lap. Reaching for her one foot, he began massaging it, his hands gentle and firm at the same time.

She closed her eyes, giving a long, rapturous sigh. "*Oh... my... gosh... you can't even imagine how good this feels. You could do this forever.*"

He stilled, smiling at the blissful expression on her face.

*If she'd let you, you would. And you'd buy her all the shoes she wanted.*

He'd buy her a pair in every color. If this is what it took to make her his, he'd give her a whole room full of shoes. He'd do this in an instant.

Thinking of this as being a possibility made him smile.

She opened her eyes, curious as to why he was no longer massaging her foot.

A wistful smile on his face, there was a tenderness in his gaze. He cleared his throat, his voice low and husky. "Angel, you know you only have to say the word, and I will."

She reached up to stroke his cheek with her fingertips. "Oh, Chester... I..."

He kissed away the rest of what she was about to say, unsure if it was what he wanted to hear. "It's okay. Just remember, I'll always be here for you. Bearing shoes by the dozens, if need be."

He reached for her other foot and, as he began massaging it, she slowly closed her eyes again, a faint smile on her face.

What he was doing for her was such a simple act, yet one that meant so much.

Without warning, she was hit with the urge to cry. Something that, as of late, seemed to be coming at her more often than not.

And, as we all know, Sophie never cries.

# CHAPTER 17

*I was looking around for love in all the wrong places.*
*Never did I think I'd find it here.*
*~ Anonymous*

Carrie and Doug were dancing.

At least, this was the plan.

But only seconds after they stepped out on the dance floor, Carrie realized she must have been out of her mind to think this would be a good idea.

All through dinner, she'd tried to ignore Doug's obnoxious behavior, his insulting comments and suggestive glances, wishing she could slide right under the table and disappear. The uncomfortable looks from the other guests at their table was the reason she suggested they dance. If she intended to retain even an ounce of her dignity, she needed to get him away from everyone.

At the time, this had seemed to be her only option. She had also hoped it might put a temporary halt to his drinking. And with the band playing all the songs so popular at events like this, the dance floor was filled almost to capacity. So, what could possibly go wrong?

*How were you to know the band would switch over to a slow song?*

Again, she grabbed his wandering hand. His attempt thwarted, he tried to kiss her. After swiftly turning her head to avoid this, she gave a frustrated sigh, pulling away from him.

She glared at him. "Doug, stop it. You're embarrassing me. Come on, aren't you the one who's been bragging to everyone at our table about what a great dancer you are? Well, I'm not seeing this. No, what you're doing is not what I call dancing."

He pulled her closer, his hands roaming all over her before he let out a long groan. "Babe, when I'm with you, dancing is the last thing on my mind."

And again, she was forced to detangle herself from his hold. But this only brought on his chuckle, his grip becoming even tighter.

She was beginning to feel like she was suffocating. And was it her imagination, or did his laugh sound sinister?

The answer to this came with his urgent whisper in her ear. "I think you're playing hard to get. Quit trying to ignore the chemistry between us, babe. Come on, can't you feel it?"

*No, you can't feel it. And you never, ever will. At least not with him.*

She blinked back the tears ready to spill. Glancing around the crowded floor, she saw Chester and Sophie were also dancing.

She watched as Chester said something to Sophie. Her response was to wrap her arms around his neck, lifting her face up to his for a kiss. After the kiss, he rested his cheek in her hair, his eyes closed as they slowly swayed to the music.

This, of course, made Carrie feel even worse.

Not because she wasn't happy for them. Or she was jealous.

No, of course not. She was thrilled for Chester.

He had introduced her to Sophie earlier and an instant rapport had popped up between them. The whole time they had chatted, she noticed how Chester patiently stood by, an indulgent smile on his face. Keeping a gentle hold on Sophie, his hand on her waist or resting lightly on her shoulder, his expression softened whenever she glanced up at him. He seemed so relaxed, so obviously happy.

She didn't know if he was ready to admit to this, but he definitely came across as a man in love.

*Totally and deeply in love.*

Her long, wistful sigh brought an immediate reaction from Doug. Stepping back from her, swaying unsteadily on his feet, he grabbed her hand. "I feel the same, babe. Come on, I'm tired of dancing. I've got a better idea."

Relieved, she smiled.

Little did she know, things weren't going to get better.

Nope, they were only going to get worse.


Thanks to the superb music and unending flow of alcohol, the reception was now in full swing.

Finishing off the last bite of cake on his plate, Chris tossed his napkin on the table. He leaned back in his chair, watching Chester and Sophie push their way onto the crowded dance floor.

He chuckled, thinking back to the lighthearted bantering that had gone on during dinner. Assigned to a table with some of Kevin's baseball buddies, he'd been seated next to Chester. They had already met at the rehearsal and he found he could relate to his dry sense of humor.

*But even the nice guy Chester seemed to be, was it necessary to give him so much personal information? What were you thinking? Talk about spilling your guts. And to someone you hardly know.*

When Chester asked if he was dating someone, a simple 'no' would have been sufficient. There was no reason to expand on it any further. But, no... instead he'd rambled on, claiming this was for the best, since he was pretty sure he'd just met the woman he was going to marry.

He had then gone on to tell Chester this woman was right here in the ballroom. And she was absolutely beautiful.

He hadn't stopped there either. Oh, no... he had gone right on to tell Chester, call him crazy, but he had a really good feeling about this. In fact, he was pretty sure this was fate. Because what else could it be?

Yep... very seriously, he had said all of this.

*Who does something like this?*

Certainly not someone who was in their right mind.

Give this Chester credit. He'd only nodded, as if he understood.

*But if you noticed, he did change the subject. Thank God for this little favor.*

And now here he was, on the sidelines and alone. He hadn't danced a single dance, nor did he feel the need for a drink. In fact, the last and only drink he had held in his hand during the evening, was the drink he'd spilled on Carrie.

But this was okay. He didn't need alcohol. As absurd as this sounded, he was already as high as he could get.

*You're high on a woman you hardly know.*

Since their chance encounter, Carrie was the one and only thing on his mind. Even now, he found he was searching the dance floor, looking for her.

*He wanted that dance.*

He wanted to know how it felt to hold her in his arms. Rest his cheek to the softness of hers. Or gaze into her beautiful eyes. And maybe, just maybe, sneak in a kiss.

He couldn't believe how much he wanted this.

*Good Lord... it's as though you're possessed.*

But it was all good.

*So good...*


Maintaining a tight grip on Carrie's hand, Doug begun pushing his way through the crowded dance floor. Moving quickly, he finally pulled her out into the hallway.

Carrie tried to pull her hand from his, but this proved impossible. She sent a frantic glance around them to see the area was deserted.

*Where was everyone? They couldn't all be dancing, could they?*

Feeling more desperate by the second, she attempted to reason with him. "Come on, Doug. I don't know what you have planned, but I have a feeling it's probably not a good idea. Let's go back and join the others." And even though she knew this wasn't true, she tried to sound convincing. "No doubt your friends are all wondering what happened to us."

He didn't answer. He was too intent on trying the handles of every door they passed. He finally gave a satisfied grunt when one opened at his touch. He pushed her into the room ahead of him and slammed the door behind them.

Carrie glanced around the room to see it was in use by the bridal party, their belongings scattered about. And now she was mad. "Doug, we shouldn't be here. This room is only to be used by the bridal party."

As she turned to leave, he grabbed her hand and began pulling her across the room.

And this was when she realized she was in big trouble. But before she had the chance to react, he pushed her down on a sofa and threw himself on top of her. He gave a long groan, burying his face in her neck.

His words came at her in a harsh whisper, his breath reeking of alcohol and heavy against her skin. *"Damn, I've wanted this with you ever since Chester brought you to the ballpark during the playoffs. You're so damn hot."* His mouth searching for hers, he groaned again. "Come on... relax, so we can do this. Don't worry, it will be our little secret. They're all too busy partying."

Now she was scared. To the point, she almost couldn't think. Doug was right. With the dancing part of the evening now in full swing and the loudness of the music, the possibility of someone interrupting what he had in mind was almost nonexistent.

*You could scream at the top of your lungs and no one will hear you.*

She couldn't believe this was happening. And even more so, she couldn't believe she had let herself get caught up in this situation.

Her fear escalating, she began to struggle against him in earnest. "Doug, you're wrong. Someone could come in here at any minute. And I know you really don't want to do this. So, come on... let me go... *please...*"

But he was already too far gone, his hunger for her clouding his judgement. He'd already pulled off his tie and was now tearing at the buttons of his shirt while he held her pinned to the sofa, unable to move. His only answer was to claim her mouth in another unwanted kiss.

It was when she felt him begin to fumble with his belt buckle, she used every ounce of strength she had to push him off her.

Miraculously, her effort seemed to work.

At least this is what she thought.


His gaze traveling over the crowded room, Chris finally spotted Carrie and Doug on the dance floor.

So, as soon as the current song ended, his plan was to cut in so they could share that dance they'd promised each other.

He wasn't one to break a promise. Especially one this important.

But as he watched, after what appeared to be a brief argument, Doug grabbed Carrie's arm, pulled her with him across the dance floor and out of the ballroom.

He took off after them, mumbling his excuses as he shoved his way through the packed room. Finally coming to a stop, and breathing hard, he gazed around the deserted hallway; the silence broken by the distant echo of a slamming door.

He was worried.

Whatever this Doug had in mind, he knew it couldn't be good. His frequent visits to the bar, becoming more inebriated with each trip, were an indication of this.

And *you still don't understand...*

*Why is she with a guy like him? She could have anyone she wanted.*

But why was he worrying about that now? He had more important things to do. Like finding out where Carrie and Doug had disappeared, which room they were in.

Breaking into a sprint, and stopping to try every door along the way, he finally came to the room reserved for the bridal party.

At the faint sound of voices, he cautiously opened the door and slipped inside. Closing the door behind him, he searched the dimly lit room.

He finally spotted Doug, stretched out on the sofa.It was only a split second before he realized Carrie was under him.

Carrie's muffled cries as she struggled against Doug had Chris seeing red.

To say he was furious would be an understatement. He seriously wanted to kill the guy.

His adrenalin kicking in and his fists clenched in response, neither Carrie nor Doug noticed as made his way across the room to stand next to them. A sound coming from him that could only be described as a ferocious growl, he reached over and grabbing Doug by the arm, lifting him to his feet.

With a surprised shout, Doug whirled around. When he saw Chris, he gave a loud curse and lunged at him, sending a volley of wild swings in his direction.

His fist flying, Chris retaliated by hitting Doug solidly in the jaw, the sound of the impact echoing loudly in the silence. This sent Doug staggering backwards, a look of complete surprise spreading across his face.

His eyes closed, he slowly sank to the floor, where he didn"t move.

He was out.

In shock—still not sure what happened—Carrie was shaking uncontrollably. Her gaze traveling wildly around the room, she finally zeroed in on the person who had come to her rescue.

*Chris.*

Dropping her face in her hands, she began to sob.

His breath coming hard, Chris was trying to calm down. After flexing his sore hand, he shot one last uninterested look at Doug before he gently pulled Carrie up from the sofa and into his arms.

He held her, shaking against him, as she cried big, gulping sobs.

His lips pressed in her hair, he whispered. *"Shhh… it's okay, it's over. You're safe now. I'm here."*

A wry smile hitched the corner of his mouth. He had wondered what it would be like to hold her in his arms, but this wasn't exactly the scenario he'd envisioned.

But this was okay.

Yeah… he would hold her forever if this was what she wanted. If anything, he was surprised she was even allowing him to touch her after what happened.

Clinging to him, she closed her eyes as his soft whispers flowed through her, calming her. And even though she didn't want to let go, after one final deep, shuddering breath, she pulled away to gaze up at him.

And like the first their eyes met, they were lost.

Her eyes were like jewels, sparking from her tears. Gazing into them, Chris knew he should say something. But as it had happened before, he couldn't, her beauty leaving him speechless.

She finally spoke, her voice filled with anguish. "I'm such a fool. I… I don't know what I would've done if you hadn't found us. Or what might have happened." Her eyes began to fill again. "I can't thank you enough. I…"

Her hand going to her mouth, she shook her head.

He pulled her back against him. "I'm glad I was here. And you're not a fool. He's the fool, more than a fool. I don't even want to tell you what I think he is."

They both looked over at Doug, who still hadn't moved. Gently extracting her hold on him, Chris went over to squat next to him. After tentatively putting his hand on him, he looked over at Carrie, his expression serious.

Her hands flying to her face, her eyes went wide. *"Oh, no… is he…?"* She couldn't even say the word.

For a moment, he seemed to hesitate. Then he came back to her, his eyes searching hers. "I may need your help here. We need to decide what to do. And more importantly, get our stories straight."

She nodded, a look of complete horror on her face. "Yes, yes, of course. I'll do whatever you say. It's the least I can do after you came to my rescue."

He took her back into his arms, the vague thought flitting through his mind how natural this already felt.

Then he put his finger under her chin, tipping her face up to his. "Oh sweetheart, he's out, nothing more. Between all the alcohol and the direct hit I gave him, he'll probably be out for a while. But he'll be fine. Unfortunately, guys like him always manage to make a full recovery and go right back to their old ways."

She stared back at him, not saying a word. And this is when he began to regret what he had done.

*Damn... you may have gone a little too far this time. What were you thinking?*

He edged her hair back from her face, an uneasy smile on his face. "I'm sorry. I shouldn't have misled you. I guess I was only trying to lighten the moment. But now I see this may have been a mistake." He smiled at her, giving her that crooked smile of his. "I must admit, the fact you actually agreed to be my partner in crime makes me feel good. It's nice to know I can count on you to be on my side."

Then the unexpected happened. Giving a small cry, she reached up to clasp her hands behind his head and, pulling his face to hers, she proceeded to give him a kiss beyond his wildest expectations.

A deep groan coming from him, he pulled her flush against him as he took over the kiss with a passion that more than matched hers. Determined to keep the kiss going, they paused only briefly to take a breath before their mouths connected again.

Was fate at work here?

Chris would be quick to tell you, the answer to this was a definite yes.


Carrie was clinging to Chris, her face hidden against his shoulder.

A horrified thought had come to her. What if he thought this was the way she'd behaved with Doug? Bringing on the reason for his attack?

So, she was afraid to look at him. Afraid of what she would see in his expression.

This was not at all what Chris was thinking. If anything, he wasn't thinking at all. No, his mind had left him the minute her mouth had connected with his.

And now, he found he was once again scrambling for something to say.

He took a deep breath, his voice unsteady. "Hey… look at me."

She lifted her face to his, wondering if her eyes showed the same awe and confusion she saw in his.

He'd be able to tell her they did.

Suddenly feeling both unsure and embarrassed, she put her hands to his chest, gently pushing away from him. Shakily running her hands through her hair, her voice was just as unsteady as his. "I'm sorry. I've never done anything like this. I didn't intend… what I mean is, I've never kissed anyone like I kissed you. Not ever."

She shook her head, her eyes pleading with him. "I don't want you to think this is what happened with Doug, because it didn't. Honest. I think with you, I got carried away and when I realized you were kidding and he wasn't… you know…"

His fingers were suddenly pressed against her lips. "Stop… Don't ever apologize for giving me… or… uh, someone a kiss like the one you just gave me."

The corner of his mouth lifted in a faint smile. "It was a wonderful, amazing kiss, one I'll treasure forever. And if you noticed, I didn't stop you. I returned the kiss just as passionately. So, if there is any blame to be handed out, it should be divided between the both of us. Okay?"

Her eyes searching his, she finally nodded.

Then she sent a worried look over at Doug, who still hadn't moved. "What's going to happen with him?"

He took out his phone and sent a text.

Within only seconds, he received an answer and was able to give her a reassuring smile. "I sent a text to Kevin. I told him to get some of his baseball buddies over here to get Doug in a cab and out of here.

They're on their way. Something tells me this won't be a new experience for them."

He slipped his phone back in his pocket and, reaching for her hand, he searched her face. "Are you sure you're okay?"

She smiled, realizing that yes, as long as he was here, she was fine. She was more than fine.

"Yes, with you, I know everything will be okay."

Both relieved and happy to see her smile, he pulled her into a hug. "Good, because if you remember, you still owe me that dance. And I'm not leaving until I get it."

Before she could respond, the door flew open, Chester, Alex and two other guys from the team charging into the room. The look on Chester's face was furious.

It was only when he spotted Carrie, his expression softened, changing to one of relief. His gaze running over her, as if inspecting her for damage—which to be honest, was exactly what he was doing— he shook his head. "*My God...* are you okay, kitten?" At her nod, he sighed. "I tried to tell you. Maybe next time you'll listen to me?"

It was only after she leaned against him, nodding into his chest, he glanced over at Chris.

A puzzled expression on his face, Chris was watching them.

*Kitten? Why is Chester calling her kitten?*

Then, for both men, it clicked—this happening at the same time.

Chester cleared his throat, the corner of his mouth twitching in an attempt to hold in his smile. "*Ah...* so I see you've met my sister."

Hoping the shock he felt wasn't showing on his face, yet at at the same time knowing it probably was, Chris groaned.

*Holy smokes! You've got to be kidding me. The guy you confided in, rambling on about how you found the woman of your dreams? He turns out to be Carrie's brother? What are the odds?*

He ran his hand through his hair, giving a slight laugh. "Yeah, I guess you could say that. Like I've been known to say, it all comes down to fate. I'm pretty sure you know what I'm talking about."

Carrie was watching them, puzzled by their behavior. Had they met before? It was almost as if they shared some kind of secret, or a private joke. But, whatever it was, they seemed to like each other. Something, she realized, was very important to her.

She put her hand on Chester's arm. She wanted to make sure he knew how Chris had come to her rescue. "I don't know what might've happened if Chris hadn't found us."

Her eyes starting to fill, she unconsciously moved closer to Chris. "I don't think I could have... I..."

Without even thinking, Chris put his arm around her. "It's okay, I'm here for you."

A small smile flickered across Chester's face at this. He held his hand out to Chris. "Thanks. I believe I owe you." He shot a stern glance over at Carrie. "We *both* owe you."

After they shook hands, Chester nodded towards Carrie. "Go on, the two of you get out of here. Get something to drink. Or share a dance or two. We'll take care of Doug."

After shooting a nervous glance over at the still motionless Doug, Carrie gave Chester a worried look. "You're not going to do anything bad, are you?"

He shook his head. "Come on, kitten... you know me better than that. I'm only want to make sure he knows if he ever comes anywhere near you again, he'll have to answer to me. It's time someone called him out on his behavior."

He smiled, gesturing towards the door. "Now, go. Both of you."

Chris nodded over at Chester. "Don't worry, she'll always be safe with me."

After Carrie pressed a kiss to his cheek, Chester watched them leave. Then he shook his head.

But he was smiling.

*"I'll be damned... fate, indeed."*


Carrie and Chris walked back to the ballroom, not a single word between them. At one point, she glanced up to find he was gazing down at her.

This time, instead of avoiding his gaze, she smiled at him. Still holding her hand, he gave it a gentle squeeze as he returned her smile.

Once they were in the ballroom, still not a word between them, he led her out onto the dance floor. It was only after she was his arms and they began to dance, he finally spoke.

His voice was a husky whisper in her ear. "A promise kept. It will be our first... and one of many, I hope."

Carrie closed her eyes, lulled by his words.

*One of many?*

Only time would tell.

Later, when Chris thought about what happened, why he'd reacted in such an extreme manner, he'd be quick to tell you there was absolutely no planning or thought involved on his part.

Nor was he the kind of guy who would respond in such a physical manner.

It was all very simple.

He believed he had been sent to protect the woman he loved.

*Yes, loved...*

And he'd gladly do it again.

*Fate?*

Let's just say he was now a believer.

# CHAPTER 18

Chester took his tuxedo from the back of his SUV and made his way into the Regency Party Center where the fashion show was to take place.

He had entered into what could only be described as a complete madhouse. The room was filled with women, too many women. Running all over the place, their chatter filled the room, sending the noise level off the charts.

He glanced around the room.

There was no Sophie.

Just as he began to wonder if he had the time wrong, he saw her coming towards him.

She was smiling.

It was a huge smile.

And it was aimed right at him.

He knew he was probably grinning like a fool right back at her, but he didn't care. It felt like it had been years since they last saw each other. This had been when he dropped her off at her townhouse after Kevin and Abby's day-after wedding brunch on Sunday.

This would be approximately forty-four hours ago.

And who would be keeping track of this? The answer to this would definitely be him. He was pretty sure it had been the longest almost forty-four hours of his life.

*Yep, it just about killed you.*

But as Sophie had explained, there were so many last-minute details she had to go over with her aunt for the fashion show. They also had a lot of work to finish up for the Paris location. This meant they would be busy for the rest of Sunday and definitely all of Monday.

*The entire time?*

Unfortunately, yes. But what carried him through those long hours was her promise. Once the fashion show was over, the remaining time they had before she left for Paris? She would be all his.

*A deal you had accepted in a heartbeat.*

And now, when she came to stand next to him, he didn't even hesitate. He dropped his tuxedo on the chair next to him, took her into his arms, and gave her a kiss that almost, but not quite, made up for the time they had been apart.

Unfortunately, the sound of Susan Carter's voice was enough to put an end to the kiss. Leaping across the room to join them, there was a megawatt smile plastered on her face,

She nodded over at Chester. "Chester Mazzori... who would've thought? When my source told me you were going to be one of the male models in this show, I insisted there was absolutely no way this was possible. But here you are, proving me wrong."

She smiled brightly at Sophie before she turned to address Chester again. "And from what I've just witnessed, it looks like you and your Paris friend are now... what shall we say? More than friends?"

Chester's sigh was resigned as he reached for Sophie's hand. "Hey Susan, how's it going? And yes, you're right. Modeling in this show will be a whole new experience for me. But as you already know, I'm always willing to help out a good cause."

He gave Sophie's hand a gentle squeeze before he went on to add. "And this beautiful woman standing next to me? I'll go on record to say she is the main reason I agreed to be here. For her, I will do anything."

Still holding Sophie's hand, he reached for his tuxedo before he gave Susan another smile. "And now I'm pretty sure I need to get changed into this tux. I take it you're staying for the show?"

At her nod, he smiled, quickly cutting off any additional questions she might have. "Great, I hope you find it enjoyable. And, *please* ... be gentle with your review if you feel the need to mention me. I have a feeling this is going to be a lot more complicated than playing ball."

Turning away from her, he glanced down at Sophie. "So, now where to, angel?"

As they walked away, he was feeling quite proud of himself. He had managed to leave Susan hanging, giving her no opportunity to obtain anything too personal from him.

But it turns out he was wrong about this.

*So wrong.*

Neither he nor Sophie had noticed the photographer Susan had brought with her. This meant they also didn't realize he'd caught the kiss they had shared, close up and almost the exact moment it happened.

As she went over to give the photographer a high five, Susan was already forming the words to her next column in her head.

She smiled.

She hit the jackpot this time around. Her readers were going to love it.

The fashion show was winding down to an end and so far, it had been a huge success. Every walk down the runway had been met with enthusiastic applause. Sophie's Aunt Louise had already gone on to claim it was the best show they'd ever put together.

Now standing at the podium next to the runway, she was waiting for the chatter to die down so she could announce the final walk of the show. It was only when the lights slowly began to dim, a hush fell over the crowd.

She sent a smile around the room. "We are now almost to the end of the show, only one more runway walk remaining. One I promise you'll love. But once again, I would like to remind you the proceeds from the tickets purchased for this show, along with what is raised by the silent auction still open for bids, will go towards scholarships to the university's fashion program."

She sent another smile around the room.

"As I look around the room at all of you who have taken time to be with us today, I can't even begin to tell you how much you're appreciated. We couldn't do this without you. I would also like to thank all the people who've worked so hard to make this possible. To the students, professors, models and everyone else who gave their time, I give you my heartfelt thanks."

She waited for the applause to die down before she continued. "As we say here in the fashion business, if you talk the talk, you better be able to walk the walk. This is exactly what is happening here today.

"Each design is the result of many hours of hard work by one of our current students. It's their final design project before they graduate this coming spring. And each design is proof of what a wonderful program the university offers.

"If I had the time, I'd give you the names of the many students in this program who have gone on to do great things in the fashion world. I can't even begin to tell you how proud I am of all of them.

"But now, as a special surprise, the final model of the show is someone many of you may recognize. Already a graduate of the program, she is now managing a boutique I recently acquired in Paris, helping me make my own dream a reality. There was never a doubt in my mind she was the person to take over the operation when a personal commitment kept me from going to Paris myself.

"Now, it would be remiss of me if I didn't let you know she's also my niece. But when you see her design, you will understand why I chose her as the last walk of this show. I'm also sure you will recognize her handsome escort. Together, they'll make every single one of you believe in the power of love. And, of course, let's not forget the need for that perfect dress."

The lights slowly dimmed until only those lining the runway remained. As music filled the room, a hush fell over the crowd.

Flashing a huge smile, Sophie's aunt held out her arms. "Without further ado, I present to you Sophie Michaels and her escort, Chester Mazzori."

Chester was standing right outside the entrance of the ballroom. A woman, her job to direct him on his entrance, was with him.

He smiled at her, not at all surprised she didn't smile in return. It hadn't escaped his notice she took her job very seriously.

Her attention glued to the clipboard she was holding, she began rattling off her instructions. "Okay... it says Louise is going to signal me when you're up. This is when you push the door open and slowly saunter up the aisle, very casual and cool-like, hands in pockets or whatever makes you comfortable."

She shot him a glance over the rim of her glasses to make sure he understood.

When he nodded, she continued. "When you get to the steps going up on the right side of the runway, you pause with one foot on the bottom step. Again, you do this in a very casual-like manner as you wait for Sophie to come out onto the runway. When she does, you are to gaze at her as if she is the most beautiful woman you ever saw. She's a vision. The woman you suddenly realize you're madly in love with. You feel almost faint with desire."

At his raised eyebrow, she shrugged. "Hey, I'm only reading what is written here." She laughed. "There is no way I could come up with something like this. Nope, this is all Louise's doing."

*Hmm... so, she does have a sense of humor.*

He grinned, relieved to finally see her smile before she went back to reading the instructions. "Now, after you wait for a few moments, you slowly go up the steps to meet her. You take her arm and walk down the runway together. Again, you are fascinated with everything about her. You only have eyes for her."

She pointed her pen at the clipboard. "According to what it says here, what you do for a finale is up to you. You can twirl her around in a dance, give her a kiss, a hug, or whatever grabs you."

She looked up at him, her eyebrows raised. "So, do you think you can do this? It says here, you should take your cue by the words to the song. Jason Bennett will be singing For the First Time. I think it's by Rod Stewart. Do you know Jason? Do you know the song?"

His nod was distracted. He was beginning to wonder if he was a little in over his head with this modeling thing. He hadn't realized there would be so much acting involved. But as far as what she was asking of him with Sophie?

*Seriously? You're supposed to gaze at her as though she is the woman you're madly in love with? You won't even have to put on an act.*

Just as he was about to tell her this, she glanced down at her phone and gave him a shove towards the door. "Oh my gosh … you're on."

As he had been instructed, Chester pushed open the door and began moving in what he felt was a very confident and casual saunter.

*Piece of cake. You've got this.*

Boy, was he wrong. It turned out being a model was much harder than he'd anticipated. Between the camera flashes and shrieks coming at him, it took everything he had to keep from taking off at a sprint, his goal now to get wherever he was supposed to meet Sophie.

*Good Lord, you'll take playing in a game, in front of a capacity crowd, over this any day.*

In what felt like hours, yet in reality was only seconds, he reached the steps to the runway. This is when he felt the mood of the crowd change, everyone joining in on one big, collective sigh as the sound of Jason's voice floated through the room.

*Is that your smile...*

Congratulating himself on making it this far, Chester glanced over to see Sophie was standing on the runway.

And he forgot everything he had been so sure he would have no trouble remembering. He could only stare, captivated by this beautiful vision in front of him.

It was only when Sophie sent him a tentative smile, he snapped to attention. After he almost tripped as he ran up the steps, but somehow managed to stay on his feet, he swiftly covered the distance between them.

His eyes never leaving hers, he brought her hand to his mouth, brushing her fingers with a kiss.

This brought another sigh from the crowd.

But Chester wasn't even aware of this. Nothing mattered except Sophie. His eyes caressing hers, his voice was a husky whisper. *"My God, angel … you look absolutely stunning."*

And she did. The dress, her own design, was a light blue satin, with silver undertones. It was fitted all the way to the floor with a slit up to mid-thigh on one side. The neckline was a wide satin band of the same color, falling slightly off her shoulders to dip down to her waist in the back. Splashes of decorative crystal beading made the dress sparkle and shimmer like a million stars in the darkened room.

> *I can't believe how much I see,*
> *when you're looking back at me...*

The music a reminder of what he was supposed to be doing, he held out his arm to her. And his eyes never leaving hers, together, they did a perfect walk down the runway.

Later, when he stopped to think about it, he decided it was a miracle he hadn't tripped over his own feet, or fell flat on his face.

> *Yes, I found you somehow,*
> *and I've never been so sure...*

After he twirled her around at the end of the runway, bringing another enthusiastic response from the crowd, he remembered the finale was up to him.

A smile spreading across his lips, and before he had time to think of what he was about to do, he bent her back over his arm.

And he gave her a long, passionate kiss.

*Now I understand what love is,*
*for the first time...*

The crowd went absolutely wild, their applause thundering in waves across the room. This continued even after Sophie and Chester had left the runway, and Jason had sung the last the words of the song

After one last group walk down the runway, models and designers alike, Chester reached for Sophie's hand, leading her to a more secluded area. He took her into his arms and gazing down at her, he shook his head. "*Whoa*, I don't even know where to start."

She grinned up at him. "So, are you ready to give up baseball for a career in modeling? Remember, I warned you."

His expression thoughtful, he gently pulled her into his arms. "Angel, if it means spending more time with you, I'd do it in a heartbeat."

He smiled. "But, truthfully? I think baseball may be the less dangerous of the two."

All smiles, Sophie's aunt came running over to them. She gave each of them a big hug. "Oh my goodness… that was just wonderful… you were wonderful! Even now, nobody wants to leave."

She clasped her hands to her heart. "Do you think you can take a few minutes to go out and mingle with the crowd? If you do, I'm sure we'll get people to stay longer and place more bids on the silent auction."

She reached over to hug Chester again. "I can't thank you enough. You and Sophie made the show a success. I know I've monopolized Sophie's time the past few days, but I if you do this one last thing, I will be forever grateful."

She winked.

"Then you can celebrate the night away."

After she walked away, Chester gazed down at Sophie.

He was smiling as he tucked her arm in his. "So, are you ready for this? I'm sure it will be quite interesting."

She nodded. "I'm ready."

After the kiss he gave her on the runway?

She was ready for anything.

# CHAPTER 19

It was snowing again.

His SUV stopped at a red light, Chester looked over at Sophie to find she was studying him.

When she smiled, he reached over to hold her hand.

He grinned. "So, tell me, what thoughts are running around in that gorgeous head of yours right now?"

"I'm wondering where you're taking me." She sighed. "I hope it's someplace nice and quiet after what I just put you through."

He leaned over to give her a kiss. "I guarantee, where we're going, it will be quiet and not crowded. And this is the only information I'm going to give you."

After the light turned green and they began to move again, he chuckled. "I thought we'd never get out of there."

"Yes, it was crazy, wasn't it? My Aunt Louise is already talking about what she wants to do next year." Sophie shook her head. "She was mumbling something about football players... or maybe hockey."

She shook her head. "I don't know..."

He smiled. "Good, that gets me off the hook. As much as I enjoyed being with you, I've decided modeling is not for me. I'm going to stick with baseball. It's definitely a safer option."

He grinned over at her. "*Geeez...* I even had a marriage proposal. From a woman who was probably in her eighties. But she did say she was a huge baseball fan. So, maybe I should have taken her up on her offer."

She laughed. "Maybe you should have. Again, you can't say I didn't warn you."

He shook his head, gently squeezing her hand. "Yes, you did. And the woman who proposed? I told her I was pretty sure I was already taken. She said she more than understood."

As he pulled up in front of the entrance to a high-rise apartment building, the concierge sprinted over to open Sophie's door. "Evening Miss, welcome to Lake View Towers."

He grinned over at Chester. "Hey, Mr. Mazzori... how's it going? Will I be parking this for you?"

Chester nodded as he took Sophie's arm to lead her over to the elevator. "That would be great, Paul. Thanks. You can drop off the keys later."

Once they were in the elevator, Sophie sent him a curious look. "I take it this is where you live?"

He glanced over at her, the tone of his voice uncertain. "Is this okay? I thought it would be a nice change. It seems like we haven't been alone since you've been home."

He wondered if maybe this plan of his wasn't the best of ideas after all. He didn't want her to think he brought her here because of, well... you know.

But to be completely honest? This was exactly what he wanted to happen.

To the point, this was all he could think about.

Sophie could see he was nervous. Hoping to reassure him, she moved closer to smile up at him. "I don't care where we are. As long as I'm with you."

*Uh oh... he's giving you that look again.*

But as he went to pull her into his arms, she backed away, a teasing smile on her face. "As long as I still get the dinner you promised. I'm starving."

"A promise is a promise, whether it be dinner or anything else." He leaned in to kiss her just as the elevator door opened. Bracing his hand against the door to hold it open, he took his time, leisurely finishing the kiss before he took her hand to lead her down the hall to his condo.

Once they were inside and he had hung their coats in the closet, he turned to see she was gazing curiously around the room. He smiled, rubbing his hands together. "So... this is where I live. What do you think?"

What did she think?

If anything, she was very much in shock. She felt like she'd walked into a model home. A model home owned by a celebrity, or someone who was very wealthy.

But come on, what did you expect? A stark bachelor type of dwelling? With maybe a big screen TV and a grouping of monstrous leather couches and chairs?

*Maybe?*

No, his condo in no way resembled that. The focal point of the large, open space was the wall of windows. Extending all the way to the cathedral high ceiling, they offered a panoramic view of Lake Erie and the skyline of the city of Cleveland. Right now, it was a hazy blur of white, with snow falling in the fading light of early evening. But it was still an amazing view.

The furnishings were a mix of both contemporary and traditional, with a neutral color scheme of creams and grey. Bursts of color came from the throw pillows scattered on the wrap around sofa and in the huge color splashed area rug. Above the stone fireplace, there was a large framed photo of the Cleveland baseball stadium.

To the right was the kitchen, a huge marble topped island separating it from the rest of the room. The different colored pendant lights hanging over the island added more pops of color.

An older woman came from around the island.

After she enveloped Sophie in a crushing hug, she stepped back, and crossing her arms, she gave her a thorough inspection before she nodded. "So you're Sophie. I'm Chester's Aunt Evelyn. I don't know if he told you, but I raised him and his three sisters. When they came to live with me, it was the best thing that ever happened to me."

She peered even more closely at Sophie before she gave another nod. "Chester is the kindest, most generous and hard-working person I know. I hope you aren't one of these groupie-like women interested in him only for who he is and how much money he makes. Carrie told me you aren't, but I wanted to hear this directly from you."

Chester groaned, running his hand through his hair. "Aunt Evelyn, please…"

A pained expression on his face, he turned to Sophie. "My aunt was kind enough to make dinner for us tonight. Which means you are in for a treat, because she's an amazing cook. But as you've just witnessed, she also has this annoying habit of saying exactly what she's thinks."

A wry smile on his face, he shook his head. "I can't tell you how many times she's embarrassed me." Then he grinned. "But we all love her to death."

Sophie smiled over at his aunt. "You remind me of my Aunt Louise. So, I completely understand how you feel. And in answer to how I feel about Chester being famous and all? If anything, sometimes it scares me."

Chester laughed. "First, I'm far from famous. And to tell you the truth, sometimes my life scares me, too. Like today, for example. Dealing with baseball fans seems like a piece of cake after what we just experienced."

At the puzzled look on his aunt's face, Sophie began filling her in about the fashion show.  While Chester, who had started opening a bottle of wine, jumped in here and there to add his own observations about the experience.

After his aunt had given him the serving instructions for the dinner she'd prepared, and she was convinced he could handle it, he escorted her downstairs to the taxi waiting to take her home.

When Chester returned, he found Sophie by the fireplace, gazing up at the photo of the stadium.

He poured out two glasses of wine and walked over to join her. But one look at the serious expression on her face, he set the glasses on the coffee table and pulled her into his arms. "*Uh, oh... what's wrong?*"

She shook her head against him. "I don't care about any of that, I really don't. I don't want you to think this is why I'm here."

At first, he was confused. But once he realized what she was trying to say, he leaned back to smile down at her. "Angel, I know you don't. And my aunt?"

He shook his head. "She would be absolutely horrified if she knew she upset you with what she said. Sometimes ... well, let's say she means well and leave it at that."

He pulled her back against him and pressed a kiss in her hair. "Come on, this is Valentine's Eve, remember? And we have a wonderful dinner waiting for us."

*Dinner?*

Burying her face in the soft cashmere of his sweater, she inhaled in the scent of his cologne, him and just everything. And suddenly, she wasn't that hungry.

At least not for food.

If she had a choice, she'd rather stay right where she was.

Chester was trying not to think about how much he wanted to kiss her. But he was afraid if he did, now in the privacy of his home, this would have him whisking her right off to his bedroom.

*Remember, you promised her dinner. And a promise is a promise. Right?*

He pressed another kiss in her hair and reluctantly released his hold. After he handed her one of the wine glasses, he held the other up in a toast.

"To us, angel. Let this be the beginning of our own special tradition."


Sophie placed her fork on her empty plate and smiled over at Chester. "Oh my, everything was so good. I definitely have to thank your aunt for such a wonderful dinner."

He poured more wine into her glass. "You will make her very happy if you do. She is never happier than when she is feeding someone."

He stood, picking up their empty plates from the table. When she moved to help, he smiled, shaking his head. "No, you stay right where you are. You're my guest, my very special guest, I might add, and I don't want you lifting a finger."

When he returned, he placed a small jeweler's box, tied with a red ribbon, on the table in front of her.

Gazing up at him, she looked like she was about to cry. "Oh, Chester... but I have nothing for you."

He leaned in to give her a kiss before he sat next to her. "Sweetheart, I didn't expect anything."

The stricken look still on her face, he gave her another kiss. Then he placed the box in her hands. "Just open it."

She undid the ribbon and lifted the lid. For a few moments, she was silent. Then she looked up at him, her eyes huge in her face. "Oh Chester, it's beautiful. Are they real diamonds?"

When he chuckled, she shook her head. "I'm sorry. I shouldn't have asked you that But, you shouldn't have spent so much. Especially when I have nothing for you in return."

He smiled as he took the box from her. "*Ah...* but I did. And this is because I wanted to. And come on, I could never give you anything but the real thing. It wouldn't be right."

He removed a necklace from the box. Hanging from a sterling silver chain were two small interlocking rings studded with tiny diamonds. Undoing the clasp, he fastened the necklace around her neck, the diamonds sparkling in the candlelight.

He gently fingered the rings, the touch of his fingers against her skin sending a shiver through her.

Instantly aware of this, his voice deepened, bordering on seductive. "The salesperson at the jewelry store told me these are infinity rings. Joined, they symbolize my promise to you, no matter where we are, we'll always be connected."

Her eyes slowly searching his face, she smiled. Then she completely surprised him, throwing her arms around him, almost knocking him over. "Thank you, thank you so much. I love it."

She held the rings in her hand, her smile brilliant. "I'll never take it off."

He raised an eyebrow at this. "So… does this mean you won't be wearing the necklace you had on the night I picked you up at the airport? The necklace with the locket? I believe you'd said a good friend gave it to you."

This had her smiling even more.

Was he jealous?

She framed his face in her hands and pressed a kiss to his cheek. She then kissed the other cheek. Only after she dropped a trail of butterfly like kisses across his face, to end at his mouth, did she finally answer him? "Oh Chester, I took the necklace off that same night. It didn't feel right to wear it after I saw you again."

He was suddenly finding it hard to care about the necklace, these kisses of hers setting off a whole new set of expectations in his mind.

But what about the dessert his aunt had made especially for her? He should let her know about this, shouldn't he? He vaguely remembered his aunt telling him it was triple chocolate or something along those lines.

*The hell with that… it can wait. The way you're feeling right now can't.*

His hands drifting down to her waist, his mouth searched for hers. She sighed against him before she slowly pulled away, her eyes meeting his. "You haven't given me a tour of your condo like you promised."

He was puzzled.

A tour? He didn't remember promising her this. This is when he saw the blush filling her cheeks, her eyes telling him what he was almost afraid to believe. A smile touching his lips , he stood, holding out his hand.

"*Ah...* of course. A tour you shall have."

Her hand in his, he began leading her down the hall, stopping to point out the bathroom and the guest bedroom. After getting an appreciative nod from her for both, they moved on to his office. She immediately walked over to look at the photos hanging on the walls, asking him one question after another.

Still not comfortable with this display of memorabilia, Chester tried to downplay the stories behind each photo, but she refused to go along with this.

She smiled at him, shaking her head. "You don't know how lucky you are to be so good at what you love."

It was then she saw a roll of Lifesavers on his desk. She laughed. "You really do have them everywhere, don't you?"

He grinned, scooping up the roll in his hand. "I'm pretty sure my aunt put these here before we arrived. She has been all hyped up since I told her I wanted to invite you here for dinner." He chuckled. "I'm pretty sure she thinks I need all the luck I can get."

Her look was puzzled. "Why would she think this?"

Leaning against the desk, he appeared deep in thought as he fingered the roll of candy. Though he gave a nonchalant shrug, she could see he was uncomfortable with what he was about to say. "She will never forget about Claire. The woman who was once my wife, for what turned out to be such a short time."

He shot her an almost apologetic look. "But this was a long time ago, about six years, in fact." His smile was wry. "Unfortunately, we got married for all the wrong reasons. For Claire, it was all about how she could benefit from my success. For me, it was all about my ego. When she left me after only a few months, well... let's just say I didn't take it very well."

A resigned expression on his face, he shook his head. "We definitely made a mess out of the whole marriage."

Sophie nodded. "Yes, this is what Helen Peters said."

He'd been tossing the roll of candy up in the air. Slowly setting it back on the desk, there was a look of confusion on his face as he gazed over at her.

Then he laughed. "Helen Peters? Who the hell is Helen Peters?"

Wondering why she had even brought this up, and to avoid answering him, she walked over to study one of the photos on the wall.

He chuckled as he reached over to pull her into his arms. "Come on, tell me. I'm curious… who exactly is this Helen Peters who seems to know so much about me?"

She sighed. "Helen is your aunt's neighbor. She came into the boutique the day after the hospital benefit, looking for a dress for her daughter's wedding. It was while she was there I got your message asking me out to dinner. I was still trying to deal with the news about moving to Paris and I didn't know what to do."

She shrugged. "For some reason, I told this Helen all about you and Paris. And she proceeded to tell me how you were inconsolable after your wife left. This made me feel even worse, knowing I would be leaving you, too."

He was silent for a few moments. Then he cupped her chin in his hand, leaving her no choice but to look right at him. His voice was so serious. "Why did you do that? Wait until that night to tell me you were leaving? If there was ever a time I was inconsolable, it was then."

She briefly closed her eyes. "Oh, Chester… I was miserable, unable to accept I might not see you again. I was almost hoping if I did see you, I'd feel differently. All these feelings you brought out in me were just a fluke, and there was nothing between us after all. Then I'd be able to go to Paris with a clear mind."

She swallowed. "But that didn't happen. I still felt the same. And then you kissed me like you did."

She finally gazed into his eyes, her voice dipping to a whisper. "No matter how hard I tried, I couldn't get your kiss out of my mind."

His mouth finding hers, the kiss he gave her was nothing like the kiss he gave her that night in July. The sense of urgency had disappeared, and there was no need to prove anything.

No, this kiss he gave her was like a promise.

It was a kiss from a man, secure in the knowledge he was kissing the only woman he would ever love.

He finally rested his forehead against hers, his voice filled with remorse. "Ah, angel… I was such a fool to walk away like I did. And even more of a fool for what I said afterwards. But if it makes you feel any better, I couldn't get the kiss out of my head either. But this was because I didn't want to let it go. At the time, it was all I had of you."

He held out his hand. "Come on, I think it's time we got on with the tour. We have only one more room to go."

He turned out the light, and they continued down the hall.

They reached the only remaining door at the far end of the hall. Reaching inside the room to flip a switch, light filled the space with a warm glow.

He stepped back, motioning for her to go in ahead of him. "And finally, this… well, this is my bedroom."

She crossed the room, drawn to yet another floor to ceiling wall of windows with a similar view of the lake and city skyline. While he remained by the door, intently observing her reaction.

She gazed slowly around the room, taking it all in.

Again, the décor was very simple, but the look more serene and almost totally masculine in design. The color combination of different shades of blue and ivory, along with the sleek lines of the mahogany furniture, were softly accented by the recessed lighting bordering the room. The calming color palette provided the perfect setting for the sweeping view of the water and sky.

For a few moments, she said nothing.

Then she tilted her head in his direction.

She smiled. "Oh Chester, this is so beautifully done. In fact, everything about this whole condo is amazing. It's so sophisticated." She shook her head. "Every room is perfect and so beautifully decorated. What you'd expect to find in an interior design magazine. I have to admit I honestly didn't expect this of you."

Now leaning back against the doorjamb, he crossed his arms over his chest, his eyes dancing with amusement.

He cleared his throat. "So, let's see if I'm reading this correctly. From what your words just implied, you expected to find me living in some unkempt bachelor pad. Maybe my only furnishings comprising a recliner and big screen TV? Then throw in a few empty pizza boxes and scatter a few beer cans about the room."

He shook his head. *"Hmm... I must say, I'm feeling a little insulted you'd even think this."*

Her expression was so guilty, he laughed before he held up his hand to stop her response. "It's okay. To be honest, I can't claim any of the credit for how everything turned out. No, this would all have to go to Carrie, who, as you can see, is very talented at what she does."

Here he stopped to give her a big grin. "She's much better at interior decorating than when she tries to act out the role of Candy, my personal assistant."

She smiled at the teasing tone of his voice before she spun back to gaze out at the view again. She was suddenly aware that she was in his bedroom. And they were alone. This brought so many images to mind, most of them having to do with the king-sized bed she was trying so hard to ignore.

He, on the other hand, was finding it hard to believe she was actually in his bedroom. Before now, the only chance of this happening would have been when she was a part of his dreams.

He decided this was a lot whole better.

They both remained silent, wrapped up in their thoughts, until he walked over to hit a button on a panel near the door. Music softly drifted through the room.

She sent him a quick glance, the start of a smile on her face. "And now we have music?"

He grinned back at her. "Yes, another unnecessary luxury Carrie talked me into. Installed throughout the whole condo, she convinced me it would come in handy when I entertained. Or, as she put it, for those special moments. I must say, I've enjoyed it so far."

Here he actually looked embarrassed. "Of course, I'm referring to being able to enjoy the convenience of having music throughout the condo. I haven't done much entertaining."

Then a small smile flickered across his face. "And I'm still waiting for one of those special moments…"

He had now slowly sauntered across the room to stand only a few feet away. The intensity of his gaze had her breath catching in her throat, her heart beating faster than it had only seconds before.

After she studied him for a few moments, she turned back to the window. She felt like she was being pulled towards him, her whole body beginning to tremble at even the thought of his touch. Wrapping her arms around herself, she closed her eyes.

Her voice was soft, hesitant. "It's so beautiful. You can see the skyline of the entire city from here. I can't even imagine what it must be like to wake up to a view like this."

He was behind her before he even realized he had moved, his arms wrapping around her. As his lips found their way under her hair to move in a leisurely trail up her neck, she leaned back against him with a soft sigh.

This brought the words right out of his mouth.

"Then stay here with me. Let me make love to you all through the night. Then, together, we can wake up to this view."

She remained silent, not moving.

Just as he wondered if he'd made the horrible mistake of assuming too much, she slowly turned in his arms, her eyes searching his face.

"Chester, I…" She stopped to rest her forehead against his chest. As he held her, he swore he could hear their heartbeats in the silence surrounding them. He was also pretty certain his was beating the more furious of the two.

He pressed a kiss in her hair, waiting.

She finally gazed up at him, her eyes wide and serious. Her voice was so faint he had to lean in closer to hear her words.

"There is something you should know. I… I've never made love to anyone before. I…" She gave a slight shake of her head, closing her eyes.

He reached out to tuck a strand of her hair behind her ear before he somehow found his voice.

"No?"

And yes, believe it or not, this was all he could come up with.

*What the hell is wrong with you? She's probably waiting for you to say something reassuring. Like this was okay, it's no big deal. Even though for you, in a way, it sort of is.*

But somehow, she seemed to understand his reaction. She opened her eyes and gave him a small smile. "No, I decided a long time ago I wanted to wait. When I finally took that step, it should be with the right person."

He nodded, a very slow nod. Again, it wasn't because he had nothing to say. Oh, he did, there was no doubt about that. But there was so much racing through his mind, here he was again, scrambling to find the right words.

On one hand, he couldn't help but want to celebrate a little, knowing if she were to stay with him, it was because he was the one she had chosen.

But overshadowing this was the fear her next words would be to inform him she was really sorry, but he wasn't the right person.

Nope, she was still waiting.

His hands gently framing her face, he placed a soft kiss to her forehead, his breath a warm caress against her skin. "This person, the one you say you've been waiting for… the right one. Have you found him yet?"

Her eyes became so bright, they were all he could see. "Oh, Chester… yes, it's you. I want it to be with you. You have to know—"

Her words were swallowed by his kiss. At first, unsure of exactly what was expected, his lips were questioning, searching. But when she tangled her fingers in his hair to pull him closer, his kiss became all-consuming, more urgent. All capacity for thought vanished, the ability to reason no longer possible.

Sophie was lost.

The feeling of his hard, muscular body pressed against hers sent her senses reeling. While his hands roamed over her, his fingers tracing the curves of her body, sending shivers down her spine. All of this coming at her all at once?

It was nothing short of intoxicating.

But it wasn't enough. She needed more. She wanted him to ease this restlessness inside of her. This craving that had been with her since the first time she had gazed into his eyes.

*You want everything with him.*

Fisting his sweater in her hands, she pressed even closer.

His mind still celebrating he was the one she had chosen, for Chester, a kiss was no longer enough. He wanted to know every single inch of her. So he could love her in a way, up until now, he'd only been able to imagine.

*You want to make her yours...*

He slipped his hands under her blouse, his thumbs caressing her bare skin. When she gazed up at him, the unconditional love shining in her eyes sent a jolt of hope to his heart and a smile to his lips.

"Ah, angel..." He reached for her hand. "Come, let me love you."

# CHAPTER 20

After Chester pulled down the covers on the bed, he turned to find Sophie was watching him, her eyes wide.

Before he could even make a move, she walked right into his arms.

He closed his eyes, burying his face in her hair. He needed to take this slow. And gentle … yes, he would be gentle. It would take every bit of self-control he possessed, but somehow, he'd do this.

After all, they had the entire night ahead of them, a night he was determined to make as one they would always remember.

But she wasn't thinking the same.

No, not at all.

She didn't want slow. And she certainly didn't want him to hold back. Or, heaven forbid, feel the need to be gentle. She wanted him to come at her with everything he had. After waiting for such a long time for this moment, and the fact it was going to be with him, made her want it all the more.

She reached for his sweater, pushing at him as she tried to pull it up and over his head. He stepped back and, coming in contact with the edge of the bed, he was knocked off balance.

Before he could right himself, he went tumbling back onto the bed, taking her with him.

They stared at each other, a completely astonished look on his face and a horrified expression on hers.

He was dumfounded.

*How did this happen? She's so small and you're certainly much stronger and bigger than she is.*

She was beside herself.

*You practically hurled yourself at him, knocking him to the bed, of all places. What must he be thinking?*

She tried to scramble off of him, embarrassment written all over her face. "Oh, no... I'm so sorry. I didn't mean..."

He chuckled, wrapping his arm around her to halt her move. His other hand tangling in her hair, he brought her face to his.

His lips, warm and tender, brushed over hers. "Angel," he whispered, "it's okay. It's fine. You can throw yourself at me anytime." When he felt her body surrender to his embrace, relaxing against him, his words fell like a gentle caress against her ear. "But we do have all night, you know. And this is something I don't intend to rush, not with you."

Her answer was to give him a slow, lingering kiss. While, at the same time, her hands crept back under his sweater. She was desperate to get closer, remove any barriers between them.

*And this will never happen if you don't get this darn sweater off of him.*

Sensing her eagerness, he quickly took over, rolling them so she was now on her back. She watched him yank his sweater up and over his head, throwing it aside before he settled next to her, his mouth swooping in to cover hers.

As if they had all the time in the world, he proceeded to give her a long, searching kiss, while at the same time, he leisurely began undoing the buttons down the front of her blouse. His lips never leaving hers, he moved on to her bra. The blouse and bra following the same route as his sweater, he continued his onslaught of kisses as he removed the rest of their clothing.

Slowly and deliberately he did this, each touch and every kiss bringing her to an even more feverish state of anticipation.

She didn't know how he could be so patient, taking the time to reassure her, seeking her approval. She wanted to tell him he had no reason to worry. If he were to suddenly stop, there was no doubt in her mind she would go insane.

When his lips slowed, she opened her eyes. He was gazing down at her, the burning intensity in his eyes sending a shiver coursing through her.

He smiled, and lifting her chin with one finger, he dropped the gentlest of kisses to her mouth, his sigh long and satisfied. "You're gorgeous, angel. You're absolutely perfect."

She reached for him, but he had other plans. He captured her hands in his, holding them captive against the bed. She could only surrender as his mouth took over, his lips trailing over her in a leisurely journey—everywhere.

When his lips finally came back to brush over hers, she sighed into his mouth. "Chester, *please...*"

Releasing her hands, he moved so he was over her. The hunger radiating in his eyes as he gazed down at her, sent a deep shudder through her. Then, slowly,... so, so slowly, his mouth came down to graze hers again.

*"More?"*

Was he kidding? She had never wanted more of anything in her life.

Her hands moving up to grip his shoulders, she managed to find her voice. At least for this one very important word, she did.

*"More..."*

His gaze never leaving hers, he lowered himself until it felt as if every inch of him was touching every inch of her. Resting his forehead against hers, he closed his eyes.

For Chester, being able to share this moment with her was almost mind-blowing. Never before had he experienced such desire, driven by this overwhelming need to prove his love. He wanted to give her everything, show her what it was like to be thoroughly loved.

There was also the knowledge he was her first, making him vow he'd be damned if he was going to let her down.

*You're going to make this night the start of many to come.*

But only after tonight would he let passion fulfill his needs. For now, here, and with this union between them, it wasn't about him.

No, this was all for her.

He opened his eyes to find hers were closed. He pressed a soft kiss to each eyelid, his whisper brushing her mouth. "Angel, look at me."

Her lashes fluttered open.

As he smoothed her hair back from her face, a sliver of doubt flitted through his mind. She was so small, so fragile. Compared to him, she was like a delicate piece of spun glass, one he could crush so easily with his weight.

His eyes held hers. "I want you to tell me if I hurt you or it doesn't feel right. So, I can stop. Promise me you'll do this."

Sophie nodded. Sure, she'd agree to this. Even though she knew there was no way this was going to happen.

*Absolutely not.*

She had no plans to stop him.

She'd already decided he was the only one who could ease this deep ache inside of her.

After all, it was because of him it was even there.

His gaze locking with hers and in one swift move, he took her.

At her soft gasp, he stilled. Bowing his head and with his heart hammering in his chest, he waited for her to give him some kind of sign.

When she arched up against him, wrapping her arms around him, a, he released a long, haggard breath before he moved to fill her completely.

Awed by this new intimacy they were sharing, they stared at each other, her eyes wide, his searching.

He rested his forehead against hers, his voice thick. "Okay, angel?"

She nodded, her lips trailing down his neck in a long, sensuous sigh. "*Oh God, yes...*"

A low growl rising from deep inside of him, his mouth came crashing down on hers. As his kisses became more demanding, his hands were everywhere, guiding her body in tune with his.

And the passion consuming them was now beyond their control, any thought of stopping no longer an option,

With her hands now free, she kept up with his every move, his every kiss. He sent her soaring, spiraling higher and higher, grasping for something just out of her reach. The knowledge he would take her there, his need as desperate as hers, she surrendered everything she'd been holding inside for so long.

His whispers urging her on, he felt her give in to the desire that had been building between them from the moment they first met. He sensed she was about to go tumbling over the edge when her cries came at him faster, more furiously, her hands gripping his shoulders to bring him closer.

His mouth searching for hers, his whisper just barely reached through the haze of desire she was caught up in.

"Let go, baby... just let go."

And she did, coming apart in his arms.

Swallowing her cries with his kiss, he held her until she finally sank spent and dazed into his arms.  It was only then, he gave in to his own release.

And as she had fallen so trustingly into his arms...

He fell into hers.


Except for the music Chester had turned on earlier, there was only silence.

He smiled. *The music...*

This would definitely be considered one of those special moments.

His face resting in the curve of Sophie's shoulder, he was lulled by the gentle touch of her fingers moving in a lazy caress through his hair. It was only when her hand drifted down his back, he lifted his head to look right into her eyes.

Her beautiful blue eyes...

For a few moments, they studied each other… as though they were seeing each other for the first time. The first to speak, the rough tone of his voice revealed this new and emotional state he found himself in.

"So… good?"

His gaze was so intense, at first she could only shake her head, everything she wanted to say frozen in her throat. It was when worry clouded his eyes, she lifted her face to his and gave him a soft, languid kiss. Then she sighed. *"Mmm… not just good, amazing."*

A smile touching his lips, he stretched out beside her. Gathering her in the curve of his arm, he pressed a kiss to her brow.

His fingers drifting through the silkiness of her hair, he gazed around the room. A quiet and cozy oasis on this snowy February night, he was thankful for this silence between them.

Because seriously? He didn't think he could find the words to explain what he was feeling right now. Never had he been taken to such heights, or filled with such completeness when with a woman. And if she hadn't told him, he never would've known this was all so new to her. Their love had come so naturally, their union so easy, leaving him in a sense of awe.

What they had together was more than what most people could dream of having in a lifetime. And now, even though everything was still the same, it was all so different.

So wonderfully different. All because of this beautiful woman he now held in his arms.

If he could, he'd keep her beside him forever. He wanted her in this bed every night so he could hold her in his arms as they fell asleep. To then wake her the next morning with a kiss before he loved her all over again.

He wanted a life with her.

Okay, so maybe there were words.

But none that would do justice.


Sophie was still trying to come down to earth.

Believe it or not, and this was a rarity, she didn't know what to say.

She only knew everything had now changed. No matter what happened next, this moment would be forever engraved in her mind. And in her heart.

And Chester?

He would always be her first love, the man who'd opened her world to such magic.

*Admit it ... he'll always be your only love. Your heart has already taken him in, closing the doors to anyone else.*

But now, in his arms, she didn't want to think of the future. She wanted to take this time to bask in what they'd shared. If only to hold on to the proof what they had was real.

It was all so perfect.

*He was so perfect.*

She closed her eyes, a smile on her face.


Chester stirred, gathering her closer. Opening her eyes, Sophie could see it was snowing much harder now. Whipped up by the wind and blowing against the windows, the swirling flakes had reduced the view to a solid wall of white.

She smiled. Sheltered in this warm and cozy haven they shared, she felt deliciously sinful. Almost reluctant to break the silence, her words were barely a whisper. "It's snowing a lot harder now."

He lazily opened his eyes at this. *"Mmm... so it is."*

When he had nothing else to add, she spoke more hesitantly. "I'm thinking... it doesn't seem fair you should have to go out and brave the snow and cold to take me home."

His fingers linking with hers, he brought her hand to his mouth for a kiss. "No?" He'd started to smile. "It's okay, I don't mind."

Her head shooting up, her mouth fell open in disbelief. He didn't mind? He couldn't possibly mean this, could he?

Then, as their eyes met, she saw the teasing gleam in his.

He laughed. "Oh, angel, I'm only teasing. I have no plans of taking you anywhere. Even if you could see every star in the sky, I wouldn't be taking you home. Nope, I'm not ready to let you go, not yet."

*Or ever...*

He moved onto his side and, after propping himself up on his elbow, he gazed down at her.

"Talk to me. Tell me what else you're thinking."

He wanted to know what she was thinking? *Wow...* this wasn't going to be easy. Not with the way he was looking at her. If anything, there was a good possibility she might melt instead.

But, after a few moments, her mouth curved in a smile. "I had no idea being with you... well, it was so amazing and I..." She briefly closed her eyes. "What I'm trying to say, I never knew it could be like this between two people. I just can't imagine... is it like this for everyone? How could it be?"

He was smiling as he pressed a kiss in her hair. If she only knew how much he loved that she always said what she was thinking. She was so open, so honest. Traits he'd never experienced before in a woman. She brought out this feeling of protectiveness from him, a need to be the person she would always turn to in need.

Stroking her hair back from her face, he smiled. "*Ah, angel...* I think we're definitely on to something. I know I've never felt like this before, not with anyone."

Noting the speculative look in her eyes, he quickly shook his head. "Not that I've had a lot of experience. Honestly, I haven't. I've been too busy playing ball. Caught up in the grand scheme of things, waiting for you to come along."

He trailed his fingers down her cheek. When she trembled at his touch, he almost lost his train of thought, his words a husky whisper. "What magic have you used to make me feel this way? You bring out all the good things in me, the person I've always wanted to be. With you in my arms, I have all I need, all that I want."

He leaned in to place a slow, open-mouthed kiss to the pulse beating in her neck. When she sighed, moving closer, his lips drifted up to settle near her mouth. "Right now, my only thoughts are of how incredibly sexy you are, how much I want you. I want to satisfy your every need, your every want. I want to make love to you like you're meant to be loved."

With the glorious way he was using his mouth on her, she was feeling lightheaded, carried away by another rising tide of desire. Clasping her hands behind his neck, she gazed into his eyes. "You asked me what I was thinking. If there's one thing I've done right in my life, it was my decision to be here with you tonight. Remember what you said? You wanted me to stay so you could make love to me until the sun rises. You can't go back on that promise now."

Before he kissed her, he had only one word in answer to this.

But it was enough.

*"Never..."*

They spent a good part of the night discovering each other, finally falling into an exhausted sleep in each other's arms.

The night was not quite ready to give way to morning when Sophie woke. Opening her eyes, she found she was alone in the bed.

Untangling herself from the sheets, she raised her hands over her head in a long, leisurely stretch. Her gaze drifted to the window, where the sky was showing a hint of dawn.

This was how Chester found her when he returned to the room. A smile lighting up his face, he crawled across the bed and leaned in for a kiss, his breath mingling with hers. "Good morning, beautiful," he said, before giving a long and troubled sigh. "How will I be able to sleep in this bed without you, now that I know what it's like to have you with me?"

He shook his head. "I don't think it's possible. What do you think?"

The longing in his voice pulled at her heartstrings. And suddenly, it was too much. To her horror, she began to cry, the tears slipping down her cheeks.

A stricken look on his face, he pulled her into his arms, holding her against him. "Oh, angel... I'm sorry, I'm so, *so* sorry. I shouldn't have said anything. Please don't cry. *Please...*"

But she couldn't seem to stop.

She wanted to tell him it was okay. Really, she did. If only to erase the sadness from his voice. But besides the fact she wasn't able to stop crying long enough to even get out the words, she wouldn't be telling him the truth if she did.

Because it wasn't okay.

*No, it was terribly far from being okay.*

Tears clogged her words. "I don't know what to do."

His hands stilled, he pressed a kiss in her hair, waiting.

She took a deep, steadying breath. "I never thought I would meet someone like you, someone who means so much to me. Every second, every minute we've spent together has been like a dream, a wonderful, unbelievably, amazing dream."

She stirred in his arms. "Since we both knew I would be leaving, maybe we shouldn't have let things get to this point. Because even though I'd give anything to stay here with you, or you would want to come to Paris, we both know this isn't even a possibility. And a long distance relationship would be so hard. I can't do this to you. You deserve so much more."

How was it possible, only a short time ago, everything had been so wonderful? Only to have reality reach out to smack them with a vengeance.

Resting her head on his shoulder, she gave a long sigh. "It all seems so hopeless."

He pulled away from her. "Angel, look at me."

She lifted her head, the tears on her face cutting him to the core. Swiping them away with his thumb, a huskiness crept into his voice. "It tears me apart to see you cry. I don't care where you are, here or in Paris. I don't want to lose you again. So, whatever you decide, I'll go along with it."

He hesitated, almost afraid to ask. "Is there any chance your stay in Paris won't have to be permanent? Could you turn the operation of the boutique over to someone else?"

She thought about this. "I'm not sure. I only know I can't walk out on my aunt and uncle until everything is running and making a profit. They've used almost all their life savings to finance this and can't afford to have it fail." Her eyes pleaded with him. "You have to under-stand, whenever me or my brother and sister needed anything, they were always there for us. I don't know what would've happened if they hadn't agreed to be ."

He pressed another kiss in her hair. He wanted to tell her if she needed help, be it money or whatever, he was here for her.

Hell, he had the money. And he had contacts. So, he might as well use them.

But he sensed an offer like this wouldn't go over very well. The last thing he wanted to do was insult her, or her aunt and uncle, by throwing money around.

*But what good is having a lot of money if you can't use it to help the people you love?*

He closed his eyes in frustration.

*Damn... why does everything have to be so complicated?*

There was one thing he was sure of, and this was he didn't want to make a stupid mistake, jeopardizing what they had. At the same time, he wanted it known he'd do anything, and he meant, anything, to make their relationship work.

"I would think, between the two of us, we should be able to work things out. But whatever happens, I know I don't want to give you up. I can't and I won't."

And this time, it was Sophie who wanted to put any talk about the future on hold. She raised her eyes to his face. "Please, let's not talk about it anymore. Just hold me."

So, this is what he did.

Together, they watched the sky gradually turn to the light of day, the sun catching the falling snow, sparkling like diamonds against the window.

The quiet beauty on display heralded the beginning of a new day, along with the promise of endless possibilities.

But for Sophie and Chester, a tenseness had begun to build between them. Because nothing had been decided, nothing had changed.

And as much as she tried, Sophie couldn't shake her feeling of hopelessness. Wrapping her arms around his neck, she placed a soft kiss to his mouth. "Love me, please? Remind me what it's like to be with you. So I can always have you in my heart, no matter where I am."

He pulled her close, his voice gruff. *"Oh, angel... the dawn will never be the same."*

So, once again, he loved her.

He gave it his all... Just as she had asked of him.

Someone was holding their finger down on the doorbell.

The annoying buzz jerking him awake, Chester sat straight up in bed. Dragging his hands down over his face, he checked the clock on the nightstand.

It was only a little after nine.

It was only after he gave one last shake of his head, hoping to shock his brain awake, he remembered Sophie.

He glanced over at her. She had pulled the pillow over her head to block out the noise.

He dropped a kiss to her shoulder. "Go back to sleep. I'll go see what's going on. Or at least stop the God-awful buzzing." He scratched his head, a puzzled look on his face. "I don't understand how someone got past the concierge without my okay."

He pulled on his jeans, and still half asleep, he was grumbling as he headed for the front door. Peering through the peephole, he abruptly took a step back, his hand going to his head.

*"What the hell?"*

And even though he knew it was the absolute last thing he should do, and he was setting himself up for disaster, he opened the door.

# CHAPTER 21

*At the end of the. day, you can either focus*
*on what's tearing you apart, or what's keeping you together.*
*~ Unknown*

Speechless, Chester stared at Claire and the little boy who was standing next to her.

And, what appeared to be a mountain of luggage on the floor beside them.

It was when she gave him a bright smile, his brain kicked in. She began to speak, but he beat her to it, holding his hand up to cut her off. "What are you doing here?"

He shot a quick look at the luggage and then back at her. "And what's with all of this? You better not be thinking you're going to stay here. Because you're not."

He knew he was getting all worked up, but he couldn't seem to stop. "If you remember, you made it quite clear when you left, you never wanted to set eyes on me again. Not even if hell froze over. I believe those were the exact words you used."

Her smile had faded. She glanced down at the child and back up at him, her eyes pleading with him. "Chester, please... not in front of

170

Hunter. Please don't say anything more until I have the chance to explain. Okay?"

She had already inched her way into the room, pushing Hunter ahead of her, as though she was using him as a shield.

He sighed in annoyance.

*Come on, she knows you well enough to know you'd never make a scene in front of a child.*

Once she was in the room, she took the child over to the sofa and removed his coat. She addressed Chester over her shoulder. "Bring the suitcases in, okay? You can set them by the door for now."

He opened his mouth, then abruptly shut it.

*What's going on here? The way she's ordering you around, it's almost as if she never left.*

He ran his hand through his hair, staring down at the suitcases. He didn't want to bring them in. Nor did he want her in his condo. What he wanted was to usher her right back out the door and lock it. Then he'd go back to Sophie, take her into his arms and pretend this had never happened.

His mind switching gears, he groaned, massaging the back of his neck.

*What about Sophie? What is she going to think about this?*

He could only pray she'd gone back to sleep, giving him time to find out the reason Claire was here.

*And give you enough time to get her and the child out of your condo and right back to wherever they came from.*

After he brought in the suitcases, he grabbed the remote from where it was on the sofa. Turning on the TV and scrolling through the channels, he found a station with cartoons.

He handed the remote to the boy. "Here, I don't know if this is a good station. If not, pick a station you like. Your mom…"

He hesitated, glancing over at Claire. He didn't even know, was this child her son? At her nod, he addressed him again. "Well, your mom and I are going to be in the kitchen so we can talk. If you need anything, let us know."

At Hunter's nod, he took Claire's arm and steered her, none too gently, into the kitchen. He leaned against the counter and crossing his arms over his chest, he directed a steely gaze right at her. "Spill…"

She was wringing her hands, refusing to meet his gaze. Unused to seeing her in this state, he waited, a flicker of unease building in him.

Her gaze shifted away from him. "I left Tom. You know, the guy I've been living with for the past five years. It wasn't working out."

Chester couldn't stop the short laugh that shot right out of him. "Ah… so history is repeating itself, huh? Is this sort of like how it wasn't working out for us?"

On a roll, his words kept on coming, laced with sarcasm. "*Hmm…* did you leave him like you left me? In the middle of the night? With a note scribbled on the back of an old receipt that said you no longer loved me?"

He briefly closed his eyes. He needed to calm down. But with her standing before him, everything he'd wanted to say to her was right there, ready to be heard. And he was powerless to stop this from happening.

He drew in a ragged breath. "So, tell me… did you also leave Tom for the same reasons you left me? If you recall, you told me was I wasn't making enough money. Or devoting enough time to you. But do you want to know what the real kicker was? When you so casually informed me I didn't know how to satisfy a woman. The one thing you told me you needed the most."

He gave another sharp laugh. "So… let me guess. This Tom didn't quite do it for you either?"

When she only kept shaking her head, he nodded. "Yes, if you recall, you said all of those things. And what a shame it was. Because right after you left, I got a contract giving me more money than even you could possibly spend."

He ran his hand through his hair. "But now, whatever your reason for coming here, you're too late. Over six years too late."

She just blurted it out. "Hunter is your son."

And… *BAM!*

Out of the blue, she threw this at him. The silence seemed to go on and on.

In shock, he could only stare at her. While she continued to watch him, anxiously waiting for him to say something.

His eyes never leaving her face, his words were a hoarse whisper. "You're lying."

She vehemently shook her head. "No, no, I'm not. He's your son. I found out I was pregnant right after I started dating Tom. We had really hit it off, and I didn't want to lose him. So, I told him he was the father, even though I knew this wasn't possible. Because I went through such an awful pregnancy, even when Hunter came over a month early, Tom didn't question it. He thought it had to do with the complications I had."

Chester took a glass out of the cupboard and, turning on the water, he filled the glass. After he drank all the water, he set the glass sharply on the counter and turned to her, his expression incredulous.

"So, what you're telling me is, because you and this Tom hit it off, and you didn't want to lose him, you lied to him? Wow, you really know how to treat a guy right, don't you?"

He shook his head, something he realized he'd been doing quite a bit since she arrived. "I can't believe you."

Leaning back against the counter, he closed his eyes. He was having a hard time comprehending all of this.

*A son? You have a son?*

How could this even be possible? Well, yeah… he knew very well how it could be possible. But Claire had always been so insistent on taking precautions to keep this from happening. Whenever he'd even brought up the subject of starting a family, her excuse had always been the same.

She wasn't ready.

But why had she decided to tell him this now? What was her motive? This wasn't the Claire he knew, the woman who did only what was beneficial to her in the long run.

*So, what was going on? What did she want?*

Her voice penetrated her thoughts. "I guess it was a rotten thing to do, but at the time I was scared. After I said all those things to you, I didn't think you'd welcome me back with open arms."

He slowly shook his head. "You know what? I probably would have. At the time, I was convinced I loved you. And with the ego trip I was on then, I would've liked the chance to prove to you how wrong you were, how great a lover I could be." He shrugged. "But now, what you do or think no longer matters to me."

She frowned. "But what about Hunter? Are you going to turn your back on him, too?"

Pinching the bridge of his nose with his fingers, he sighed. "I don't know. Seriously? I don't know. Give me some time to process this, okay?"

He shot her a sharp glance, his look piercing. "Is it money you want?"

"No." But she refused to meet his eyes, a sign she wasn't telling the truth. "What I want, what I really want, is to start over. Us … you, me and Hunter as a family. I want the three of us to try and make it work this time."

"No, absolutely not." This came flying out before he could rein it in. He glanced quickly over towards Hunter, relieved to see he was watching TV and wasn't listening to their conversation. "No, it's out of the question. Things are different now, I'm different."

Just as these words came out of his mouth, he heard the door to his condo slam.

He groaned. *Now what?*

Carrie came running into the room, out of breath and a worried expression on her face.When she saw Claire, her shoulders slumped, her gaze going to Chester.

"Oh, Chez… I thought I'd get here before she did, but I see I haven't. I'm sorry… so sorry. I wanted to warn you." She glared over at Claire. "I can't believe the concierge let you in."

Claire shrugged. "I didn't have a problem at all. I've learned, with most men, a few tears will get you just about anything. And having a small child in tow doesn't hurt either."

Carrie was ignoring her. A concerned look on her face, her focus was on Chester. "Where's Sophie? I thought she might still be here with you."

He nodded, briefly closing his eyes.

Sophie…

*Yes, she is still here. In your bed, so warm and loving. And what you need now more than anything.*

This earned a sharp look from Claire. "Sophie? Who's Sophie?"

Claire swiftly answered. "She's Chester's girlfriend. More than a girlfriend, actually. I wouldn't be the least surprised if they get married in the future."

She directed a meaningful look over at Chester. "The very near future. Right?"

Claire sent him a swift glance. "Is this true?"

With both women watching him, waiting for his answer, Chester felt trapped. He also didn't feel the need to explain. In fact, the only thing on his mind was how much he wanted to be with Sophie.

He wasn't going to do this. Shaking his head, he turned to walk away. His abrupt words discouraged any response.

"I'm not discussing my relationship with Sophie with either of you. It's none of your business. Now, if you will excuse me, I am going back to bed."

Then he stopped to wave his hand around at the kitchen. "If you need anything, food or whatever, help yourself. The guest bedroom and bathroom are down the hall."

His next words were delivered directly to Claire, the threatening tone of his voice stressing how serious he was. "But don't get too comfortable. Because no matter what you've been planning in that devious mind of yours, you will not be staying here."

Again, he remembered Hunter. After he glanced over to see he had fallen asleep, he sent Claire a curt nod. "We'll discuss him later."

Carrie followed him, grabbing his arm right before he went to open the bedroom door. "Chez, stop. I'm so sorry. I had to tell her where you lived. I didn't know what else to do."

He turned to stare at her, his look one of disbelief. "You told her how to find me? Why? I don't understand. Why would you do this? You know how I feel about her."

He tried to pull his arm from her grasp, but she wouldn't let go. It was then he noticed the disheveled state she was in. Devoid of makeup, her hair was uncombed, and she was wearing pajama pants and a tee shirt, with only baggy sweatshirt for a coat.

He glanced down at her feet. At least she was wearing her fleece-lined boots, and not her favorite fuzzy kitty slippers.

She also looked like she was on the verge of tears.

He drew a deep breath. "I'm sorry, Kitten. I'm a little shook up right now. I didn't mean to yell at you. But tell me, why did you send her here?"

"She called me. I almost didn't answer when I saw it was her, I knew whatever she wanted, it wasn't going to be good. After all, we both know she never liked me. Remember how she used to treat me? Like I was some kind of pest, or beneath her."

She was scowling, getting all fired up. "Why, I remember the one time…"

He sighed.

*This is what Claire does. She has a way of getting everyone riled up before they even know what the hell they're doing. How well you remember this.*

He grabbed Carrie's chin in his hand, bringing her to face him. "Carrie, stop it. Come on, you need to focus. We both remember how she treated you and don't need to be reminded. At least not now."

When she nodded, he dropped his hand. "Now, tell me what she said when she called you."

She sent him a hurt look, dramatically rubbing her chin before she answered him. "She left the message she needed your address as it was important she talk to you. And if I didn't get back to her, she would contact the player's office. She had news concerning you that might interest them."

She shrugged. "She sounded so menacing, I panicked. After I sent her what she wanted, I jumped in my car and drove over here. Unfortunately, she beat me to it."

She looked so upset, he couldn't be mad at her. After all, she did try. And he, for one, knew how Claire could get people to do what she wanted, no matter how she had to go about it. One minute, she was all smiles and total sweetness. The next, she was like the devil on a rampage.

He patted her hand that was holding his arm. "It's okay, kitten. I know you tried. But now I need to get back to Sophie and figure out how to explain all of this to her. Do me a favor and go talk to Claire. See what you can get out of her, what her plans are. Okay?"

She nodded, but she didn't move, still gripping his arm. He raised his eyebrows. "Yes? Is there something else?"

She hesitated a moment before she spoke. "What did she want to tell you? What is this news she's talking about? Is it bad?"

For a split second, he considered not telling her. But then he realized if he didn't, Claire would. Which wouldn't be good.

He sighed. She was going to find out eventually, wasn't she?

So, it appeared he had no choice but to tell her.

He couldn't hide the despair in his voice.

"You saw the little boy sleeping on the sofa? Claire just informed me I am his father. And because of him, she wants us to be a family again. So, it now seems my life has suddenly taken a turn in a whole new direction. Am I a lucky guy, or what?"

He gave a sharp laugh. "Now, if you'll excuse me, I need to be with Sophie."

He slipped inside the room, closing the door behind him with a very decisive click. Leaving Carrie standing there, her mouth hanging open in shock.

Very similar to how Chester had reacted when he got the news.


Sophie was confused.

And a little worried.

Even after holding the pillow over her head, she still couldn't block out the sound of Chester arguing with someone.

A someone who was a woman. So, as you can imagine, this was very concerning,

A door slammed, followed by another woman joining in on the conversation.

So, now she was really beginning to worry.

Because, come on… when you spend the night with someone, only to wake up in the morning to find him no longer in bed with you. To then hear the sound of not only one, but two women arguing outside the bedroom door? It would be insane not to be at least a little worried, no?

She was also feeling pretty vulnerable right now. After the night they spent together it's understandable this new development hit her so hard.

She sat on the edge of the bed, and after staring down at the rumpled sheets, smoothing them with her hand, she gazed around the room.

She sighed. Why was everything always so complicated?

Should she get dressed? To then go ask Chester why he and his friends felt the need to have such a loud conversation so early in the morning? Or to at least let everyone know she was still here?

Or should she breeze nonchalantly into the room, cheerfully informing him it was all okay, he had no reason to worry about her. It had been great and now she should probably head for home.

Dragging her hands through her hair, she gave a frustrated sigh. First things first… she needed to get dressed.

She had come to the last button on her blouse when she realized Chester was now right outside the bedroom, the voice of the woman with him belonging to his sister, Carrie. She was about to go over and open the door, when he spoke, his words brutally clear.

> *"You saw the little boy sleeping on the sofa? Claire just*
> *informed me I'm his father. Because of this, she wants*
> *to be a family. So, it seems my life has taken a turn*
> *in a new direction. Am I a lucky guy, or what?"*

She froze in her tracks. giving a strangled cry. Her hand going to her mouth, she slowly sank down onto the bed.

And this is how Chester found her when he walked into the room.

*Yes… things had changed*

# CHAPTER 22

*D*amn ...

When Chester saw the look of anguish on Sophie's face, he was at her side in record time. Pulling her up from the bed and into his arms, he pressed desperate kisses in her hair.

At the same time, he sent a wild plea up to God. He had just one wish. This would be to erase everything that happened, taking them back to where they had been only minutes before. Blissfully asleep, and wrapped in each other's arms.

*This wasn't too much to ask, was it?*

His mouth against her hair, his voice was strained.

"Angel, you heard, didn't you? I'm so sorry, I had no idea. Please believe me when I say this is a complete surprise to me."

She was silent, giving a brief shake of her head against him.

He let out a ragged breath. "You have to know Claire means nothing to me. But if what she says is true and Hunter really is my son, I have to figure out what I need to do next. It isn't his fault it's come to this. And God knows, I could never turn my back on him."

He pulled away from her and, framing her face in his hands, his eyes pleaded with her. "Please, please don't look like this. We can work this out."

She could only keep shaking her head.

*No, no... they couldn't.*

No, she couldn't do this anymore. She was beginning to think they had been doomed from the very start. She didn't know a lot about relationships, but she was pretty sure being in love with someone shouldn't involve all of this heartache.

Taking a slow, shaky breath, she gently pushed away from him. "I think it's best I leave."

She could feel her eyes filling with tears, threatening to spill over. Willing this not to happen, she averted her eyes as she began to back away from him, her gaze going to the windows. She saw the sun was shining, the sky now a brilliant blue.

*How could this be when you're both so miserable? It just didn't seem right.*

And with this, the tears began to fall, her voice barely audible. "Oh Chester, I'm beginning to think, you and I? We're not meant to be." Shakily wiping away her tears away with the back of her hand, she gave him a watery smile. "Being with you was wonderful, everything. But, I don't know... maybe..." She shrugged, the tears now flowing even faster.

He stood where he was, almost paralyzed by her words.

*Noooo... this can't be happening.*

His mind was in a complete turmoil, wanting to deny everything being thrown at him. In fact, he was almost to the point he wanted to cry right along with her.

Her name coming from him in a groan, he moved to take her back into his arms, but her hands came up to stop him.

"No, please don't." If he touched her, she'd lose it completely. The only thing that could save her right now was if she were to leave.

She was shaking now, her voice coming out in a whisper. "I really need to go. You need time alone to work this out."

She pushed her way past him, and with him following right behind, she left the room and made her way down the hall. Vaguely aware Carrie, and the woman who must be Claire, we're both watching from the kitchen, she headed for the door. It was only when her hand was on the doorknob, she realized she didn't have her coat.

Or her shoes and her purse.

*Oh, God… and now, you don't even have him.*

Momentarily at a loss what to do, she leaned her head against the door before she turned to find Chester was right behind her. She tried not to look at him as she spoke. "I need my coat. And my purse and shoes."

Without saying a word, he brought them to her. It was only when she began struggling into her coat, he moved towards her, hesitantly reaching out to help her.

"Angel, how are you going to get home? Remember, I brought you here. Let me take you."

In his mind, he was thinking if he could spend more time with her, even minutes, they could talk. Then he could get her to understand leaving wasn't the answer.

But she shook her head. "No, don't worry about me. I'll figure it out."

He groaned, running his hand over his chin. "Come on, please don't do this. Let me take you home. We can't leave things like this."

Just as she was about to refuse him again, her hand reaching out to grasp the doorknob, Carrie's voice came from behind them.

"Sophie, I can take you home. I'm leaving now, too."

At Sophie's nod, Carrie gave a sigh of relief. She was still trying to process the news Hunter was Chester's son. Or that he even had a son. And now, feeling even worse about her part in the whole mess, offering to take Sophie home was the least she could do.

She slipped into her coat and grabbed her keys, "Are you ready?"

But Sophie wasn't there. She'd gone down the hall and back into the bedroom. Once there, she unclasped the necklace Chester had given to her. For one moment, she held it tightly in her hand before she slowly set it on the nightstand. As she came back out of the room, she nearly collided with Chester. At the concerned look on his face, she shook her head. "I… it's only something I forgot." Offering no other explanation, she moved past him to where Carrie was waiting.

Carrie gave her a hesitant smile. "Okay?"

Sophie nodded before she slowly turned back to Chester. For a few moments, she studied him, almost as if she was trying to memorize everything about him. Then she walked over to put her hand against his chest and going up on her tiptoes, she placed a soft kiss to his cheek. She could barely get out the words.

"Thank you. For the dinner, for everything."

When he closed his eyes, a look of such pain on his face, she swiftly turned away. She walked over to open the door and after giving him one last look, she was gone.

Carrie opened her mouth and turned to Chester as if she was going to say something. Then she gave a helpless shrug before she followed Sophie, closing the door behind her.

Chester remained completely motionless, his eyes closed and his hands clenched at his sides. Only when he felt the presence of someone beside him, he finally opened his eyes.

It was Claire.

Before she could say a word, he turned away from her and let out what sounded almost like a long, agonized growl. As he began walking down the hall, his harsh words came back to her.

"If you need anything, the housekeeper is due here shortly. Otherwise, you're on your own. I can't talk to you now. I need to be alone."

He walked into his office and closed the door.


After Claire checked on Hunter to see he was asleep, she gazed appraisingly around the room. She frowned, shaking her head. If this was to be her new home, the décor was going to need a complete overhaul. Because it certainly wasn't her style.

She made her way to the kitchen. Even though it was only morning, she could really use a glass of wine after the recent drama she'd witnessed. She'd drink it while making out a list for the housekeeper.

She opened the refrigerator, knowing she could count on Chester to have a bottle of wine on hand. Her eyes were immediately drawn to a miniature chocolate cake, covered in a thick fudge icing. And conveniently, right next to it was an unfinished bottle of wine. An obvious sign, at least to her, they were meant to be enjoyed together.

She eyed the cake. Maybe it was for something special? Then she shrugged and took both the cake and wine out of the refrigerator.

Why shouldn't she treat herself? She needed something to lift her spirits after the surprise of finding Chester had a woman with him.

Unfortunately, any additional information she tried to get from Carrie about this supposedly serious girlfriend of his had gone for naught. Carrie had remained completely tight-lipped. The only thing she volunteered was the woman's name was Sophie.

Then the dramatic scene between this Sophie and Chester before she left? What was that all about? Seriously? It had soap opera written all over it.

She frowned.

Things would need to change. With the road her life had taken right now, she had no other recourse than to get back on Chester's good side. She couldn't take any more of Tom moaning about layoffs and cash crunches. Or his not-so-subtle hints she needed to cut back on her spending. Or how he kept promising her things would eventually get better.

She wasn't willing to wait around to find out if this was going to happen. There were so many things she needed. And she wanted them now.

She poured out a glass of wine and popped a forkful of cake into her mouth. Then, giving a long sigh of pleasure, she took a sip of wine.

Yes, this was exactly what she needed right now.

She scooped another piece of cake into her mouth. As she slowly licked the fudge icing off the fork, she wondered if Chester's Aunt Evelyn had made this cake for him. Because if she remembered right, Chester had never shown a fondness for sweets.

She frowned. She didn't even want to think about who this cake was for. Instead, she drank more wine.

It appeared she had her work cut out for her. If Chester was really serious about this Sophie, it was going to take her a little longer than she'd planned to sway him over to her way of thinking.

And Carrie? She needed to figure her out. Because she definitely needed her as an ally.

Suddenly feeling restless, she picked up her phone to check the time. It wasn't even noon yet. She put what remained of the cake and the bottle of wine back in the refrigerator and glanced around the kitchen.

Chester had left his wallet on the counter. She picked it up and, holding it in her hand, she looked over at Hunter. He appeared to be still sleeping.

She smiled.

Things weren't looking so bad after all.


Carrie merged her car out onto the main highway.

She glanced over at Sophie to see she'd rested her head back against the seat and her eyes were closed. A stray tear still lingered on her cheek.

Saddened by this, Carrie reached over to pat her hand, happy to see this gesture brought a slight smile to her face. Unfortunately, this was then followed by another tear.

This made her angry. Why had she caved into Claire's demands? If she hadn't, maybe things would be different right now.

But again, this probably wasn't true. Claire's threat of contacting the team office with this information about Hunter could have resulted in a fiasco.

Once the news got out about Chester having a child, the media would've had a field day, blowing everything out of proportion. With Claire playing the part of the heartbroken and jilted ex-wife. While Chester would be portrayed as the absentee and irresponsible parent. A professional athlete who didn't think rules applied to him.

Thinking about this made her scowl. Everyone who knew Claire knew she was just plain evil. Status and money meant everything to her. And anyone who got in her way? They were quick to back off once they learned how nasty and conniving she could be when things weren't going as planned.

There was one thing Carrie found puzzling, though. Why had Claire waited so long to come to Chester about this child? It didn't make sense.

Sophie's voice cut into her thoughts. "My place is the next one on the right."

She pulled into the parking space for Sophie's townhouse and put the car in park. Before Sophie could even unbuckle her seatbelt, she turned to her.

"Sophie, before you get out of the car, I need to say something. Please, please don't walk away from Chester because of this. It would about kill him. He needs you now more than ever."

Slowly turning to meet her gaze, Sophie shook her head. "Oh, Carrie… I don't want to walk away from him. This is the absolute last thing I want to do. But I heard what he said. Claire wants the three of them to be a family. And he has to give this a chance, if only for the sake of the child."

Carrie shook her head vehemently. "No, he could never be with Claire again. She's not good for him. She has a way of egging him on, almost as if she enjoys making him mad. Then when he reaches his limit, she comes back all sweet and sorry like to make him feel guilty." She shook her head again. "Sophie, she ruined his confidence to the point he almost gave up playing ball. Why, it wasn't until after she left, his career took off. And now with you in his life, he's finally back to the brother I remember."

She smiled. "He's happy. And more relaxed."

She laughed. "When Chester goes to our Aunt Evelyn and asks her to teach him how to cook… and a romantic dinner at that, it says only one thing. He's in love."

The look on Sophie's face, filled with such anguish, Carrie spoke even more earnestly. "Come on, it's so obvious you're in love with him, too. And, yes… things will be different now that Hunter is in the picture, but Chester will make it work, I know he will."

For a few seconds, Sophie remained silent.

Then, her gaze focused on her hands, she began to speak. "When I was eight years old, my father gathered me, my sister and my brother together to tell us he was leaving. He told us he and my mom couldn't live together anymore because they didn't agree on anything. He also told us none of this was our fault, and he'd come see us as often as he could.

"I can still remember how my sister kept hanging onto him, sobbing as she begged him not to go. But that didn't stop him. We saw him maybe four or five times after that before he eventually faded out of our lives completely.

"My mom later told me the real reason he left was because he met another woman. I never had the opportunity to meet this woman, but I would've refused if given the chance. And even though I knew nothing about her, I hated her. As far as I was concerned, it was her fault we were no longer a family."

She looked over at Carrie and shrugged. "I don't want to be that woman. Because I know what it's like to be the child who was left behind."

Carrie reached over to hug her. "Oh Sophie, I'm so sorry. And you would never be that woman. Because Chester wouldn't let this happen. Why, you and he would be better parents to Hunter than Claire could ever be."

They sat in silence until Sophie gave a long sigh and opened the car door. She looked over at Carrie, a sad smile on her face. "He needs to make Hunter his main priority, without me there to complicate things. It's probably for the best that I'm leaving tomorrow. Fate must have other plans for us." "

After she was out of the car, she turned back to Carrie. "Thanks for bringing me home. And tell Chester..." She paused, her voice becoming choked. "Tell him I'm sorry, so sorry. Everything was... I..." Her face crumpled, and unable to finish, she closed the car door. and ran up the walk to her townhouse.

As Carrie waited for her to unlock the door and go inside, she vowed, if it was the last thing she did, she would find a way to get the two of them back together again.

# CHAPTER 23

Chester didn't know how long he'd been sitting at his desk, staring blindly out his office window. He didn't even notice the snow had stopped, the clouds making way for blue skies and sunshine. In his mind, he was back with Sophie, holding her in his arms as they watched the snow swirling past the windows, sparkling like diamonds in the early dawn light.

He finally stirred, wearily dragging his hands through his hair. He picked up his phone, his fingers hovering over the keypad as he contemplated calling her. His excuse he wanted to make sure she got home safely.

But this was stupid. Of course, she was home by now. Carrie would've made sure of this.

He tossed the phone back on his desk, watching as it slid across the smooth surface, stopping right next to the roll of Lifesavers still there.

Was this a sign of some kind? He hoped so …

Leaning back in his chair, he stared up at the ceiling. The silence in the room was beginning to feel overwhelming, making it too easy to think. Thoughts of what should be, could be and everything that wasn't and why.

And none of this was doing him a damn bit of good.

Glancing over at the clock on his desk, he saw he had been in this comatose state for over an hour. The only interruption had been a short time ago when someone knocked on the door.

Something he'd refused to acknowledge. Because he didn't want to talk to anyone.

But this wasn't entirely true. There was one person he would talk to, and this was Sophie. In a heartbeat, he would do this. He had to believe, between the two of them, they'd be able to figure out how to handle this newest roadblock thrown in front of them.

And what a roadblock it was. A son…

*He had a son.*

For a little over five years, this little person, part of his own flesh and blood, had been in existence and he hadn't known a single thing about him.

But this was something else he didn't want to start thinking about, because it only brought on this deep rage inside of him. Claire had done some pretty questionable things in the past, but never would he have imagined she'd keep something like this from him.

His laugh was sharp. Of course, there was only one reason for this sudden disclosure. She wanted something. And by presenting this child, *his son*, to him, she knew he wouldn't turn her away.

He put his head down in his hands. There had to be a way to persuade Sophie to talk to him. And he needed to do this as soon as possible. Because once she left for Paris she would no longer be his.

As it was, she already felt lost to him.

And this was something he didn't even want to think about.


Sophie couldn't seem to stop moving.

Ever since Carrie dropped her off at her townhouse, she had tried to keep busy. She took a shower, washed her hair, changed the sheets on her bed and now she was cleaning out her refrigerator.

She didn't know why. There wasn't really anything in it to clean.

She removed a jar of pickles to check the expiration date. It slipped out of her hand, and crashing to the floor, pickles, pickle juice, and broken glass went flying everywhere.

This is when she finally lost it.

With a frustrated cry, she slammed the refrigerator door and sank down to the floor. Putting her head down on her knees, she began to cry… heart wrenching sobs.

She wanted Chester.

She wanted him to look into her eyes and tell her everything was going to be all right and back to where it was before Claire made her appearance.

One image, however, refused to leave her, rising above everything else, monopolizing her mind. As she was about to leave Chester's condo she glanced over at the little boy, Hunter. Their eyes met, and she saw the sadness in his. As if he understood what she was going through.

Glancing over at the clock on his desk, he saw he had been in this comatose state for over an hour. The only interruption had been a short time ago when someone knocked on the door.

Something he'd refused to acknowledge. Because he didn't want to talk to anyone.And this was when she knew she had to do the right thing.

She leaned her head back against the cabinets and, closing her eyes, this was how remained for the longest time. Finally, she stirred, wiping away her tears with the back of her hand.

She gave a frustrated sigh. She hated these tears that kept coming at her. They came at her so fast, she didn't know quite how to handle them. If this is what happened when you fell in love, maybe she would be better off without Chester.

*Yeah, like you really believe this.*

Wearily getting up off the floor, she cleaned up the broken glass and pickle juice. After she had a cup of tea and a piece of toast, most of the toast left uneaten, she decided to go see her aunt. There were still a few things they had to wrap up before she left tomorrow.

Who knew? Maybe once she was back in Paris, she'd be able to get back to the life she had known before.

*Yeah... maybe you only need a change of scenery. And time.*

She was going to need lots and lots of time.

Chester had finally ventured out of his office and, after taking a long hot shower, he got dressed and headed for the kitchen.

He found Hunter still in the great room, completely immersed in cartoons on TV.

Claire was nowhere in sight.

Slowly strolling over to sit on the sofa next to the boy, he gave him a tentative smile.

Cautiously, Hunter smiled back at him.

Chester cleared his throat. "So, how's it going?" At Hunter's shrug, he glanced over at the empty kitchen and then back at Hunter. "I don't see your mom. Do you know where she is?"

Hunter pointed to the kitchen island. "She told me to tell you she left a note on the counter."

Chester nodded, a slow nod. It was taking everything he had not to ask Hunter if this was a common occurrence, to be left alone.

But before he made the mistake of doing this, he walked over to the counter to read the note.

> Chez,
>
> I called for a cab so I could go get my hair and nails done. They are long overdue. I hope you don't mind I took some money from your wallet. You left it out on the counter so I figured it was free game. I knocked on your office door to let you know I was leaving, but

*you didn't answer. Hunter will be fine. He doesn't mind staying alone. He might get hungry. But he's not picky, so I'm sure you'll find something for him to eat. XOXO Claire*

He glanced over at his wallet, still on the counter. It was probably a lot lighter now, knowing Claire.

He gave a frustrated sigh, rubbing the back of his neck.

*Damn, you don't want to do this again... you can't do this again.*

He glanced over to see Hunter was watching him, a worried expression on his face. Immediately sending him a smile, he made his way back to the sofa.

"So, are you hungry?"

Hunter shook his head, his gaze shifting back to the TV.

Leaning back on the sofa, Chester nonchalantly clasped his hands behind his head. He stretched out his legs. "Okay. So, I take it you only want to watch TV. We can do this if you want."

Hunter nodded, his eyes still glued to the TV. Then he suddenly turned to face him and Chester was dismayed to see his bottom lip was quivering. "I want to call my dad. But mommy said he's not my dad anymore. You're my dad." As he said this, two big tears began to roll down his cheeks. "I... I want to keep the dad I have."

Chester hoped the fury he felt wasn't obvious. He wanted to throttle Claire. The same Claire, who right now, was more interested in getting her hair and nails done than she was about the turmoil she was causing in her child's life.

He scooted next to Hunter and put his arm around him. "Hey buddy, you can keep the dad you have for as long as you want. I have no intention of taking over that role, if that's not what you want. When your mom comes back, I'll make sure she knows this. Okay?"

Hunter nodded, the relief so apparent on his face, Chester smiled. Settling back on the sofa to watch TV, he was soon laughing along with Hunter at the antics of the cartoon characters. He couldn't even remember the last time he'd watched cartoons.

When another episode came to an end, he reached over to rub Hunter's shoulder. "So, are you hungry now? I'm not much of a cook, but I can make a mean peanut butter and jelly sandwich. I might even be able to rustle up some chips."

This time, when Hunter nodded, he was smiling. This made Chester feel pretty good.

*It looks like being a dad wasn't going to be so hard after all.*

He stood and reaching over to pick up the remote, he turned off the TV. He gestured for Hunter to follow him. "Come on, I want you to sit in the kitchen with me while I make the sandwiches. Then you can tell me all about yourself."

Reaching over to ruffle his hair with his hand, he smiled. "But first, let me ask you a question.

Hunter nodded.

"How do you feel about baseball?"


This was how Carrie found them when she stopped by Chester's condo after she dropped Sophie off at her townhouse earlier.

Worried about him, she wanted to see how he was doing.

She also wanted to give him Sophie's message. It might make him feel better. Then again, it might make him feel horrible. But whatever the outcome, she hoped it would at least galvanize him to go see her.

*They. Needed. To. Talk.*

She smiled over at Hunter as she sat next to him at the island. "Wow, you got him to make you lunch? Very impressive. He doesn't do something like this unless he really, really likes you."

A pained look on his face, Chester turned and began loading the dishwasher. This is when she remembered the special dinner he'd planned for Sophie.

Her intention to change the subject, she smiled brightly over at Hudson. "Where's your mom?"

"Out." This was the extent of his answer.

Now wiping down the counter, Chester looked over at her. He rolled his eyes. "I inadvertently left my wallet on the counter. So, she decided to get her hair and nails done. Compliments of yours truly." He turned to grin at Hunter. "But it's worked out great. The two of us have spent the time getting acquainted. While sharing some chips and peanut butter and jelly sandwiches. Because a man's gotta eat, right?"

Hunter nodded, a big grin on his face, before he stuffed the rest of his sandwich in his mouth. After he washed this down with a big gulp of milk, he slid off the stool.

He looked over at Chester. "Can I be excused to watch TV?"

At Chester's nod, he ran over and picked up the remote. Diving onto the sofa and curling up in the corner, he turned on the TV.

After they watched him for a few seconds, Carrie gave Chester a curious look. "So, are you okay? I had to come here because I was so worried about you. And just so you know, Sophie's a wreck."

He groaned, closing his eyes. "Gee, thanks for telling me this."

She rested her arms on the counter and relayed the message Sophie had asked her to give him. "You needed to hear this. Just like you need to go talk to her. Before it's too late. Unless you don't care for her as much as I think you do."

He studied her for a few moments before he spoke. "I probably shouldn't even be telling you this, but last night was the best night of my life. Not because of… uh…"

He paused, his face turning red with embarrassment. He wasn't used to sharing this kind of personal information with anyone, let alone her.

*She's your little sister.*

He didn't even want to think of her knowing anything about sex. Or, God forbid, asking him questions.

He cleared his throat. "Well, I'm sure you know what I'm talking about. With her, well, it was different. There was something almost magical about what we shared, almost as though it was all a dream. But a real dream. A perfect dream."

He stared into space, his voice becoming soft with the memory. "It was so right. I wanted to keep her with me forever."

He glanced back at Carrie, giving a self-conscious laugh. "I can't tell you how many times I almost blurted out 'marry me' to her. But I was afraid she'd say no. Then the whole evening would be ruined, all the magic disappearing into thin air."

He snapped his fingers. "Just like that."

Observing his sad expression, Carrie was puzzled. "But why would you think she'd say no? You didn't know about Hunter then."

He shrugged. "Paris, she's flying back there tomorrow. When we first realized something was happening between us, I told her I didn't want to talk about her leaving. We would deal with things as they came up, I said. But now I realize this was a stupid mistake on my part because by ignoring the inevitable, nothing has been resolved."

His look bleak, he ran his hand through his hair. "And now this new development with Hunter complicates everything even further. But I know we can make it work. What I'm having a hard time with is understanding why she doesn't think the same."

He swallowed. "This scares the hell out of me..."

He closed his eyes, a look of such pain on his face, she reached over to cover his hand with hers.

"There's something you should know." She told him what Sophie shared about her father.

He shook his head, a bewildered look on his face. "But this isn't what's happening here, not at all."

Carrie shrugged. "I know this, and you know this, but unfortunately, Sophie seems to believe differently. So, this is why you need to talk to her. And you need to do this now."

She pushed away from the counter. "And while you do this, I'm going to watch TV with Hunter. After all, if he really is my nephew, I should get to know him better, right?"

At Chester's questioning look, she shrugged. "I'm sorry, I don't trust Claire. Why did she show up now to tell you this? It doesn't make sense."

He shrugged. "Nothing makes sense where Claire is concerned."

They both took the time to think about this. Then, reaching into her jeans pocket, she pulled out a roll of Lifesavers and tossed it to him.

"Here, take these for good luck. I'm pretty sure you're going to need plenty of that. I brought a roll for Hunter, too." She grinned. "Like you, I seem to have quite a collection of them. So, go… I'll stay here until you or Claire returns."

She made a face. "Let's hope you come back first. My nerves always get on edge when Claire is around."

He watched as she settled next to Hunter on the couch, whatever she said to him, making him laugh. As he put on his coat, he smiled, thinking how lucky he was to have her as a sister. After he slipped the roll of candy in his pocket, he grabbed his keys from the counter and headed for the door, sending both Carrie and Hunter a wave as he left.

He was feeling hopeful. In fact, it was almost as if he was on a mission.

One that could very well determine the rest of his life.

# CHAPTER 24

Sophie finished writing out the list of things she needed to discuss with her aunt. She was stuffing it in her purse when her front doorbell rang.

She opened the door to find Chester standing in front of her. A hesitant smile on his face, his voice came out husky with longing.

"Hi ..."

Unable to answer because of the sudden lump in her throat, she only shook her head as she stepped back so he could enter. After she closed the door, she turned to find he was gazing at her with an intensity that made her look away.

She swallowed.

*Don't cry... don't you dare start crying.*

When the silence between them became almost unbearable, she finally spoke, her words aimed right at his chest.

"I was just leaving. To go to the boutique."

When he said nothing, she looked up to find he was still watching her. She continued, her words barely audible. "There are some things we need to talk about. My aunt and I. Orders for the Paris store. And a few other things ... little things. Like the promotion we have coming up next month. And..."

Her voice trailed off as she pushed her hair back from her face, nervously tucking it behind her ears. Why was she telling him this? He didn't care about orders or promotions.

This wasn't why he was here.

He wanted to talk about Claire and Hunter. But talking about the situation wasn't going to change anything. It wouldn't make her change her mind.

*Even though you want to... so, so, much.*

Chester knew he wasn't helping by remaining silent, but right now, truthfully? He didn't want to talk. He wanted to take her into his arms and hold her close. So, he could bring back the magic they shared only hours before.

*If only just for a little. Enough to get a start at finding the way back to where you were.*

But he was afraid if he did try to take her into his arms, there was a good chance she'd push him away.

So, talk it would be.

He cleared his throat. "We need to talk about what happened this morning."

She dropped her gaze to her hands, clasped together at her waist. Dismayed to see they were shaking, she clutched them even more tightly together.

Taking a deep breath, she looked right at him. "Chester, I'm not going to change my mind. I can't. It would go against everything I believe."

When he started to open his mouth to say something, she cut him off. "Please, let me finish. You have a son and he's what matters the most. He needs Claire's and your total attention. Can you even imagine what must be going on in his mind right now?"

The sadness in her eyes was killing him. In order to keep from reaching out to smooth away this pain showing on her face, he jammed his hands in his coat pockets.

His eyes holding hers, he spoke. "Carrie told me about your father. Angel, you must realize this is a whole different situation. Hunter already told me he doesn't want me as a dad, he wants the dad he has.

I'm hoping this will change and he'll eventually come to like me, but I won't push it. I'm willing to wait until he's ready."

At her silence, he struggled on. "And Claire and I together again? This will never happen. Trust me, she's not the woman I love. And I would never, ever be able to pretend she is. Even for Hunter."

At this, her head jerked up, her eyes intently searching his. "You had to have loved her at one time."

He shook his head, slowly moving closer. "But this was so long ago. In a different time and place in my life."

Her next words were so soft, he had to move even closer to hear them. "But maybe if you get back together again, things will change. After all, she is the mother of your child. You may find you still love her after all."

Immediately, he realized where she was going with this. The possibility his interest in Claire might be rekindled. This prompted him to move even closer, tentatively reaching out to stroke her cheek.

"Angel, you have to know you're the woman I love."

He was taken completely by surprise when she jerked away from him, her expression becoming angry.

*So, so angry.*

He, in turn, stepped back, confusion taking over.

*What the hell? What's going on here? Didn't you just tell her you love her?*

Yes, Sophie was angry. She was so furious her words came out in a sputtering mess. "How would I know this when you've never come out and told me?"

He was stunned. How could she not know he loved her? Not only because of what they shared last night, but with all the time they'd spent together. And then there were the many conversations they had about what they were looking for in a relationship. Was he wrong to have assumed they were on the same page, with both of them wanting the same thing?

*Nope, you don't think so.*

As usual, he didn't quite get it, his next words coming out wrong.

*So terribly, horribly messed-up and completely wrong.*

"I guess I thought by my actions you'd realize this. But if you want me to say it, then yes... I love you."

And now it was her turn to be stunned.

Had he lost his mind, or what? If this was his way of making it all better, well... he was in for a big surprise.

She began backing away from him. "I can't believe you. If you think what you just said is going to send me right into your arms, you're wrong."

And this is when her anger spiraled out of control, and she let loose the words she knew she shouldn't. Words she herself didn't even believe.

"Maybe this explains why you and Claire didn't make a go of it. Evidently you don't think at all, do you? Instead, you take everything for granted. And if it doesn't work out? Well, it's no big deal, is it? You move on. Because we all know there will always be plenty of other women out there for you to choose from."

As soon as these words left her mouth, she knew she had gone too far.

Yep, this was a mistake. *A huge mistake.*

What she accused him of wasn't what she believed, but what she feared. A small part of why she'd been holding back, afraid to commit to him completely.

She wanted to grab those words right back and pretend they were never said. But by his expression, she knew it wouldn't matter. It was too late, the damage was done.

For a few moments, they didn't move, glaring at each other.

She spoke first, her words barely above a whisper. "It seems I've... we've said more than enough. So, maybe it would be best if you left." She stepped back, wrapping her arms around herself in an effort to stop her violent trembling. "I guess... I guess we should've seen this coming. There's just too much working against us."

Still reeling from her words, at first, he didn't respond. Then, after dragging his hand through his hair, the look on his face was one of total disbelief.

"*My, God* ... I don't even know what to say here. Except, I hope you don't really believe I'm the person you just said I was." Then he slowly shook his head. "No, I think the real problem is you don't trust me, do you?"

She closed her eyes. The fact he'd been able to know what she was thinking made it impossible for her to deny what he said. She could only helplessly shake her head.

With her silence, he became overcome with emotion, the threat of tears making it almost impossible for him to continue.

He blinked, his voice far from steady. "I want you to know I do love you. More than you could ever possibly know. And God help me, this is something that will never change."

He struggled on, his voice becoming even more unsteady. "Maybe I did start taking things for granted, but only because I thought you felt the same. I'd even dared to imagine spending the rest of my life with you, starting a family and eventually growing old together. But now? It appears what I foolishly thought was the real thing was, instead, only a dream."

His smile was sad. "So, it looks like you're right. I haven't been thinking clearly at all, have I?"

He studied her, drinking in every detail, every emotion he was struggling to overcome, showing in his expression. "I want you to know, once I walk out this door, I will not be back. I can't do this anymore, Sophie. The ball is now in your court."

He reached into his pocket and pulled out the roll of Lifesavers Carrie had given him. After staring down at the candy in his hand, he set it down on the hall table.

His smile was sad. "Carrie gave these to me right before I left to come here. She said I needed all the luck I could get. But it looks as though they no longer have the ability to work their magic on me. So, take them, they're yours."

He turned and walked out, closing the door behind him.

Sophie stayed where she was until she heard him start up his SUV. She made an abrupt move towards the door, but then she stopped, her gaze falling on the roll of candy. She walked over and picked it up. Holding it tightly in her hand, she closed her eyes.

There was only one thing going over and over in her mind.

*He called you Sophie... not angel.*

And this was what was breaking her heart the most.

After Chester started up his SUV, he rested his arms on the steering wheel and putting his head down, he closed his eyes.

*Well, that certainly didn't go very well, did it?*

He felt like the ground had been pulled out from under him. But after what he said to her, this shouldn't come as a surprise.

*"I guess I thought by my actions you would realize this. But if you want me to say it... then, yes... I love you."*

*My, God...* what had he been thinking when he blurted out those words? Could he have been even any more insensitive?

Obviously, Sophie was right. He hadn't been thinking.

But he'd been so frustrated. The fact she didn't trust him, hurting the most. Prompting him to go on and say something even more incredibly stupid, making things worse. But hadn't he warned her he wasn't good in this kind of situation?

*The bottom line is you're a fool. You've said this before and you'll say it again... a damn fool.*

He opened his eyes and staring at her front door, he willed it to open. To then have her come running out, waving at him as she called out to tell him she'd changed her mind. She wanted him to stay.

But knowing there wasn't a chance in hell this was going to happen, he put the SUV in gear and drove at a snail's pace through the parking lot. He pulled out onto the main road, with no clue where he was headed. He only knew he didn't want to go back to his condo.

No, there was no way he was going to go back there. He couldn't face Carrie. The possibility of having to deal with another lecture, or even worse, her look of pity, would be more than he could take.

And God knows he wanted nothing to do with Claire. After all, it was because of her everything was now in such a mess.

He decided to head for the gym. Where he would work out until he dropped. He wanted to become so exhausted he wouldn't be able to think.

After that? He didn't know what was going to happen.

Nor did he care.

# CHAPTER 25

*Don't be pushed around by the fears in your mind.*
*Be led by the dreams in your heart.*
*~ Unknown*

Chester pulled into the parking garage.

He had stayed at the gym, pushing himself until he couldn't move another muscle. Unfortunately, this hadn't been enough to dull the pain of knowing he might never see Sophie again.

*You can only blame yourself if this happens. This is the second time you've given her an ultimatum. To then turn around and leave. You'd think you would have learned your lesson the first time.*

And now? He couldn't even escape into the privacy of his condo because Claire and Hunter would be there.

With an enormous sigh, he hauled himself out of his SUV.

There was no getting around it. Without Sophie?

Nothing would ever be the same again.

When he first entered his the condo, it was so quiet, he dared to hope no one was there.Then Claire came out of the kitchen.

A glass of wine in her hand, her smile was overly bright. "Well, hello. I was wondering if you were ever going to come back. Carrie wouldn't tell me where you went. Or if you were even planning to return. In fact, she really didn't talk to me at all."

Her lips were pressed together in anger.. "She hasn't changed one bit. Still the moody Carrie I remember so well."

Chester hung his coat in the closet before he turned to study her for a few moments. She just didn't get it, did she? She had absolutely no idea how she came across to people.

When he finally spoke, he was surprised at how steady and calm his voice sounded. "Carrie chooses her friends very carefully. But once she lets you in, you're her friend for life. On the other hand, if you hurt her, or those she loves, she'll drop you in a second. As old-fashioned this may seem, she believes in loyalty. I guess it's one trait we both value very highly."

Claire gave him a sharp glance. "*Ah…* I get it. Point taken. I wish I could be so perfect."

When Chester didn't seem to have a comment to this, she turned to go back into the kitchen, gesturing for him to follow her.

"I've made dinner if you're interested. Now that I have a child, I've been forced to learn a thing or two about cooking. Though I'm sure my simple attempts won't be enough to satisfy you or your Aunt Evelyn. But Hunter seems to be happy, so I guess this is all that matters, right?"

Chester sighed, running his hand wearily through his hair. It was starting already. This is what she did. The constant jabs and insults bringing out the worst in him.

*What about the comment you made about Carrie and loyalty? Doesn't this make you just as bad?*

Seriously? Now he was doubting himself? He sent a longing glance over at the door. If only he could walk right back out of his condo and keep going.

*You'll go anywhere.*

Instead, he decided he was going to make the effort to be nice.

He followed her into the kitchen, where he took a glass out of the cupboard and filled it with wine from the bottle she'd opened. It didn't escape his notice the wine she'd chosen was one of the pricier brands he had. Or that she was drinking it out of one of his expensive Irish crystal wine glasses.

*Nope, no surprise here. Only the best for Claire.*

It was when he went to put the bottle back in the refrigerator he noticed the half-eaten chocolate cake, right there at eye level for him to see. Next to the unfinished bottle of wine he and Sophie had shared.

And for some reason, this hit him hard.

*The cake is for Sophie.*

He knew Claire had arranged this, if only to let him know she was staking her claim. He turned to her, giving a nod towards the cake.

After a slow sip of wine, she eyed him over the rim of her glass. "Yeah, I hope you don't mind. You know how I need to satisfy my chocolate fix every once in a while."

He couldn't help it... he slammed the refrigerator door. It was suddenly very important he let her know she was not going to take over. He knew he was overreacting, but as far as he was concerned, there was only one person who would be allowed to do this.

And this would be Sophie.

"It wasn't yours to take. That is Sophie's cake."

"Well, Sophie isn't here, is she?" She put her wine glass down on the counter.

*Hard.*

He also set his glass down, but more carefully. Then he leaned back against the counter, briefly closing his eyes.

When he opened them and began to speak, the controlled anger in his voice made her take a step back, a wary look in her eyes.

"Do you even know anything about love? What it's like to find someone whom you feel this immediate connection? Then, in less than an instant, you realize they're the person you've always been waiting for, the person you're meant to be with. And for them, you'd do anything. Because they complete you like no one has ever done before."

His voice became soft with emotion. "All of this is what Sophie is to me. She has become my reason for living, for every breath I take. But because of the compassionate person she is, she refuses to come between me and Hunter." He shrugged. "And I don't know what I'm going to do. Because honestly? Now that I've lost her, I don't know how I'll be able to go on without her."

He pushed away from the counter and walked out of the kitchen.

He didn't even turn around when he spoke. "I'm sorry. Suddenly, I'm not very hungry."


Claire watched until he disappeared into his bedroom, closing the door behind him.

After drinking the rest of her wine, she carried the glass over to the trash can. She threw it in, a satisfied smile on her face at the sound of breaking glass.

*So there...*

She leaned against the counter. Tightly crossing her arms over her chest, she found she was blinking back tears.

Angry tears.

*Scared tears.*

Nothing was turning out like she'd planned. And as much as she didn't want to admit, she had been moved by what Chester said about Sophie. But it also made her angry. Because she knew, no matter what she said or did, he would never say anything like that about her.

"Mommy?"

Hunter had come into the kitchen. He had a worried expression on his face, the same look he'd had ever since they left Tom. In fact, he looked like a miniature Tom right now.

She gave him a bright smile. "I hope you're hungry, because Mommy just finished making dinner. Come and sit down. It looks like it's going to be only the two of us."


A late night commercial woke Chester.

For a few seconds, he stared at the TV. Then suddenly, fully awake, he looked over at the space beside him on the bed.

It was empty, the sheets still rumpled from the night before.

He groaned, dragging his hands down his face. How was it even possible, less than twenty-four hours ago, this same space had been occupied by Sophie? A warm and loving Sophie, the message in her eyes telling him everything was as it should be.

He searched the bed for his phone, finally finding it under one of the pillows. Checking the time, he saw it was a little past midnight.

There was no call from Sophie. No text either.

*Did you really expect there would be? After the ultimatum you gave her?*

Should he swallow his pride and call her?

*You know she won't answer. Why make yourself even more miserable? And didn't she make it clear there was nothing more to say?*

Suddenly feeling very irritated, he went to set the phone on the nightstand. His hand brushing against something, he glanced over to see it was the necklace he'd given her.

A deep and overwhelming sadness settling in his chest, he picked it up.

*But she told you... no, she promised you... she would never take it off.*

His head falling back against the pillows and the necklace still in his hand, he closed his eyes.


He must have dozed off, the soft knocking on his door bringing him to open his eyes. When the knocking persisted, becoming louder, he placed the necklace back on the nightstand and wearily crawled off the bed to go open the door.

It was Claire.

Without a word, she pushed past him, leaving him to watch as she crossed the room to sit on his bed.

Instantly on alert, he closed the door and remained where he was. Still not quite awake, he knew this wasn't the best state to be in when dealing with Claire.

*What the hell does she want?*

She patted the space by her on the bed. "Come, we need to talk."

He shook his head.

The fact she was sitting on his bed, the same bed he'd shared with Sophie only a short time ago, was not an easy thing for him to swallow. He wanted to tell her to go sit somewhere else, anywhere but on his bed. But this was being crazy.

After running his hand nervously through his hair, he cleared his throat. "I'm fine right where I am. Go ahead, say what you have to say."

She opened her mouth. But then she dropped her gaze down to her hands, remaining completely silent. Right as he was about to ask her what was going on, she lifted her head to face him.

She took a big breath. "I lied. Hunter is not your son. Tom really is his father."

The silence in the room seemed to go on forever before he cleared his throat again.

"Why?"

Yep... just one word. If anything, he was surprised he'd even managed this. With what she just said, it was almost as if she'd slapped him, her words knocking him completely senseless.

She was refusing to look at him. "I don't know. I guess I thought it was a good idea. A way to get a new start."

His hands going to rub the back of his neck, he stared at her, an incredulous expression on his face. Did he hear her right? A good idea? How the hell would telling him something like this ever be a good idea? And for whom?

When she saw the fury building in his eyes, she began twisting her hands together. Then she began to talk. Fast... very fast. Scared fast.

"I didn't know what else to do. Lately, it seemed like Tom was drinking a lot. I think there are some problems with his business, I don't know. He doesn't like to talk about it."

She shrugged, while managing to look annoyed at the same time. "Over the past few weeks, he started spending more time at work, When he did come home, he'd go directly to his office and shut the door. If I tried to talk to him, he became angry, lashing out at me."

Okay, so maybe she was exaggerating a little. She was the one who got mad, not Tom. But she was walking on thin ice here. This meant she needed to convince Chester she'd been right to leave.

Yeah, it probably wasn't the smartest thing to do. But at the time, it felt like it was the only choice she had.

At his questioning look, she shook her head. "No, he never physically hurt us, but I didn't want to stick around to see if it might come to that. Though I know he'd never hurt Hunter. He's always been really good with him."

She sighed. "But Hunter was becoming more like the parent, always watching Tom. Almost as if he was waiting for things to change." She shrugged. "For his age, he's very perceptive."

She gave a frustrated sigh, pushing herself off the bed. After she wrapped her arms tightly around herself, she began pacing back and forth.

"So, I packed up a few things, and we left. At first, Tom kept calling me, leaving all these messages. But as of yesterday, I haven't heard from him."

Her eyes began to fill with tears. But, by the tone of her voice, he knew they were angry tears. "It really doesn't matter, though. Because I know it's not me he's worried about. He only cares about Hunter."

Again, she was refusing to meet his gaze. But after a long and tense filled silence, Chester nodded.

*Ah... now it's all perfectly clear. Hunter has bumped her off the pedestal Tom had her on. And you know how she always wants to be number one.*

But none of this mattered, because everything had changed.

As far as Claire was concerned?

She was no longer his problem.

She was done.

He was done.

*They were done.*

A harsh laugh escaped him. "You haven't changed a bit, have you? It's always been, and always will be, about you. But do you know what? From now on, count me out as someone to come to with all of your lies. Because once you leave here, and you will be leaving *very* soon, you and I are through. For good."

He reached over to open the door, gesturing for her to leave. "I want you to go make flight reservations for you and Hunter. I don't care where this takes you. Back to Texas, where I know you have family or back to Tom. It's your choice."

Her head shot up, her expression angry. "I'm not going back to Tom."

His mouth twisted into a wry smile. "This is for you to decide. And, since I know money is the number one concern of yours right now, I'm going to set up a bank account with enough money to last you for a year."

He gave a short laugh. "But don't think I'm going to be funding your extravagant lifestyle. What I give you will be what I consider a more than generous amount a normal person would need with a child to support."

He saw her eyes light up at this. There was no doubt in his mind she was already calculating how much money this would be.

He shook his head. "And don't you think it's about time you start thinking about turning your life around? Not only for your sake, but for Hunter as well. You can start out by telling him Tom really is his father. The poor little guy is traumatized by all of this."

He studied her for a few moments before he went on to add. "In fact, if I find out you aren't making a genuine effort to change, I'll cut off the money. Immediately."

Crossing his arms across his chest, he waited. He could almost visualize the wheels turning in her head as she tried to decide if she should accept what he was offering.

Finally, she nodded. After she came to stand next to him, she gave a nervous laugh. "I want you to know I'm not all bad. I told you the truth because I was so moved by what you said about this Sophie… or whatever her name is. You made it very obvious how much she means to you."

She swallowed, her comment almost a whisper. "I can only hope, someday I'll find such a love. You're lucky."

She kissed him on the cheek and left the room.

He closed the door. For a few moments, he took the time to let everything sink in. Then Claire was completely forgotten, leaving only one thing on his mind.

*Sophie... you need to tell her this. Then you have to let her know you'll agree to anything she wants. You don't care. You only want her back.*

A sudden lightness filling him, he picked up his phone from the bed.

Everything was going to work out.

It had to… right?

# CHAPTER 26

The latest boarding announcement blared loudly over the PA system, startling Sophie out of her zombie-like state. She checked the overhead screen for flight updates, relieved to see her flight was still on schedule.

The airport terminal was almost deserted. Evidently Valentine's day, or what was now only a few minutes into the day after, was not a popular time to travel.

*No, everyone was probably with their special sweetheart right now. Like you had so foolishly hoped to be. Instead, here you are, alone.*

It had taken a lot of fast talking on her part, but she had finally convinced her aunt she should leave the airport and go home. She didn't mind being alone while she waited for her flight, she told her. She would be fine.

If anything, the silence was a welcome relief after the hectic and emotionally exhausting time they spent together, leaving her with a pounding headache and feeling completely drained.

Her aunt hadn't reacted favorably to the news Sophie had changed her flight, booking an earlier red-eye back to Paris. After her initial shock, she'd hit Sophie with a barrage of questions. All of which Sophie refused to answer. The only information she volunteered was that she and Chester had parted, and it would be best for everyone if she left.

Paris was her life now, she told her aunt. She was more than ready to get back to running the boutique. After all, they both knew this was the life she had always dreamed about.

*Then why do you keep checking your phone? To see if he called? Hadn't he made it perfectly clear, from now on, it was all up to you?*

Blinking frantically, willing herself not to cry, she pulled her phone out of her coat pocket and turned it off.

*There... this makes it official. Now there's no reason to check your phone.* Or be disappointed.

Restlessly shifting in her seat, she glanced down again at the newspaper on the seat next to her. It was opened to the Arts and Entertainment section. Her aunt had pulled the paper out of her purse when they first arrived at the airport, insisting there was something Sophie needed to see. And even though Sophie had asked her to take it with her when she left, her aunt refused.

With a sigh, she picked up the paper to look at it again, her eyes reluctantly going to the bottom of the page where there was a photo of her and Chester. His arms around her, they were both smiling at each other, just about to kiss. Evidently, Susan Carter had arranged for this moment to be photographed without their knowledge.

She studied the photo closely. Closing her eyes, she could almost feel that exact moment, the anticipation building for his kiss.

*Stop it, you can't go there. You don't need to be reminded of how happy you were.*

Even though she almost had the caption memorized, she read it again.

*Well girls, it official. You can cross Chester Mazzori off your list of eligible bachelors here in Cleveland. Remember the woman I mentioned only a few days ago? The one I saw him with at the airport? It turns out she really is his angel. So much so, he agreed to take part in a fashion show put on by the Chic Boutique yesterday where Sophie Michaels, aka angel, is a co-owner. Together, their walk down the runway together was the highlight of the show.*

*Let's just say, love was in the air. Or more fittingly, for Chester and the woman he calls angel, it was a match made in heaven. Happy Valentine's Day to all! Until next time, Susan*


After tracing their smiling faces in the photo with her fingertip, she carefully tore the article from the newspaper and folded it up. She slipped it in her pocket, her fingers coming in contact with the roll of Lifesavers.

Holding on to them, comforted by the fact they had once been his, she glanced over at the windows to see it had started to snow again

She hoped to God her flight wouldn't be delayed.


Sophie wasn't answering her phone. What was even more concerning, not only was she not answering, Chester kept getting the damn recording she wasn't available and her phone had been turned off.

Which meant he couldn't leave a message even if he tried.

*So, what the hell are you supposed to do now?*

Pacing back and forth in his bedroom, he stopped to glance over at the windows. It was snowing again. And it was coming down pretty hard.

*Yeah? So? What are you waiting for?*

It took him all but one second to make the decision. There wasn't even an option. It looked like he needed to go to her.

Slipping on his shoes, he grabbed his keys off the dresser. Once he was at the door, he hesitated. Practically sprinting back through the room, he picked up the necklace from where he'd left it on the nightstand and stuffed it in his jeans pocket.

*Just in case.*

There was only silence as he made his way to the door, grabbing his coat from the closet. Filled with a sudden sense of urgency, he took off in a sprint all the way to the parking garage, pulling his coat on as he went.

Once he was in his SUV, maneuvering it over the deserted and snow-covered roads, his mind was focused on only one thing.

*Please, God... let this have a good ending. We need this, we really, really do. I need this...*

He wasn't one to bargain with God, but if there was ever a time he was willing to try, this would be it.

Wearily yanking open the door of his SUV, Chester sank back into the driver's seat, slamming the door shut in his frustration.

Throwing his head back against the head rest, he closed his eyes.

*Where was she?*

If Sophie was in her condo, she wasn't answering her door. He had knocked on it, softly, loudly and to the point he was banging on it like a madman. He had hit the doorbell more times than he wanted to count. And he had tried to call her again and then again on his phone. All of this happening as he stood on her front steps with the snow coming down around him. Testimony of this was how cold he was and the layer of white covering him.

He shook his head, sending a shower of wet snow over the inside of his SUV.

*Where could she be? Had she gone to stay with her aunt?*

Or the unthinkable... she knew it was him, and was refusing to acknowledge him, sticking with her claim they had nothing left to talk about.

Finally, after giving her townhouse one more searching look, he backed out of the parking space and headed for home. Since her flight to Paris wasn't leaving until late afternoon, he would try again in the morning. And if he still couldn't get ahold of her in the morning?

He'd stop by the boutique. She was sure to be there.

Then everything would be back to the way it was, and he'd have no reason to worry

*No... no reason at all.*

Chester had a sleepless night, The memories of the previous twenty-four hours running over and over in his mind, he was relieved when the morning light finally began to fill his bedroom.

Once he showered and got dressed, he made his way to his office.

He tried Sophie's number.

Again, there was no answer, the same unavailable message beginning to sound like a bad omen in his ear. Drumming his fingers on his desk, he tried to ignore the worry pooling inside of him.

Abruptly pushing away from the desk, he went down the hall to the kitchen, thankful to find Claire and Hunter weren't up yet. He ate a quick breakfast and after skimming through the morning newspaper, he decided he couldn't wait any longer.

His first stop, Sophie's condo.

Hopefully, a second stop wouldn't be needed.


Forty-five minutes later he pulled into the parking lot of the boutique. He shut off the engine, glancing around at the almost full parking lot.

*Great... just great. The last thing you want right now is an audience.*

He got out of the SUV and marched over to the building. A determined expression on his face, he pulled open the door and walked inside.

As had happened the last time, everyone turned around to stare at him, their chatter falling off into silence. After all, it wasn't very often a man was brave enough to venture into a place like this. A very handsome man who, going by the sudden excited whispers, was quickly recognized for who he was.

A nervous smile on his face, he scanned the room. But unlike the last time, he recognized no one.

There was no Sophie.

No blue eyes to meet his, to ground him with the promise she would always be the one waiting for him.

The hope he had been holding onto, well, just like that, it was gone. And now he wanted nothing more than to turn around and walk right out the door. In fact, not even aware of his actions, this was exactly what he started to do.

A hand grabbed his arm, bringing him to a halt. He turned to see it belonged to Sophie's Aunt Louise. Immediately concerned when she saw the distraught expression on his face, she tightened her hold.

"Chester… wait. Don't go." Her gaze sweeping the the room, she gestured to a woman who quickly came to join them. She leaned over to whisper in her ear. "Do me a favor and take over for me, Pat. This handsome gentleman and I need to talk."

Still holding on to his arm, she took Chester to the back of the store and into her office. After she closed the door, sat behind the desk, pointing to the only other chair in the room.

"Sit."

The tone of her voice brooking no argument, he sat.

She studied him for what seemed like a very long time. Then leaned forward, giving him no other option than to look right into he eyes.

Confusion sounded in her voice. "Chester, what happened? I have never, ever seen Sophie so upset. She wouldn't talk to me. What was even more concerning, she would hardly talk at all, which for Sophie just doesn't happen. The only way I can describe her behavior is that of a broken woman."

Finding his voice, he spoke, but it wasn't in answer to her question. "Where is she? I need to talk to her before she leaves."

When only silence followed his words, stretching out much longer than it should have, he closed his eyes, a sick feeling settling in his gut. He braced himself, waiting for what he feared she was about to say.

But Louise wasn't ready to give him that information yet. Because, to tell the truth? She was angry. And extremely frustrated.

She didn't understand. What was wrong with the two of them? It was obvious they were so in love with each other. Yet here he was, sitting across from her and looking like death. While Sophie was on her way, if not already in Paris, probably looking close to the same.

It had to be an issue of stubborn pride on the part of one of them and she was willing to place her bet on Sophie.

She shook her head. Sophie was always one to do the right thing.

Not that this was a bad thing, but in some situations, it was best to let go and give in a little.

This especially holding true when it came to love.

But taking pity on Chester's miserable state, she put her feelings aside and broke the news to him as gently as she could.

"Oh, Cheste… she left already. She changed her flight. She's probably already in Paris as we speak. I tried to talk her out of it, I really did." She shrugged. "But she was so insistent on leaving. The only thing she would tell me was she had to do the right thing. And this is why you and she had to part."

With a groan, he slumped back in his seat.

"If only she would've waited. Or, for God's sake, hadn't turned off her phone. I can't even tell you how many times I tried to call her. Or how I went to her condo looking for her. At least twice I was there. And now this was my last hope, coming here. I wanted to let her know everything has changed and it's going to be okay."

He leaned forward, his elbows on his knees as he raked his hands through his hair. Lifting his head, he gave Louise a wry smile.

"We parted with such angry words, saying things we shouldn't have." His laugh was sharp. "Apparently, it appears I'm quite good at saying the wrong thing. And, unfortunately, I just keep on doing this, over and over again."

He gazed over at her, his look one of total frustration. "Why can't I ever get it right? What do I have to do? Tape my mouth shut?"

She shook her head, a look of compassion on her face. "Oh Chester, this is what love does to us sometimes. It makes you crazy, messes with your emotions. But real love always finds a way to get you through both the bad and the good times. And if you both want it bad enough, it will only grow stronger,

She sat up straighter in her chair, clasping her hands together in front of her. "Let's not give up hope just yet. Maybe we can fix this. Why don't you start out by telling me what happened and then we'll try to figure out what steps you should take to make it right.

"Because, as much as I am so disappointed in both of you right now, I really like you. And I can see how much you love Sophie. Your eyes give this away when you look at her." She shook her head, a knowing smile on her face.

So, this is exactly what he did. He told her everything. Going all the way back to when they first met. How their problems started when Sophie completely threw him for a loop with the news she was leaving for Paris, prompting him to foolishly give her an ultimatum. Something he realized almost immediately was a very bad move.

*But don't forget the kiss you gave her. If you were to rate that kiss on a scale from one to ten, it would be a fifty. Or hell, let's bump it up to a hundred. It was by far the best kiss you ever shared with anyone. It was only what you said afterwards that was a mistake... a huge mistake.*

He went on to tell her when Sophie came home for the wedding, he realized his feelings for her hadn't changed. If anything, they were even stronger. He also told her how he convinced Sophie they should ignore the fact she would be leaving, something he now realized was probably his second bad move.

He didn't go into great detail about the night they spent together, putting more emphasis on the Valentine's Day dinner he arranged. After all, she was Sophie's aunt, so there were some things, private things, he couldn't share. But by the way she was nodding, a slight smile on her face, he had a feeling she knew exactly what he wasn't telling her.

He did tell her, for him, the night had been one he would never forget. And that he thought of it as a turning point in their relationship. A time they both came to realize what they had was the real thing.

They had fallen in love.

*At least you thought this at the time. How were you supposed to know it only counted if you said it out loud?*

Caught up in these thoughts, he stared into space. It was only when Louise tactfully cleared her throat, he continued.

He told her how Claire had come on the scene, with the news Hunter was his son. The timing of this coming at the worst possible time, it was literally, a wake-up call.

Not that this news would have been easier to take at another time.

Of course, it wouldn't have. But Sophie saw this as the end of them. Even when he went to see her, she'd refused to change her way of thinking.

It was during the last time they were together, he made his final and most damaging move with what he said to her. But to be fair, he wasn't the only one handing out the insulting remarks. She started it off when she accused him of taking love for granted.

Even now, thinking about how she ha accused him of taking love for granted, his anger made a comeback.

*Really? Did she ever stop to think your actions might be on the*

Louise cleared her throat again, prompting him to reveal Claire's confession that Hunter wasn't his son. And how this changed everything.

But now this didn't matter. It was too late, He was too late.

Sophie was gone.

"I just want her back." Despair written all over his face, he shrugged, leaning back in his chair.

She waited, not saying a word.

And suddenly, it was if a lightbulb went off in his brain.

*My God... the solution is so obvious.*

She watched his expression shift from utter despair to a sudden flash of hope before she opened her laptop.

She smiled. "So, it looks like you'll be taking a trip. I hope your passport is up to date?"

At his nod, her fingers began moving swiftly across the keyboard "Good. Let's check out what flights are available. I'm thinking the sooner we get something set up, the better.

# CHAPTER 27

*The hardest thing to do,*
*is watch the one you love,*
*love someone else.*
*~ Anonymous*

Sophie turned the key, locking the door to *Sophie's*. Then she flipped the sign from Open to Closed.

She was alone in the little shop. Emma, her assistant, had taken the afternoon off. She deserved a rest after manning the store twenty-four-seven while Sophie was gone.

Since then, business had almost been almost non-existent.

But now, watching as everyone scurried past, their collars turned up and their heads down against the driving rain, Sophie wasn't surprised. This was the kind of day to stay home. Maybe even curl up in a comfortable chair with a good book and a cup of hot chocolate. Or better yet, a glass of wine.

*This won't be happening for you if don't finish adding up today's receipts so you can call it a day.*

With a resigned sigh, she went over to sit by the counter, the receipts in hand. It was after she added them up for a third time, each time coming up with a different amount, she gave a frustrated sigh, pushing everything across the counter and away from her.

She couldn't do this. It didn't matter.

*Nothing really mattered anymore. Not without Chester.*

She dropped her head down on her arms.

*How long are you going to feel this miserable? And how is it possible you miss him this much?*

Because she did… so much. She missed everything about him. The sound of his voice, his smile and so, *so* much more.

She wanted to see him. If only to be able to stand next to him so she could slip her hand in his. Or feel him press a kiss in her hair like he always did.

Throughout the day, every time the bell chimed, a sign someone had opened the door to the boutique, her heart beat quickening, she had glanced over to see if it was Chester. And when it wasn't, she was left feeling even more disappointed.

She didn't want to think about how many times she had gone over what happened the last time they talked. How she'd give anything to go back and re-live that time all over again. She'd take back all the terrible things she said, and everything would go back to the way it was.

*Time…*

She only needed time.


The tapping noise was barely discernible over the sound of the heavy rain. When it sounded again, louder and more urgent, Sophie looked over to see someone was standing outside the door of the boutique, waving to her.

It was Julian.

She opened the door to be wrapped in his hug. "*Ma chérie*! I've missed you. Have you missed me?"

And this, for some reason, made her want to cry.

Peering into her face and seeing the tears pooling in her eyes he, of course, thought this was because she was so happy to see him.

He pulled her closer. "Ah… so, you did miss me, no? What they say is true then. Absence really does make the heart grow fonder."

He kissed her firmly on the lips. "This is good. This is really good. Because right this very minute, I have a proposition for you. We are going to go up to your flat, where you will pack a bag. Then you will accompany me to my aunt and uncle's house in the country for the impromptu gathering they've arranged to take place tomorrow. It is to celebrate my cousin's recent engagement."

She shook her head. "I can't… the boutique…"

"I already told Emma I was planning on taking you with me, so this is not a problem." He looked down at his watch. "Come, if we leave now, we'll be there in about an hour. Just in time for a late supper. It will be fun. I promise to have you back here by tomorrow night."

When he saw she was still hesitant, he gave her a knowing smile. "Ah… and you'll have no reason to worry, because I'll be on my best behavior. I promise we will be like friends, nothing more."

But she didn't want to go. She wanted to go up to her apartment, put on her pajamas and curl up in bed. Maybe even finish the last few chapters of the book she'd been reading. Anything to stop from thinking about what she'd left behind, what was no longer hers.

But Julian was gazing at her with such a hopeful expression on his face, she was finding it hard to refuse him.

And he did say it was a party. So, they'd be with a lot of people, giving her a chance to forget about everything she didn't want to think about.

So, she gave in. She nodded, this bringing another enthusiastic hug from Julian. After all, she really had no reason to refuse, did she?

No, she didn't. If she were to compare her life to a book, the last chapter certainly hadn't turned out as she expected. So maybe it was time to start a whole new chapter and hope for a better ending.

And what better time to start than right now?

*Remember when Chester asked if you believed in fairy tales? You said you did. But the happily ever after part? This had a lot to do with luck, you told him.*

She sighed. It looked like her luck had more than run out.

This wasn't at all what Chester thought Paris would be like.

Because, come on… could it be even more of a miserable Saturday morning?

His hands buried deep in his pockets and his collar pulled up against the freezing rain, he could only pray this wasn't an omen of what was to come.

*Cleveland is looking pretty good to you right now. You'd pick snow over this lousy rain any day.*

A woman hurried past him, her umbrella flinging a cold spray of water right into his face. He shivered, digging his hands even deeper into his pockets before he gazed up at the name above the door of the fashionable little shop.

*Sophie's*

Now that he was here, he couldn't believe how nervous he was. Afraid of what he'd find when he entered the boutique, he had been standing in the same place for about five minutes, rain and all.

He had no idea what had become of all the confidence and hope he'd carried with him through the long flight and up to this moment. It appeared to have left him, washed away by this depressing rain. Leaving him with an overwhelming feeling of self-doubt.

When yet another person bumped into him as they tried to skirt around him, he decided enough was enough. Before he could change his mind, he walked over and pulled open the door.

The tinkling bell announcing his entrance immediately caught the attention of the young woman behind the counter. She was talking on her phone.

She waved to him, flashing a big smile. "Une minute, s'il vous plaît." At his nod, she gave him another big smile before going back to her phone conversation.

He sighed, trying to ignore the curious glances of the other shoppers in the store. He was feeling way out of his element. What man wouldn't feel the same, standing in a boutique filled with women.

Women who, by the way, were all speaking in a language you couldn't understand.

*You wouldn't wish this on any man...*

Of course, he'd expected the challenge of dealing with a different language, but it was starting to get to him. Everywhere he went, he was surrounded by people he couldn't understand. Which, he learned, tends to make one suspicious.

Even now, glancing over at the woman on her phone, by the furtive glances she kept sending his way, punctuated by her soft giggles, he couldn't help but wonder if he might be the topic of her conversation.

But why was he even worrying about this? Because it looked like he might have a much bigger problem right now.

*Like, where was Sophie?*

Having already sent a searching glance around the room, he saw no sign of Sophie. Hopefully she was in the back? Or had gone out on an errand?

Evidently, showing up without any kind of warning wasn't one of his better decisions.

And now? Well, let's just say he was beginning to have a really bad feeling about the way things were going. Yes, unfortunately, he had envisioned this moment so differently.

His version had Sophie glancing up, a look of pure joy coming over her face when she saw him walk through the door. This would send her running right into his arms. After they shared a long and passionate kiss, she would tell him since they'd parted, she had realized no problem was too big for them to overcome. And she didn't, couldn't, or wouldn't ever want to live without him.

*Ah yes, the perfect ending. Like a movie. Or those fairy tales the two of you talked about. As Sophie had put it, you're both hoping to get lucky.*

The woman had finished her conversation and now came from behind the counter and over to him, a questioning smile on her face.

He cleared his throat. "I, *umm...* Sophie?"

She proceeded to let out a long string of words.

All of which were in French. "Sophie? Ell n'est pas là. Elle est allée au pays avec Julian pour le weekend. Pour une fête de famille."

Unfortunately, the only words he recognized were Sophie, Julian and weekend. Three words, when put together, could only mean trouble.

At least, this is the way he saw it.

Holding up his hands, he smiled. "*Whoa...* hold on. I'm sorry, I don't understand. Unfortunately, my French is very limited."

She nodded before she answered, this time in perfect English. "Sophie is not here. She went to the country with Julian for the weekend. For a family celebration."

Chester could only stare at her.

You know the phrase... you felt like you were hit by a ton of bricks?

Well, this was exactly how he felt.

He swallowed.

To then slowly repeat what she said, if only to make sure he understood. "She went to the country. With Julian. And this would be for the weekend."

She answered just as slowly. "Yes, Julian is her boyfriend. As I believe you Americans would say, they're very serious." This was followed by her long, dramatic sigh. "She is so lucky. I can only hope someday I will have a man love me as much as Julian loves Sophie. He idolizes the ground she walks on. And since he's such a successful artist, she'll never want for anything."

He'd started to back away from her, a voice in his head telling him he needed to leave... fast. Before he did something stupid. Like ask her if she knew where in the country Sophie and Julian had gone so he could go charging out there like a crazy man and confront the both of them.

Or at least get the chance to witness the two of them together. Then he'd be able to see with his own eyes, Sophie was no longer his.

It was when he reached the door, his hand on the doorknob, she called out to him. "Wait. Do you have a message for Sophie? At least tell me your name so I can let her know you stopped by."

He shook his head, attempting a smile. "No, no message. It's not important." He didn't recognize the voice coming out of him. He sounded like an old man. A weary and defeated old man. This had his next words coming out almost in a whisper. "As it now appears, neither am I."

Opening the door, he slipped outside.

He was beyond noticing it was now raining even harder.


For Chester, the rest of his trip was a blur.

Later, when he thought about it, he had to believe, if travel Gods existed, they had blessed him with their presence. With the state he was in, there was no way he would've made it home on his own.

Somehow, he'd been able to book a return flight within only a few hours. Now granted, there was a layover in Seattle, of all places, but he didn't care. He just wanted out of Paris.

In fact, he didn't want to step foot in any part of the city ever again.

*The city of love? Yeah, you'd beg to differ with this.*

On the plane, his dejected air and disheveled state helped discourage interaction from any of the other passengers. And for this, he was grateful. Having to converse with anyone was something he knew he'd be incapable of during this time.

Though he wished he'd reassured the woman, who kept sending him worried looks from across the aisle, he was harmless.

*The only person you're a threat to these days is yourself.*

He had plenty of time to think during the long trip, a series of delays making it even longer. This was when he'd made the decision he was going to leave earlier than usual for spring training, maybe even in the next day or two.

Because there was really no reason to stay in Cleveland, was there? Why not go where he could soak up some sunshine and try to forget.

Leaning back in his seat, he'd closed his eyes, a frustrated sigh coming from him. He was still finding it hard to believe, after all they shared, it had come down to this.

He should've heeded his own advice, relationships weren't for him. And, if there was anything to be learned from the past few days, this was there was no way in hell he could go through something like this again.

*Yep, you're done for good. And you mean it this time.*

So, as you can imagine, it was a different Chester who walked off the plane at the Cleveland airport.

A Chester who no longer believed.

A Chester who decided he was now going to simplify his life.

From now on, he was only going to concentrate on playing ball. After all, baseball had always been good to him.

It hadn't let him down yet.


When Sophie opened the boutique on Sunday, there was a note on the counter from Emma.


Sophie,

You had a visitor come into the boutique yesterday looking for you. I tried to get him to leave his name, but he refused. He said it wasn't important.

I can't wait to hear all about your trip with Julian when I come in on Tuesday.

Thank you for giving me today and Monday off.

Until Tuesday,

Emma


Sophie read the note again, a puzzled expression on her face. She had no idea who this visitor could be. For a very, *very* brief moment she wondered, could it have been Chester?

But what was she thinking? This was impossible. He'd never travel all the way to Paris, to then leave without talking to her.

She stared down at the note.

*Would he?*

No, she was being silly. Whoever this visitor was, he'd said it wasn't important. It was probably a friend or husband of a customer of the boutique, wanting to buy a gift or merely looking for advice. It could be anyone.

*But as much as you might hope, it probably wasn't Chester.*

With a resigned shrug, she tossed the piece of paper in the trash can before she walked into the back room. Boxes of merchandize, delivered while she was gone, had almost completely taken over the space. This meant she had a lot of work to do. But she was okay with this.

She had come to the conclusion keeping busy was the answer. The weekend she'd spent with Julian had been fun. And as promised, he had treated her only as a good friend.

So, maybe things could change. She'd change. To eventually find she could love Julian as much as he seemed to love her.

They had plans for a late dinner on Tuesday after she closed the boutique. This is when she planned to tell him what she had decided. But for this to happen, she was going to need more time.

She stared down at the unopened box in front of her, slowly shaking her head.

*If you were actually thinking, even daring to hope, Chester had come all the way to Paris just to see you, you're certainly not ready to jump into a new relationship.*

Julian wasn't going to be happy. Because it was obvious she was going to need a whole lot of time.

More than he'd want to give her.

# CHAPTER 28

The haunting country melody filled Chester's car.

*I can't win, I can't rule.*
*I will never win this game without you...*

His gaze veering from the road, he glanced over at the audio screen on the dashboard.

This turned out to be a bad move. Sailing right past the entrance to the parking lot of the training complex, he slammed on the brakes. Bringing the car to a stop on the side of the road, he stared over at the dashboard. *My God, this song could have been written for you.*

*I can't rest, I can't fight,*
*what I need is you...*

Mumbling under his breath, he swung the car around, still listening.

*I can't take one more hopeless night*
*without you, not without you...*

He turned into the lot and pulled into a parking space. After he put the car in park, he rested his head against the headrest. His eyes closed, he continued to listen.

*I can't look, I'm so blind,*
*I lost my heart, I think I've lost my mind...*

He reached over and hit the button, silence instantly filling the car. He groaned, running his hand over his chin.

*What the hell are you doing? This isn't you, listening to songs about unrequited love. Isn't it bad enough you're already living one of your own?*

But, *damn*... if he needed a theme song, this one would fit the bill. Especially the lost my mind bit. He could definitely identify with that line.

He jerked his head up. Giving a swift glance around the parking lot, he was relieved to see no one was around to witness his dramatic display.

Most of the time, when he drove into this parking lot, he was flying, not a care in the world. After coming to a screeching halt, he'd jump out of the car, filled with enthusiasm and ready to reconnect with the guys on the team. After all, it was the start of a new season and all things were possible.

And this car of his? Come on, it was made for speed and a grand entrance was expected.

But things were different now.

The car didn't matter.

That it was a new season wasn't bringing the excitement it usually did.

And he really didn't want the company of the other guys. In fact, the fewer people he had to talk to, the better.

*You just don't care. Nope, you don't give a damn about anything.*

A car pulled up beside him. A mumbled curse coming from him, he remained as he was, hoping whoever it was, they wouldn't notice him.

But no such luck.

At the knock on the passenger window, he glanced over to see Alex motioning for him to unlock the door.

After he slipped into the passenger seat, Alex remained silent for a few moments. Then he cleared his throat. "It's good to see you. We've been wondering where you've been."

When Chester merely grunted, Alex tried to think of what to say next. Finally, he spoke, his voice overly cheerful. "So, here we are, the start of a new season before us. Exciting, isn't it?"

The look Chester gave him spoke volumes. This prompted Alex to go a completely different route.

He chuckled, slowly shaking his head. "Women are hard to figure out, aren't they? Love is pretty much the same. And when you put the two together? *Whoa...* all at once it gets really complicated."

When he saw this brought a slight nod from Chester, he plowed on. "You go along thinking, no problem, you can live without either of them. Then... BAM! You're suddenly thrown into this life you have no idea of how to deal with. You do stupid things, words come out of your mouth you had no intention of using in your lifetime and your pride takes over at the most inopportune moments.

"But... if you sit back and face each new phase head on, falling in love with someone is the most exhilarating and wonderful feeling you'll ever experience. It makes everything in life worthwhile."

He glanced over at Chester to see he was staring at him. His mouth hanging open, he had a look of complete shock on his face.

This brought on his embarrassed laugh. "*Umm...* I guess I got a little carried away, huh? And believe it or not, I'm not done yet. I guess what I'm trying to say, don't give up on Sophie just yet."

He sighed. "You gotta give her a little time to get over this. From what you've told me, the two of you have been handed some pretty tough challenges. Which means you have your work cut out for you."

He shot him a stern look. "And when I say you, I mean the both of you. It's got to be a joint effort."

Chester ran his hand through his hair, his voice resigned. "I went to Paris."

At Alex's look of surprise, he nodded. "Yeah... I wanted to let her know Claire lied about Hunter. I also wanted to tell her, whatever she wants, I'd do it. Because I don't want to lose her."

He slowly ran his hand over the steering wheel. He was stalling, reluctant to say out loud what he found so hard to believe. "But, as it turned out, I didn't even get to see her. When I finally got there, she was gone."

He nodded at the questioning look Alex gave him. "Yeah, it seems she went to the country for the weekend. With this Julian guy. Who, according to Sophie's assistant, idolizes the ground she walks on. Evidently, he's a catch. A successful artist and every woman's dream guy." He shrugged. "So, since that made it pretty clear she's already moved on, I turned around and left."

He looked over at Alex, a pained expression on his face. "It didn't take her much time, did it? Something I'm having a hard time trying to understand."

"No. ..." Alex vigorously shook his head. "You can't go by what this assistant said. You need to talk to Sophie in person. And seriously? Why the hell didn't you ask me to go with you? Because it sounds like you left your brain behind and could've used some help."

Chester took his keys out of the ignition and pushed his door open. He didn't want to talk about this anymore. It wasn't doing a damn bit of good.

His response to Alex came out in a growl. "Thanks for your advice, but I think I'm done. I'm going to stick with baseball. It's the only thing I can count on anymore."


An hour later, while manning first base, Chester watched as one of the new guys came up to bat. His name was Greg.

The thought crossing his mind this guy could put some distance on the ball if he got the right pitch, he adjusted his stance.

The pitcher threw a fast ball and with one swing of his bat, Greg made the connection, sending the ball shooting through the air like a rocket. Unfortunately, it sailed right at Chester.

Slamming into the side of his face, the pain was excruciating.

And then everything went dark.


Chester was pretty sure he was in a hospital. Or a clinic of some kind. The air had that antiseptic smell, the type of smell you don't want to wake up to with a headache. A headache you'd swear was the absolute worst you'd ever experienced in your life.

He was floating in a pool of darkness. He'd tried to open his eyes, only to shut them almost immediately against the bright lights they seemed to have positioned to shine directly into his eyes.

There was also all this crazy stuff going on in his head. If he moved, even a fraction of an inch, it was as if fireworks exploded in his mind. Then the shooting pain that followed? *Damn...* the excruciating pain seemed to reach out to every part of him.

He had already decided he'd wait a little while longer before telling whoever was in charge he was ready to go home.

It turned out he didn't have to worry about this.

The medication they gave him finally kicked in and he was out like a light.

# CHAPTER 29

*When I first met you, I was afraid to kiss you.*
*When I first kissed you, I was afraid to love you.*
*But now that I love you, I'm so afraid I'm going to lose you.*
*~ Anonymous*

Sophie was waiting for Julian.

According to his text, he was going to be about twenty minutes late.

The boutique now closed for the day, she was absentmindedly wandering around the sales floor, stopping here and there to make sure everything was where it was supposed to be. After she adjusted the hangers on one of the display racks, she moved on to rearrange the jewelry laid out on a scarf draped over one end of the sales counter.

She checked her phone. Only ten minutes had passed since Julian's text. Running her hand through her hair, she took a deep breath.

She was nervous.

After thinking about this almost constantly over the past few days, she knew she couldn't put it off any longer. It was time to tell Julian what she should've told him as soon as she'd arrived back in Paris.

And this was, even though she'd tried, and she'd tried so very hard, she'd never be able to return a love like he so passionately declared for her.

It didn't matter how much time she had or what Julian did to convince her otherwise, her feelings for Chester were not going to go away. He would always be the one who would have a place in her heart. Somehow, he had managed to find his way in there for good, and she knew she'd never be able to let him go.

She was leaning against the counter, deep in thought, when Julian finally arrived. When she opened the door, he immediately took her into his arms, his lips moving in her hair.

"Ah, *So-pheee*... how good it is to see you after such a day. I hope you are hungry, because I am starving. We've been so busy at the gallery, I didn't even have time to eat a single thing all day. I've been existing on coffee... too much coffee, I fear."

She gently pulled away from him to study his face, a face she'd come to grow very fond of over the past few months. Hesitantly, she began to speak. "Julian..."

But his attention was no longer on her, His gaze going to the counter, he reached over to pick up her phone. "I think someone just left you a message. Maybe you should check it out."

She sighed. Everyone who knew Julian knew his obsession with his phone. For him to miss a text or call was unthinkable. Knowing he wouldn't rest until she checked it out, she took the phone from him to see she had a text message. It was from Lisa.

> Sophie, you need to call me. It's important.
> Something has happened.

Her smile faded, her first thought something happened to someone in her family. But then she realized Lisa wouldn't be the one to call her about this.

This was when a deep fear slowly began to spread through her.

*Chester... it's about Chester.*

Something had happened to him.

Julian saw her worried expression and, taking the phone from her, he read the message. He gave her a reassuring smile. "I'm sure it's nothing bad. But you should probably call her to make sure."

He took her arm, and leading her over to sit in the chair by the dressing room, he handed her the phone. "Now, go ahead, make the call."

Lisa answered on the second ring, starting right in with the reason for her text. "Sophie, I'm so glad you got back to me so quickly. Abby and I both thought you'd want to know what happened. There's been an accident."

After a short pause, she continued. "It's Chester. He's been hurt pretty bad."

For Sophie, everything came to a crashing halt, except for her heart, thundering in her chest. She closed her eyes, her voice barely audible. "How? What happened?"

"He was hit by a ball during a practice game. The ball was a direct hit to Chester's face, right below his left eye, knocking him unconscious. They rushed him to the hospital, but as far as we know, he's still out. Alex promised to call as soon as he had any news, but we've heard nothing yet."

There was another pause, this one longer. "We're all very worried."

Sophie was having a hard time breathing, her whole body beginning to shake. The phone clutched to her ear, she kept shaking her head.

*No, no, no... this didn't happen. Not to him. Baseball isn't supposed to be a dangerous sport. Not like football .. or hockey. What if...*

She swallowed, her voice barely audible. "This is all my fault. It's because of me this happened to him. I never—"

Lisa interrupted her. "*Oh Sophie, no...* It's not your fault. It just happened. It was an accident. Chester would be so upset if he heard you say this. He would never want you to blame yourself. Why, you weren't even here."

At this, Sophie began to cry. "That's what I mean. I'm not there and I should be. So, I can tell him I didn't mean all the awful things I said."

She took a deep breath, dragging her hand over her face to wipe away the tears. "I'm sorry... I'm so sorry. Pease send me all the information, what hospital he's in. And call me as soon as you hear anything. Promise me you'll do this."

"Of course, I will. And Sophie, know he's not alone. Alex, Kevin and Abby are at the hospital. And everybody—the guys on the team, the staff—they've all been coming and going to check on him. So, he has a lot of people pulling for him. But he could still use lots of prayers, as many as he can get. So, pray."

Feeling as though her heart was lodged in her throat, Sophie had to take in a big gulp of air before she could answer. "I will... oh, I will. And thank you for calling me." She swiped at her tears again, unsuccessfully trying to steady her voice. "Again, please send me the information as soon as you can."

"I'll text it to you as soon as we end the call. We all miss you, Sophie. Take care."

"You, too... take care. And I miss you, too. I miss everyone. So, so much..."

She was left staring down at the blank screen, willing it to ring again with a call from Lisa that Chester would be okay.

But this didn't happen.

Julian cleared his throat. "What do you want to do?"

She gazed up at him, the tears beginning to flow again, her voice filled with anguish. "*Oh God,* Julian... this is all my fault. I don't know what I'll do if something happens to him. The last time we were together, we shared such angry words. And now I'm so far away."

Julian reached over to cup her chin in his hand, forcing her to look at him. "Ah, chérie... you need to go to him. I can see how much you love him. And I have to say, even with the state he is in, I envy him. He is a lucky man to have your love."

A choked sob escaped her lips. Then she was in his arms, clinging to him, desperate for some kind of reassurance. While, his eyes closed, he held her as she cried.

She finally pulled away from him, swiping at her tears with shaking fingers. "I'm so sorry. I really wanted to like you, but for me, it will always be Chester. I truly believe I gave him my heart the very first moment we met. And he still has it, he always will."

She reached up to caress his cheek. "And you ? *Oh, Julian*, you deserve so much more than I could ever give you, someone who loves you for the amazing man you are."

His smile was faint. *"Ah, So-pheee...* how I'd hoped it would be you. But you're right. I want a love like the love you have for this Chester of yours." His expression became serious, almost threatening. "He better return your love. And if he ever hurts you in any way, you come right to me. I will make him rue the day."

"I think..." She gazed up at him, shaking her head, "Well, I'm pretty sure I'm already guilty of doing that to him."

A faint smile on his face, he nodded. "You do keep a man guessing. I can certainly attest to that."

He glanced over at her phone. "I believe your friend has sent you the information. So, while I work my magic to get you the next available flight to wherever you need to go, you have to pack. Hopefully we'll have time to grab something to eat before we need to be at the airport. Because even with all this going on, I'm still famished. And you need to eat, too. We can't be sending you off on an empty stomach."

He looked down at her phone, then at her. "We also need to charge your phone. It's almost out of power."

As she began to thank him, he waved her away. "No, there's no need to thank me. This is what friends do. So, go and pack."

After she left, he called out to her. "And *So-pheee?* Make sure you pack those lucky shoes of yours." He winked. "You know which ones I'm referring to... those *oooh-la-la* red heels of yours."

She was already gone, running up the stairs to her flat, her mind on what she needed to pack.

In what felt like many, many hours later, Sophie was trying to sleep. But for some reason, someone was shaking her and they weren't being very nice about it.

This prompted her to burrow even further into the corner of the back seat of the taxi. She tucked her face under her arm, hoping this would persuade whoever it was to go away and leave her alone.

But this didn't happen. Instead, the shaking became more insistent, the voice even more urgent.

"Miss, come on. You've gotta wake up. We're here. This is where you wanted to go, right? Phoenix General Hospital?"

Sophie slowly opened her eyes to see a man was peering down at her, a very concerned expression on his face. For a moment, she was confused.

Then it all started to come back to her. He was the taxi driver who'd picked her up at the airport. The last thing she remembered was resting her head back on the seat and closing her eyes. She'd meant to do this for only a few minutes, but apparently, she slept through the entire drive.

The taxi driver was trying to get her attention again. "Hey, are you all right? Do you need me to walk you to the door?"

She could tell by the tone of his voice this was the absolute last thing he wanted to do. She struggled to sit up, giving a big yawn as she reached up to push the hair out of her face.

Now that she could actually see him, he looked pretty annoyed.

*Oh my God, he's probably wondering if you're going to pay him.*

Grabbing her purse and digging through it, she searched for her credit card. This was when she finally found her phone. Unable to find it earlier, she thought she'd left it behind when she went through security at the airport. She pulled it out to see there was no charge left.

*But, it's okay... you're here. That's all that matters.*

The taxi driver cleared his throat, a reminder of why she was looking through her purse in the first place. She finally found her credit card and held it out to him.

He shook his head. "No, you already paid, remember? And now I really need to get going. I got another call. So, if you don't mind...

Still in a fog, she nodded and half slid, half stumbled out of the taxi. When she finally turned around to thank him, he had already driven away.

Shivering in the cool night air, she glanced down at her suitcase. Almost too exhausted to pick it up, she wanted to sit right down on the pavement and cry.

*You need to get a hold of yourself. You've come too far to break down now.*

She straightened her shoulders, and dragging her bag behind her, she entered the hospital. The woman on duty at the reception desk looked up from her magazine, a resigned expression on her face. "Yes? Can I help you?"

Sophie responded with a big smile. "Hi, I'm here to see Chester Mazzori. May I please have his room number?"

One eyebrow raised, the woman crossed her arms over her chest. "*Oh... my... God...* Are you kidding me? Another one? Do you women have any pride? Just so you know, you're about the fifth woman who has come waltzing in here today to see him." She shook her head again. "Let me guess, you're his sister? Cousin? About-to-be-fiancée? A wanna-be-girlfriend? Which one is it? Because, let me assure you, I've heard it all."

Her gaze dropping to Sophie's stomach, she laughed. "Well. at least you're not pregnant like the last woman that was here. I gotta give her credit, she put on quite a show."

Picking up her phone, she proceeded to ignore that Sophie was even there.

Sophie slowly shook her head. "I guess I'm really just a friend. I heard what happened to him and I just arrived here from Paris."

She closed her eyes. "It was a long trip, an awful flight. And I've hardly slept for I don't know how long. I'm exhausted."

The woman didn't seem to be impressed. Nor did she seem to care.

Now on the verge of tears, Sophie wearily ran her hand through her hair. "*Please...* I need to see him. If only for a minute, to make sure he's all right. Then I'll go away. Honest."

Peering at her more closely, the woman gave an overly dramatic sigh as she picked up her phone. "Okay, okay. Let me see what I can do. Just don't start crying on me."

Relieved, Sophie watched her talking on her phone as she paced back and forth. After plunking the phone down on the counter, she looked over at Sophie. She pointed to the nearest chair. "Sit down right there and don't move."

Sophie did as she was told.

Alex was sitting next to the bed in room 112, the hospital room assigned to Chester. In the ten minutes since he'd arrived, Chester had only opened his eyes once.

He was a sorry sight. Motionless and his eyes closed, he had the start of what was going to be a colossal black eye.

Alex cleared his throat. But even after doing this, he still couldn't hide the trace of emotion coming through in his voice. "Man, you scared the hell out of all of us. I've never seen anyone go down so fast and stay so still. Then, to top it off, Greg was so shaken up, he almost started hyperventilating. I thought he was going to have a heart attack. Not the best way for a rookie to start out their first spring training in the major leagues, knocking out one of the big stars on the team."

His eyes still closed, Chester's only response was a faint grunt.

*Yeah, you're a big star all right. If you're so good, why didn't you get out of the way of the ball? Evidently you weren't paying attention?*

He appreciated the fact Alex had come to stay with him, but at the same time, he wanted to be left alone. His head was throbbing and as much as he hated to even admit this, he was feeling very sorry for himself.

*Life doesn't seem to be on your side right now, does it? You thought base-ball was your friend. But now, it looks like even that is out to get you.*

Now that Chester was finally conscious and somewhat responsive, Alex thought about leaving. But then he decided he would stay a little longer.

Just to be sure.

The whole episode had scared him to death.

He could only watch in horror as the ball sailed off the rookie's bat like a rocket, smashing into Chester's face before he had the chance to react. When he hit the ground so fast, remaining so deathly still, everyone on the field had rushed over to him in a panic.

It was something he hoped to never again witness in his lifetime.

Both he and Kevin had followed the ambulance to the hospital, where they paced away the time as they waited for news. Joined by an almost continuous stream of concerned players and staff who came to lend their support, there was nothing they could do but wait.

Only an hour ago, they were finally given the news that Chester had regained consciousness and was responding positively to their tests. To be on the safe side, he would remain in the hospital overnight. But once he was transferred to a room, they would be allowed to see him.

As the last couple of weeks had been such a roller coaster of emotions for Chester, they didn't think it would be right to leave him alone. So, while Kevin stayed to keep him company, Alex went home to have dinner with Lisa and Chloe.

Now back in the hospital, he glanced over at Chester, who was still holding the card Chloe had made for him. He was glad he'd be able to report back to her this had brought a smile to Chester's face. Even if only for a few seconds.

He sent Lisa a text he didn't know when he'd be home. Then, settling more comfortably in his chair, he checked his phone for messages, responded to those asking about Chester.

After he slipped the phone back in his pocket, he glanced over at him. There was no change, his eyes still closed.

Tapping his fingers on the arm of the chair, he blew out a long breath. He couldn't understand why Lisa had been so adamant about calling Sophie. And why she seemed to think this was going to bring them back together.

He didn't know if he agreed with this. Not after Chester told him about this guy Sophie was hanging around with in Paris.

And after what happened? The last thing Chester needed, was to get his hopes up, only to be shot down again.

Because, come on… a guy can only take so much.

A nurse came into the room, and making her way over to Alex, she kept her voice low. "We have another woman in the reception area who's insisting she needs to see Mr. Mazzori. Do you think you can talk to her? She seems quite desperate."

He groaned.

The last thing he wanted was to deal with a hysterical female who had a crush on Chester.

He let out a long sigh and slowly rising from his chair, he glanced over at Chester. His eyes slightly open, he was observing this.

He smiled at him, adopting a cheerful tone of voice. "Well, it appears you're pretty popular. I've just been informed another adoring fan is trying to get in here to see you. So, it looks like it's my job to turn her down easy."

He shrugged. "Unless you want me to bring her in?"

Chester closed his eyes, an expression of pain flashing across his face. "You know there's only one woman I want."

Alex grimaced, running his hand through his hair.

*Good job. Nothing like hitting a guy when he's already down. Why the hell don't you think before you open your mouth?*

He sent Chester a salute. "Okay, got it. No woman for you, no matter how sexy and beautiful she is. I'll be back, so don't go anywhere."

He was whistling as he walked out of the room.

After Alex left, Chester cautiously moved his head, wincing at the pain.

He was trying not to dwell on how awful he felt, but with the condition he was in, it was pretty hard to do anything but.

He appreciated the fact Kevin and Chester had stayed. He did, he really did. And he knew how hard they were trying to cheer him up. But honestly? This was almost making him feel worse.

*Like you're a loser. A big, pathetic loser.*

Let's face it, even before this happened, he had already begun to question the path his life was taking. Lately, it was as though everything had begun to spiral out of control, completely falling apart as he knew it.

He'd been reduced to hanging out alone in his condo, mindlessly staring at the TV until he dozed off. He'd also started eating cereal for almost every meal, if only because it was easy and required no real preparation of any kind.

At least he hadn't resorted to ordering random stuff advertised on the infomercials or home shopping channels. But A few times he'd come pretty damn close.

And that damn song… he couldn't get it out of his head, no matter how hard he tried. Without you, without you… enough already. It was driving him crazy.

But more than anything, he was haunted by memories of Sophie.

He missed her chatter… about anything and everything.

He missed how she always showed such a sincere interest in everything he did, making him believe he could climb the tallest mountains if he so desired.

He missed how she would become so flustered when he caught her looking at him, his only recourse to pull her into his arms and kiss her until they were both completely kissed out.

*Hmm... do you think that's even possible? I don't think so.*

And even though he knew this was silly, he missed how she always wanted to share her dessert with him.

There were just so many damn things he missed.

But it was when he turned out the lights at night, her absence hit him the hardest.

The memory of her soft curves against him, her hair spread out in a golden cloud over the pillow. The breathy sound of his name on her lips. Or the gentle touch of her hands, roaming over him, caressing him. Right before she tangled her fingers in his hair, pulling his face to hers for a kiss.

*And, yes... then there were her kisses.*

How they'd come at him, fast and furious when they made love, her eagerness sending a thrill through him he couldn't even begin to describe.

He missed every single one of these things.

*He missed her.*

Without thinking, he turned his head, giving a frustrated sigh. He was immediately hit by another wave of dizziness.

He closed his eyes.

He needed to get some sleep. And he needed to get out of this damn hospital. Then he could go home and wallow in this misery his life had become.

*Alone.*

Taking long, deep breaths, he finally dozed off.


Still whistling, but a little apprehensive about this woman he was about to meet, Alex strolled into the hospital's main reception area.

Because of the lateness of the hour, there was only one person in the visitor's section. A petite woman with blonde hair, she was seated in a chair near the sign-in desk, her head bowed.

The woman manning the desk glanced over at him, acknowledging his presence. This is when the blonde lifted her head and looked right at him.

He came to a dead stop.

"Sophie, what are you doing here?"

With a small cry, she flew across the room and right into his arms.

"*Hey, hey, hey... don't worry, everything is going to be okay.*" Murmuring these words of comfort, Alex kept patting Sophie on the back.

She abruptly stepped back, her eyes desperately searching his face.

Before he could say a single word, she began talking, non-stop, Sophie style. "I'm sorry. So, so sorry. I didn't mean to come at you like I did. I think I'm a little out of it. Right after Lisa called to tell me what happened, I booked the next flight here. And it seems ever since then, I've been living a nightmare."

Her hands shaking, she ran them through her hair. "The turbulence was horrible almost the entire flight, and the man seated next to me began some kind of chanting as soon as the plane left the ground. He kept this up until the plane landed. I seriously thought I was going to lose my mind."

She ran her hands through her hair again. "I must look like a mess. I feel like I haven't slept for days and I haven't had anything to eat for I don't know how long."

Alex started to say something, but she cut him off. "Then I thought I lost my phone somewhere in the airport, which meant I had no way of knowing if Lisa had tried to call or message me about Chester."

She spun around, running over to pick up her purse. Digging through it, she held up her phone. "But, look... I found it."

She frowned down at the phone. "But it has no power."

After she stared at the phone for a few seconds, she gazed back up at Alex. "But I'm here. And this is all that matters, right?"

Her eyes again searching his, desperate for reassurance, no matter how little, her voice was choked. "I had to come. If only to make sure he's really okay. I've been so afraid, I..." The beginning of a sob rising in her throat, she brought her fist to her mouth.

He took her arm and, after leading her over to the seating area, he smiled down at her. "Hey, it's going to be okay. The doctors told us he's going to be fine. It was touch and go for a while, but for now, everything has checked out good. They plan on keeping him here tonight so they can keep an eye on him, but there's a good chance he may be discharged as soon as tomorrow."

For a few moments, she only stared at him. Then, wrapping her arms around herself, she took a deep gulping breath, her words barely audible. "I don't know what I would've done if..."

And before he even knew what was happening, she closed her eyes and began to sway.

She had passed out.

With Alex catching her just before she hit the floor.

Sophie opened her eyes to find she was now stretched out on a sofa in the reception area, Alex's anxious face hovering above her.

She watched relief flood his face before he smiled. "Welcome back."

When she only gazed back at him, a dazed expression on her face, he reached down to brush the hair out of her face. "You fainted. I think everything finally caught up with you. So, I asked for someone to bring you something to eat and a cup of coffee. But until it gets here, I want you to stay right where you are. *Thank God* you passed out here instead of in the parking lot, or who knows where."

He ran his hand through his hair before he gave her another smile.

*"Geeesh…* first Chez and now you, both passing out on the same day. If this isn't enough proof, the two of you are made for each other, I don't know what is."

Closing her eyes, she whispered. "I'm sorry."

He chuckled. "Don't be. If anything, I believe you coming here is the absolute best medicine for him right now."

Then he grew serious. "Promise me you won't run off on him again. I don't think he can handle much more right now." He shook his head. "The guy is so in love with you, he doesn't know whether he's coming or going anymore."

He watched a faint smile come to her face. While at the same time, shaking her head, her eyes began to fill. "I promise, I never…" Her words trailed into a long, shaky breath.

Noting her impending tears, he grew nervous, searching the room. Where was the person with the food?

He wasn't good at dealing with women when they cried. Young or old, it didn't matter. Their tears always had him handing out promises he normally wouldn't even think of making.

Relieved to see a woman coming in their direction carrying a tray, he took Sophie's arm to help her into a sitting position. "Here, let's have you sit, because it looks like your food is here."

After the woman left, he sat beside Sophie. "Now I want you to eat. Because it looks like you'll need to be the strong one. At least for now."

He gave her an encouraging smile. "So, eat up."


Alex kept up a casual commentary about anything he could think of as he waited for Sophie to finish her sandwich.

He was worried about her.

She looked so frail. And, with the dark circles under her eyes, it was obvious she was beyond exhausted, just barely hanging on.

It was only after she'd finished eating enough to satisfy him and had made a visit to the bathroom to, as she put it, make herself look halfway presentable, he showed her to Chester's room.

As they stood outside the door, she gave him an anxious glance. "Wish me luck."

He reached over to give her a hug. "*Ah, Sophie*... it's going to be okay. Like I said before, you're what he needs. And more importantly, what he wants."

He left, turning back to give her one more smile and a wave.


Sophie quietly made her way into the dimly lit room. His eyes closed, Chester appeared to be asleep. The left side of his face was swollen and bruised, already sporting all shades of purple.

When she moved closer, he stirred. She whispered his name. "Chester?"

Chester was dreaming.

*They were on a beach. It was sunset and everyone had left, leaving Sophie and him alone. On a blanket spread out over the sand, they were wrapped in each other's arms as they shared a bottle of wine. Talking about simple things, they'd watched as the sun slowly sank into the horizon. With darkness now upon them, the only light coming from the moon above, and the sound of the waves as their background music, he leaned over her and...*

He stirred restlessly. Was he still dreaming?

Because he was almost positive he could feel Sophie's presence, the scent of her perfume so familiar, so real.

But it was the sound of her voice, calling his name, that had him struggling to come awake. Granted, it was only a whisper, but it was enough to make him smile.

*Yes.*

He opened his eyes and, for a moment, he stared right at her.

*Are you hallucinating? You must be.*

He groaned, quickly shutting his eyes. "No, please… I can't do this."

Then it dawned on him.

He wasn't caught up in a dream after all. No, if anything, he was more awake than he'd ever been.

He opened his eyes again, everything in him praying what he saw was still there. He was just in time to see Sophie's face crumple as a deep sob escaped her. After a second sob, this even louder, she clasped her hand over her mouth and turned to leave.

Chester would later claim he didn't know how he managed this without passing out, but diving from the bed, he lurched across the room and pulled her into his arms. Her face pressed against him, she began sobbing uncontrollably. All the while telling him she was sorry… *so, so sorry.*

Over and over, she repeated this.

His mind still trying to process she was real, *damn* if he didn't feel lightheaded. And again, with no clue of how he gathered up the strength, let alone take her with him, he moved them both back to the bed. Where he fell onto it, dragging her with him.

After he managed to pull her into his arms, he settled her next to him, where she continued to cry. He tucked the blanket more securely around her, and running his fingers through her hair, he began whispering words to calm her.

Just as he was beginning to wonder if she was ever going to stop crying, she grew silent. Then she sighed, easing her grip on his hospital gown. This was followed by the sound of her slow, even breathing.

She had fallen asleep.

He pressed a kiss in her hair before he leaned his head back against the pillows. He couldn't stop smiling. Strange as this may seem, never in his life had he been happier than he was at this moment.

*And relieved…*

He was just so damned relieved.

He placed one more kiss to the top of her head before he gave a long, contented sigh. This was then he realized the song playing over and over in his head? It was gone. He couldn't remember the words for the life of him.

The smile still on his face, he closed his eyes.

He was out like a light.


"Mr. Mazzori. Mr. Mazorri, wake up. Can you hear me?"

This hissing whisper kept coming at him. Groggily opening his eyes, he saw there was a nurse standing by the bed. A huge frown on her face, when she realized she had his attention, she shook her finger at him.

"Mr. Mazzori, you ought to be ashamed of yourself. You are in a hospital because of a serious head injury. That you would even think of entertaining a woman in your room is out of the question. You need to take this more seriously. We certainly don't want any setbacks, do we?"

She pursed her lips together, shaking her head. "I'm here to give you the medication prescribed for you. If you sit up, it will be easier to take."

Squinting at her i.d. tag, he saw her name was Nora. Then he glanced down at Sophie. Her mouth slightly open, she was out completely.

*Entertaining women? Did Sophie look like she was in the midst of being entertained? If so, it certainly isn't much of a compliment to you or your ego.*

He gave her his best smile. "Nora, come on... you have to see nothing is going on here." He nodded at the pill and cup of water she was holding. "And I don't need those. All the medicine I need is right here in my arms."

He tilted his head, trying to leverage in as much charm as he could. "I wonder if you could do me a big favor. I want you to walk out of this room, close the door and forget we're even here. Put a do-not-disturb sign on the door, if you have one. Whatever... we just need to get some sleep. Then we'll be fine."

"*Hmm...*" Her arms crossed over her chest, she studied him for a few moments. He'd swear a flicker of a smile passed over her face before her mouth settled into a frown again.

"Okay. But, please be careful. Remember why you're here." She then cracked out an actual smile. "I'll see that you're not disturbed. But only if you promise to behave."

He put on his most serious expression and nodded. "You have my promise." He considered adding a wink, but he wasn't quite sure what she was thinking. Which meant the wink could very well backfire on him.

So instead, he sent her a smile as she made her way over to the door. Where she turned to send him one more warning glance before she closed it behind her.

Chester sighed with relief.

*Good grief, you'd hate to work for her. But maybe now everyone will leave you alone.*

Sophie stirred in his arms.

He glanced down to find her gazing up at him, a dazed look on her face.

He leaned in to place a gentle kiss to her forehead, a huskiness in his voice. "*Hey...* are you feeling a little better?"

At her nod, he hesitated, his eyes searching. "Angel, I'm finding it hard to believe you're here. At first, I thought you were part of a dream I was having."

He tenderly brushed the hair back from her face. "But now that I know you're real, I can't tell you how damn good it feels to have you in my arms again. *God*, I've missed you. I can't even begin to tell you how much."

At first, the only thing that registered with Sophie was that he called her angel. Then everything hit her all at once. She closed her eyes, her voice choked with tears. "I had to come. I was so scared. When Lisa called to tell me what happened, you were still unconscious. And when I thought I could lose you—" Knotting her fists in his hospital gown, she pulled him against her as she began to cry.

He rested his cheek to the top of her head. "*Shh... shh...* I'm okay. I'll be fine. Even more so, now you're here. So, please don't cry."

His hands gently stroking her back, they became lost in the feel of each other.


Sophie was the first to move. Still clutching his hospital gown, she lifted her face to his, her lips parted.

Unable to pass up this invitation she was offering, Chester shifted until he was leaning over her. He kissed her slowly, gently. Then he kissed her again, his lips hovering over hers, teasing her with the promise of more.

When she responded by tangling her hands in his hair to pull him even closer, he groaned, his voice a deep rumble in her ear. "Angel... I want to make love to you. *Here... Now...*"

After claiming her mouth in another kiss, almost stealing her breath away, the roughness of his voice traveled through her like fire. "I want this more than I've ever wanted anything." His voice dipped to a whisper. "I want to get lost in you."

Her voice was hushed. "Chester, we're in a hospital. In a hospital bed. We..."

Her words trailed off as his mouth traveled down her throat before skimming along the neckline of her sweater. Then his hands were sliding under the sweater to unhook her bra. In one quick move, he pulled both the bra and sweater up and over her head, tossing them both to the floor.

Her eyes wide, she gripped his shoulders. "Chester..."

"*Shh...*" She could feel the smile on his lips as he pressed a kiss to the pulse beating at the base of her neck. At the same time, he slipped his hand under the waistband of her leggings. After a quick downward tug and a brief struggle with the zipper of her one boot, he sent both the leggings and boots flying to the floor to join the rest of her clothing.

He was driving her insane.

His lips were so hot, leaving a trail of heat wherever they touched. While his hands roamed over her, everywhere, bringing her to arch up against him in her need to get closer. As close as she could get.

She was frantic to get closer.

*"Oh my God… Chester… I want, but I can't… you…"*

He gazed down at her. After he gave her another kiss, his voice came out in almost a growl. "We belong together, angel. The love we share has been a part of us since we first laid eyes on each other. You're mine. As I am yours. *I will always be yours."*

Somehow, she found a way back to her mind. And her voice. And miraculously, she was able to get them to work at the same time. It wasn't that she didn't want this. *My God,* she couldn't believe how much she wanted him right now. But she couldn't stop thinking about what could happen.

*Because, again? Who does something like this? In a hospital, of all places.*

It seemed so risky.

She pressed her hands against his chest, her words a frantic whisper. "What if someone finds us like this? What are they going to think?"

His hand, now resting on her hip, his answer was to pull her closer. His kisses becoming bolder, she reached down to tangle her hands in his hair.

*"Chester, please…"*

His hands stilled as he looked up at her. "Ah, yes… you're worried about someone walking in on us. Since I told the nurse we didn't want to be disturbed, I'm pretty sure we'll be fine. It's just you and me, angel. No one else."

He suddenly moved to frame her face in his hands, the look in his eyes raw with emotion. "Weren't you the one who said you wanted to be so in love with someone, it would take only one look and you would do anything for them? Knowing they felt the same? There would be no thinking, no hesitation, it would be spur of the moment, you said. Only then would you know it was right, it was the real thing."

The intensity of his gaze messing with her senses all the more, she could only nod.

A smile spread across his lips, his whisper like a vow. "We are those two people, angel. Everything I have, is yours. Everything I want, I want it with you. And all that I am, my heart, my body and my soul… they all belong to you. There is nothing, *nothing* more real than what we have together." His mouth coming down on hers, his kiss backed his words and anything else she might need to know.

And she was gone. Helpless. She could do nothing but give in to the passion taking them by a storm.

She forgot all about the fact they were in a hospital. Nor did it matter they were in a not-so-accommodating hospital bed.

And if someone walked in on them?

She could care less.

She reached up to undo the back of his hospital gown and, after pulling it down over his shoulders, she threw it over to join her clothing on the floor. Urged on by his whispers, she eagerly explored the body she had so recently learned to love. She became lost in the feel of him, something she'd feared would become only a memory.

He was right. This love had been with them from the very first. And like him… all that she was, her heart, her body and her soul…

*They all belonged to him.*


Since opening his eyes about a half hour ago, Chester had been content to watch Sophie as she slept in his arms.

He heard a loud click and, glancing over at the door, he watched as it began to open. When a nurse peeked cautiously into the room, he pulled Sophie closer, covering her more securely with the blanket.

Once she saw he was awake, the nurse made her way over to the bed, skirting around their clothes still scattered on the floor. After averting her eyes from the sleeping Sophie, she gave him a cautious smile.

"Mr. Mazzori, I'm Erin, the day nurse. I've come to see on how you're feeling, and to let you know the doctor usually makes his rounds about eight. I know it's only six-thirty now, but I thought you'd like a heads up."

She glanced over at Sophie, then at him. "Do you think it would be possible for me to do my morning check? Then I'll leave you alone."

He smiled, holding out his arm when she pulled out the blood pressure cuff. "Sure, here you go. And thanks for the heads up about the doctor. And though my black eye might not show this, I am feeling much better." He smiled down at Sophie. "I consider myself a lucky guy."

Concentrating on her task, it was only after she finished, she nodded. "Everything looks good. And yes, you're definitely very lucky."

She was walking away when she turned back to him. "I'll have someone bring breakfast for both of you in about forty-five minutes. Would you like me to close the door on my way out?"

He nodded. "And thanks for putting in the breakfast order." He grinned. "Suddenly, I'm starving."

She laughed. "I bet you are."

After she left, closing the door behind her, he chuckled. "You can come out now. She's gone."

Sophie gave a soft groan as she pushed the blanket aside and struggled to sit up against him. Hoping to bring some kind of order, to what she was sure was her disheveled appearance, she began combing her fingers through her hair.

She avoided his gaze. "I can't even imagine what she must be thinking. I should have slept in the chair. Or on one of the sofas in the waiting room."

He reached for her hands, pulling her up against him. "Leave it. You look beautiful. You look like a woman who has been thoroughly loved. And so very, *very* sexy."

Watching the blush spread across her cheeks, he leaned in to give her a kiss. "And in answer to what you said, once I accepted you were actually here, there's no way was I would've let you sleep anywhere but here with me." Stroking the hair back from her face, he smiled at her. "I've learned my lesson. I'm never going to let you walk away from me again."

She studied him. How was it, even in the early morning light, he could still be so handsome? His hair was all over the place, going off in every different direction. And his face was rough and in need of a shave. Then there was his black eye, giving him an almost devilish, come-hither look.

He was perfect.

*Just so, so Chester…*

She pulled her hand from his, tracing the bruised area of his face with her fingertips. "Does it hurt?"

Lulled by her soft whisper, he shook his head.

She slipped her hand back in his. "Every time I'm with you, I can't believe how lucky I am to have found you. You… I…" Here she stopped to shake her head, her gaze dropping to their hands.

Cupping her chin in his hand and lifting her face up to his, he wondered… was it possible to fall even more in love every time he looked into her eyes?

Because he did.

*Every single time.*

And… lucky?

His answer came out in a husky whisper. "No, this isn't about luck, angel. There's so much more. I don't think there's an explanation or reason for what we have, only that it's more real than anything we could've ever imagined."

He smiled. "Better than any fairy tale."

As he watched all the different emotions cross her face at what he'd said, he had to close his eyes. A surge of desire raced through him, almost blindsiding him.

*Damn… you want her again. What is it about her that brings on this overwhelming need to love her?*

Thinking about how only a few days ago, he'd foolishly thought he'd be fine without her, he almost laughed.

Obviously, he had been wrong.

*So wrong.*


Sophie wanted him to open his eyes.

*Then you can ask him to kiss you again.*

Because right now, more than anything, she needed all the proof she could get he was real, and she was even here with him. God only knows how many times in the past few days, he'd only been part of her imagination and in her dreams.

She leaned in closer, the breathy tone of her voice drawing him in. "Kiss me..."

At first, he didn't respond. Then he leaned in to meet her.

She sighed, her lashes fluttering shut. But there was no kiss. She slowly opened her eyes, to find his mouth was drawn up in a smile, his gaze one of such tenderness.

He cleared his throat. "If I kiss you, I'm going to want more, angel. I'm going to want it all... every single inch of you."

His smile growing, he pulled her against him.

"You can't get any more spur of the moment than this, can you?"

# CHAPTER 31

Sophie was a nervous wreck.

The steering wheel gripped tightly in both hands, she was staring straight ahead as she drove.

In order to convince the medical staff of the hospital, he was ready to be released, Chester had made all kinds of promises. And one of these promises was Sophie would drive him home.

This was before he told Sophie what kind of car he had. The fact it had some fancy Italian name to match its ridiculously expensive sticker price was more than she needed to know.

So, to say they were taking it slow would be an understatement.

After he turned his head to see the long line of cars trailing behind them, he felt he should say something. He glanced over at her and, clearing his throat, tried to hide the amusement in his voice.

"You could go a little faster, you know. In fact, this car would probably be a lot happier if you did. It's made for speed."

She shook her head, still staring straight ahead. "No, I don't trust myself." She frowned. "Certainly not after you told me how much this car costs."

She gave a frustrated sigh. "I told you we should've called for a taxi."

He tried not to smile. "I can see giving you this information was a mistake on my part. But, if you remember, you did ask." When she didn't respond and noting how tense she was, he sighed.

"Angel, it's only a car. Like any other car. But since you seem so nervous, maybe you should pull over and let me drive? I'm sure I'll be fine."

She shook her head, this time more vigorously. "No, I can't. The doctor said you shouldn't drive. And didn't you say, only a short time ago, we were almost to your condo?"

"*Umm… yeah. I did say that. But this would only hold true if you drove the speed limit and not ten miles below.*" He shook his head, adding under his breath. "If even that."

Maybe it was only his imagination, but he had the distinct impression there was something bothering her. Something more than her reluctance to drive his car.

He glanced over at her again, startled to see a tear slowly making its way down her cheek.

*Damn… what did you do this time?*

Quickly leaning over to grab the wheel, he began steering them to the side of the road.

"Put on the brakes, angel."

Which she did, bringing them to a screeching halt. Something he found rather confusing with the slow rate of speed they had been traveling. Once he put the car in park, he reached over to cup her chin in his hand, turning her to face him.

"What's wrong? Why are you crying?"

She shrugged her shoulders as she tried to avoid his gaze. She didn't know how to answer him. And this was because she really didn't know why she was crying.

It was almost as if all the tears she'd been holding inside for most of her life had suddenly decided it was time to make an appearance.

To the point, she wanted to drop her head down on his shoulder and cry her eyes out.

This explained why her next words came out in a long wail. "I don't know… Honest, I don't. I never cry. But for some reason, now I can't seem to stop."

She was gazing at him, her expression one of such anguish, for one brief moment he thought he was going to break down and cry right along with her. Swallowing past the lump in his throat, he reached over to wipe her tears away with his thumb.

"Hey, it's okay. Nothing could be so bad. Not with me by your side."

This seemed to set her off even more, the tears falling even faster as the words began to pour out of her mouth. They came out in such a rush, he almost couldn't understand what she was trying to say.

"No, it's not. It's not okay. I keep thinking about everything that's happened since I met you, and how it's probably all my fault. I should've never left after I said such awful things. Then, to make things even worse, no matter what I do, you're still so nice to me. And I don't deserve this. I don't deserve you…"

She started shaking her head. "What if I goof everything up again and…" She stopped to take deep, gulping breath.

Concerned, he swiftly put his fingers to her mouth. "Stop. Just stop. Nothing is your fault. And you're not going to, as you claimed, goof things up." Smoothing her hair back from her face, he smiled. "I think you've been working too hard and you're exhausted. Then you've had to put up with all my shenanigans. I've acted like a jerk, getting jealous and making all these demands. I certainly haven't made it easy for you."

She searched his face, her expression frantic. "*No, no, no…* it's not because of you. Nothing you would ever do could change how I feel about you."

She closed her eyes, her next words barely a whisper. "You are everything to me. You have to know I've been yours from the very beginning."

His hands sliding in her hair to bring her closer, he captured her mouth in a kiss that seemed to go on forever. Then, his eyes holding hers, the heat of his gaze leaving her even more breathless, he pressed a gentle, almost revered kiss to her mouth, his voice deep with emotion. "Angel, I love you so damn much. You are everything to me, too. And I am going to keep on loving you for as long as you let me."

His lips brushed against hers. "This is all you need to think about now. What's happened in the past, none of that matters anymore."

Her gaze locked with his. Everything she ever wanted showed in his eyes… tenderness, love, passion… sweeping aside all the tension and guilt she'd been carrying inside.

She blinked and between them, everything fell into place.

*And it was so right. No, it was amazing...*

Wrapping her arms around his neck, her smile was brilliant. "Oh, Chester… I love you, too. I love you so, so much."

And he was kissing her again.

And again… and then again.

Chester lifted his head, his gaze traveling in a slow journey over her face. Almost reverently, he traced her bottom lip with his thumb. His voice was deep with emotion. "You realize it's official now."

At her nod, he continued. "And you can't change your mind. Ever."

She nodded several more times before she leaned in to kiss him again.

He suddenly shifted in his seat, digging for something in his jeans pocket before he turned back to her.

He smiled. "Close your eyes."

He took the necklace he'd given her, the one she'd left behind on the nightstand, and fastened it around her neck.

Her lashes flying open, she reached up to clutch the diamond rings in her hand.

This set off another round of tears. "Oh Chester, I thought I'd never see this again. I didn't want to take it off, but it didn't seem right to…"

He pressed his fingers to her mouth, shaking his head. "This necklace was made for you, and only you. It's yours forever. Think of it as my promise to always love you. For eternity, like the two rings symbolize. I've been carrying it around with me ever since I found it on the nightstand. Hoping for a miracle, I guess."

He grinned. "And now, here you are."

She reached into her sweater pocket and pulled out the roll of Lifesavers he'd left with her the last time she saw him. She held them up to him.

She smiled. "I guess they really do work."

"*Oh, angel...*" And he was kissing her again.

The cars flying past a reminder of where they were, he tucked her hair behind her ear. He was smiling. "You know what you have to do now, don't you?"

She shook her head, her look uncertain. He placed her hand on the gear shift. "You're going to put this in drive, pull out on to the highway and show everyone how you're supposed to drive a car like this. Can you do this?"

For a moment, she stared at him. Then a mischievous look coming over her face, she nodded. Very slowly, she did this.

Suddenly wondering if he should be nervous, he leaned back in his seat, his hand searching for the armrest. He glanced over at her. "So, whenever you're ready...

She sent him a big grin and put the car in drive. At the first break in traffic, she pulled out, hesitating for a brief moment before she stepped down on the gas pedal. With a slight jerk, the engine roared into life to send them sailing down the highway.

*Whoa...*

He dragged his hand down over his chin, a smile spreading across his face. He glanced over to see she was grinning from ear to ear. Her hair blowing in the breeze coming in through the open windows, she had to shout for him to hear her words.

"Music... we need music!"

He reached over to turn on the audio player, turning up the volume. She sent him a nod, right before she started singing along with the song.

He shook his head, while at the same time, he began to laugh.

*It looks like you've created a monster. But this is okay... because right now, only one thing matters.*

She loved him.


When they arrived at Chester's condo, Sophie was thrilled to have free rein of the bathroom.

While he made what he told her were some necessary phone calls.

Now running her brush through her just washed hair, while watching this in the mirror, she had to stop and close her eyes.

Did she dare believe what she'd hoped for had really happened?

She smiled, wrapping her arms around herself in a hug.

*He loves you...*

Closing her eyes, she could still hear the emotion in his voice, proof that he meant every word.

*"Angel, I love you so damn much. You are everything to me, too. And I am going to keep on loving you for as long as you let me. This is all you need to think about now. Everything else, all that's happened in the past, none of this matters anymore."*

"I hope this smile I see on your face is because of me?

Chester was standing behind her. His arms coming around to pull her against him, he pressed a lingering kiss right below her ear.

A shiver running through her, she turned to rest her face against him. Her voice was muffled. "I was thinking about how you said you love me."

He kissed her again, this to the top of her head. "Remember, we've already decided it's a done deal. No going back on that now."

Even though she knew he was kidding, she could hear the hint of anxiety in his voice. She pulled away from him, a big smile on her face as she shook her head. "Nope. I'm afraid you're stuck with me now. You couldn't shake me even if you tried."

But he didn't seem to be paying attention. Slowly backing away from her, a grin spread over his face as he reached out to straighten the collar of the robe she was wearing. The hem almost dragging on the floor, and the sleeves rolled up, he recognized it as his.

He reached for the sash she'd tied into a big bow.

She grabbed his hand, giving him a guilty look. "I left my change of clothes in the bedroom and I found this. I thought you wouldn't mind if I wore it for a just little while."

*Uh oh...*

He was giving her that look again. The look that made her want to go into his arms and melt right into him. After he ran his fingertips slowly down the inside of the collar, he cleared his throat. "You can wear it whenever you want. As long as I'm the one who always gets to take it off you."

He smiled at her flustered expression, reaching for her hand. "Come with me."

He took her over to the bed, where he propped up the pillows against the headboard. Settling comfortably against them, he patted the space beside him. "Sit here with me."

After she crawled across the bed to sit next to him, he put his arm around her. "We need to talk."

A worried expression on her face, she backed away from him. "Oh, no you don't. When someone starts out a sentence with those words, nothing good ever follows."

She closed her eyes, a dramatic sigh escaping her. "I should have known this was too good to be true."

He chuckled, quickly pulling her back. "Hey, come back here. That came out all wrong. I only want to get everything between us out in the open. As you women like to say, we need to communicate our feelings."

She nodded against him. "Well, it's true. And always a good thing to do. Surely, you must agree."

*"Hmm..."* He raised an eyebrow. "Maybe not in such detail? But right now, we need to talk about Claire. And Paris."

When she didn't say anything, only moved closer, he continued.

"Let's start with Claire. From what she told me, things weren't going well with Tom, the guy she's been with over the past five or six years. So she decided to leave, taking Hunter with her.

"Tom retaliated by cancelling all of her credit cards. Desperate, and nowhere to turn, she came up with what she thought was a brilliant plan to convince me Hunter was my son. She knew I wouldn't turn my back on him and then the three of us would become a family."

He sighed. "But she saw how upset I was and decided to tell the truth." He paused to press a kiss in her hair. "Angel, I'm so sorry this happened. I promise I'll make it up to you next Valentine's Day. And every Valentine's Day to come."

"It's okay. Don't you remember what you told me earlier?"

She was gazing up at him, her eyes so incredibly blue, any chance of this happening was almost entirely out of the question.

*Geeez, you can't even remember what you said only a second ago.*

He gave her a blank stare. "I think I do?"

She laughed, shaking her head. "You said the past doesn't matter. And you're going to keep on loving me. This is all I need to know." This being said, she settled back next to him. "So, go on. What happened next?"

After an incredulous look, he pressed another kiss in her hair. "Uh, yeah… back to Claire. She admitted she'd lied. Tom is Hunter's father."

Here he grew silent.

When she glanced up to see the wistful smile on his face, she reached over to stroke his cheek. "He's such a cute little boy." She frowned. "I felt so bad for him. He looked so sad and so terribly lost."

He hugged her closer, a sigh coming from him. "Yeah, in a way, I was a little disappointed when Claire told me I wasn't his dad. I'd already started to imagine how much fun it would be to take him the ballpark. Or do all the things dads do with their kids"

He shook his head. "Oh well, someday. But back to Claire, I told her I would give her enough money for one year if she promised to get her life back on track. Once she agreed, I set up a bank account for her. Then I put her and Hunter in a taxi and sent them off. I think she was heading to Dallas, where I know she has family."

He remained silent for a few moments. "Angel, Claire and I were both so young when we got married. I thought I was in love, but now, looking back, I know I wasn't. I don't think I even knew what love was during that time of my life. It was so crazy back then, my career just starting to take off and everything coming at me from all directions. Grasping at some sense of normalcy, a wife, and maybe even kids, looked really good to me. Unfortunately, Claire was more into what was in it for her. Thinking back, I feel embarrassed about how we both behaved."

Sophie burrowed closer to him, slipping her hand in his. "I think it was nice of you to help Claire and Hunter."

His laugh was short. "I'm not that nice. I made sure she can only withdraw money out of the account twice a month so she doesn't spend it all in one shot. I guess it's true, old habits die hard, because I still don't trust her."

For a few seconds, they were silent. Then he sighed. "And now, about Paris..."

When he felt her grow tense in his arms, he rested his cheek to the top of her head. "I want you to know, whatever you do, wherever you go, I will stand by whatever decision you make. I've realized I can't expect you to give up everything you've worked for so long, just for me. And I admire the commitment you made to your aunt and uncle. Somehow, we'll make it work. It's not going to be easy, especially when the season kicks off, but I'll do anything to keep us together."

Here he stopped to shake his head before pressing another kiss in her hair. "I can't give you up. I'd rather have you for only a little at a time, than not have you at all."

She was silent. When the silence grew, he gazed down at her. "Sophie?"

"What if I decide not to go back to Paris?"

He closed his eyes, unable to trust himself to speak. His immediate impulse was to tell her this would be the absolute best news she could ever give him. But this would be putting all the pressure on her. And as much as he even hated to admit this? He didn't know what he would do in the same situation.

When she moved in his arms to gaze up at him, he gave her a hug. *"Ah, angel...* I want you to do what you feel you have to do. Of course, if you did decide not to go back, I'd be a very happy man. But, as I just said, I'm totally committed to doing everything I can to keep us together, wherever we are. I never want to be the one to stand in the way of your dreams."

Moving out from under his arm and sitting back on her heels next to him, she reached over to frame his face in her hands.

For a few seconds, she gazed into his eyes. Then she gave him a brilliant smile.

"Oh Chester, I'm not going back. I can't. I can't leave you. I used to think living in Paris was what I wanted, a dream come true. But now I know this is what it is... only a dream."

Giving him a kiss, she smiled at him. "Where you? You're the real thing. You're so, *so* much better than a dream. I love you, Chester Mazzori. I love you more than anything in the world, Paris included. And I will go anywhere, follow you everywhere. Always."

Then she grinned. "But, just to warn you, if you ever leave me, I'll make you regret it for the rest of your life."

Filled with an overwhelming feeling of relief, he pulled her into his arms. Burying his face in her hair, he closed his eyes.

Then he laughed. A deep, happy laugh. "Regret it, huh? Is that a threat? Well, I'm not scared, because it's never gonna happen. At least not if you keep doing things like wearing my robe. You're too tempting for me to even think of leaving you, baby."

And before she even knew what he planned, she was on her back, with him gazing down at her.

"Have I told you lately how much in love I am with you? Because I am. So, *so* much." This was delivered in a whisper between the soft kisses he dropped to her face.

That familiar heat building inside of her, she closed her eyes, a long sigh escaping her. "You can tell me as often as you want. I love you, too"

He was smiling. *"Mmm... that's good."*

Urged on by her response, after leaving a trail of kisses along the opening of the robe, he pulled at the sash, unraveling the bow.

When his hand drifted under the robe, she gave a soft, breathy moan, trying to pull him closer. "No fair... you have an advantage here."

She could feel his smile against her lips as he slid the robe down over her one shoulder. *"Mmm... I told you what the consequences could be if you wore this robe."* His hand went to her other shoulder. *"More?"*

Her only response was her kiss.

But this didn't matter. He already knew what her answer was.


It was much later when Sophie woke, the sun low in the sky, the fading light of early evening coming in through the window. When she realized she was alone in the rumpled bedding, she stretched her arms above her head, giving a big yawn.

This was when she noticed the wonderful aroma coming from the direction of the kitchen. Someone was cooking something that smelled absolutely heavenly. This made her realize how hungry she was.

She slipped out of the bed and rummaged through her bag, searching for something to wear. She finally settled on a long, royal blue sleeveless knit dress and her metallic flip flops.

After she ran a comb through her hair and put it up in a casual twist, she applied a touch of mascara and lip gloss.

She ventured out into the hall. The mouth-watering scent leading right to the kitchen, she came to a stop, taking in the scene in front of her.

While something was sizzling on the grill top stove, Chester, wearing a white cook's apron, was slicing a tomato on the butcher block top of the island. He was humming, but then began to sing.

He had a beautiful voice. Completely mesmerized, she closed her eyes as she listened.

*"Only minutes ago, I saw you.*
*I glanced up when you came*
*through the door.*
*My head started spinning,*
*You gave me the feeling*
*The room had no ceiling or floor."*

She quietly made her way over to the island.

Chester looked up and right at her, the words he was singing abruptly falling into silence. She could see he was embarrassed, a redness slowly spreading across his face.

She smiled at him, her words a whisper. "Please don't stop."

For a moment, he hesitated. Then, giving her a slow smile, he came around the island and pulled her into his arms.

His eyes never leaving hers, and taking her with him, they danced around the kitchen as he sang.

*"Yes, I found her! She's an angel,*
*The sparkle of starlight in her eyes!*
*We are dancing, we are floating,*
*And I like it so well, for all I know,*
*I may never come back to earth again..."*

He ended the song with a kiss.

She sighed against him. "Oh Chester, that was beautiful. You have an amazing voice. And the song... isn't it from Cinderella?"

He grinned down at her. While at the same time, he pulled at the clip in her hair, watching as it tumbled to her shoulders in a riot of curls.

Framing her face in his hands, he smiled down at her. "There, that's better." Then he nodded. "Yeah... the song is from Cinderella, but I guess you could say it's my version. When I was a junior in high school, the drama club put on the musical, Cinderella. My sisters talked me into trying out for the part of the prince and I got it."

Caught up in the memory, he chuckled. "They were thrilled, but my friends razzed me like you wouldn't believe. They dared me to put my own spin on the song. Never one to pass up a dare back then, I did. The choral director almost had a heart attack."

He shook his head. "I was a know-it-all teenager at the time. I wanted to be this big, macho sports star, not a singing prince."

Her hands going up to clasp behind his neck, she smiled. "You will always be my favorite macho sports star *and* singing prince, rolled into one."

She sighed. "I'd give anything to be able to sing like you can. I'm sure you've noticed singing is not one of my better traits."

A teasing gleam came into his eyes. *"Hmm...* I'm not quite sure how to answer that?"

As she started to back away from him, her eyes widening in mock horror, he chuckled, pulling her back into his arms. "Angel, I love your voice. If you only knew what the sound of it does to me when we're together and I, well..."

Here his voice dropped down to a whisper. "I'm unable to think of anything except how much I want you. Like right now. How is it you always manage to look so beautiful?"

After he confirmed his feelings with another kiss, she gazed up at him. "I don't want to ruin the moment, but can we please eat? Whatever you're making smells heavenly. And I am so, so hungry."

She sent him a teasing smile. "After that, I'll do anything you want."

He laughed, slapping his palm to his forehead. "Do you mean to tell me, all along, all I had to do was feed you in order to have my way with you? If only I had known..."

He pulled out a stool by the island, patting it with his hand. "Please, have a seat. Even though I've now been bumped up to a princely status in your eyes, I'm going to wait on you. We're having a salad, steak, baked potato and green beans. All prepared by me, especially for you."

He nodded over at a cookbook setting on the counter. "My aunt gave this to me. She told me the next time I wanted to invite you over for dinner, I would have to make it myself. So, bear with me."

He reached over to run his knuckles lightly down her cheek.

"You're probably wondering what I have planned for dessert, aren't you?"

She grinned. "Oh, my… dessert, too? Please, do tell."

After giving her one of those looks of his, he cleared his throat. *"Hmm…* I think I'll keep that as a surprise for now. But before you ask, yes, I plan to share it with you." This he followed with a wink.

He had poured out two glasses of wine. Handing one to her, he held up the other in a toast. "To us, angel. "

She leaned over to kiss him. "To us… forever."

# CHAPTER 32

hester arranged the logs in the fire pit, moving them around to bring on a roaring fire on this cool night. The only other light came from the millions of stars in the jet black sky.

Curled up in a lounge chair, a fleece blanket wrapped around her, Sophie smiled when he joined her.

She rested her head on his shoulder. "Dinner was wonderful. But then everything is wonderful, you most of all. I can't believe, only yesterday, I was so miserable. And so afraid I might never see you again."

She sighed, moving closer. "When I went back to Paris, every time the door to the boutique opened, my heart would start racing like crazy. I kept hoping it was you, only to become so upset when it wasn't."

She shrugged, smiling up at him.. "I was looking for a miracle."

He pressed a kiss in her hair. "I did go to Paris."

At her shocked expression, he nodded. "Only to have the woman running the store inform me you had gone to the country with Julian. I can't even tell you how much I disliked this Julian at that moment. I also couldn't understand how you had forgotten me so soon."

He frowned at the memory. "I was such a fool. A fool who wasn't thinking straight."

She reached up to kiss his cheek. "Oh, Chester... you had no reason to worry about Julian. He's nice, but he isn't you. From the very first moment I met you, I couldn't imagine being with anyone else."

She laughed. "I think your Aunt Evelyn might be on to something with the Lifesavers. I carried that roll you gave me everywhere I went."

At his silence, she looked up at him. He was gazing down at her, a bemused expression on his face. She reached up to stroke his cheek. "Chester? What are you thinking about?"

He cleared his throat. "Speaking of those magic candies..." Reaching into his pocket, he was smiling as he pulled out a roll of Lifesavers. "I just so happen to have a roll of them right here. And I believe the one on top is for you. So, here, take it."

His look was so intent, she was hesitant to take what he was offering. Instead, she peered even more closely at him.

What was he up to?

When she didn't move, he took her hand and placed the roll of candy in her palm.

He smiled at her, an eagerness in his expression. "Go ahead, shake it in your other hand. It won't fall out by itself."

At her wary glance, he chuckled, giving her another nod.

So she shook the opened end of the roll over her palm.

But t wasn't her favorite pineapple flavored candy that fell into her hand.

It was a ring, the diamond sparkling in the light from the fire.

*An engagement ring.*

In a state of shock, she almost dropped it. Clutching it tightly in her hand, she watched Chester sink down on one knee in front of her.

He was smiling as he gently pried the ring from her hand and slipped it on her finger. "Angel, I love you. I know we've only been together for a short time. But for me, it's long enough to know you're the one I want. You've become the light of my life, and my reason for living."

Bringing her hand to his lips, he brushed a kiss over her fingers. "I want it all… I want to be your groom for the beach wedding at sunset. Your husband on the honeymoon trip to Italy. To then spend the rest of my life with you, loving you."

He took a deep breath. His gaze was serious, yet at the same time, filled with such tenderness. "So, Sophie Michaels, will you marry me? Say yes, and you will make me the happiest man in the world."

She came to life. Flinging herself into his arms, she gave what was both a cry and a laugh, all rolled into one.

He waited, her answer the only thing that mattered. Muffled, and right up against his heart, it was the answer he'd hoped for.

*"Yes, yes, yes… Oh, Chester, of course, my answer is a yes."*

She was still clutching the roll of Lifesavers in her hand.

# CHAPTER 33

*I look at you and see the rest of my life in your eyes.*
*~ Unknown*

Sophie opened her eyes to find Chester leaning over her, gazing into her face.

He grinned. Right before he swooped down, covering her mouth in a kiss. "Hey, sleepyhead… wake up. We have a busy day ahead of us. It's the start of the weekend and we don't want to waste a minute."

Now totally awake, she smiled up at him, "We do?"

Settling next to her, his head propped up on his hand, he reached over to tuck her hair behind her ears. "Yep, I've made a few plans and as soon as you get dressed, we'll be off. You'll need to pack a bag."

Puzzled, she stared at him. "Off? Off to where?"

He smiled again. "It's a surprise."

She nodded very slowly. "Okay, but…"

He raised an eyebrow at the slightly worried expression on her face.

She shrugged. "I didn't bring a lot of clothes. In fact, I couldn't even tell you exactly what I threw in my suitcase, I packed in such a hurry."

After planting a quick kiss to her mouth, he left the bed. "No need to worry. If you find you need something, we'll stop and get it."

He smiled down at her. "Now, come on. Get ready so we can leave. We have about an hour drive. So, we'll stop somewhere on the way for a quick bite, or have lunch when we get there."

As soon as he left the room, she jumped out of bed. Once she was in the bathroom, she turned on the shower.

As she reached for the shampoo, the flash from the diamond on her finger caught her eye. Even though Chester had given her the ring four days ago, she was still having a hard time believing they were engaged.

It felt like a dream.

*But it's not a dream... you're really going to marry this man.*

The bruise on Chester's face, along with his black eye, had almost completely faded, the headaches, far and few between. But since he still wasn't allowed to report to practice, they had spent all their time together.

And a good portion of that time had been spent discussing their immediate future.

Beginning with the wedding.

She was still sticking to what was her idea of the perfect wedding. No matter where or when they got married, she didn't care. She only wanted it to be with him you know, the groom. And with their close friends and family there to celebrate the day.

And if Chester had his way?

What was his idea of a perfect wedding?

If he had his way, they'd go big. This was only because he wanted to share his happiness with everyone he knew.

But, as he'd assured Sophie, he completely agreed with her. All that mattered was that they got married.

The sooner, the better.

Like her, he was eager to start their life together.

She smiled, thinking about their long talks about their future. She had a feeling life with him was going to be an interesting journey, every single step of the way.

Gazing down at the ring, she felt her heartbeat quicken in anticipation, wondering what surprise he had planned now.

She finished her shower, got dressed, and packed in record time.

Just as Chester predicted, an hour later they pulled up to the entrance of an impressive cedar log-built lodge. This backed up to a lake, the dazzling expanse of clear blue water seemed endless.

This explained the name Crystal Lake Lodge.

The hand-carved wooden doors swung open, two cheerful lodge employees running down the steps to greet them. After they unloaded the luggage and escorted them inside, Chester checked in at the reservation desk,

Sophie gazed around the enormous space, taking it all in.

The interior was all wood, from the polished cedar planked floors, to the huge cedar beams supporting the high, open wooden ceiling.

A huge river stone fireplace was the focal point of the room with floor to ceiling windows on each side, these offering perfect view of the lake. The cozy groupings of overstuffed sofas and chairs upholstered in jewel-toned fabrics were an invitation to relax, take time away from the hustle and bustle of the outside world.

The clerk handed Chester the keys. "Here you go, sir. Dave will show you to your cabin. And so we can make sure things go as planned, when do you expect the others to arrive?"

Chester gave a swift shake of his head. "I'm afraid you have us mixed up with another party of guests. It will only be us."

The clerk seemed confused, but before Sophie had time to think anything of this, Chester took her arm and whisked her back outside. Once Dave loaded their luggage into a small jeep and settled Sophie and Chester in the backseat, he started up the jeep.

Chester smiled down at her. "So, what do you think? Isn't this place amazing? I know you thought the dinner I made for you the other night was as gourmet as you could get, but wait until tonight. The chefs here are some of the best around."

She glanced back at the lodge, then at him. "But where are we going now? We're not staying in the lodge?"

With the jeep now on the move, bouncing over the uneven ground, he put his arm around her, holding her close. "Nope, we're in a cabin. It's not far, you can walk to the lodge easily."

In mere minutes, Dave pulled up in front of a small picturesque cabin, almost a miniature replica of the lodge. After he brought in their luggage and informed them he was leaving the jeep for their own personal use, he left.

Chester was smiling as he watched Sophie gaze around the interior of the cabin, checking out every detail. "So, do you like it?"

She loved it.

It was a blend of rustic charm and luxurious comfort. Like the main lodge, the floors, walls and ceiling were all cedar paneled. There was also a fireplace flanked by large windows, offering another magnificent view of the lake.

The bed was of hand-carved wood with a plaid comforter and quilted pillows to match. An efficient and well-stocked mini-kitchen, along with a bathroom equal to that of a luxurious master-bath in a five-star hotel, completed the space.

She glanced over at Chester to see he was watching her, that look in his eyes. She walked right into his arms, sighing against him. "It's beautiful. I love it."

He gazed down at her. "What would you like to do? We can go for a hike along the lake." Here, he stopped to give her a leisurely kiss. "Or... we can stay here and enjoy each other's company. It's your call."

He pulled her closer, his choice of activity obvious in his eyes.

She wound her arms around his neck, her fingers tangling in his hair as she pretended to think about her answer before she reached up to give him a kiss. "How about a late lunch, with a hike to follow?"

He was more than happy to go along with this plan.

After lunch at the lodge restaurant, they strolled hand in hand along the trail bordering the lake.

Sophie sneaked a glance up at Chester. She was trying to figure out why he'd brought her here. Not that she wasn't enjoying their time together. Of course she was.

But she was puzzled by this air of expectation he had about him, as if he was waiting for something to happen.

He chuckled, putting his arm around her. The tone of his voice was teasing. "My goodness, what could you possibly be thinking, that merits such a serious expression?"

She waved her hand at their surroundings. "All of this… and why you brought me here. Is this a favorite place of yours?"

He shrugged. "A favorite? I guess it happens to be one of my favorite places. But what about you? I know how you feel about your beach wedding and all. What do you think? Would this place meet your expectations?"

She turned to him, her expression serious. "Oh Chester, I really don't care where we get married. We can go to a courthouse or anywhere. It doesn't matter to me. The most important thing is you're the man standing next to me to exchange our vows."

She grinned. "You know, as the groom."

Now at the door to their cabin, he gazed down at her for a few moments. Then he grinned. "I'm very happy to hear this. Because I have a surprise for you." He opened the door, gesturing for her to go ahead of him.

She was met by a choir of excited voices.

*"Surprise!"*

Chester reached over to frame her face in his hands, his whisper for her only. "Happy wedding day, angel. The next time I see you, it will be at sunset. When you walk across the beach to meet me at the altar.

After a quick kiss, he was out the door and gone.

Sophie was surrounded.

Abby and Lisa were there. Chloe was with them, hopping up and down with excitement.

Her Aunt Louise, emotional as always, was dabbing at her tears with a tissue. When Sophie's sister Hannah saw their aunt was crying, she began to cry, too.

Chester's sister Carrie and his Aunt Evelyn were standing off to the side, watching everyone. There were two other women with them, who had to be Chester's other two sisters, Carolyn and Livy.

Quickly moving from one person to the next, Sophie gave everyone a big hug.

Everyone was chattering all at once.

Everyone, that is… except Sophie. In shock, was still trying to take in this surprise Chester had arranged.

It was Lisa who finally got everyone to quiet down, a silence falling over the room as she spoke. "Girls, we need to stop talking and get to work. Because we have a lot to do, with only about four hours to get it all done. In these four hours, we're going to turn Sophie into the beautiful bride Chester will fall in love with all over again."

Sophie sent a wild glance around at all the smiling faces. "But how? I'll need a dress… and shoes… and everything else."

Her hands to her face, her expression was one of pure panic. "I have nothing. At least not what a bride would need."

She gestured at her simple blue and white flowered sundress. "Look at me… I certainly can't wear this." She sent a smile around the room. "Even though Chester likes me in blue."

Then her face scrunched up in thought. "There is this blue knit dress I brought with me, but he's already seen it."

She shook her head, her hands going to her face. "But shouldn't I have something new? You know, something new, something borrowed, something blue… all those traditional wedding things."

She turned to Abby. "Abby, you know what I'm talking about. I remember at your wedding…"

Lisa came over and clamped her hand over Sophie's mouth. She was laughing. *"Stop… Calm down.* We've got this."

Her hands on her hips, Aunt Louise sent Sophie a stern look over the rim of her glasses. "Sophie… I can't believe you have so little faith in us. Everything has been taken care of, mostly by Chester. When he called to tell me what he was planning and if we'd be willing to help, we all put our heads together and got to work. Your dress, along with dresses for Hannah, Abby, Lisa, Carolyn, Carrie and Livy, were all sent by overnight delivery. Thank goodness I had most of the measurements from Abby's wedding."

Noting the anxious expression on Chloe's face, she sent her a smile. *"Ah,* little one... don't look so worried. I personally brought your dress with me. I even carried it on the plane so it wouldn't get lost. So, let's see a smile on your pretty little face."

Smile received, Louise continued. "And someone will be arriving in only a few minutes to do hair and makeup."

She reached over to hold Sophie's hands, her expression suddenly serious. "Love, are you sure this is what you want? Chester assured me this is exactly the wedding you wanted, but I've found he can be a very persuasive man. And I know how much he wants to marry you." She laughed, shaking her head. "If only so you don't disappear on him again."

A hushed silence fell over the room. As Sophie gazed around at the sea of faces, all the people she loved, she didn't have to think about her answer. Enveloping her aunt in a big hug, the smile she gave her was radiant. *"Yes... oh, yes. I do, I do. I really do."*

Wiping away the start of new tears, Louise gave her a watery smile. "Well, this sounds like a yes to me. You even have the 'I do' part down."

Once again, Lisa stepped in to take charge. "Okay, girls... listen up. This is what we're going to do..."

The wedding was on...


Chester had instructed all the guys to meet at the bar in the lodge.

This included Alex, Kevin, Sophie's brother Brian, her Uncle Paul and his sister Carolyn's husband, John.

The only person who was missing was his sister Livy's boyfriend, Zack. According to Livy, he was in the middle of closing on a big work deal and couldn't take the weekend off.

Chester frowned. There was something about this Zack he didn't like. He was too smooth, too evasive about what he did for a living.

*Another big deal, huh? It's always the same excuse. Sort of suspicious, you'd say.*

Maybe later, he'd talk to Livy about this. But now, headed for the lodge, his mind was on other things.

He was feeling a little nervous. If he were honest, he'd admit he was more nervous than he'd ever been.

This wasn't because of what he and Sophie were about to do.

*God, no…* he wanted to marry her more than anything. She was all he wanted, all he needed. He was more than eager to be the groom she'd so often referred to, more than willing to agree to all her plans.

*Whatever, you're in.*

So, what brought on this case of the jitters?

For starters, he wasn't sure if she was totally on board with this impromptu wedding he'd planned. He knew she wanted to marry him, but was this still the wedding she wanted? Having grown up as the only male in a house of four women, he knew how quickly they could change her mind.

He also hadn't quite mastered the connection between what a woman said and what she meant. Or more importantly, what answer was expected of him. Something went on between those two things that was way over his head.

This was why he'd left so quickly after he dropped Sophie off at their cabin.

*You only know you love her. For you, this is enough.*

Someone tapped him on the shoulder. Holding a beer out to him, it was Alex. Holding his own beer up in a toast, he grinned. "Here's to the man of the hour. Life is good, no?"

When this was met with a loud cheer, for the life of him, Chester couldn't stop grinning.

Yes, life was not only good… *it was amazing.*


Sophie studied herself in the full-length mirror.

Then she closed her eyes.

*It's true... you're marrying Chester Mazzori, the man you fell in love with the moment you met him.*

And after today? She would never have to leave him again.

She knew she was being silly, but she was still worried she was going to wake up and find it was all a dream. So, for her, the ceremony couldn't come soon enough. And that Chester had planned this wedding just for her?

*This makes you love him even move.*

The need to tell him this, she picked up her phone from the bed. Once she thought about what she wanted to say, she typed it out and sent it to him.

Her aunt had come into the room. A smile on her face, she came over to Sophie and gave her a big hug.

"Sweetheart, you look beautiful. But it's not the dress that makes you look this way. It's your face. You are glowing with love for this man of yours. I pray the two of you will have a long and wonderful life together."

She shook her head. "I will never forget how upset Chester was when he came to the boutique that morning. This was when I knew the two of you were meant to be together." She frowned. "You should've told me what was going on. It would have saved so much heartache if you had."

Sophie sighed. "I know. But I was so confused. And so scared. I think I needed to get away, if only to clear my head." She searched her aunt's face. "But, now that I'm not going back to Paris, are you sure you're okay with this? I feel like I'm letting you down."

"Sophie, don't even think like this. We'll work it out. I would have loved for you to stay there to run the boutique, but I would never, *ever* stand in the way of your happiness."

She smiled. "Paul and I have already decided once he gets the okay from his doctor, it's time we made a return visit to Paris together. Maybe for a month or even more. While we're there, we'll make sure the boutique is running as it should be. From all the good things you've told me about the assistant you hired, we should be okay. And since Chester assured me he has no intention of leaving Cleveland, his plan to keep it as his permanent home, you'll be able to take over the boutique while we're gone. So, everything will work out just fine."

Sophie's answer was to give her a long hug.

Her aunt was the first to pull a way, dabbing at her eyes with a tissue. Then, after inspecting Sophie's dress, smoothing out a few wrinkles in the skirt, she smiled. "But we have no more time for tears. We need to make sure everything is perfect. Every detail , no matter how small, must be flawless."

She glanced down at Sophie's feet, shaking her head. "I'm still a little on the shelf with these red shoes."

Sophie adamantly shook her head. "They are my lucky shoes. I have to wear them." She grinned. "And Chester will understand."

She laughed as she twirled around in front of the mirror. "Everything is perfect. Now I know how Chloe felt in the dress she wore for Abby's wedding. This dress makes me feel so happy. I love it. I couldn't have made a better choice."

The dress was a pale ice blue, almost appearing white with flashes of iridescent blue when she moved. This was because of the fabric, a sheer chiffon with just a hint of shimmer. The thin-strapped bodice was the same fabric, intricately pleated and tightly fitted with a natural waistline.

The skirt of the dress was tea length and made up of layers and layers of the same chiffon. When she moved, it fluttered around her like fragile flower petals in a soft breeze.

The hair stylist had pulled her hair back with a sparkling rhinestone comb, the back a cascade of soft waves and curls. The only jewelry she wore was her engagement ring and the necklace Chester had given her.

And the finishing touch? Her red shoes. Adding a pop of color and a bit of whimsy, they were totally Sophie.

"Something's missing..."

This came from Louise, who was studying Sophie, a thoughtful expression on her face. Then she clapped her hands together. "Oh, my... how could I have forgotten?"

She hurried over to where her gigantic travel bag was setting on the bed. After digging through it, she pulled out a small wrapped jewelry box. She handed it to Sophie. It was the same kind of box that came with the necklace Chester had given her. She read the attached card.

> *With love to my bride-to-be on our wedding day. With all of my love, Chester. (And in case you're wondering ~ yes, they're real.)*

Slowly opening the box, she stared down at the diamond earrings nestled inside. Blinking back tears, she was at a loss for words.

She gazed up at her aunt. "How did I get so lucky?"

"Oh, sweetheart… it's not luck. It's a gift. And for the both of you, it couldn't be a more perfect match. Anyone can see this. Promise me you'll treasure every moment."

She followed this with a big hug. "Now, I'm going to check on the rest of the girls. Try to take this time to relax a little, okay? I'll bring everyone back in a little while."

Chester saw he had a text from Sophie.

> Do you know anyone who could use a roll ofLifesavers for good luck? I've found I don't need them anymore, because now I have all I could ever want. And this is you. love you so much. P.S. This is the best surprise... EVER!

A huge smile on his face, he glanced up from his phone. Faced with the knowing looks from his friends, he nonchalantly began making his way over to the door. "*Uh…* I need to answer this. I'll be right back."

Alex chuckled, leaning back against the bar. "Well, look at Mr. Tough Guy. His silly grin can only mean the text is from Sophie. Not even married yet, and already he's at her beck and call." He held his beer up in a toast. "Looks like another one has joined the club, eh? Who here will drink to this?"

The laughter and comments following him out of the bar, Chester headed to the main room of the lodge. He sank down on the sofa in front of the fireplace.

He read the text again. Then he typed out his answer.

> You are my Lifesaver. And, I love you, too. More than you could know. P.S. Maybe you should hold on to those Lifesavers. One can never have too much luck.

A big grin on his face, Kevin plopped next to him on the sofa, patting him on the back.

"Guess who got voted to check up on you, make sure you're alright?"He nodded. "Yep, I'm the lucky guy. But you look like you're doing just fine."

"Yeah, I'm good. I was worried I went too far, springing the wedding on Sophie like this. Even though I made it as close to the wedding she wanted."

He grinned. "But it looks like I nailed it. Her text just confirmed this."

Kevin nodded. "That's great. And you?"

Chester slipped his phone into his pocket before he looked over at Kevin. "I don't care how it happens, I just want to know she's mine." Then he shook his head, an almost bewildered expression on his face. "Who would've thought?"

"There's no need to explain, I know where you're coming from." Coming to his feet, Kevin grinned. "You've got this. Like I said, I'm at your disposal. If only to make sure you don't goof up."

"You?" Chester burst out laughing. "Lord, *help me*… I'm doomed."

They were still laughing when they joined the rest of the guys in the bar.

# CHAPTER 34

The sun was just beginning to set over the water, painting the horizon in a glorious combination of pinks and reds. Sparkling like crystal sequins in the sky, a few stars had already made their debut.

The ushers had seated the guests in the rows of chairs facing the flowered covered arbor serving as an altar. The candles lit in the lanterns lining the sandy path, now serving as an aisle, flickered in the evening breeze. Almost as though they were dancing to the music played by the string quartet.

Sophie was standing at the top of the steps leading down to the sandy beach. She was with her brother Brian, his job to walk her down the aisle, and Chloe.

After Chester escorted both his Aunt Evelyn and her Aunt Louise to their seats, he took his place at the altar with the ushers.

The tempo of the music by the string quartet shifted, a cue for the bridesmaids to begin their slow walk down the aisle.

Hopping on one foot, Chloe was mumbling to herself. Thinking she was nervous, Sophie put her hand on her shoulder. "Are you okay? I would think you'd be a pro at this, since you just did the same thing for Abby's wedding."

Chloe shrugged. "I'm actually pretty good at it, now that I know what to do. It's a very easy job. You only need to remember to walk slow and smile." She frowned. "And always make sure you don't throw flower petals in someone's face by mistake. I don't want to do that again."

She peered up at Sophie. "What about you, are you okay?"

Sophie kept a straight face as she answered. "I'm fine. And very excited. Why do you ask?"

Chloe sighed, a very long and dramatic sigh. "Momma told me I might have to give you a pep talk, since this must be such a big surprise for you. She said she can't even imagine what Chester was thinking. She also said men tend do crazy things sometimes, and this is certainly one of those times. But daddy said this is only because women send mixed messages."

She scrunched up her face in thought. "I'm not sure what daddy meant when he said that? But momma also said it's romantic. So, that's good, right?"

After she sent Brian a warning look when he laughed, Sophie gave Chloe a hug. "Oh sweetheart, I'm fine. Really, I am. And yes, this is crazy. But very romantic, too. It's also nice to know I can count on you if I need help."

She glanced over to where her aunt was waving her arms at them. "I think Aunt Louise is letting us know it's your time to start. So, go ahead, we'll be right behind you."

After Chloe began her walk down the steps, Brian patted Sophie's arm. "Okay, I'm going to ask you this one more time… are you sure this is what you want? It seems sort of sudden."

Sophie's smile was brilliant. "I've never been so sure of anything in my life." She reached up to press a kiss to his cheek. "Thank you so much for being here."

His answer was lost in the beginning chords of the wedding march floating up to them in the evening breeze.

But this was okay.

Sophie was ready… more than ready.

How could she not be?

She was marrying the man of her dreams.

As Chester watched Sophie slowly make her way to where he was waiting for her, he was relieved he wasn't expected to say anything.

Because honestly?

He didn't think he could.

And if he did manage to get out a few words? They probably wouldn't make any sense.

She was, by far, the most beautiful bride he'd ever seen.

Believe it or not, Sophie was as speechless as Chester. The moment their eyes met, she was lost.

When asked afterwards what they most remembered about the ceremony, they both agreed this would be when they were pronounced husband and wife.

This might sound as if they hadn't taken their vows seriously. But of course, they had. Only because everything was as it should be.

*Because it should all be simple, don't you*
*think? All about the bride and groom, the love*
*they share, and the life they're about to start*
*together as husband and wife.*

If you recall, if she was ever to become a bride, this was Sophie's wish. With Chester more than happy to claim his place as the groom.

When Sophie first reached Chester's side and held out her hand, he leaned in to place a kiss to her mouth instead. Only then did he take her hand.

*Kiss number one...*

He didn't mean to do this, it just happened.

And after they repeated their vows and Chester had placed the ring on her finger, he impulsively leaned in to give her another kiss.

*Kiss number two...*

He still denies he had any intention of doing this. He swore it was beyond his control.

So, you can imagine how eagerly both Chester and Sophie were waiting for the priest to say those magic words…

*"With the blessing of everyone gathered here today, I now pronounce Chester and Sophie as husband and wife."*

Then he chuckled, nodding over to Chester. *"Now* is when you kiss your bride."

Chester didn't disappoint. Taking Sophie into his arms, the kiss he gave her was an -I-love-you-madly-show-stopping-and-bend-over-backwards-kind of kiss.

A kiss that left no doubt she was the love of his life.

*And, there you have it, kiss number three…*

So, it goes without saying… good things really do come in threes.


After Cester and Sophie walked back down the aisle to the base of the steps, he took her into his arms. And, softly, for only her to hear, he sang.

*"Yes, I found her! She's an angel,*
*The sparkle of starlight in her eyes.*
*We are dancing, we are floating,*
*And I like it so well, for all that I know,*
*I may never come back to earth again…"*

Resting his forehead against hers, he whispered. "Ah, angel… I truly may never come down to earth again. I love you, Sophie Mazzori."

Reaching up to frame his face in her hands, she also whispered. "Not only did you give me the wedding of my dreams, I do believe I've found the perfect groom. I love you, Chester Mazzori."

And she was the one to initiate the kiss this time.

# CHAPTER 35

*You are enough.*
*A thousand times more than enough.*
*~ Anonymous*

The reception was in full swing, everyone dancing to the music of the band. Unfortunately, it wasn't Jason's band, as he had already been booked for months for this particular night. But those who were dancing had to admit the band Chester founs was almost, but maybe not quite, as good.

So, there were no complaints.

All the speeches had been made, and there were quite a few. With only Chester and Sophie's closest friends and family in attendance, almost everyone had something they wanted to say. This meant there were so many shared memories and stories, resulting in lots of laughter and even a few tears.

The wedding cake had been cut. Knowing Sophie's love for chocolate and, per Chester's request, Abby had made a cake that could only be described as a chocolate lover's dream. The dark chocolate cake was layered with a chocolate chip cheesecake filling and frosted with a decadent chocolate ganache frosting.

There was also a small groom's cake in the shape of a baseball bat and mitt holding a baseball.

And, yes, this cake was also chocolate.

The verdict was in. The traditional white wedding cake was over-rated. And, with all the compliments she received, Abby was wondering if maybe it was time to add cakes to her now rapidly growing cookie business, Sweet Abby's.

Always ready to give his opinion of Abby['a newest creations, Kevin greeted this news with a thumbs-up. He considered himself as Abby's official taste tester. A job —after baseball—he took very seri-ously. S

After saying good night to her aunt and uncle, Sophie made her way over to the huge fire pit, where the flames provided a welcome heat in the now slightly chilly night air. Holding her hands over the fire to warm them, she smiled as she gazed up at the star-studded sky. It was the perfect night to celebrate a wedding.

Someone grabbed her hand. It was Chloe. Laughing, Sophie hugged her close. "Hey, are you having fun?"

"I think she's had about all the fun she can handle. And now she's about ready to drop. Which means it's bedtime." This came from Lisa, who had come to stand beside them. She smiled at Sophie. "This has been such a wonderful day, and I can't even begin to tell you how happy I am for you and Chester. You have made him into a new man, Sophie. A man who has finally found what he wants in life. The two of you are just so perfect together."

"I know." Sophie blinked at the threat of tears. But it had been a very emotional day. And as the bride, she was pretty sure this was allowed.

She waved her hand around them, her voice trembling with emotion. "I can't believe Cheater did all this. It was the best, most romantic, and sweetest thing anyone has ever done for me. The wedding of my dreams." Her laugh was shaky. "I love him so much."

Chloe tugged on her hand. "I guess I should be glad everyone is happy, but I'm not. I'm sad. Because now there is no one else to get married, only me." She frowned up at Sophie and Lisa. "And I won't be getting married for a million years. Or as Daddy said, not for a very, long, *long* time."

Sophie laughed. "Oh Chloe, you always make me laugh."

Lisa was shaking her head, a resigned smile on her face. "Chloe, I can't even imagine how Daddy will be able to handle your first date, let alone walking you down the aisle when you get married."

She reached over to give Sophie a hug before she took Chloe's hand. "Come on, Chloe, you'll see everyone again at brunch in the morning. You're about ready to fall asleep on your feet." She grinned over at Sophie. "For that matter, so am I."

As Sophie watched them walk away, a breeze ruffled her hair, billowing her skirt out around her. She shivered as she gazed around at the dwindling crowd, searching for Chester. She finally spotted him where the band was set up, talking to Alex.

As she watched him, almost as if he could sense this, he glanced over in her direction. Their eyes meeting, he gave her a slow smile, that look coming over his face. You know the one. Then he turned back to Alex.

She closed her eyes, almost overcome by the sudden rush of desire that surged through her. She wondered, was she always going to feel this immediate attraction, this hunger for him when she saw him?

*God, she hoped so...*

She shivered again, wrapping her arms around herself for warmth. But it wasn't enough. She longed for Chester, his warmth, his arms holding her close.

Right now, more than anything, she wanted this.

Like a blanket falling from heaven, a jacket was draped over her shoulders from behind. She turned to go right into Chester's arms, his lips claiming hers in a long kiss.

Resting his forehead against hers, he sighed.

"Hey..."

*I love you.*

She pulled him closer.

"Hey..."

*I love you back.*

He took her hand, leading her from the patio and up the steps to the lodge before she stopped him. "Chester, are we leaving? If we are, shouldn't we let everyone know?"

His hold on her hand tightened. "I'm sure everyone will excuse our absence. And I really want to be alone with you." He pulled her back into his arms and proceeded to give her another kiss, leaving her with no doubt what he had in mind.

Without a single word between them, they continued on to the main entrance of the lodge where a lodge employee was manning the front door.

He sprinted over to greet them, flashing a huge smile. "Good evening, Mr. and Mrs. Mazzori. And congratulations. Would you like me to drive you to your cabin?"

At Chester's nod, he opened the back door of the waiting jeep. Once they were all settled in, he drove them to the cabin, where he waited for Chester to open the door before he drove away.

Chester turned to Sophie and, with a big smile, scooped her up into his arms. "I've been waiting all day to do this. Carry my beautiful bride over the threshold." There was a teasing glint in his eyes. "So, tell me… do you know how this tradition came about?"

She had wrapped her arms around his neck, now pressing soft kisses across his face. "No, tell me… how did it all come about?"

He groaned as she continued her onslaught of kisses, her mouth now hovering over his. "*Ah…* angel, you're not playing fair with these kisses. You need to listen to me, so you'll see I'm actually doing you a favor. There is a reason a husband carries his wife over the threshold, and this is to keep her from being kidnapped. And to foil the evil spirits she might be bringing with her."

"*Hmm…*" This was her only answer, her fingers tangling in his hair so she could pull his face even closer. After she kissed him, she smiled. "The only person I'd let kidnap me would be you. And you say I'm an angel, right? Well, evil spirits know to stay far away from angels. So, I think we're safe."

After he leaned his shoulder against the door to close it, he carried her across the room and laid her gently on the bed. He settled next to her, remaining completely silent as she slowly—close to driving him crazy slowly—unbuttoned each button of his shirt. It was only after she pulled it down over his shoulders, and he shrugged it off, he took her hands in his, placing a kiss in each palm.

His breath brushed against her cheek, his voice husky with emotion. "I love you, angel. I can't wait to see what life has in store for us." He smiled. "Starting with tomorrow night, when we board a plane to Italy. For the first step of our honeymoon."

She threw her arms around him, her eyes shining with excitement. "*Chester... are we really going to Italy?*"

He nodded, laughing at her excitement. "Paris, too. I was able to convince management I'd be more productive this coming season after a honeymoon with my wife. And even though I'd vowed never to return to Paris, I know with you it will be the city of love it's claimed to be. I want to make every one of your dreams come true, angel."

She pulled back to search his face. Her expression thoughtful, she traced his lips with her fingertip. "It's probably a good idea to take this trip now. Because, I've been thinking... maybe we should get to work right away on a little Mazzori. Someone for you to take to the baseball games and all the other places you want to share with him." She grinned. "Or her... because, after all, we don't have control over that."

He framed her face in his hands, an incredulous look on his face. "Angel, are you serious?"

At her nod, he laughed, pulling her back against him. "My God, how did I get so lucky? I'll do whatever you want." His expression turned thoughtful. "*Hmm...* maybe we should plan on having enough for a whole team?"

The expression on her face was priceless. "Chester... that's nine." This was when, even though he was trying so hard to be serious, she saw the twinkle in his eyes.

He tucked her hair behind her ears. "That's a good point, since that would give us an uneven number. Maybe we should plan on ten? And who knows? We might get lucky and wind up with five of each, boys and girls."

He had an extremely satisfied smile on his face. "I believe this would be the best way to go about it."

She could only shake her head as she tried not to laugh.

After pressing soft, urgent kisses over her face, his lips then went on to trail down her throat and along the neckline of her dress. He was searching for the zipper when she reached up to run her fingers through his hair.

She gave a soft little sigh. "Okay... ten."

His hand stilled as he gazed down at her. "*Ah,* angel... we're not going to worry about that right now. Not today, on our wedding day." He smiled. "But I promise we'll get to work on that soon. No matter how many tries it takes."

Right before he claimed her mouth in a kiss, they both spoke... and at the same time.

*"I love you."*

Mini Triple Chocolate Cakes

*When Chester's Aunt Evelyn found out Sophie never had the chance to taste the dessert she made for her on their first Valentine's Eve celebration, she was very upset. So, when Chester called her with the news he and Sophie were getting married and she was invited to the wedding, she decided she was going to bring the dessert with her. They were carefully packed in her special Tupperware cake holder, which she held on her lap the entire flight. Sophie couldn't thank her enough. And of course, Chester was more than happy to share them with her.*

- Ingredients:
- Cakes:
- 1/2 cup butter, room temperature
- 1-1/2 cups sugar
- 3/4 teaspoon salt
- 2 teaspoons vanilla
- 1/2 teaspoon baking powder
- 2 teaspoons instant coffee
- 2/3 cup cocoa
- 2 large eggs
- 1-1/4 cup flour
- 1/2 cup sour cream
- 1/4 cup milk
- 1/2 cup mini chocolate chips

- Chocolate Ganache:
- 1 cup heavy cream
- 1 teaspoon vanilla
- 8 ounces semisweet chocolate, broken into pieces
- Garnish: 1/2 cup mini chocolate chips or shaved dark chocolate, optional

- Directions:
- For the cakes:
- Preheat oven to 350°F.

- Coat six 1-cup mini fluted cake molds with nonstick cooking spray for baking.
- In a medium bowl, beat together the butter, sugar, salt, vanilla, baking powder, instant coffee and cocoa until blended.
- Add the eggs, one at a time, beating well after each addition.
- Add half of the flour, beating at low speed to combine.
- Whisk together the sour cream and milk until blended.
- Add to mixture in bowl, beating at low speed to combine.
- Add the remaining flour, beating just until batter is smooth.
- Stir in mini chocolate chips.
- Pour batter into prepared cake pans, filling about 3/4 full.
- Bake for 25 to 30 minutes or until a cake tester inserted comes out clean.
- Let the cakes cool for 10 to 15 minutes before turning out onto a wire rack placed over a baking sheet.
- For the Ganache:
- In a small saucepan, heat the cream until very hot.
- Add the vanilla.
- Place the chocolate pieces in a heatproof bowl.
- Pour the hot cream over the chocolate and stir until chocolate is melted.
- Pour ganache over the cakes. If desired, sprinkle with mini chocolate chips or shaved chocolate.
- Let ganache set before serving.

Yield: Six individual cakes.

# ABOUT THE AUTHOR

L. B. Joyce lives in Chagrin Falls, Ohio. A freelance artist by day, with designing Christmas ornaments her specialty, she's also a writer by night. She loves getting lost in a good book, has redecorated almost every room in her house more times than she'd like to admit, loves baking up a storm in her kitchen, hates housework with a passion and will drive just about anywhere because of her fear of flying.

To keep up with news of the first nine novels of the series -

*A Million Decembers*
*For the Love of July*
*February's Angel*
*Promise Me November*
*An Unexpected June*
*A January to Remember*
*September's Moonlight Serenade*
*Goodbye Heartbreak, Hello May*
*March, a Song and a Dance*

(*Along with A Grand Slam Kind of Christmas, the first book of the series, Holidays in White Oaks Valley*)
*check out the* website/blog: lbjoyceauthor.com
Facebook: https://www.facebook.com/AuthorLBJoyce/
Or send her an email at: lbjoyce12@gmail.com
And, if you have a chance, check out the latest post on Facebook for L. B. Bear Christmas Ornament designs and about everything you ever wanted to know about Christmas at: @LBGlitterGirl

And finally, let's give credit where credit is due: Inspired by the following songs:

*For the First Time* - Songwriters: Jud J. Friedman/James Newton Howard/Allan Rich

*Ten Minutes Ago* - Songwriters: Rodgers and Hammerstein

*Without You* - Songwriter: David Guetta

Cover by Soxsational Cover Art